JULES & ROM

JULES & ROM

Sci-fi meets Shakespeare

Pete Mullineaux

Matador
9 Priory Business Park,
Wistow Road, Kibworth Beauchamp,
Leicestershire. LE8 0RX
Tel: 0116 279 2299
Email: books@troubador.co.uk
Web: www.troubador.co.uk/matador
Twitter: @matadorbooks

ISBN 978 1800462 519

British Library Cataloguing in Publication Data.
A catalogue record for this book is available from the British Library.

Printed and bound in Great Britain by 4edge Limited
Typeset in 11pt Minion Pro by Troubador Publishing Ltd, Leicester, UK

Matador is an imprint of Troubador Publishing Ltd

In memory of Isaac Asimov

For Moya & Cass

PROLOGUE

"...where we lay our scene..."

J anitor AJFX72 paused from vacuuming the empty corridor to acknowledge the first human presence of the day – Rob Bennett, the teacher with overall responsibility for the school's android workforce.

'Good to see you're getting a head-start on things AJ,' said Rob.

'Better than playing catch-up later on,' replied the android, offering the teacher a stock "smiley".

'I just looked in on the learning buddies – all fully charged and ready to go.'

'That's very good to hear, Mr Bennett,' said AJ, holding the same expression.

The young African-American projected a hologram timetable from his wristband, sharing his thoughts as he checked it through: 'I need to re-assign a few of the drones; one of the learning hubs is being fitted with a new console. You might give the space a quick look-over when they've finished AJ. Oh, by the way, you're probably aware our Principal is at a physical presence meeting this morning with the Education Board, so I'll be in and out of his office keeping watch on the monitors to make sure everything's running smoothly.'

'Yes, I was aware of his enforced absence,' said AJ, with a small frown.

'And I guess we'd better keep a special eye out for Mr Milton now that he's been tasked with the drama presentation for open day; *Romeo and Juliet,* no less.'

AJ raised both eyebrows to indicate mixed feelings.

'I'm reading you, AJ – tenth grade English aren't an easy group to work with, especially for a rookie teacher; he's got a few wild cards in there.'

Howard Trent came jogging up to them, still in his tracksuit, his normally pallid face flushed after an early morning run. The long-serving sports-teacher wore a pair of old-style ear-muff headphones bookending a grey head of hair.

AJ took this as a cue to return to his vacuuming.

'Sucking up with the enemy as per usual?' said Howard, with deliberate provocation, addressing Rob while nodding disdainfully towards the janitor.

Rob sighed and shook his head, well-used to Trent's antipathy towards the school's android population.

Howard continued: 'I guess it's easy for a foot-loose fancy-free guy to throw his virtuous liberal PC values around. Wait 'till one of these units moves in next door and has its telescopic arms around your only daughter.'

Rob was about to say something in protest, but found himself instead addressing a polite 'Good morning' to Miss Angelou, as she passed by on her way to the staffroom.

'Good morning, gentlemen,' said the android English teacher, rotating her head to include everyone, her distinctive light-blue skin-tone augmenting the white, black and silver already present. 'The three wise men,' she remarked with a smile, continuing on her way.

'What's the world coming to,' grunted Howard. 'This will all end in disaster, mark my words. Anyway, no hard feelings, Mr Tin Man,' he added, aiming a last dig at the janitor, before shuffling off down the corridor.

'I'd better leave you to it, AJ,' said Rob, heading in the opposite direction.

'OK, let's get this show on the road,' said the android, cheerfully returning to work.

ACT ONE

"...if you with patient ears attend..."

J im Brady was heading back to school in his eco-
friendly replica cream and green 1957 model Chevy,
having just escaped from a fractious meeting of
fellow high school principals, where they'd laboured
and sweated their way through a long list of pressing
issues, from buildings infested with mould because of
the warmer-damper climate to the equally hot topic that
impacted particularly on his patch: artificial intelligence.
Thankfully they'd found some common ground in
complaining about reluctant learners and despairing at
how both country and planet were fast falling apart. After
all the doom and gloom, to lift his spirits, he'd stopped
off to make a small purchase at the local garden centre,
aiming an admiring glance at the riot of coloured flowers
emanating from the heat-loving cactus now occupying
the car's passenger seat.

Coming to a stop light, he examined the queues
of carriers left and right, all driverless; the occupants
happy being taken for a ride. A few were empty, most
likely on their way to a pick-up. Realising he was the
only one actually at the wheel he felt a glow of inner

contentment almost matching the external temperature. It was worth paying the modest carbon tariff to have a sniff of independence. Stealing a glance in the rear-view mirror at the pleasing angle of his retro-Rockabilly quiff, he mused on how many of his forty odd years it took off? His fingers began to tap out a rhythm in response to the enhanced purr of the otherwise soundless electric engine as he looked again at the empty vehicles either side before ramping up the imaginary revs and belting out a chorus of Eddie Cochran's immortal, *"C'mon Everybody!"*

With the lights turning to green and his hand reaching for the gearshift, the upbeat mood music was rudely interrupted like a needle scratching across an old vinyl record, when Rob Bennett buzzed through a serious incident report.

Brady hurled a pile of curses at the universe, switched the car to auto-drive and flicked on its monitor, jabbing a finger at playback.

❖

"Oh Romeo, Romeo, wherefore art thou Romeo?" protested Juliet from her balcony, helplessly in love with a guy from the wrong side of the tracks.

Brady's screen revealed Mr Milton's tenth grade English class in learning hub 23 doing their first read-through of Shakespeare's timeless play. As far as the Principal could make out, everything had been moving along swell at that point; the rookie teacher didn't look to be in any obvious difficulty, in fact the class seemed remarkably alert and engaged.

Brady ran the recording forward to where the trouble began, with what was on the face of it, an innocent enough remark:

'But what is love, exactly?' asked fifteen year old Harper Richards, looking up from the play-text in her iGlobe and using two index fingers to divide the twin curtains of her dyed-blonde hair.

'A profound question indeed and very interesting in the context of the drama,' replied Mr Milton appreciatively.

The girl left her learning station and strolled over to the command desk where the teacher was standing. 'I mean what's going on inside Juliet's head when she first sees Romeo?'

'We will have to refer back to the text,' said Mr Milton, his smile broadening; encouraged by such active interest.

Harper grinned at her classmates then turned back to the teacher. 'Isn't she thinking in the back of her mind, that this is a boy she might be going to have amazing sex with?'

Mr Milton considered it for a moment before replying. 'We cannot answer your question conclusively, because Shakespeare does not use an aside in this instance to allow us into the character's thoughts.'

'Hmm,' said Harper, 'maybe you can help us in that case, Mr Milton. Tell us if you please, what *you* think is going on inside Juliet's head: we're all very innocent and we want to know about sex and love and how it fits together.'

'Yeah, *you* tell us!' chorused two more girls, backing Harper up; swooning theatrically to add to the fun.

'Come on, Mr Milton!' whooped a couple of boys wearing retro-military jackets circa The Beatle's *Sergeant Pepper* album – aiming air kisses at one another.

'Tell us what you know about sex and love!!!' demanded another boy wearing a Jimi Hendrix headband, leaning over his work station and rapping out an insistent rhythm with his knuckles.

'My own experience is not relevant in this context,' said the teacher awkwardly, his lips noticeably tightening.

'It's a fair question Milt,' said Little Stevie Marvin, who'd been playing Romeo – shuffling up in his Cuban-heels and flares. 'Quit the old prevaricating, if we're doing some kind of show-off presentation we need to know what's going down man – it's all about males and females right?'

'That is correct,' the teacher replied. 'Boys and girls who have to cross a great divide to patch up an ancient feud –'

'Yeah, we know all that,' Harper interrupted. 'But right now we want *you* to tell us about their sex lives.'

Mr Milton glanced towards the row of android learning buddies placed on standby at the back of the hub as if he was hoping they'd self-activate and bail him out. 'Sexual activity needs to be understood in relation to the norms and taboos of the historical times in which the drama is set...'

'But we're not back in old Shakey's time,' groaned Chuck Harrington, a good-looking but overweight boy with long fair hair, wearing a droopy striped Beach Boys shirt. 'We're stuck here in f...'d-up 2040! So we don't know what those freaks got up to – *you'll* have to tell us.'

'We really would like to know all about it,' insisted Wanda Jones, flicking her earrings wickedly and buffing up her towering Afro.

Harper stood on tip-toes as her hands reached up to

almost touch the teacher's ultra-smooth neck. 'Did *you* ever fall in love yourself Mr Milton? Can you imagine what it would be like to have actual sex?'

'This is not appropriate behaviour, please you must stop it immediately...' said Mr Milton feebly, his voice beginning to slur...

'Stop what exactly?' asked Harper, rolling her eyes; really playing to the gallery now.

The atmosphere in the room had changed however. So far most kids had been content to be passive spectators, but several in the class were now looking concerned at where this might be leading them.

'Forsooth, you must have heard of the big "O" Mr Milton?' asked Harper. 'Didst thou perchance ever have an orgasm?'

'I have asked you to desist. You must PLEASE, STOP IT NOW...' the teacher pleaded again.

'Oh Romeo,' sighed Harper dreamily from her imaginary balcony. 'Oh, Oh, Oh...'

'Oh, Oh – Oh!' chorused those pupils still backing her up.

The boy rapping his knuckles added some vocalised guitar power-chords: 'It's a *"Purple Haze"* man...'

'...**STOP** IT NOW – STOP **IT** – **STOP** IIIIIIIIIIIIIIIT...'

Mr Milton's voice finally gave way to a pitiful electronic screech – followed by a sharp "pop" like a champagne cork exploding as his head dramatically lifted itself upwards and flipped over to one side, pulling with it a messy tangle of electronic and organic matter, much of it now dangling down sadly over his smart linen jacket. Numerous micro bits and pieces of his memory and logic circuitry lay scattered over the floor: all the great works of world literature and much more, just there for the picking.

❖

It was August 1969 – the *summer of Woodstock*. At least it was for Greta and Gaia as they grabbed themselves a seat looking out at the geometric patterning of the artificial flame resistant carbon-gorging trees lining the campus recreation area. Greta took out her earpiece and held it close to her companion's ear, sharing the song she was listening to.

'*Stardust*: that's what we are!' declared Greta, opening up her sixteen year old heart. 'And what else?' she added.

"*Golden*?" said Gaia, with a slight tilt of the head.

'Right on, babe!' said Greta. 'And where do we have to get ourselves back to?'

'To the *garden*,' replied Gaia, again showing a little more reserve.

Greta's heartfelt expression contracted into a small frown. 'You have to admit it's kind of amazing how Joni only wrote that song after watching the festival on TV from a hotel room. I mean she wasn't actually there.'

Gaia cocked her head at the remark.

'Still, I guess we weren't there either,' Greta added on reflection.

After a pause for consideration, Gaia nodded affirmatively.

Greta's face brightened again. 'But hey flower girl, aren't we there now!' She looked around to check no one was watching then gave the back of her friend's hand an encouraging pat.

With recess now in full flow more students continued to spill out for air, turning the whole scene into something reminiscent of the 1960's, albeit a jumbled up representation of that iconic decade given the extraordinary multiplicity of retro fashions on show. Set against the modern design of the learning hubs, this grand parade appeared more than incongruous, practically dream-like, as if these were figures exiting from a time warp: actors from a movie made eighty years or so earlier. But these young people were typical for 2040, all experiencing a disconnect from the present tense not to mention the messed up future being handed down to them by the adult world. While there were still some who found a spark inside themselves to engage with the issues and be active participants in trying to change things for the better, a great swathe of the youth population had simply given up the ghost and switched off to current reality. To express their united discontent, nearly all had chosen to take on these superficial trappings of what was perceived by them to be a golden era from the past.

Despite this homogeneity there was clearly plenty of leeway in terms of dress-code: hairstyles alone displayed a dizzy mix of Afros, beehives, mop tops, flipped bobs, pixie-heads, and a wide variety of hippy-styles. For an overall effect some had gone for the earliest years, adopting a "Peggy Sue Got Married" look, while others leaned more to the mid-decade "mod" fashions associated with Soho and Carnaby Street in the UK. A few chose the surfing image of California's Beach Boys, contrasting with young African-Americans in particular making a connection with the more urban pulse of Tamla Motown. Yet more free spirits went with the flowers, beads and sandals of the "Drop out of the System – Make Love not War" hippie movement.

Two middle-aged female teachers emerged to join the throng, their costume also reflecting the current fad. Many in the adult world, suffering the same feeling of dislocation, had allowed themselves to be swept up by this drift into nostalgia, although amidst the general consensus there was elbow room for the odd contrary individual: one young male teacher appearing now wore sensible slacks along with a shirt and tie, more like someone in a play from the 1950's. In fact the school principal himself was well-known for drawing a line at the tail-end of that same decade.

The two figures on the bench were looking out onto an artificial lawn; the original turf having been torn up during an infamous military intervention on campus back in the angry summer of 2034, when troops had been called to break up student protests against the suicidal direction society was heading in. The overall sense of containment had since been reinforced by a looming thirty foot perimeter wall topped with razor wire and a necklace of electro-magnetic sensors; plus four watchtowers looking in as well as out, monitored by a private security company employing mostly robots.

The lawn's illuminated artificial grass offered a continuous incandescent light-show, changing now from orange to red…yellow to violet…

'If the world could only be one colour, what would you pick?' Greta asked as she chewed her thumbnail.

'It should be you that chooses first,' Gaia insisted.

Greta reflected for a moment: 'I guess it has to be green for renewal?'

Her companion nodded: 'Well, then let it be green for me too.'

'Or then again…blue maybe? I was just thinking there used to be a drinking fountain here once upon a time.'

Gaia sat up a little taller. 'Yes, let us not forget you have a presentation on water conservation to make immediately after the break. We should focus our full attention now on what you have prepared.'

Greta released a big grin. 'You're outasight learning buddy; what would I do without you!' Looking around, she noticed a small group of students from her class gathered in a huddle around Harper Richards. 'More gunpowder-plotting going on there I reckon.'

The pair continued to watch the changing colours against the dull background of a heavy grey polluted sky.

'It's all so ugly and beautiful at the same time,' said Greta, stretching out her arms with a teenager's yawn and more than a touch of sadness. 'But it's our world, the only one we have.'

Gaia nodded in acknowledgement, tilting her head thoughtfully before repeating the words: "Our world…"

❖

As Jim Brady's Chevy turned into the avenue leading to the school, noises up ahead alerted him to a protest taking place. Demonstrations against the threat of AI taking over the planet were an ongoing occurrence, with those attending often supported by others concerned with a wide range of issues from climate change to species destruction, war, human migration, pollution and pandemic diseases.

Getting nearer, he spied an all too familiar "People before Androids" banner – fuelled no doubt by the fast-spreading news of Mr Milton's classroom meltdown, one of their placards now asked: 'Are our kids safe?' Brady wasn't unsympathetic, but he decided to avoid any awkward questions on this occasion and turned off the avenue, bringing him round to a side-entrance where he screeched to a halt and held a palm out the window to a checkpoint sensor.

'Good morning Mr Brady,' a cheery female robotic voice declared. 'Identification verified. Today is Tuesday April 24th, two zero four zero; a leap-year no less: now is the time Mr Brady! The actual time is 11.05. Weather outlook mixed: some light rain expected; temperature currently a pleasant 34 degrees; medium humidity; pollen count minimal; pollution levels stable at close to orange level, although filter masks are advised from mid-afternoon. In case you haven't heard, there has been an incident involving Mr Milton and his English class that has been taken care of in your absence. Oh, and I notice your personal carrier's battery needs re-charging soon; you should probably check how many indulgence credits you have left –'

'I don't want to know! ' Brady yelled, wiping beads of sweat from his brow. 'Do you think I can afford to sit here and chew the fat all day,' he added bittersweet, before lowering his foot gratifyingly on the life affirming pedal, a feeling worth all the indulgence tariffs going – letting the Chevy ease forward like candy sliding into an open mouth, as car and driver entered Big Rock High School…

In learning hub 23, Brady found Android JFX72 carefully vacuuming up the last scattered micro bits and pieces of Mr Milton. The elongated extension hose whirred and whistled with a high-pitched screech. Brady grimaced at the sound then flinched at the sight of what looked like an eyeball being sucked up. He put down the potted plant he was carrying and waited respectfully until the janitor was finished.

'All of Mr Milton's parts have now been recovered, Mr Brady. The main sections were taken away earlier for inspection. I see you had a successful visit to the garden centre. I hope your meeting with the education board was equally rewarding.'

Brady paused to study the janitor for a moment. Unlike the school's android teaching staff, AJ's more obvious mechanical limbs made him closer to being a humanoid robot. Instead of possessing fully naturalistic features, his digital face formed the front part of a Perspex head mounted on a cantilever neck. Expressions appeared as rapid arrangements of pixels, usually delivering stock emotions akin to old style emojis, although occasionally this process took a moment or two when there were conflicting choices. The Principal had noticed some novel alignments appearing of late; he wasn't sure if these came from a deeper layer in the software or if the android was improvising and moulding new responses itself. Right now AJ was showing what appeared to be a sad, regretful smile.

'A fine mess we've got ourselves into, AJ,' said Brady. 'So, what's your informed take on this?'

There was a marked delay while the android endeavoured to pin down an appropriate response, finally offering something that suggested bemused detachment, although the words that followed were in a slightly forced voice-tone: the overall effect akin to someone trying to remain calm in the midst of a storm. 'Mr Milton was a diligent and hard-working teacher, Mr Brady – however the pupils were not so fond of him so I gather.'

'*So I gather* – is that empathy or irony I'm hearing AJFX72?'

'My own observations have led me to believe that all is not always well between staff and students?' said the android, now getting up to speed with the conversation.

Brady did a double-take. 'All is not well, period!' he declared.

'Let's hope it ends well,' the android quipped with a nimble shift of voice register and a stock "smiley".

'Was that supposed to be a wisecrack?' asked Brady, raising both eyebrows.

'I did not mean to cause offence, Mr Brady. You yourself have the habit of throwing away such a line,' said the janitor humbly.

Brady released a short whistle. 'Ah, but the timing AJ, that's something else…maybe just a whisker too quick with that one: you really should come along to one of my extra-curric stand-up classes.'

'I think I would be most out of place at a microphone Mr Brady,' said AJ with a modest shrug.

Brady grinned. 'Anyway, your honest humour is much appreciated AJ, a little comedy always lightens the load. But I don't know where half of that clever stuff comes from: who knows what other mysteries are going on inside that old janitor's head?'

'It was merely wordplay on the title of another Shakespeare play the students did at one time,' said AJ. 'Remember that I have you personally to thank for permitting me access to a selection of the Bard's texts.'

'And why not,' said Brady, 'no reason why an honest blue-collar guy can't have the same fanciful notions as anyone else round here.'

Rob Bennett gave a cough as he appeared in the doorway. 'Mr Milton's gone into the pre-lab ready for transport back to company headquarters. I feel really bad about what happened, but I just didn't see it coming.'

'Tell me about it,' said Brady, downbeat.

'I was watching the monitor: the class looked like it was going really well; OK the kids were a bit animated, but they were doing a play after all. I turned the volume down for a moment to tune into the other screens, then I was called away to attend to an incident in the canteen…'

'Anyway, I caught it myself on flashback,' said Brady. 'It all happened in a…flash.'

'Not good for the school's image,' said Rob with understatement.

'Yes, a fine mess we've got ourselves into,' said Brady for a second time.

After Jim Brady and Rob Bennett had excused themselves and left the room, AJ waited a moment or two for their footsteps to recede then moved behind the command desk at which Mr Milton had last addressed his wayward students. The android janitor looked down at the vacated work space – then out at the empty hub. Finally, AJFX72 produced an expression that was neither a smile nor a frown; something different altogether.

2

Kerry Tracker sat on the shuttle-bus, feeling a little apprehensive as it approached the school. It was less than a week since she'd spotted an ad for a specialist drama teacher; a rare enough job opportunity in these times. The post was only short-term, barely three months and part-time at that, but having been out of work for quite a while she wasn't in a position to be picky. Anyway, who knew what could happen, they might like her, extend the contract. Applying online she'd found herself immediately engaged in a virtual interview with a very pleasant but thorough android interrogator, and then within minutes she'd been accepted. The proficiency of algorithms!

She wondered why there'd been such urgency; and how they'd chosen her from what must have been a good number of eager applicants. Maybe at the tender age of twenty-six she was a little more mature than most newly qualified teachers, which might say something about the challenges that awaited her. At the same time she was still at the youthful end of the spectrum and against the background fatalism of the day had managed to cling onto some blind hope and idealism. For Kerry personally the moment felt right, having arrived at this point via a circuitous slow route: taking a time-out after getting her degree to see a bit of the world before it sank beneath the waves. It did mean she'd been out of the educational loop for a while and this might mean playing catch-up a little. She twisted the Tibetan yin-yang design bracelets on her wrists to help herself focus. Anyway here she was, about to take up her new employment, tasked with supervising some form of dramatic showcase: "a presentation of scenes from Shakespeare's *Romeo and Juliet*" according to the job specification. Her robot interviewer had been tight-lipped about the detail; but regardless of that, it was something she was already looking forward to.

She'd been sitting next to the aisle: even with her dark skin it was wise to avoid the full glare of the harsh sun, but then hearing loud voices outside, moved over by the window to see what was going on. There was clearly some kind of protest taking place up ahead; a few members of the group, "People before Androids" were making their way in that direction, chanting and carrying banners. It wasn't a surprise to her – the school was well known nationally for having a particularly heavy deployment of android teachers at the expense of humdrum human beings.

Although Kerry was well-used to handling robotic teaching aids and had some experience working with android teachers, this would be her first time being placed alongside them practically as their equal – and as part of a minority to boot. She was conscious of how this set-up was made possible through the benevolence of the state's former governor, multi-billionaire Charles Richards, boss of Allied Robotics, one of the prime movers and shakers in the rapid development of AI across the US. Kerry felt a twinge of unease remembering he carried a reputation for being as hardnosed in business as he was charming in politics.

The bus drew closer to the main gate and she could hear voices chanting: "PBA, PBA – We Won't Go Away!" With the crowd pushing up against the restraining barriers and someone waving an information leaflet at her, she felt a stab of guilt at not being out there amongst them.

Kerry didn't need a leaflet to tell her the broad history of how even before the advent of robots and androids, there'd been a steady shift towards AI via online interfaces; this development coinciding with a strong promotion of individualised tuition at the expense of collective learning, dismissed and downgraded by many at the time as "group-think". Conventional classrooms had morphed into learning hubs with each student allocated a work station and given a touch screen along with a personal "learning buddy" app to guide them through whatever educational programmes had been sourced from department supplies or bought from private companies. Policy makers had argued that with access to the best educators nationwide, students wouldn't have to suffer being held-back by poorly performing local teachers: in fact the physical presence of an actual "teacher" was no longer required, only a technical supervisor and soon enough even this position was allocated to robots, with a few security guards on call in some of the rougher areas.

Eventually however the whole thing had come off the rails. Individualised tuition may have worked hunky dory when the learning environment was less pressured, with the cosy feeling the world centred around you, "was your oyster", but the growing impact of AI meant narrowing of employment prospects and consequently constraints on the curriculum, so freedom of choice ended up counting for little, encouraging disillusion and alienation rather than assimilation into society. And as general trust in the adult world dropped off the edge of a cliff with each new global catastrophe, more and more young people saw studying hard to get somewhere in life as simply not worth the effort. They mostly came to school now for their attendance credits, a necessity for graduation and to see their friends. Many fell asleep during classes or daydreamed within the privacy of their earphones, tuned into their own music, chat-rooms and online games. As earplugs morphed into ear-studs and then implants it was even easier for them to live out a parallel existence in the clouds. Internet blockers were belatedly applied to thwart such distractions but that often resulted in them doing nothing, staring off aimlessly into the void.

Heading into the 2030's a grudging reassessment had taken place, policy makers finally admitting this unhealthy mix of individualism and artificiality might be contributing to the alienation felt by so many of the younger generation. In an attempt to restore a feeling of old-fashioned communality, some schools returned to the old classroom setup with pupils learning together as one group. As to the second issue, a few institutions even managed to put a brake on the use of robots, taking on more flesh and blood teachers. But for a school like Big Rock there could be no going back, the march of progress was only in one direction: full-silicon ahead.

'PBA, PBA – we won't be going way!'

As the bus slowed almost to a standstill, painfully making its way past the protesters towards the main entrance, Kerry didn't know whether to wave and indicate her support or duck down out of sight. Thankfully, at the last moment the shuttle veered away sharply and took off down a side avenue.

❖

'Welcome to Big Rock,' said Jim Brady into the intercom for the side gate he'd taken to using himself recently. He wanted this particular visitor's arrival to be under the radar, certainly not via the main entrance where she'd have to pass through the crowd gathered outside, the last thing the embattled Principal wanted was for them to see a human face and offer the impression the school had caved-in under pressure and done a U-turn on recruitment policy.

The monitor revealed a sweet-faced young black woman with a big smile. She wore a string of beads around her throat and Brady could just see the neckline of a Moroccan style tunic. There was an open but determined look about her. 'Hippie inclined, but smart, focused and ambitious,' he muttered to himself, hoping this was just the right combination for taking over supervision of Mr Milton's tenth grade English class and their contribution to end of year Open-Day.

On this important date in the school calendar, all age and subject groups were invited to offer something by way of visual art, literary readings, science exhibits, craft and other examples of what had been achieved, depending on how much enthusiasm for the challenge their tutors could muster up. Being a private boarding institution with limited public funding, everything depended on philanthropic donations from a few well-heeled individuals, chief amongst them Charles Richards, who'd just been on the phone bending Brady's ear over what had happened to Mr Milton. The unfortunate incident carried the potential for serious reputational damage to both school and company: the android teacher had been at the very cutting edge of AI development, a pioneering hybrid model no less, complete with organic parts operating in tandem with the more traditional electronic components. Moreover, the school's intention had been to show off this ambitious innovation by entrusting Mr Milton with delivering the drama presentation. While Brady was able to contain and downplay the incident within the school, background fear and suspicion in the outside world was harder to deal with.

Brady's first thought had been to hand responsibility over to one of the more tried and tested android English teachers such as Mr Wilde or Miss Angelou, but to most of the general public all androids were superficially alike and so they'd only be coming up against the same fears and suspicions. Bearing in mind what the students had done to Mr Milton, the school couldn't afford even a small risk of a repetition, so to be on the safe side as well as help shift attention away from the android presence, he'd decided on a rare U-turn in recruitment policy and the call had gone out for a regular old-fashioned flesh and blood human-being; preferably someone relatively young who might stand a better chance connecting to these disaffected youngsters.

Jim Brady wiped sweat from his brow. There was a lot at stake and on top of everything else they'd have to pay her: a modest enough challenge perhaps to the school's finances, but an irritation he could still have done without, especially when you could get an army of androids working for nothing.

❖

The new teacher sat in the chair offered to her as Brady took a moment to slide a comb through his hair, giving a few final flicks to the sideburns. 'Welcome to Big Rock High Miss Tracker, more affectionately known as "Candy" – our ancient sacred motto which you'll now have to swear an oath of allegiance to being "*OK, so it's a mountain, get over it!*" He added a grin, before adjusting his voice to sound less flippant. 'Please don't mind my occasional tongue in cheek manner; it's just one of the things you'll have to get used to. And be warned, I do have my darker side.'

Brady took a glass of water from the purifier and handed his guest one. As they lifted them to each other in a symbolic toast, he continued: 'Sorry by the way Kerry for bringing you in the tradesman's entrance; thought I'd save you having to pass by the protest going on outside the main gate, unfortunately there's still a degree of negativity from some towards what is perceived as our over-promotion of AI.'

The young teacher returned Brady a cryptic look. 'You'd have thought they'd been glad to see me in that case?'

Brady threw her a broad smile, glad the young woman seemed sharp and on the ball. 'It's clear you have no issues yourself with artificial intelligence,' he said, glancing at her profile up on his screen. 'You've worked alongside robot teaching staff before.'

Kerry offered an easy shrug. 'Whatever my own feelings are, it's the times we're living in. Anyway I'm truly excited about working in such an AI focused environment; it offers new challenges and hopefully some interesting openings artistically.'

Brady looked satisfied. 'Anyway, your presence will no doubt be a moral boost to the few remaining traditional members of staff we have here.'

The Principal leaned back and filled her in on how he wasn't that long in the saddle himself. He'd originally trained as a science teacher, then taken a masters in psychology, but had subsequently become disillusioned with some of the changes going on in education not to mention the shrinking job opportunities. Someone had given him a birthday present of a course in comedy improvisation and he'd quickly become hooked, progressing on to becoming a solo stand-up. A couple of hard grafting years later, he'd been doing reasonably well on the circuit and building a modest reputation as a satirist, when someone from the education board had seen his act. It had occurred to them that here was someone with an education background, but also with a thick skin and able to handle a tough crowd. OK he was a little off-beat but the school was desperate at that stage and willing to take a gamble on something a bit different to inspire the increasingly disinterested students.

As a lover of early rock and roll Brady had been taken by the serendipity regarding the school's name and as an ex-science teacher he was genuinely interested in what they were trying to achieve with their AI program. He'd been reluctant to give up the blossoming comedy career but had felt obliged to answer what appeared to be a higher calling.

Having enlightened Kerry with some of his own personal history, Brady switched the conversation back to her appointment.

'You're already aware the state's former Governor no less is fully behind our grand project, in fact it's the androids from his illustrious company that make what we do here possible. The good man has even provided a further show of faith by offering up his precious daughter instead of sending her to a fancy Ivy-league establishment befitting her station. Harper Richards – you'll meet her soon enough, her class are the ones presenting a selection of scenes from *Romeo and Juliet* for open-day.'

'Yes, it was what first attracted me when I saw the post advertised,' said Kerry with a confident smile, smoothing her tunic and adjusting the bracelets on her wrists.

Brady looked around the room for a moment. 'You'll hear the full story about this soon enough – we did have an unfortunate incident involving a technical breakdown of one member of our android teaching staff who'd originally been given the task of delivering the drama showcase.'

Kerry's ears pricked up. On first hearing about the job she'd checked for references to the school on the web and read about a new state of the art android model that had recently been assigned to the English department. But strangely, when she'd then checked the school's own site, there was no mention of this good news story and she'd wondered at the time whether it had been deleted. And if so why? She said nothing and waited.

'A systems fault of some kind, I guess not unusual with any innovative prototype,' continued Brady, perhaps sounding a little too casual. 'One of our more seasoned android teaching staff, Miss Angelou will cover Mr Milton's regular English classes until the end of term. Regarding the showcase, the crucial thing now is we repair any reputational damage by continuing to present a positive image of how things are done here.' Brady paused to consider the all-too human form sitting in front of him. 'Obviously inviting you to take up the director role might appear to show us admitting defeat – representing a row-back on our philosophy. But I've been talking this through with Charles Richards himself, deciding how we can still best set this up to show-off android involvement in the learning process; keep that right at the centre of the drama presentation.'

Kerry's eyes lit up. 'You said the right thing: "*process drama*" is exactly where I'm coming from.'

'Well I'm certainly glad to hear that,' said Brady, more encouraged. I was half-afraid you might be disappointed we're not going for a grand full production.'

'No, that's not a problem,' said Kerry, with an easy shrug, 'I gathered that from the job-spec. This kind of thing is right up my alley.'

Brady leaned forward. 'OK, so here's what we're looking for. If we can effectively demonstrate exactly how our android learning buddies are helping the kids to explore the play: researching their characters, learning their lines, that sort of thing; actually put all that positive interplay right up there on display, then follow it up with some sample scenes to illustrate what they've accomplished together...'

Kerry smiled and took a sip of her water: 'That all sounds great.'

Brady nodded. 'Of course you won't have had experience with the advanced model android learning buddies employed here: in a lot of schools it's still the original cute avatar character on a touch-screen; OK, in a few more advanced establishments you might get a hologram figure projecting from your wristband or even a free-roving robot, but we're proud to say we're pretty unique in this respect.'

Kerry was familiar with the general role played by all AI learning buddies in helping students through their educational assignments, it mostly involved asking appropriate questions to encourage forward movement and progress – sometimes it might involve a little coaxing. A partnership then of sorts, like having a personable coach you could talk to and bounce ideas off; with slow learners, an LB could even act as a pacer, working through a task with the student observing, until he or she got up to speed. If someone was recovering from illness or suffering general hopelessness, expectation levels could be lowered even further to offer encouragement; in short bursts this practise was useful in building self-esteem, especially in remedial education. Kerry imagined things would be straightforward enough at a relatively affluent school like Big Rock.

'Anyway, I'm sorry to drop you straight in it,' Brady continued, glancing at a 1950's themed calendar on the wall showing Bill Halley & the Comets and the words underneath, *"Rock Around the Clock"*. 'But you do have around ten weeks leading up to the date we've earmarked in mid-July. Again, I stress we're talking about something fairly modest: it's something you should be able to accomplish in the number of sessions we've allocated for you to take over Miss Angelou's class –'

'Actually,' the new teacher finally interrupted, keen to get a few of her own thoughts into the mix, 'taking on board all you've just said about highlighting the process, I was wondering if it might be better if I met with them outside their formal class times, maybe even during lunch hours? It might give us more freedom to play around a little?'

Brady resisted a cynical response and settled instead for a sober "let's be realistic" tone: 'That would very likely cut down the numbers who'd agree to be involved. Our students are never too happy about giving up their precious leisure time.'

Kerry sat up straighter, showing off her light but sprung frame. 'I'd be willing to take a chance; even if it meant a smaller number.'

Brady sat forward assertively...but then paused, sensing an opportunity. 'Would a group of say eight kids, along with their learning buddies be too small?'

'No...' said Kerry, 'that would be a reasonable number in fact. With a presentation of scenes there's going to be lots of room for doubling up on the play's characters.'

Brady stroked his jaw thoughtfully. 'OK...so leave this with me – I'll see what I can sort out for you.'

Kerry would have liked to continue the conversation, but Brady abruptly got to his feet and opened the door: 'Anyway, enough of the preamble, time you met your fellow staff.'

Outside on the landing they met Android Janitor FX72 cleaning graffiti from a wall. Just before they were wiped out Kerry flinched a little on seeing the words: "everything sucks, so why bother..."

'Miss Tracker, this is AJFX72,' said Brady, 'or "AJ" for short. After me he's by far the most important figure around here. Anything you want, just ask *him*.'

'Pleased to meet you Miss Tracker,' said AJ, with a hearty smile. 'I hope I can be of assistance at some point.'

'Good to meet you too,' said Kerry, returning the smile, still a touch bemused by it all.

Kerry followed as the Principal led her along a raised gallery that loomed above an open plaza below. Looking down, she could see a dizzy mix of human beings and androids moving to and fro.

3

On entering the staffroom it took Kerry a moment to take everything in. The place was a cross between a space-mission control centre and a hotel suite hosting a wedding reception. Around one large round table, divided up into cake-like slices hosting personal touch-screens, sat a mix of human and android teachers: the latter outnumbering the former at a rough count, two to one. Kerry noticed how they were interspersed, suggesting at least a veneer of communality.

'Welcome to the new Camelot,' Brady quipped.

Circling the room were more ports occupied by basic-grade robot teaching units, or "drones" as they were commonly referred to: essentially plastic shells in elemental-human form with their software designed specifically for the subjects they taught. Here in the staffroom they downloaded material for lesson plans and received fresh updates from the more senior teaching staff. Kerry was already familiar from her work experience while at college how these robots entered the learning hubs and simply hooked themselves up to a teaching console.

She smiled warmly as Brady introduced her to the pitifully small group of traditional teachers still in attendance, numbering just four: Inez Martinez (life sciences) Meera Patel (languages & geography) Howard Trent (sports and fitness) and Robert Bennett (conjectural history* optional). Rob's subject had been downgraded only a few years earlier after finally succumbing to pressure from the "alternative facts-fake news" brigade. Luckily for him he'd been able to double-up here as supervisor of the android workforce.

Both female teachers looked to be in their mid to late-forties and Kerry wondered why they'd chosen to turn down any incentivised offers of early retirement. Maybe they enjoyed working with androids? Howard Trent had the veneer of someone just plain stubborn, a seasoned trooper refusing to quit his post on a sinking ship; but again she could be guilty of a false perception. Brady also mentioned the absent Belle Olsen (moral guidance/sex education) who was out on long term sick leave.

The Principal singled out Inez and Meera as "wise women" who'd look after Kerry and "show her the ropes".

'Welcome to the sisterhood,' said Inez cheerily.

Kerry also said hello to Liza Woodley, a personal counsellor who visited the school one day per week. Liza immediately launched into dismissing the myriad online chat-box therapists available; how she'd been seconded as a result of growing unease regarding these non-human interfaces. Back in the early days of the first psychotherapy-bots, many people had been attracted to the novel idea of sharing their problems with a non-human presence, where the relationship appeared to offer a guaranteed non-judgemental perspective and for those operating in confined social circles, a more secure level of anonymity. But with the alarming rate at which AI was infiltrating so much of the human sphere, along with some serious issues concerning alleged misuse of personal data, distrust had seeped in: a growing suspicion they were not as neutral and detached as first appeared.

'Lucky for you Kerry that Liza's here today, she can block-book you in for a few sessions,' said Meera with a wry smile.

Brady grimaced good-humouredly and moved quickly on to introducing the android representation waiting patiently and attentively around the table: Mr Wilde and Miss Angelou (English) Miss Curie and Mr Hubble (science/maths) Mr Globe (geography/travel/languages) Miss Kahlo (art/design/fashion) Mr Tchaikovsky (music) Miss Hideko (sports/personal fitness/body-toning) …

The new teacher got a somewhat stiff handshake from each of them as they stood up to greet her: but she was conscious maybe that was coming from her? She also received a polite smile and a uniform, "Welcome to our humble school, Kerry." Thankfully she was able to detect enough subtle variation in expression and voice-tone to make it feel more natural, helping to put her at ease.

As she was about to take a seat, Rob Bennett whispered for her to avoid "Mr Milton's chair" which was being left vacant out of respect.

'*The Siege Perilous*,' Brady remarked, adding to her general bemusement.

Howard Trent overheard, guffawed and declared, 'He means it's jinxed!'

The sports teacher received a communal frown of disapproval for his indiscretion.

Either way, it was clear no one appeared to want to break this informal rule, including Mr Milton's fellow brethren, not normally prone one supposed to such irrational thinking.

Kerry chose a ginseng tea when Inez offered her a drink from the nearby dispenser. Brady helped himself to a soya milkshake with a straw, pulled up a stool and for the new teacher's benefit offered a "quick toast" to what he called his "complimentary workforce" and Charles Richards's benevolence which allowed such a pioneering enterprise to operate. He leaned in closer to Kerry to make the droll observation that with their enhanced emotional intelligence software along with sophisticated external design features, these elite model androids in attendance were indeed a fairly reasonable match to their human colleagues.

Looking around the table Kerry was able to appreciate how highly flexible facial features did help to suggest a modest degree of personality, perhaps as much as you'd expect to get amongst human beings in an average supermarket checkout queue or business boardroom. These emboldened individuals had also been given a few token items of clothing to help distinguish them: Mr Rembrandt, who'd just entered, wore an artist's scrub cap along with a smock daubed in fresh paint. Miss Kahlo had her namesake's famous flower headband; Miss Angelou of course presented a distinctive headscarf, while Mr Wilde flaunted a debonair velvet jacket and silk cravat. Hanging around Miss Hideko's neck was a replica of her Olympic gold medal. Mr Hubble had even been allowed his iconic wooden pipe as a prop. With Brady taking a moment to use his straw to get at the last of his milkshake, Rob chipped in, recalling fondly how Mr Milton's title had, like Mr Globe's, been more of a nickname: rather than assume 17th century attire he'd adopted a modern, yet "classic" English-professor look – beige linen jacket complete with hand-sewn brown leather elbow patches, along with a pair of vintage brogues; a set of spectacles and a flamboyant mop of hair in slight disarray.

Beyond the individual personalisation, what couldn't be missed was of course their uniform blue skin-tone. Kerry wondered if it had actually been the manufacturer's intention or an accidental by-product of design and marketing, but it was intriguing how this served to instil a look of neutrality that initially by-passed identification in terms of race or nationality. Perhaps reading her thoughts, Inez took the opportunity to point out how their personal identities had been chosen by the Principal and an education board advisory panel, aiming to achieve a broad spectrum regarding gender, race, sexual orientation, as well as historical representation.

Having satisfactorily set the scene, Brady excused himself to get back to his office and with everyone falling into small talk, Kerry was now able to witness how adept these android teachers were at holding up their end of a conversation, even whilst downing modest amounts of herb teas. Lowering his voice, Rob discretely pointed out how the primary focus was on listening, but with a full allowance to be pro-active whenever their highly attuned EI told them they had something useful to offer.

Wit and wordplay were definitely encouraged along with appreciating a good joke. A few things were banned, such as mindless chit-chat about the weather; their human colleagues suffered enough having to listen to their own kind droning on. Despite their elevated status, androids also had to forego a few more basic human entitlements such as the freedom to lounge around and grumble, be bad tempered; curse and swear. All forms of anti-social behaviour were of course missing as a default in robot programming. This might have left someone like Howard Trent feeling a touch isolated had it not been for a tweaking in their software allowing them to differentiate boorish behaviour in pupils from what could be magnanimously viewed as harmless excess from fellow staff. So now as the grouchy sports teacher propped his feet up on the table, scrunched up a coffee carton and propelled it past Mr Hubble's nose several feet into the bin, the android teacher barely raised an eyebrow. Trent duly trotted out what was by now likely a well-worn joke: how it was an improvement on his ex-wife. Even the normally obliging androids joined their fellow-staff in failing to smile at this one.

Kerry accepted a cookie from a plate offered to her by a beaming Miss Angelou and mindful of what had just been said about superficial conversation, proceeded instead to ask the android teacher about her subject area, keen to hear how students were engaging with the current English syllabus.

4

'Welcome to tonight's show!' announced Jim Brady. The "Candy Cabaret" represented the school's informal assembly, held irregularly, but usually on a weekday evening from 7 to 10 pm, with Brady himself as resident MC. Attendance was considered mandatory as this was the main forum for airing hot topics and sorting out any pressing school business, with the more serious items presented alongside various forms of lighter entertainment. After taking over as Principal, it hadn't been long before he'd abandoned the more traditional gatherings, seeing them as a waste of time, few appeared to be moved anymore by long-winded motivational speeches; even for the staff they'd become tedious. Anything connected with organised religion had also been dropped as too contentious and divisive. Along with his passion for early rock and roll, Brady was also a big fan of great old-time comedians like Lenny Bruce, a 1950-60's icon currently enjoying a deserved revival. He also employed an offbeat reading of Zen teaching: out of all the people in the room the secret was being the only one truly in the moment; it was all about *presence*.

Outside celebrities might occasionally be invited along to perform, but it was essentially an opportunity for students themselves to offer contributions in the form of music, comedy, dance, spoken word or whatever else came to mind. Sometimes a member of staff might also be cajoled into presenting something. The set-up consisted of a non-alcoholic bar, a small intimate stage, soft lights and Brady's pride and joy, a retro microphone on a stand, adding to the high-tech ones built into the auditorium. He used his command of the stage both to entertain and at times to intimidate, based on a belief that the most effective way of keeping troublesome teenagers in line was less by promises, threats and sanctions and more through the ancient art of satire: plain old personal embarrassment allied to an eternal fascination in the collective unconscious with public humiliation. This mostly came down to the art of manipulating the crowd dynamic, whipping up just the right level of hysteria then maintaining a delicate balance between comfort and discomfort. Anyone who'd seriously stepped out of line was invited up onto the stage to take part in an open-ended improvisation with Brady as the other half of an unpredictable double-act. He was aware of course how risky this was in potentially alienating these kids even more than they already were, but in a counter-intuitive way, they'd shown themselves open to such a crazy off the wall approach. They even put up with having to squirm around at his often juvenile jokes; if nothing else it appeared to place him nearer to them than the so called sensible but discredited adult world. While it might be momentarily painful for those thrust into the spotlight, it was fun for everyone watching. Overall, Brady was accorded a grudging respect for at least trying to be different.

He liked to rotate his MC outfit. It might be an imposing 1920's gangster style look, or if he was really in a madcap mood, a medieval jester's costume. Sometimes it was the red nose and white face of a traditional circus clown; if he wanted to be extra mean, he'd take on the persona of the fairground puppet, Mr Punch, complete with noisy wooden ratchet. Tonight he was going with the current retro trend, combining his two great passions, music and comedy: wearing a late 1950's-early 60's style suit and moving around the stage in freewheeling jazz-inspired mode aka Lenny Bruce, oozing a cheery mix of improvised mayhem and calculated intent. Despite willingness to occasionally play the fool, Brady was at the same time, no fool; consequently there were no serious heckles during the Candy Cabaret: put downs and take-downs were his department only.

'I believe we have a few volunteers for our next item?' he said with a grin, staring down from the stage.

An audible intake of breath identified a small section of the audience, each with his or her eyes fixed on the floor, hoping they wouldn't be invited up. Everyone else could afford to relax, knowing that tonight's "open spot" had been reserved for the ringleaders in the assault on poor Mr Milton.

This small group of rebels had of course already been spoken to immediately after the incident, when all but one of the eight kids had expressed some level of remorse, saying they'd only been trying to test the teacher, not knowing their actions would have such a violent effect.

They were conscious of the fees their parents paid and not all of them were from well-off backgrounds so Brady was able to wave the threat of bringing their folks in to make financial recompense as back-up to whatever else he might decide to throw at them. The main complication was Charles Richards's own daughter Harper, who'd clearly led the whole thing and possibly knew exactly what she was doing in provoking one of her father's precious androids into having a meltdown. She alone had been largely unapologetic, shrugging it off as "accidents happen" – there was certainly no fear of her being expelled, although that would have suited her fine had it been the outcome. The way she saw it, being sent to a school she hadn't chosen herself made her into an unwilling sacrifice simply to demonstrate her father's confidence in his android products.

How to deal with this conundrum had posed a challenge for Brady, but his contrary streak was like a Zen form of colour blindness: faced with a red traffic light, he tended to see only green. His earlier conversation with Kerry about meeting the drama group in their own time had presented an opportune way to kill two birds with one stone: he could isolate this small band of rebels from having any further bad influence on the rest of their class and as an appropriate punishment for what they'd done, offer them up tonight as "volunteers" for the redefined showcase, ready and willing to give up their precious lunch hours for the cause.

'I see a few of our good people praying down there,' Brady drawled, milking the moment. 'So who's it gonna be? I spy with my little eye, I wonder if someone here is going to *lose their head*; have one of those *out of body* experiences!'

There were a few groans and laughs from those not under threat. Everyone understood the pointed references to poor Mr Milton.

The room fell into an expectant silence.

Not able to bear it any longer, Harper Richards looked up to see Brady's curled finger beckoning.

As the wayward teenager rose from her seat to a modest scatter of pitying applause, a spotlight swivelled and lined her up in its sights. Flushing instinctively, her face hardened in a gritty show of defiance.

Brady invited the other seven to stand.

'Let's hear it for *all* our volunteers!' said Brady, whipping up some hearty clapping.

With all eyes on her to take the lead, Harper began to shuffle slowly along her row to the central aisle.

'Oh…but wait a moment, I think there's a better way of doing this…' Brady announced abruptly, surprising everyone not least Harper. 'Maybe we won't be inviting these guys up on stage just yet…'

There was a cheerful groan of disappointment as the audience played its part at being robbed of immediate entertainment and gratification.

Brady concluded: 'I think they have some serious rehearsing to do first.'

5

Kerry looked around the fringe activities hub for positive signs. She'd missed out on the cabaret the night before due to exhaustion from the long train journey from California (doing her bit to reduce her fossil footprint) and what was probably a rogue stomach bug, but Inez Martinez reported how the Principal had kept his word and provided her with a group of "volunteers". Dispersed around the space, Kerry could see a small number of students: three girls, five boys – two African-American, two white, two Hispanic, one Chinese and one Arabic – all of them lost in their virtual worlds behind tinted iSpecs.

She was about to introduce herself when Rob Bennett stepped in through the entrance and addressed the kids: 'Why aren't your learning buddies in here with you?'

Kerry remembered the line of androids she'd just passed outside in the corridor, the sophisticated DAK models Jim Brady had talked about.

'We left them out there till we know what's happening,' replied Tania Castro with a dismissive click of her tongue.

'Maybe we won't need them today,' added Little Stevie Marvin, sourly.

Rob frowned. 'You know iSpec shades aren't allowed during school activities.'

The group collectively sighed as they made their specs transparent. 'This is our lunch break,' said Wanda Jones, almost reasonably.

'I understand from the Principal the LBs are to be an essential part of this,' said Rob. Kerry watched as he instructed the learning buddies to file in and line up over to one side. The kids immediately turned their backs on them, sulkily.

So these were the bold offenders against Mr Milton, whose arms had been twisted into turning up; it was clear they were here only on sufferance. Kerry felt some annoyance with Brady for going about it this way, but maybe she'd invited it on herself by saying she wanted to meet them out of normal class time.

She suspected they'd now be hoping for an easy ride: find out which characters they'd be playing in any particular scene and leave it to their learning buddies to absorb the relevant sections of text, feed it back in bite-sized chunks; then organise much of the prep work to sort out cue lines, even act as understudies for the really boring bits, those dull chorus moments standing around waiting for your "star" turn. Bearing in mind the Principal had stressed the main objective with the showcase was to present the kids and their android assistants working creatively together, certainly not let it happen "offstage" as it were, right this moment she was acutely aware of the multiple challenges facing her. Her most immediate task though was to win them over to the project so they actually wanted to be here, not feeling like they'd been press-ganged.

Kerry offered a polite 'thank you' to Rob as he retreated through the door, then she turned to face the group. 'Hi, it's great to meet you all. And thank you for coming. Today will be a quick chat just to touch base before we get going properly. Anyway, I gather from that revealing snippet of conversation with Mr Bennett you've already taken the initiative and divided yourselves up into Montagues and Capulets?'

The kids stared back at her.

'Two tribes?' she prompted.

'You mean those goons over there?' Chuck Harrington tilted his specs upwards so you could see his full face. 'They can't be *in* the play.'

'I don't see why not,' Kerry replied calmly.

The group looked to one another, clearly not sure how to take the new teacher.

'You do know why they were left out there in the cold?' asked Wanda.

'Actually, no I don't,' replied Kerry, genuinely.

'Jeez, she knows nothing!' snorted Harper.

'Didn't the Principal tell you anything?' said Chuck, derisively.

'He told me you'd already started reading through the play? I know he's also very keen on involving the learning buddies, so I thought…'

Harper placed two hands on her mini-skirted hips. 'OK, even if we did agree to do this, I was already reading Juliet. I'm not falling in love with a dumb Montague droid!'

'Of course you're not,' replied Miss Tracker. 'This is fiction right – *acting*?'

All eyes looked to the leader of the brat pack. Despite

the girl's open hostility, she appeared to be caught in two minds; hovering on the brink of walking out, but at the same time curious to find out more.

'You've been brought in special to do this thing?' asked Wanda quizzically.

'That's right; I'm taking over from where Mr Milton left off.'

A chorus of guffaws went around the room like a spinning top.

'So Mr crazy-man Brady's depending on you to pull this off?' said Little Stevie, shuffling around and rubbing his chin inquisitively, examining Kerry like an explorer discovering a new species of exotic creature.

'And on you too,' replied Kerry, as she looked again to Harper, who did appear to be wavering a little.

'You're actually thinking of using the droids like they're one of the two tribes?' asked Omar, one of the three boys who hadn't spoken until now. Turning to the other two he received a non-committal shrug that at least looked like it wasn't an outright dismissal.

'Does that mean we get to act out the feud with *them* as the sworn enemy?' said Chuck, suddenly sounding keener.

'I'm sure we can explore that as a possible scenario,' said Kerry, trying to ride this interest while at the same time wary of over-committing to one angle.

'Will it always have to be during lunch break, we do have lives to lead,' said Tania.

Kerry tried to sound sympathetic: 'I'm aware it's a big sacrifice. But after your forty-five minutes with me you'll still have a chance to get something to eat.' She looked again at Harper, who was still clearly sizing up the situation. 'OK, this might involve a little hard work, but it might also turn out to be enjoyable and rewarding.'

'Sure, what the hell, let's go for it then,' Harper said finally, to looks of genuine surprise from the others.

'Is that the same for everyone?' asked Kerry.

There was a collective shrug in response.

'Well, that's great you're all on board,' said Kerry. 'And thank you for your mature attitude. So, can we begin with a full session tomorrow at the same time?'

The group offered another choral look that simply said, 'OK'.

'So, I'll see you then.' Kerry threw them a last smile as she left.

'So what changed your tune?' asked Wanda, as soon as the teacher had gone.

'Who said I've changed anything?' said Harper. 'Sure it sounds like the dumbest thing ever. That's why we're gonna do it – and make sure the whole thing's a disaster so Mr not-so-funny Brady can come down hard on his big fat butt and bring this whole crap-assed school with him!'

❖

'So, will someone please give me some background on why the kids here are so down on their learning buddies, apparently they see them as the enemy? And why our dear Principal left that bit out of his briefing?' Kerry was playing catch-up later in the staffroom.

'I guess he just didn't want you going in there with your head filled with too much negativity,' said Inez sympathetically. 'Remember he used to study psychology before he became a comedian.'

'Sure,' said Kerry, nodding. Thinking about it, maybe it was better she'd met the kids feeling upbeat and not overwhelmed by the multiple challenges.

Inez recapped on why the "cold war" had come about: at some point the education authorities had become concerned over what they'd come to perceive as over-sympathetic programming in all learning buddies right across the board, resulting in these units being way too soft when dealing with the fast-growing numbers of disaffected students refusing to knuckle down and apply themselves to their studies. Most schools had voluntarily introduced empathy boundaries into the learning buddy software, making them more distant and impersonal, complete with a neutral voice-tone replacing what had once been a more coaxing "child-friendly" delivery. As far as assignments were concerned there would be no more indulging students with any "poor me" nonsense, goodbye to these units as babying "soothers" – they'd simply reverted to what they were always intended to be, a useful learning tool and no more. Here at Big Rock they'd felt compelled to go along with the general consensus despite it being something neither Brady or Charles Richards were too keen on doing; after all the latter's reputation was built on the superior empathetic qualities of his android products, particularly the DAK models. But they were unwilling to isolate themselves at a time when the school was at the head of the firing line regarding public criticism and scrutiny around AI.

Predictably of course, the student body's reaction

had been outright resentment. Kids had always liked the way their personal helpers didn't guilt-trip or admonish them in the way a parent or teacher might have done, instead nudging them gently along while shouldering responsibility for much of the workload providing study plans, simplified outlines, handy summaries and best of all without a complaint!

In the blink of an eye each learning buddy went from being an easy-going friendly companion to a cold-hearted humourless know-it-all, constantly pulling you up for not trying hard enough. The worst part of it was it felt like they no longer belonged to the students, had simply been reclaimed as school property. This disconnection cut deep psychologically: it was bad enough having to hand your "friend" back at the end of term; some even found it difficult leaving them overnight in their recharging bays. These units had clearly extended the companion role played in earlier times by smart-phones and their various tech descendants, with many young people feeling bereft when separated from what they felt were intimate extensions of who they were as individuals.

The inevitable backlash had taken the form of social banishment, the one thing the students could fully control. Henceforth all learning buddies would only be engaged with for mandatory study purposes, outside of that, sent to Coventry: kept at arm's length and generally ignored as the goody-goody pains in the ass they'd become.

'OK…so this is the "ancient grudge" I was introduced to earlier,' said Kerry, taking it all in. 'But maybe then my off-the-cuff suggestion for the two tribes could turn out to be even more useful and apt than I thought. The play ends with the two sides coming together, so as well as uniting the fictional warring factions, our process might offer a way of healing this real life conflict closer to home and allow me to deliver on the Principal's request to show students and learning buddies working together in creative harmony?'

'Please tell me you're kidding?' said Meera Patel, mock-awestruck as she sat down to join them.

'Why not?' said Kerry, after getting her breath back. 'Anyway, it might be something to aim for, hang onto as a reference point; a guiding star?'

Meera smiled mischievously as she stole a glance at Mr Hubble who had been sitting there quietly chewing his pipe and half tuned-in to his own internal processes. With a wink to her two fellow humans, she said: 'Anyway, back to the play and all that delicious conflict – I'm thinking especially about all those fight scenes, where are you going to get the blood?'

Kerry picked up on the ruse, tapping her cheek with one finger as if giving her answer deep consideration. 'Hmm, maybe I should go for the real thing; ask the cast to volunteer the red stuff themselves; take transfusions throughout the rehearsal period? It would be really authentic and we wouldn't be wasting valuable ketchup.'

'I assume you're pulling our legs?' said Mr Hubble, taking the pipe from his mouth.

'Yes, I am,' said Kerry with a smile, pleased their android colleague had cottoned on.

'Should get a full house anyway,' chirped Inez.

Kerry relaxed back into her chair, allowing in some modest hope. At least her fellow members of staff were warming to the project. She could just imagine them sitting in the school's amphitheatre, eagerly waiting to give the thumbs down as Harper alias Juliet pondered on whether or not to use Romeo's dagger.

6

'So you can forget about auditions; I'm still Juliet, that goes without saying,' Harper announced the next day, laying down the law at the start of their first full session.

'In that case, I wonder who would be your Romeo?' mused Kerry, choosing to sidestep the challenge for the moment.

Harper puckered her lips. 'What's it matter, so long as he's a cool far-out kisser.'

Kerry looked at the learning buddies waiting on stand-by. 'How about you?' she asked the nearest one.

'Hey no way!' the girl squealed, getting doubly annoyed because Chuck and a few of the others were snickering. 'And that's my own tin can in case you didn't know.'

'What would be the problem with that?' said Kerry innocently. 'In fact with DAK 49 and yourself already aligned –'

'Are you kidding me!' pronounced Harper, probably more outraged this time at being upstaged.

As more giggles rippled through the group, the teenage terror turned a murderous shade of crimson to match her lipstick.

Kerry hadn't set out to tease, but she needed to establish who was boss here. Anyway, she felt she'd won a small but important round in asserting herself and that it would be wise now to back off. 'OK,' she said, sympathetically, 'how about DAK 17?'

'Fine,' said Harper, offering a token pout, trying not to look too rattled in front of everyone. 'Just ditch what I said about the kissing. I forgot about the crazy casting idea.'

'Anyway, we're running way ahead of ourselves,' said Kerry, switching the focus. 'I want to do plenty of exploration work as an ensemble before we even think about individual casting for whatever scenes we end up showcasing. So let's get started with a simple warm-up: can we form ourselves into a circle.' As she clapped her hands, the learning buddies came to full attention, almost embarrassingly willing and organised themselves into a small ring. In marked contrast, the kids stayed rooted to where they were, offering only a vague shuffling of feet. 'Thanks, but I did mean everyone? Can we make one big circle? And by the way, can anyone who hasn't done so already, please get rid of their gum?'

'Why?' drawled Little Stevie, 'it helps me concentrate.'

'Because they didn't have bubblegum in Shakespeare's time you dumb-ass!' said Chuck with a smirk. 'But they did have swords!' he added, stepping into the centre of the ring and showing off a fanciful fencing routine, duelling with an imaginary opponent. 'There's lots of crazy fighting in this play, right Miss Tracker?'

Although grateful Chuck was at least displaying some enthusiasm, Kerry was reminded of something she needed to attend to regarding school safety protocol when doing physical activities such as drama. 'Actually, since we're talking of weapons, I meant to ask you all to leave your stunners to one side while we're working.'

Carlos, one of the two remaining boys who hadn't spoken up until now, shook his head. 'Hey come on, what if some nutcase comes in and...'

Kerry was all too familiar with the tragic history of shooting incidents in US high schools. Yet another spate of killings in the late 2020's had finally ushered in taser-style stun guns for personal protection; it was now compulsory for each student to carry one. These quasi-weapons possessed identity codes to prevent them being turned on fellow students or staff; bad luck if you missed the first day of term was one morbid joke that did the rounds. The authorities had previously experimented with employing armed security guards, but that had proved ineffective, too many were required to shield an entire school against an assailant carrying an arsenal of assault rifles. Arming teachers had also been proposed but even with their unions weakened they'd managed to resist that as a solution. Another idea had been to bring in war veterans and others familiar with firearms and re-training them as teachers: this too was rejected – if a "Mr Milton" exploding was scary it would be nothing compared with one of these hired hands suffering a classroom meltdown. Even arming the learning buddies had been muted but that was dismissed due to ethical concerns around what a robotic device should or shouldn't be allowed to do with regard to using force, especially in relation to humans: definitely a grey if not a red no-go area.

'Anyway, they didn't have gum *or* guns back then,' added Chuck, with a lunging stab.

Kerry nodded her agreement. 'Yes, just one of the many things we'll have to consider in our approach to the play.' Taking further note of the boy's continuing athleticism with his imaginary sword she added: 'Of course, whatever implements we choose we'll certainly need to apply some disciplined choreography.'

As the group relented and placed their stunners on the table, Kerry continued with her preamble: 'So, following up on the idea we had last time, I'd like to explore a little more how we can best involve the learning buddies in helping us develop the play.'

'Hey, less of the "we" – that was *your* crazy notion!' said Harper, making an exaggerated show of chewing imaginary gum.

'But it was you that put it into my head with *your* clearly defined segregation…' Kerry broke off, noticing a frown on another face. 'You also look a little unsure, Li Jing?'

Jing adjusted his headband. 'I'm just thinking – if they didn't have gum or guns back then, they definitely didn't have droids.'

'Yo – good point,' cheered Little Stevie, punching the air. 'What does that say about having robots in the play?'

'OK,' said Kerry, 'maybe we should think of our android actors portraying people, not necessarily playing themselves?'

Wanda's hand shot up. 'It'll be weird though; whoever they're playing they'll still look like droids.'

'True,' said Kerry. 'In that case the audience will appreciate all the more how the learning buddies are acting – and that they're being asked to play something they're not. It'll help show off their performance skills.'

'Did you say skills?' Chuck snorted as he did a mocking imitation of a robot trying to juggle an oversized sword.

Kerry ignored Chuck and took a moment to examine the make-up of her group: 'Let's consider for a moment how the play is set in late 16th Century Italy. OK, so there were no androids in that society, but I doubt if there were any Afro, Arab, Asian or Hispanic Americans either. Also there were no female actors – and most of you will have to pretend to be a lot older than you are: so one way or another the audience will be asked to take a leap of faith.'

Kerry got a half-hearted group shrug in response; Wanda looked thoughtful at the reference to African-Americans, but none of them looked fully convinced.

'So the audience sees an android playing a human character and maybe they're a little surprised at first, but then they just get used to it, accept it as a theatrical conceit.'

'Maybe you could say that last item again in regular English!' said Tania, clicking her tongue Latino style.

'It just means the audience will appreciate all the more how the learning buddies are joining with us in common cause to present this play.'

Harper shook her head dismissively. 'OK, whatever all that highfalutin stuff means – maybe it's time for someone to get real here.'

'What did you have in mind?' asked Kerry, reasonably.

'For a start I need my droid on my own case to –'

'– Do all the hard work?' interjected Chuck, while at the same time sending Little Stevie a sly wink. Whether this was an open snub to Harper, or simply a willingness to back

Kerry on this occasion wasn't clear. Either way it stopped the girl in her tracks, leaving her silently fuming again.

'OK,' said Kerry, 'going back to what I was saying, let's try and think outside ourselves for a moment. Integrating the learning buddies into the play will offer a positive reflection of the broader set-up we have here in school, show everything off in a good light. That's supposed to be the main focus of this project; Mr Brady for one will be very pleased I'm sure.'

They all stared back at her, seeming to be weighing up the last factor in particular.

'And if you yourselves are a little uncomfortable with the idea, let's see if we can transfer some of that discomfort to our audience: challenge *them* to think.' She took a moment to make eye contact with all of them individually. 'I'm just asking you to stick with it for the moment, be willing to wait and see. What we're looking to present has to involve creative tension, the life-blood of drama; you can't have good theatre without it.'

Wanda looked around at the others; then decided to take the lead, offering a shrug of resignation. 'OK Miss, I guess you just *talked* us into submission, for the moment anyway.'

'Thank you so much for that,' said Kerry, hugely relieved. 'And I'm glad we had this discussion now, good and early, it will stand to us in the long run.' She was tempted to add her favourite mantra: "It's the process not the product" but quickly changed her mind, better to stop while she was winning.

Anyway, she was aware of what her responsibilities were. *Process* was all well and good, it was what Jim Brady had said he wanted to highlight. But Kerry also knew that he, the school and no doubt the whole world sure as hell also wanted *product.*

❖

'No pressure, but how are we getting on with the play?' asked Jim Brady as he joined Kerry later in the corridor. 'You haven't forgotten what's at stake here?'

'I'm simply here to save the school – something like that? Pull it back from the brink of self-destruction?' said Kerry with a smile.

Brady winced then continued good-humouredly: 'By the way, sorry not to have filled you in earlier on the full situation with the learning buddies.'

'No problem,' said Kerry, well over it by now.

'Anyway, by all accounts you handled it pretty well. So what can I say, Miss Tracker? How about, *"Be-bop-a-lula!"* roughly translating as, 'you're doing mighty fine so far'.

❖

'See how everything is always changing,' Greta observed, as the school's floodlights swept bands of shadows across the lawn's artificial surface, now a deep pink – adding a mesmeric rippling effect to the otherwise stillness of the evening.

'Yes, that is how it might often appear,' Gaia replied, tilting her chin thoughtfully.

'And one day *we* will change the *world*,' Greta continued encouragingly, giving her friend's arm an affectionate rub.

'You're not s'posed to sit out here doing weird stuff like that,' announced Harper curtly, as she and Wanda approached. 'Getting personal with an android, I could easily report you. It's bad enough you being a traitor to our cause.'

The two figures got up from the bench and without saying anything, wandered back towards the main campus buildings.

'Those two are freaky,' Wanda said, linking her own friend's arm as they walked on, before turning to enquire: 'So tell me, are you still against us doing this play or what, Harper?'

'Why are you asking?' said Harper, trying to appear disinterested.

Wanda shrugged. 'After all you said right at the beginning. Now you seem to be kind of going along with it?'

'If that's what you and everyone else thinks, that's fine by me,' said Harper, returning the shrug.

Wanda gave it some further thought. 'Miss Tracker goes on a bit, but she's sort of OK at the same time.'

This time Harper said nothing, offering a non-committal toss of the head.

Wanda continued: 'I was talking to the others; seems they're willing to wait and see what happens.'

'Sure, we'd better let it run then so, for the moment anyway,' said Harper, this time accompanied by a yawn.

It was getting dark. 'Guess it's time for us to go in,' said Wanda, as she spun around to steer them back towards the dorms.

'Yes, lead the way good gentlewoman!' declared Harper, changing her voice to a put-on theatricality. She even threw Wanda a grin, appearing to have broken out of her sombre mood for the moment.

Wanda pulled her friend's arm closer, relieved.

As they walked on, Harper allowed herself a private conspiratorial smile.

The following Monday Kerry began her second week at the school. In the main corridor she bumped into Liza Woodley who was in offering her usual support to anyone facing mental and emotional stress. The old song, "*I don't like Mondays*" entered Kerry's head: she had to admit to experiencing a little rawness herself having spent a first weekend in her new surroundings feeling a touch lonely, far from home. The news reports coming in concerning ever more awful things happening in the world had only added to her overall discomfort, even if it put her own challenges in perspective.

The fringe hub was due to be taken over through the lunch break that day for a Fair Trade event so Kerry had given the drama group some time off. She decided to go along to the venue anyway hoping for some uplift and a chance to observe the student population in a different social setting. On arrival she was encouraged to see a modest number of stalls and was particularly pleased to come across one manned by Carlos, Omar and Jing, who chuckled amongst themselves on first seeing her but then offered "peace" signs and an invitation to buy something.

While she was choosing, they dropped their guard further and revealed they were enjoying working on the play, at least so far. In gratitude, she took away a bag of coffee, some joss sticks and a decorative African necklace.

Unusually, at one stall the girl behind it had her learning buddy with her. Kerry knew this to be Greta Pearson who was in the same English class as the drama group. Greta had been talked about in the staffroom as a determined go it alone type who'd resisted the consensus in staying loyal to her LB, who she called "Gaia". As well as various food items, they'd laid out a number of paper plates with an invitation for anyone to write something on them.

'Write anything you like on the theme of "food"', said Greta, 'it could be a simple thought, or a poem maybe?' The girl smiled at her learning buddy who nodded back.

Kerry looked at what had already been offered, flinching at seeing the word "traitor" scrawled on one plate. As she caught Greta's eye, the girl shrugged and said: 'Free speech?'

Greta checked in again with her LB then said: 'We're thinking maybe we could follow this up by laying all the plates out in the canteen, just like it was a real table-setting?'

'I like it,' said Kerry, touched by the girl's almost painful enthusiasm.

'Like a kind of installation? Making a statement about the world we're living in?'

'Even better,' said Kerry.

'We all know about Martin Luther King right, especially with this whole retro 1960's thing – he's most famous for that "I had a dream" speech, but a lot of people don't know about him saying: "When I sit down for breakfast, I engage with half the world?"'

Kerry had an inspired thought: 'OK…I guess following on from that and then thinking about all the challenges facing him with the civil rights issue, he might then be thinking, "what's on my plate today?"'

'Oh yes, write that down, Miss Tracker!' said Greta, delighted.

'What do we do with these?' asked a boy wearing a long mod-style parka jacket covered in badges, circa UK 1963. 'Maybe they're Frisbees?' he added, bending his elbow as if about to try his luck.

Kerry said politely but pointedly: 'Maybe after you've written something you could go outside and pass it around like a Frisbee?'

The boy thought about it. 'Maybe later,' he said, giving Greta and Gaia a cold stare before wandering off.

Kerry wrote her piece onto one of the plates.

'Thank you so much,' said Greta, 'a lot of people are saying "why bother" but it can still be our moment if we can grasp it, right?'

'Yes, I think it can,' said Kerry.

'By the way, how's the drama presentation going? The rest of us in Miss Angelou's class are going to be reading from Emily Dickenson and other poets.'

'That sounds great, I'll look forward to it,' said Kerry, smiling as she picked up two extra-large bunches of bananas to take away with her.

Later on, Kerry was in the staffroom recounting her visit to Greta's fair trade stall, and how it was so sad that only a few of the plates had been filled in.

'You have to admire the way she's sticking by her learning buddy,' said Rob.

Meera shrugged. 'It probably didn't help having to write your piece by hand; hardly anyone does that anymore, especially the youth.'

'Not easy when you're used to letting AI do everything for you,' confessed Inez sitting down to join them. 'Look at me, I've got all the latest fancy gadgets, hardly need to do anything for myself anymore. My whole apartment's fully set up with EI too, so it knows all my moods, sensors everywhere picking up my vibrations, it even knows how I'm feeling from my wristband so when I get home it can be ready with some consoling words and a nice tall glass of wine.'

I usually order an android nurse when I'm off sick,' admitted Meera.

Howard Trent raised his iSpecs, taking advantage of an ad break in the baseball match he was watching. 'I had a droid maid come in for a short while: made me paranoid, couldn't help that creepy feeling it was watching over my shoulder all the time.'

Across the table, Mr Wilde looked at Mr Hubble for the briefest of moments; neither said anything.

'Funny to think,' said Inez, almost nostalgically, 'once upon a time there were only emails from a computer driving you crazy with reminders about who to get in touch with or maybe send a birthday message to. Now it's all slap there on your wrist or in your specs, you'd feel naked and lost without it.'

Kerry had been following the conversation with interest. 'With the drama presentation I'm expected to focus on the positive side to our connection with AI – but maybe within the tensions of the actual play there's room for showing how it's also contributed towards us becoming more detached and distanced from ourselves?'

8

The next day, Kerry entered the fringe hub for her third meeting with the drama group and was once more relieved to see they were all there.

Jing, Omar and Carlos were near the door engaging in a rapid-fire alphabet game, naming bands from the 1960's.

'*Animals* –' said Jing.

'*Byrds* –' said Carlos.

'*Country Joe and the Fish!*' said Omar. They all chimed together: "And it's 1 – 2 – 3…"

The boys noticed Kerry hovering nearby taking an interest.

'*Dead* – the *Grateful* kind?' she offered: "Anthem to the Sun?"

All three missed a beat then soft-punched the air in unison.

'Hey, here's our cool teacher!' declared Jing, waving a two-fingered peace sign.

Kerry returned the sign, happy with her modest success. Looking to the whole group, she sensed the girls had been watching and weighing her up; re-assessing her perhaps? It even crossed her mind fleetingly what the learning buddies thought of it all.

'Hi, all you cool dudes,' she said, chancing her luck further. 'OK, we've done a lot of talking the last two sessions; I think it's time to get physical. And just to get us started I have in mind a trust game? This should be fun but I think it will help too with our general focus.'

'When do we get started on the actual play?' said Little Stevie.

'Don't worry we'll be getting onto it in due course. I'm asking you to be patient for a little while. This is all part of the exploration "process" – believe me you'll see its worth as we go along.'

They all shrugged, seemingly content to wait and see what was on offer.

'For this I need everyone divided in two lines facing one another; you kids in one line will be the A's and your learning buddies opposite you in the other line will be the B's.'

'Is this how it's going to be in the play?' asked Jing.

'OK,' said Kerry patiently, 'let's really try to put the play completely to one side for the moment. This exercise is more to do with our actor training and to help underline how we're all working together as an ensemble.'

'Let's get on with it then,' said Chuck, cheerfully cutting her dead.

'So partner A will turn their back to partner B and close their eyes. Why? Because it takes away our normal reliance on sight, improving the other senses: hearing and touch in this instance.'

'Sure, kindergarten stuff,' drawled Harper as she turned around; trying to act casual.

'The B's can stand in a bit, maybe a short arm's length behind.'

The androids duly took a step in closer.

'What's going to happen?' asked Tania, looking anxious. 'Are *we* going to be the ones falling?'

'Yes, this first time round I want the learning buddies to do the catching.' Kerry wasn't sure herself why she'd made this choice, was it because she trusted them more? OK, everyone was on a learning curve, including her. 'You have to trust that you'll be caught. It's as simple as that.'

'So why the rubber mats?' asked Omar with a frown.

Kerry smiled, forced to accept the obvious contradiction. 'They're just a precaution, to keep Mr Brady and the school happy.'

Omar looked baffled. 'I still can't help thinking of this being about two tribes – aren't we supposed to hate one another's guts?'

Kerry nodded to acknowledge fair comment. 'Yes, that's why we're continuing to establish a clear distinction between character conflict and actor co-operation.'

'She's got an answer for everything,' groaned Wanda, raising her eyes to heaven. Kerry smiled, that was a compliment in her book.

'So, A's – when you're ready, just fall very slowly backwards...'

And it worked; each android receiver did its job: the kids swooned and fell – and despite some giggles and hysterics, no one came even close to hitting the mats.

'Good,' said Kerry, disguising her own relief. 'I think you'll all agree that was a success?'

❖

'What in heaven's name are they doing in there, AJ?' asked Meera Patel, pausing in the corridor – hearing a mixture of shrieks and screams coming from inside the fringe hub, 'sounds like torture.'

'I believe it means they are having fun,' replied android janitor FX72 with a smile.

❖

'So – now it's the turn of the learning buddies to do the falling,' said Kerry, after they'd all caught their breath.

'What if I drop my droid?' Chuck asked with a grin.

'The lightweight design should make them easy enough to catch,' said Kerry. She was comforted too by their possession of a latex skin, making them soft to the touch.

'Is it clear what I'm asking you to do?' she said to the nearest learning buddy.

'Some information required,' replied DAK 16. 'How fast would you like us to fall?'

Kerry paused. 'I'm not sure I fully understand your question?'

'Should we fall with the same speed that our partners did?' the android clarified.

Kerry thought about it. After Chuck's last remark she felt more cautious. 'OK…maybe make it a good bit slower this time?'

All the learning buddies stood poised and ready to

fall, with the kids waiting to embrace this communal challenge.

'OK,' said Kerry, '3-2-1 – and fall…*slowly*…'

'Jesus – it's like watching a clock!' groaned Carlos.

And it *was* slow…super-slow – with the learning buddies barely moving…

'Maybe not quite *so* slow,' said Kerry, trying to remain unfazed. 'Let's step it up say, five-fold?'

This time the naked eye could actually see them falling, each one ending up supine in the arms of their saviours.

'Hey, this guy's light as a feather,' said Tania.

Except for one pair: DAK 49 had clearly sensed Harper's supporting arms were not going to arrive in time; at the last moment the android had spun like a cat onto its front, landing in a press-up position.

Kerry held up a hand. 'OK, let's take a timeout and talk about what happened.' She looked to the android first.

'Necessary action was required to avoid self-harm,' said DAK 49 in a flat, reasonable tone.

Harper folded her arms. 'I just wanted to find out the truth. This was meant to be all about trust, right Miss Tracker: question answered wouldn't you say?'

❖

Howard Trent had his feet propped up on the coffee table. It was the end of the school day and Kerry was enjoying some wind-down time with her fellow staff.

The sports teacher scoffed: 'All droids are hard-wired to avoid self-harm unless it clashes with protection of a human life. It's in the basic manual, every lawnmower, vacuum cleaner and waste-disposal has it. Ain't that right, Mr Bennett, you're the android-lover, the so-called expert?'

Rob ignored the barbed remarks and continued stirring his coffee.

Inez stopped sipping her own drink. 'But Harper was right in a way: her android wasn't willing to fully trust her. Maybe she wanted to show that up.'

Kerry had momentarily drifted away from the conversation onto another train of thought connecting to her growing discomfort at the way her human companions blithely talked about their android teaching colleagues as if they weren't present. Maybe it was an attempt to uphold a status divide and hang on to some level of superiority? On the other hand, Mr Hubble and Mr Wilde sitting right there amongst them appeared oblivious to any offence caused. So maybe it was just her, Kerry, being ultra-sensitive. She decided to park these thoughts for the moment.

'Supposing I intended having another go at that exercise, but wanted to give the learning buddies a clean slate – could I re-programme DAK 49 not to anticipate a breakdown in trust?'

Rob put down his cup and flexed his fingers. 'First thing is you can't mess around with a DAK's hardwiring, that's out of bounds even to me. So there's no way around that compulsion to self-protect. And let's say you do this experiment again. Yes, you might even have an added problem because your android has by now self-adjusted to half-expect the girl to drop him.'

Howard snorted. 'Guaranteed, a *Harper Richards* will always drop you in the shit, given half a chance!'

Rob added: 'Plus the other LBs will have observed what happened and their evasive-action programming will also contain the new data.'

'In that case could I get permission from the Principal for a temporary override to their automatic self-defence systems?' asked Kerry.

'Then your dumb droid will surely walk into the first wall it comes to,' jeered Howard, notching up an imaginary victory point in the air with his finger.

Kerry stole another glance at the two android teachers sitting with them, as another idea popped into her head: 'What would happen if I got two learning buddies to do that exercise together?'

Mr Hubble and Mr Wilde lifted their heads simultaneously and looked at one another. Miss Curie, sitting across from them also looked over. All three looked as if they were about to say something, then changed their minds. But they remained attentive, waiting to hear the question answered.

Rob stroked his chin. 'I guess that shouldn't offer any problem; as long as the instructions were clear, they'd carry out the task you set for them to the letter.'

'So they *are* already programmed to protect one another?'

'Hmm,' said Rob, more cautious, 'only to a limited degree. Intervening to prevent damage to a fellow AI device will be in their hard-wiring, but not if that puts them in a situation of potential conflict with a human being, or involves taking sides in a conflict between two or more persons.'

Mr Hubble and Mr Wilde both nodded knowingly.

'I guess that's why the learning buddies didn't try to help poor Mr Milton,' said Inez.

Rob looked more thoughtful. 'He actually had them in passive-attentive mode at the time, following the play line by line via the play-appreciation download he'd given them. But that wouldn't have precluded them from becoming fully active if there'd been a threat to one of the students, like if someone was about to faint. Nor would it have stopped them in principle from assisting another AI device that was in danger.' Rob made his fingers into a temple of thought. 'The problem there was the deviousness of the assault: OK you had an inappropriate invasion of the android teacher's boundaries which might have rung warning bells, but against that there was no apparent threat of actual physical harm. While some kind of intervention from the LBs might have been expected in the form of a verbal caution, the event occurred primarily at an existential level above and beyond their restricted EI and therefore capacity to respond.'

Howard smirked. 'My God there you have it all – the whole goddamn story!'

Rob shrugged, indicating he had nothing else to add.

'I'll have to come up with something,' said Kerry, a touch despondent. 'I'd like any future exercises we do to be open-ended; free of baggage.'

'In that case you might be better off working out how to re-programme a certain somebody's daughter,' said Meera with a smile.

That evening, Kerry lay on the floor of her on-campus condo, staring up at its fractal stress-remover while using her wristband to activate her personal globe's voice recorder, ready to say her thoughts out loud. She still found doing this a little uncomfortable, recognising the contradiction of being a drama teacher who was self-conscious about hearing her own voice. Maybe that's why she'd never seriously considered becoming an actor herself? She hoped it wouldn't be long before technology was available in schools to allow her to record directly from her brain patterning, but in the meantime she'd have to put up with this discomfort. Anyway, it was great having her own learning assistant, capable of de-scrambling rambling thoughts into neat subject headings; identifying keywords that were already being projected from the globe's screen, ready now for her to review.

"Trust" – she focused her mind on what had happened at the end of the last session: Harper's action, or rather inaction, along with her follow-up pointed comment had served to provoke an enlightening discussion in the staffroom, but it still left Kerry with some key questions concerning how she was going to proceed in exploring the play. If the learning buddies really were going to take on playing characters in addition to fulfilling their roles as learning assistants, the first task would be enabling them to switch between the two functions, free to temporarily put aside their usual roles as the selfless facilitators of the needs of others to having the focus fully on *them*.

Then they faced the no small task of learning *how* to act for the stage. OK, they already had access to all the lines of the play and would obey any movement command from her, but to engage with all the underlying themes alongside the kids, they needed to be flexible and open to give and take. She'd certainly need to release them from the basic software programme they'd been given by Mr Milton and let them operate in freeform mode under her guidance. But as the incident with Harper and DAK 49 had starkly revealed, while the kids were in theory free to do what they wanted, these android actors were still handicapped by fundamental safety features compelling them to intervene when either they or a human being were at risk. With a tragic work like *Romeo and Juliet*, based on conflict and a good deal of pain and hurt, surely this would restrict how they were going to inhabit many if not most of the play's persona unless they were able to operate like their human counterparts with the capacity to distinguish between actor and character, move fluidly between truth and pretence, reality and fiction.

Kerry also had to face up to the obvious limitations posed by their general stiffness. She wondered if she could dare to ask Jim Brady for special permission to restore their previous empathy settings, maybe even grant her a temporary EI upgrade. It wouldn't have to be at the level of a Mr Wilde or Miss Angelou, in fact she'd be happy with whatever emotional intelligence was built into the school's android janitor, who certainly appeared very much on the ball. Enough anyway for them to interact with the kids and at least give the impression of having a free will and able to display some warmth even if it was simulated. How else were they going to "feel" their way into their parts, help bring the play to life?

9

Jim Brady turned away from the surveillance monitors to give Kerry his full attention. 'OK, this is no small request: you want your LBs back to their previous empathy settings and maybe even add an EI upgrade to boot so they can be more open and put some emotion into their acting?'

'Both would really help, given what we're trying to do.'

Brady frowned. 'You think it's a good idea, them being more "open" – look what happened to poor old Milt.'

Kerry gave an involuntary flinch at the thought.

'I was only kidding,' said Brady, 'Mr Milton was a special case, way different to anything else we have here.'

'It's just I could do with them being more flexible and spontaneous; good acting requires that small level of uncertainty: y'know, like Heisenberg?'

Brady smiled at the science reference. 'OK, you're doing well so far in a blatant attempt to soften me up. But any changes would have to be run by Charles Richards; after all it's his babies you'd be messing with.'

'Would you be so good as to ask him for me?' said Kerry sweetly.

Brady rubbed his jaw. 'I know his company's got a lot of important stuff going on at the moment, including some kind of hush-hush government contract coming down the line. You're asking me to go back on our previous decision to downgrade the LBs when we're under enough pressure and scrutiny as it is.'

Kerry tapped her fingers on the armrest of the chair. 'You know yourself how this drama showcase could be so important, not just for the kids in the group, but for the whole school. Maybe we can be showing the way here, shining a light?'

Brady leaned back rubbing his chin, obviously sympathetic. 'OK, it's clear how this would aid our overall objective and maybe if it turned out well and the kids demonstrated a new maturity towards how they relate to their learning buddies, yes I guess we could be seen as a beacon of positivity...'

While Brady was considering, Kerry ran her eyes around the room, noticing there was a new calendar on the wall, this time with a 1960's theme: the page for "May" showed The Loving Spoonful band from California. 'Nice calendar and a band from my neck of the woods no less, maybe that's a good omen.'

Brady read out the words under the image: "What a day for a daydream." He sighed and sat forward. 'It was a present from the staff back in January; I finally gave in and put it up instead of the other one. See what a big old cuddly bear I am?'

Kerry bit her tongue and waited.

'OK, fine,' said Brady at last, 'I'll do my best to catch Richards at a good time. Maybe he'll agree if it's just the ones in your charge; at least for now anyway.' He allowed himself a grin before adding, 'Hell, I was always against that downgrade anyway: can't do any harm to loosen those stiff-lipped stuffed-shirts up a bit.'

'Oh, I almost forgot,' said Kerry, deciding to push her luck, 'I was also wondering if you'd relax the usual rules and allow the kids to dress them up a little?'

❖

'So how is it all coming along?' asked Inez over mid-morning coffee. 'Is it still going to be humans versus androids?'

Kerry had joined the small group of staff gathered around the table, eager to share her current thoughts and get some feedback. 'Hmmm, I'm not sure about that initial idea for the two warring tribes – maybe it's too clichéd and predictable; too *West Side Story?*'

'That excellent old movie is enjoying yet another revival,' said Mr Wilde.

Miss Angelou raised a finger. 'The English National Theatre did an interesting one recently with the Montagues as Mods and the Capulets as Rockers, set in the seaside town of Brighton.'

'Yes, by the sea would be nice,' said Meera wistfully. 'I still love that old movie where they used Verona Beach, back in…' she snapped her fingers trying to remember, 'you know, the crazy punk version with a very youthful and cute Leonardo what's his name…'

'Di Caprio,' said Mr Hubble. '1996 I believe.'

'Wasn't there a popular TV series one time with the

Capulets as vampires and Montagues as werewolves?' asked Inez.

'Hell, why not just make half of them zombies!' declared Howard from behind his iSpecs.

Kerry looked even more doubtful. 'I don't want it clichéd *or* superficial. I'm hoping for something that will challenge cultural stereotypes.'

Inez took a moment to pass round a plate of cookies.

'Thank you...yummy,' said Miss Kahlo who'd just joined them along with Mr Rembrandt. 'Is it going to be set it back in the 16th Century?' she continued, while passing the plate on, 'imagine that gorgeous historical decor?'

'Sure,' said Kerry, 'but again I'm kind of reluctant: I was hoping for something I don't know...different, more innovative.'

Inez looked inspired: 'Well, how about you place it in the future?'

'Science fiction,' said Miss Angelou with a nod. 'But we still mustn't lose sight of the initial question concerning the nature of the divide: the cause of the conflict.'

'Shakespeare didn't exactly bother,' said Inez, 'kept it all pretty vague.'

"*Two households both alike in dignity...*" quoted Mr Wilde.

'Why not really throw the can among the pigeons and divide them into red and blue voters?' said Howard rubbing his hands together.

'I don't know about anyone else but my head is spinning with it all,' said Meera, reaching for the cookie plate only to see it was empty.

Kerry checked the time. 'Anyway, I guess we'll have to come back to it. But thanks for the brainstorming everyone, that was really helpful. There's plenty there for me to chew over, I'm confident something will work out. Meanwhile maybe I'll just tread water a little by doing some work on make-up.'

❖

Kerry scrutinised the learning buddies. Essentially androgynous, their perfectly proportioned bodies were for the moment unadorned by any cosmetic additions or costume accessories. Personalised items had been allowed once upon a time, but unfortunately many students had gone overboard with decoration and the school had considered it a distraction from focused studying as well as feeding social competition and peer-pressure. Even before the empathy downgrade, dressing them up had been banned.

'As part of the process of exploring the play, I thought we might give some broad attention to character building,' said Kerry as she rolled out her yoga mat and started to cover it in odd pieces of material, some cheap jewellery, artificial hair; a few hats and scarves – along with scissors, Velcro patches, ribbons, markers, tape.

'I don't get it,' said Jing, looking at the various objects.

Kerry glanced at the learning buddies, standing at ease, but attentive. 'And more importantly, for this to be a real acting ensemble, we need to do something to help bring our fellow actors a bit closer to our own level, if like yourselves they're going to extend their personalities into developing characters for the play.'

'What personalities?' Chuck guffawed, making a face at the others.

'Exactly Chuck,' said Kerry. 'You have it there in a nutshell.'

'Are we going to be dressing *them* up?' said Tania. 'You mean it's allowed?'

'Yes, thanks to how well we're doing so far, I was able to get a special dispensation earlier from Mr Brady, just while we're working on the play; and so long as we keep it within the confines of the rehearsal room.'

Wanda's face brightened. 'Hey, that's cool; it'll be like they used to do with those old Barbie dolls!'

'Isn't it kind of early days for this sort of thing?' asked Carlos, confused. 'We don't even have a clue what we're doing yet.'

'True, we don't even know who's playing what,' said Omar.

'Or *what's* playing *who*,' said Chuck, looking sideways at the learning buddies.

'Yes, I'm fully aware we haven't decided yet on what parts anyone will be playing in any of the scenes, soon enough I'll be asking you to take on the challenging task of inhabiting all the characters on offer. But in the meantime I thought we could just have a bit of fun playing around with how externals can help reflect inner identity. Think of how much importance you attach to this whole retro 1960's thing.'

'Hell,' said Jing, scratching his head. 'You sure can talk Miss, maybe you should be in the play yourself.'

Kerry allowed herself to enjoy the back-handed compliment for a moment. 'Anyway, shall we get started?'

'I hear the Principal has given Miss Tracker permission for her cast to clothe and decorate their learning buddies?' said Mr Globe, sounding a touch stuffy as he joined Mrs Martinez at the drinks dispenser.

'So what if he has?' replied Inez, 'maybe it gives them all a chance to let their hair down.' She had a further thought, staring at Mr Globe's bald head. 'Even give guys like yourself some hair to think about!'

Mr Globe smiled back, perhaps picturing himself similarly endowed.

Inez was clearly in a playful mood: passing by Mr Wilde sitting in his usual place, on impulse she leaned over and expertly adjusted his silk scarf. 'There, that's better Oscar,' she said mischievously as the android teacher returned her a bemused smile.

Meera looked up from something on her screen. 'I guess it's only fair the LBs get a chance to show off their personalities like everyone else.' She herself was wearing a loose cotton tunic over flowery silk trousers accompanied by a hippie headband. In contrast Inez was showing off a more tailored outfit reminiscent of Jackie Kennedy-Onassis when she was still a president's wife. Howard Trent sported a cowboy shirt and neckerchief circa the 1960's *Rawhide* TV series, while Rob Bennett was dressed in his usual smart slacks along with a formal shirt and tie, looking something like the straight-laced kid in the movie *Rebel Without A Cause*.

As Kerry entered and headed for the drinks dispenser, Inez called over to her, 'How goes it with the dressing-up?'

'Really well,' said Kerry, quickly filling her cup. 'I decided to leave them on their own, just for a minute – allow them some space.'

'Is this an extension to your earlier trust game?' asked Miss Curie, looking over.

'Yes, I guess so,' said Kerry, pleased it could be perceived that way, checking the time and leaving them with an upbeat wave.

Inez turned back to the others. 'I'm really looking forward to this play – especially the balcony scene: *"What light through yonder window breaks?"* she intoned, mimicking Romeo gazing upwards adoringly: *"Is it the fairest Juliet?"*

Meera inserted imaginary gum into her mouth, chewing it around before stretching it out in a thin line with her fingertips the way teenagers do and tried to capture the enunciation of a gummed-up Harper: *"Is that you my lurve? Oh, Romeo, where 'fart' thou Romeo!"*

Inez sputtered and almost choked on her coffee. 'Now, that's going too far Mrs P; more decorum if you please, we have Mr Globe in our company today.'

'So what?' challenged Meera with a wicked chuckle, 'isn't he a man of the *world*?' She started to snort uncontrollably at her two little gems of wit; her face contorting with the exertion.

Mr Globe smiled but at the same time managed to look somewhat morose. No doubt he could appreciate the creative wordplay that had just taken place, cognisant of the subtle dynamics of both jokes: but how was he to process the way Mrs Patel was now almost doubled-up, clutching at her heart and wheezing, barely able to get her breath back? He could never experience what he knew to be the masochistic pleasure of having what was known as one's "funny-bone" tickled until it became almost unbearable; feel that exquisite pain extend into the ribs, approaching the very limits of ecstasy; leading finally to the unimaginable bliss of release from such torment…

❖

Kerry stared eyes wide at the new-look learning buddies, all wearing various combinations of hats, caps, ear-rings; with lots of wild make-up designs. It was weird to see some of them with hair. Be careful what you wish for she thought: before this an android couldn't have a bad hair day.

'Hey – my one looks almost cute,' cooed Tania.

DAK 16 was looking thoughtfully into a mirror held up by Wanda. 'What's the matter,' the girl said, 'you want that fringe longer?'

Harper's learning buddy had acquired her shaded iSpecs; along with some dazzling earrings and bright orange lipstick. 'Cool huh, Miss Tracker?'

'Yes, I like it,' said Kerry, genuinely. Turning to the boys, they'd obviously come to a collective decision as all of theirs wore improvised bandanas; eyes and mouths exaggerated with make-up to appear menacing: like a cross between crazed zombies and a gang of B-movie martial-arts villains.

'What do you think Miss Tracker,' asked Jing, obviously not sure himself.

'I think it shows great imagination and offers much food for thought,' said Kerry, with a diplomatic smile.

'Would be almost cool if we could keep them like this,' said Carlos with a carefree shrug.

'Maybe we can bring in a bunch of different outfits and really finish them off?' added Wanda.

'Well, I'm sure we'll have more opportunities to continue our experiments once we start getting deeper into the play's characters,' said Kerry, pleased but not wanting to get too distracted from the main objective.

'It's like they almost belong to us again,' said Tania, verging on nostalgic.

'Fine, let's not go overboard,' said Harper. 'Maybe it just looks that way on the surface.' It was meant as a dampener, but lacked the usual edge, almost as if she was only going through the motions of being difficult on this occasion.

'Progress?' thought Kerry, allowing herself an inner smile.

'Anyway, we won't be bragging about it outside of here,' said Chuck, 'I've got a reputation to protect.'

10

Jim Brady was tucking into a bowl of breakfast muesli and getting started into a new day by "consulting his oracles" – that's what he called watching old classic-comedy movies. Right now he had one of his all-time favourites, *Punchline*, from 1988 running in the main hexagon of the office globe: the scene where Tom Hank's stand-up character has a meltdown on stage. Brady found himself thinking of Mr Milton, wondering if the agony was in any way comparable.

The globe pulsed with an incoming call as Charles Richards's face appeared and relegated the movie to a smaller honeycomb. Brady lowered the sound. 'Hello Sir, what can I do for you?' he said to Richards's hologram, projecting into the room.

'I got a call saying you wanted to talk to me about something, Brady? I've been meaning to check in anyway and see how everything is settling down again after recent events.' Richards rubbed his neck as he made an effort not to look and sound too sheepish. He was bare-legged, wearing only a bathrobe. 'It goes without saying I'm still none too happy my own daughter was so involved.'

Brady nodded sympathetically but said nothing, retaining a diplomatic silence, conscious of his own fully clothed virtual presence in what appeared to be a shower room.

'Anyway,' Richards continued, 'thankfully we seem to have survived the initial negative reaction coming from outside the school.'

Brady eased back a little in his chair. 'Yes Sir; and things are looking good and relaxed here inside, in fact pretty upbeat all round. One positive thing I can report: the open day drama presentation of *Scenes from Romeo and Juliet* is firmly back on track, with our fine new director in charge.'

'Well that's good to know,' said Richards, also relaxing a little. 'And Harper is one of those on board?'

'Yeah, she's very much a key member of the team by all accounts.'

'I'm very relieved to hear that. Good work Brady.'

'You'll also be pleased to hear that Miss Tracker has come up with some excellent ideas for showing off the LBs to full effect.'

'Well that's more good news,' said Richards, perking up even more. 'As I said before, they're sure to prove their worth when it comes to assisting the young actors with learning their lines, researching their parts; maybe help too with moving props around and that sort of thing.'

'Actually, she plans to have them up on stage taking part in the actual scenes.'

There was a small pause as Richards took this in. 'You don't say…yes, I guess there might be a call for a few walk-ons.'

'In fact, she's thinking of assigning them full speaking roles.' Brady deliberated before deciding to be fully upfront: 'She wants the two warring factions to be made up of humans and androids...'

Richards immediately frowned at a notion too far. 'Come now, do you really think that's wise Brady? Having the LBs on stage is one thing but surely taking that slant only feeds the divisions we currently find ourselves facing down there – not to mention attracting more negative attention from the public.'

'Like we were saying before, don't forget this is all about the process: her argument is that by the end of the play itself the divisions are healed and so the hope is that through working on it together, it will also deal with the real cold war going on between the kids and their android assistants.'

Richards nodded, seeing the merit. 'And the kids are OK with all this? Working alongside their learning buddies practically as equals?'

Brady shrugged. 'So it seems; she appears to have got them past that first hurdle.'

Richards pondered on it some more then shook his head. 'I'm still wondering though Jim if this is the wisest thing: you already know my feelings on this, at the moment we could do without unnecessary attention being focused on our android family, Allied Robotics has some sensitive government contracts coming up that I wouldn't want to jeopardise.'

Brady offered a helpless shrug. 'The kids are already hooked on the idea; it might be hard to pull back now without risking another teen rebellion.'

Richards considered the potential reputational damage from such an outcome; especially the likely-hood his daughter would be mixed up in it again. After a moment's further reflection he reluctantly gave way. 'OK, I'll have to trust your instinct on this. I just hope your new teacher knows what she's doing.'

'I think this one has her head well screwed on,' said Brady, deadpan. 'I'll be keeping a close eye on her anyway.'

Making a mental note of this, Richards asked: 'Was there anything else you wanted to update me on?'

Brady considered briefly whether to bring up Kerry's request for an EI upgrade to the learning buddies – that was what his initial call to Richards had been about after all. No, better to stop while he was winning, the moment didn't feel right; as a comedian he knew it was all about timing, there would be other opportunities to slip it into the mix. 'No, I guess that's all for now.'

❖

After concluding his conversation with Richards, Jim Brady stepped out of his office onto the viewing gallery to stretch his legs and get a change of scenery. He gazed down at the mix of people and androids moving across the plaza like two forms of exotic wildlife, while beneath their feet the floor's pink and white pattern changed to green and red, then to purple and orange; then to a sudden scattering of many colours as the image appeared to shatter – like in one of those antique toy kaleidoscopes.

Brady felt unimpressed, even if he was the Principal. Such attempts at stimulation via distraction were surely indicative of what had gone wrong in society as a whole with mass addiction to so-called "reality" TV, online games; social media and myriad other forms of escape, resulting in people living less and less in the real world. Once screens became portable this alternative reality was even harder to get away from; now with iSpecs it was literally stuck to your face. Here at Big Rock it had been a questionable decision to go along with, rather than try to stem the flow towards oblivion.

Another switch in the floor pattern reminded him of underwater wildlife films showing shoals of fish. He'd so loved seafood, now only a memory due to the global ban on marine products following the 2037 'fish-flu' pandemic. This had followed on the heels, or rather wings and trotters of several waves of bird and swine flu running through the early-mid 2030's. Humankind had sadly learnt little from the coronavirus disaster of 2020. Each outbreak had eventually been brought under control, but with a substantial loss of human life and at the expense of billions of chickens and pigs, not to mention uncountable numbers of birds and fish.

The sad case of the chicken had been especially poignant to someone with Brady's off-beat scientific mind: tragic-comic to think how the closest living descendant of the great reptile, Tyrannosaurus Rex, to escape the first wipe-out 65 million years earlier, had evolved into a creature that survived purely by becoming indispensable to the new top predator, *Homo sapiens*. It had in fact been a remarkable feat of adaption and endurance: before the more recent catastrophe, they'd represented eight out of ten birds on the planet. But now, sadly, the noble bird-reptile had succumbed to a second extinction, albeit not total – there were still a few left in zoos under strict quarantine behind infection-proof glass. The current "chicken" you got in eateries was a vegetable substitute – and maybe that would be extinct too the way things were going.

Jim Brady blinked at another switch in the kaleidoscope – then became aware of Miss Tracker moving across the floor like a cursor across a computer screen. He wondered if there would ever be a day he could invite her out for a fish dinner.

❖

'Everyone freeze!'

Rob Bennett pointed his stun-gun as Chuck lay on the ground with DAK17 looming over him.

No-one moved.

❖

'I have a *feeling* about this drama presentation,' said Meera Patel, to no-one in particular as she absent-mindedly pushed away her lunch plate.

'I suppose I don't,' said Miss Angelou, as she got up to go to her next class. It was a straightforward reply, a simple statement of fact. But why the android teacher chose that moment to become lost in thought while she paused to pick a small crumb from her sleeve wasn't immediately clear.

❖

'So what happened exactly?' Jim Brady sighed as he put aside his sandwich and swivelled his newly installed 1950's vintage barbershop chair around to face Kerry. 'I hope you realise this is eating into my lunch,' he said dolefully.

'I thought I'd prepared them well for this session, taking time establishing clear ground rules. We also warmed up with a *feelings circle*.'

Brady raised an eyebrow. 'You'll have to fill me in on that one.'

'Someone picks an emotion such as "happy" and says it out loud. They all repeat it back as a chorus. Then we go round again, this time adding a physical gesture to go with each feeling. Again, the whole group repeats it back.'

'OK, I see the reasoning…this is all about "acting" as in pretending to feel something?'

'Everyone gets a chance to express a range of emotions, including what might be termed "negative" feelings.'

'So an LB might show "anger" for instance without actually getting angry?'

'Exactly, I think we're on the same page here.'

'Fine,' said Brady. 'Now let's go back to what happened.'

'I thought it was time to look at an actual scene, reward them for their show of faith so far. It made sense to start at the beginning: *Act One, Scene One* – the opening encounter in the street firstly between the Montague and Capulet servants and then their noble masters?'

'OK, so take me through it, blow by blow,' said Brady, leaning back.

'It was working fine until Chuck got a little carried away as Tybalt.'

Brady stroked his chin. 'You'll have to remind me, I have that old Baz Luhrmann movie in my head – was Tybalt the crazy Latino with the handgun?'

Kerry grimaced: 'We were going by Shakespeare's version where they have *swords* – definitely not guns.'

'I hope you're not using real ones?'

'*Imaginary* ones for the moment: just to be really on the safe side.'

Brady shrugged. 'Imaginary weapons, what could possibly go wrong?'

'OK, we have to back up a moment to when Benvolio, who is master to the servants on the Montague side, appears on the scene –'

'This is the guy wearing the Hawaiian shirt in the same movie, kind of punked-up hair?'

'That's the one. I wanted to try out one of the learning buddies to see how it worked out, so I had DAK 17 playing the part. He tries to act as a peacemaker but foolishly draws his own weapon as a show of authority –'

'Maybe not such a good idea,' said Brady.

'Because in comes Tybalt, master to the Capulet servants, played by Chuck; he sees Benvolio and raises his…'

Brady put up his hand: 'You don't have to say it.'

'Next thing, Lords Capulet and Montague appear and stick their noses in, waving their fists and flourishing their –'

'"*Awopbopaloobop – awopbamboom!*" that's a lot of imaginary weapons flying around!'

'Thankfully, Prince Escalus arrives; he has a sword too by the way, but doesn't need to use it because his authority is enough to put an end to the fighting.' Kerry paused to take a breath. 'Anyway, that's what *should* have happened according to the script. Unfortunately, Chuck couldn't resist one final lunge at DAK 17.'

'And the android took evasive action for self-protection, inadvertently causing Chuck alias Tybalt to end up flat on his backside?'

'Yes, that's exactly what happened. But hey, here comes the best bit.'

'You've been saving that till last,' said Brady, deadpan.

'Don't you see? DAK 17 instinctively went into self-protect mode, but "in character" as Benvolio instead of responding to what would have been the normal impulse to protect Chuck from harm; in other words the android temporarily switched its loyalty to the pretend situation, i.e. the play.'

Brady couldn't help being impressed, even if he still looked wary. 'I suppose the obvious irony here being Chuck rather than DAK 17 getting his reality-pretend boundaries in a muddle?'

Kerry made an attempt at a joke: 'You win some you lose some?'

Brady managed to smile and wince at the same time. 'Anyway, the long and short of it is you're presenting this as a human failing – the android wasn't to blame?'

'Yes, I guess that's what I'm saying.'

Brady sighed. 'OK, so no one was hurt, maybe I don't have to make a formal report. On the other hand I've been waiting for the right moment to approach Charles Richards about your upgrade, but if I ask now I feel I'd have to mention this incident and he may not see the whole thing quite as positively. So unfortunately we may have to sit tight on that one for a little while longer.'

'Sure,' said Kerry, feeling her hopes somewhat dented.

❖

After Kerry had left his office, Jim Brady resumed to eating his lunch and sat for a while thinking through what had happened. This idea of hers to give the learning buddies actual parts in the play: did it have the potential to badly backfire? Not to mention an EI reversal and upgrade that would set her team of LBs apart from the others and might further threaten the school's already fragile social cohesion.

He got up and went over to examine his collection of old DVDs and vintage vinyl records, running his eye over the titles. When it came to big questions that entered higher philosophical realms, he could do no better than check out a master guru like Lenny Bruce, or find inspiration in one of the early rock and roll greats: Elvis, Eddie, Buddy...Chuck?

Brady stuffed down the last morsels of food and shuffled over to one end of the room and turned. Balancing low he proceeded to traverse the floor in a series of one-legged manic hops while holding an imaginary guitar in impersonation of Chuck Berry's famous duck walk. It felt stir-crazy but also mighty liberating; needy relief from having to play the part of a responsible human being.

❖

Kerry descended via the glass drop-pod onto the plaza and watched for a moment as human and android bodies intermingled through various patterns of movement. She noted how even within the latter population there was a distinction between teacher androids that were free to roam and learning buddies forced to stick close to their assigned student despite being given the cold shoulder. Keeping up wasn't easy, compared to its advanced intelligence a DAK's locomotion was limited, so in order to match strides with a student moving at even a moderate pace, tiny rollers in the soles of the feet had to be employed, so the android appeared to skate rather than walk.

A number of students were enjoying a timeout at rest tables fringing the area. Most had their LBs parked off to one side, but a tiny minority still kept theirs close by. Such "traitors to the cause" inevitably had to face banishment for letting the side down: Kerry could see Greta Pearson and her learning buddy sitting together away from everyone else. Some of these "oddballs" were considered to be beyond the reach of peer-pressure and so were generally ignored: right that moment "child-prodigy" Norman Hale was playing a game of high speed checkers with his learning buddy. While he took no more than a few seconds over each move, his android opponent made instant replies, demoralising for anyone else, but all in a day's work for Norman, battling it out on behalf of humankind. In fact every now and then he managed to achieve a respectable draw.

Kerry became aware of another contest taking place around which a small crowd had gathered: two learning buddies were engaged in a game of power-chess, which in itself wasn't unusual, androids had long been used in exhibition bouts to show off their skills with everything played out in a blur of lightning moves, leading to inevitable stalemate as both players could download all the major tournaments ever recorded, so neither could be taken by surprise and beaten.

But on this occasion something was noticeably different, an electrical charge hung in the air akin to the atmosphere surrounding a playground fight; gladiatorial: the collective unconscious responding to the thrill of danger and the unexpected. Opposing one another were DAK 14 and DAK 27 – learning buddies assigned to Omar and Carlos from the drama group. Both boys were trying to display an air of detachment, yet it was obvious they were keenly interested in what was happening.

Kerry made her way over to get a closer look, trying to figure out was giving this particular game its edge. Was it the body-language? She detected a barely perceptible holding of eye-contact after each move: androids didn't normally look at each other so intently. There was a subtle yet palpable tension in these brief moments of non-verbal communication, reminding her of certain plays she'd studied at college for a dissertation on 20th Century Western Theatre: works by David Mamet and Harold Pinter with his "Theatre of Menace". It also brought to mind what was possibly an apocryphal story concerning the infamously pernickety Irish playwright Samuel Beckett who, on witnessing a rehearsal of *Waiting for Godot* had gone so far as to lecture the actors, urging them to pay closer attention to the varying number of dots he'd inserted after each *pause...*

Kerry moved her attention back and forth between the seated androids playing the game and the human observers who loomed over them cheering and goading, stoking the fires of competition and conflict: or maybe this was just more projection on her part?

❖

"Happy birthday Mrs Patel – happy birthday to you…!" At the end of a school day there was simply nothing to compare with a staffroom full of teachers singing when a number of them happened to be androids. Expertly conducted in four-part harmony by an animated Rob Bennett, at the centre of it all Messieurs Hubble, Globe, Wilde and Tchaikovsky offered themselves up as a strange form of male barber-shop quartet. Mr Rembrandt had opted out from the singing to do a quick sketch of the happy scene.

Likewise, the female songbirds led by Inez and Kerry along with Miss Angelou, Miss Curie and Miss Hideko also acquitted themselves admirably. Not to be outdone, Miss Kahlo was adding paint to her own canvas.

For the special occasion, Meera Patel was dressed in traditional Indian costume complete with a colourful sari accompanied by lots of bracelets and other jewellery.

'You do look extra lovely today,' said Inez, 'so nice to be oneself for a change.'

'The big five zero,' whispered Meera, cutting into her cake, 'but don't tell anyone!'

'I guess we won't be celebrating too many more birthdays in here, Mrs P,' said Inez whimsically, before turning to the younger teacher next to her. 'If you stay on Kerry, it'll be up to you to carry the torch; you're definitely the baby of the gang.'

'I'll be twenty-seven this year and already I feel ancient,' said Kerry good-humouredly.

Mr Hubble coughed politely as he sat down to join them. 'Without wishing to compete, I do believe I entered this world even more recently: eleven months, five days, three hours, four minutes, eleven point five seconds ago to be almost precise.'

'Heavens!' said Inez, but was then lost for something else to add.

'In that case we'll have to light a single candle when it's your *first* birthday,' said Meera. 'Here Mr Hubble, you can have a share of *my* cake for the moment.'

Howard Trent had entered the staffroom; he sidled over and rudely helped himself to an oversized chunk.

'And not so much as a "thank you very much" to the birthday girl!' declaimed Inez, scowling at the interloper. 'Where were you anyway for the singing?' she added.

Howard glanced at the three members of the android quartet still standing huddled together. 'Happy returns,' he grunted to Meera through a mouth-full of cake. He then plonked himself down in Mr Milton's old seat, receiving daggered looks from everyone.

'What's the matter? Don't tell me I'm stepping on someone's oh so sensitive toes?' he said, staring in Rob's direction.

The younger teacher looked away, saying nothing.

'Cat got your tongue?' said Howard. 'Or should I make that *droid*?'

'I could say plenty if I chose to,' Rob replied impulsively, but then appeared to regret the comment, withdrawing behind the safety barrier of his cake.

'Well is that so?' said the older man, sensing an opening. 'Sure, we don't know the half of what's going on around here. I dare say there might even be someone among us with a number of things he's not telling?'

As Rob continued to ignore the taunts, the sports teacher swiped the table-top touch-screen in front of him. 'Oh my, now look who we have here?' said Howard, eyes wide as he displayed on the nearest wall what appeared to be a newspaper shot of Rob looking like a hippie with long hair and beard and flowers in his hair. A second figure materialised itself alongside him: an android, similarly attired. Both had big grins on their faces and were making peace signs.

'That was a good while back,' said Rob awkwardly.

'Looks recent enough to me,' said Howard, dismissively, before launching into a few nasal lines of a song from the 1960's – "*They may say…*"

Inez wiped a line of cake icing from her lip. 'Don't let him rile you Rob; you looked good with all that "flower-power and long hair"; this fool doesn't know his elbow from his hairy ass.'

The sports teacher glanced over at Miss Hideko wearing her Olympic medal. 'I deserve gold just for turning up here every day,' he moaned before turning his attention to the ranks of android "drone" teaching aids glued to their monitors. 'Look at them all, do they ever stop trying to better themselves! Give a monkey a spanner along with a banana and what happens next? You're flat on your backside looking under your car for missing wheel-nuts!' The "joke" sounded like it might have been passed down through the Trent family generations and by now lost whatever sense it might ever have contained.

Inez released a weary sigh and turned back to Kerry. 'By the way, we heard what happened with Chuck Harrington and one of the learning buddies: another silly boy getting a little carried away with himself.'

'Oh yes, the infamous "imaginary" weapon,' said Meera. 'You'd better call those improvisation sessions of yours *thrust* rather than *trust* games,' she added with a chuckle, spearing herself another helping of cake.

❖

Later, as she was about to leave the main building and head for her condo, Kerry passed AJ hovering near the doorway sucking up litter. 'Is the play going well, Miss Tracker?' asked the janitor.

'Yes very well in fact; and thank you for asking, AJ,' the teacher answered, somewhat touched by the android's keen interest.

11

aving finished her evening meal, Kerry was enjoying a glass of wine while lolling against a plumped up cushion and indulging herself with the balcony scene in Franco Zeffirelli's 1968 movie version of *Romeo & Juliet*. After the incident between Chuck and DAK 17 she was keen to remember the play wasn't all about violence and conflict – it was principally about love.

A while later the action had moved on to *Act Three Scene Five* – the early morning "post-consummation" bedroom scene, reminding Kerry that love also meant sex, for not only did the hero and heroine fall in love, get married and finally die in each other's arms – along the way they also spent one whole night together.

So how to view social conventions and taboos contained in a 16th Century play through the lens of current attitudes and norms? Kerry was keen to take on board the views of her 21st century teenage cast while being mindful they were still aged between fifteen and sixteen.

She reminded herself that in Shakespeare's day it was quite normal for a girl to be married at that age: the Bard had even gone so far as to reduce Juliet's age to fourteen in his version of what was already by then a well-known story. Wanting to be true to realism in his own film, Zeffirelli had made a point of choosing underage actors for the two principal roles, a decision that had raised a few eyebrows at the time, even back in the "permissive" 1960's.

Thankfully as far as school productions were concerned, Shakespeare had been old-fashioned enough to make the actual event happen offstage between scenes. The audience is only witness to the morning after the night before. It probably kept the wolves from the door in presenting the play as appropriate for younger age groups. There would always be some who still felt awkward about it however.

Kerry mused further on what she considered to be a perverse contradiction: how a much darker work like *Macbeth* was deemed perfectly acceptable for young impressionable people to study and stage, even though its main protagonist was a multiple killer – of men, women, even children. The play was a blood-fest and still held its own against contemporary displays of extreme violence on stage and screen.

But getting back to *Romeo and Juliet* and the theme of love, she hoped it wasn't being over-ambitious to imagine some kind of "chemistry" developing between whichever actors played her star-crossed lovers. Whoever took on these roles would have to be capable of portraying a wide range of feelings from desire and passion to hurt, loss, anger, guilt, remorse. With each emotion there was also a flipside – without desire there could be no threat of rejection; no heartbreak. And without these elements being present there could be no friction or suspense; in short no drama.

Kerry had to acknowledge her own limited experience in the courtship department. True she'd suffered a few unsatisfactory encounters, maintained one longish relationship with someone only partially compatible, enough anyway for her to feel a reasonably sized jolt when they'd both finally given up the ghost and separated. Whatever the future held she currently felt OK at being without a regular partner, sustained by her passion for her work.

And passion wasn't overemphasising it: she loved teaching drama, even had to admit to being a little obsessed. There was no doubt that it brought its own rewards, already there'd been moments with the group when she'd felt moved by what they were doing together and while working with the learning buddies was a challenge it was also proving to be an enlightening experience. She allowed herself a flight of fancy, imagining one of them trying out a few of Romeo's lines and despite the monotone delivery, somehow managing to come across as genuinely charming; even attractive? Yes, their acting so far had been predictably wooden, or should she say "robotic" but given the wonderful lines of the Bard she hoped beauty and meaning might yet find a way of shining through. By working with them on speech patterns, experimenting with variation in rhythm using the in-built musicality of the poetic lines, Kerry hoped these rookie players would be able to compensate for their limitations. She planned anyway on keeping performance levels low key for all of her cast: go for a sustained dynamic rather than topsy-turvy highs and lows. She mused on how another of Shakespeare's heroes, Hamlet would have approved of this restrained approach.

Kerry gave herself a pat on the back for what they'd

achieved so far. She was aware she might be straining the kids' patience a little with so much focus on the process, but knew from experience how invaluable it would be further down the line. What the audience saw on stage, the final words and actions, were only the tip of the iceberg beneath which were deeper layers of rich sub-text she hoped to discover in these early sessions. Moreover it was this aspect of their work that Jim Brady and Charles Richards wanted to highlight.

She was also keen to give the play the respect it was due; it was a tragedy after all with important social and political themes that needed to be taken seriously. On the other hand she couldn't ignore how it contained some genuinely standout funny moments. If called on, would her learning buddies be able to handle comedy?

Serendipitously, the next day had been designated a "Fun Friday". There was another event happening in the fringe hub at lunch time, so Kerry arranged to meet the group at the end of school during the short time-gap leading up to that evening's scheduled Candy Cabaret. She was keen to follow through on her thoughts from the night before, so as an experiment, asked DAK 43 to try out the part of Juliet's Nurse in a read-through of *Act One Scene Three*, conscious of how this character was the source of much of the play's pathos and comedy. In this scene the Nurse is talking to Lady Capulet, cheerfully reminiscing on her role as wet-nurse to baby Juliet and the challenge of having to wean the child off the breast.

"*When it did taste the wormwood on the nipple of my dug...*" declared the android nurse, arms held rigid and with an absolutely straight face.

The kids immediately began nudging one another, trying not to laugh out loud.

"*Dug?*" guffawed Chuck, sniggering.

Kerry could see there was comedy, but not of the type she was looking for, with the kids laughing at the actor, not the character. She cradled her own arms to demonstrate: 'DAK 43, can you present yourself like this, as if gently holding a baby at your breast?'

The android tried again, but with a flat chest adding to a total absence of facial expression to show tenderness, it made a mockery of the whole thing.

Most of the kids burst into giggles. Harper remained the obvious odd one out: hands on hips, scowling, more annoyed at being made a spectator for so long in the scene, given her starring role as Juliet.

DAK 43 pressed on with the speech undaunted, recalling a time when an older Juliet had tripped and fallen forwards onto the floor and how the Nurse's husband had joked crudely: "*Thou wilt fall backwards when thou has more wit.*"

Wanda just about managed to stop laughing and find her next line: "*Enough of this, I pray thee hold thy peace!*" declared Lady Capulet, trying to put a stop to such crude allusions to sex and setting her daughter a bad example.

At last Juliet had a line of her own. "*And stint thou too, I pray thee, Nurse, say I!*" pronounced Harper, with too much vehemence, allowing her own irritation to override what should have been a much gentler chiding.

"Thou wast the prettiest babe that ere I nursed," continued DAK 43, without missing a beat.

With Harper barely able to force a tight-lipped smile in response and everyone else giggling, Kerry called a timeout to take stock. In an ironic way it *was* almost comic. 'OK,' she said, holding up her hands to call a halt. 'Maybe we'll park this scene for now. I guess we're all on a learning curve here.'

❖

'At least we'll be getting some laughs in there one way or another,' said Jim Brady, before adding deadpan: 'Go easy mind, that's my department.'

After the session, Kerry had bumped into the Principal coming along the corridor and with her spirits a little low begun unburdening to him over what had just happened, describing DAK 43's primitive attempt at portraying Juliet's nurse as well as how while observing the scene, the other learning buddies had presented blank expressions in response to the witty wordplay, missing out completely of course on the sexual innuendo and overall exhibiting a clear lack of whatever emotional intelligence was required to actually get it all.

Clearly sensing where all this might be leading, Brady, looking a little wary, rubbed his chin thoughtfully. 'So what are we saying now: saddled with low-level-empathy, how can any humble-pie android expect to pick up on all that tricky inter-human sub-text?' He paused to take in the hustle and bustle in the busy corridor, the way facial expressions and bodily reflexes allowed everyone to skilfully negotiate a crowded shared space. 'I wonder, did you ever come across an old manual on comic acting from way back when, it was simply titled *Improv* –'

'Hey, yeah!' said Kerry, 'That was one of my bibles at college.'

Brady gave her a broad smile. 'I think I still have an old hard copy somewhere.'

Kerry crossed her fingers…

'OK,' said Brady finally, 'I hear what you're saying Miss Tracker and I'll formally put your upgrade request to Charles Richards at the earliest opportunity. Hell, what harm can come from asking.'

But right now the Principal had to excuse himself – tonight was Cabaret night and he too had to get into role.

ACT TWO

"Ancient grudge break to new mutiny..."

The school was in lockdown, with security personnel and uniformed police roaming and bossing the learning hubs and corridors. Confusion reigned while everyone sat tight and waited to be interviewed – students and staff alike.

At some point in the evening, while the cabaret was happening, a fatal accident had taken place. Rob Bennett of all people had been found dead at the bottom of a staircase by AJ doing his rounds. Android JFX72 immediately reported it to Jim Brady who received the news through his ear-piece while on stage. Forced to abandon the show mid-flow, Brady had to face the ignominy of being cross-examined while still in his jester costume by a supercilious police officer accompanied by an equally un-empathetic robot assistant.

By the following morning rumours and conjecture were rampant and the investigators had quickly zoned in on two key questions: cause of death and whether anyone else might have been involved. Could this even be a homicide? First indications suggested an injury to the head had killed Rob, but it wasn't clear if this was solely due to a heavy fall down the stone steps, or if it involved a separate blow of some kind.

Without any witnesses, probability would have favoured a tragic accident except for the subsequent discovery the school's internal CCTV system had failed to operate during that crucial part of the evening, plus the previous twelve hours had somehow been wiped clean.

While the police were working with internal security and technical support to discover the cause of the systems failure, discussion inevitably moved on to speculation surrounding Rob. Had he fallen out with anyone recently? Were there any unusual circumstances in the school of late? Howard Trent's open hostility was immediately raised but that soon connected to Rob's role as the androids' supervisor and it wasn't long before the conversation moved on to Miss Tracker's drama production and her unconventional deployment of the learning buddies. The leaking out of the recent incident involving Chuck Harrington and DAK 17 was enough in itself to raise a few eyebrows.

And if there had been foul play then everyone in attendance that evening was a potential suspect, even androids had to be taken into consideration as they too lived in the building, if that was quite the right term. With yet more loose talk in the air regarding Kerry's plans to have the learning buddies on stage, imaginations were soon running rife over what these units might be capable of. How close were they anyway to free-will? Who knew what went on after dark? Maybe they woke-up during the night and had secret parties where they danced around and mocked their human superiors. Perhaps their surface behaviour, all that polite deference during the day was simply a mask – a front, hiding deeper malevolent intent.

Time of death was calculated to be around 7.30–7.45pm. Rob had been seen by other members of the cabaret audience earlier on, but must have slipped out at some point: a few people thought they could remember him leaving, but couldn't say exactly when. Others had come and gone, but again times were vague. It was still too early to conclude anything; the only limitation on potential suspects was that it would have to have been an insider as no outside guests had been present that night, a situation confirmed by the external security cameras which had remained operational, unlike the internal CCTV.

❖

Special Agent Floyd Linton from Homeland Security had originally been sent down to the school over the ensuing weekend just to lend the regular officers of the law a helping hand and keep an overall eye on things. But then following the initial interviews and taking of statements, everyone else had been withdrawn and he now found himself facing into the new school week with sole responsibility for pursuing the investigation. Linton had no idea how or why this had happened: it was damn puzzling to say the least.

He looked around the Principal's office and homed in on the surveillance monitors: all now working perfectly with every classroom and corridor, nook and cranny covered. First examination of the system had revealed some kind of interference at precisely 7.15 pm on the fatal evening. It was still unclear as yet how this had actually happened – whether it was tampered with manually or hacked. Either way the whole thing had to be more than a little suspicious.

For his part Jim Brady wasn't exactly enthusiastic about being quizzed a second time, still feeling emotionally raw at what had happened. He was obviously personally in the clear regarding the fall on the stairs, given he was fully engaged in the cabaret throughout the crucial time period, but then again the monitors were his responsibility and Agent Linton was looking to be thorough.

'OK, we have your initial statement but I want to go through this again, maybe in a little more detail,' said the detective, 'just for the record.'

Brady released a deep sigh: 'We only kept those old stone steps as exercise for the students. The guy would be still alive if he'd taken the lazy way and used the drop-down pod.'

Linton nodded sympathetically while he made a quick appraisal of his interviewee, contrasting Brady's sizeable Caucasian body with his own lean and mean, somewhat worn and weathered African-American torso. They obviously shared an affinity for the late 1950's – Brady's rockabilly-look mirroring the detective's Harlem-sleuth image for that time: sharp retro suit matched with shiny two-tone shoes and a felt fedora hat.

Brady looked again at the monitors, still perplexed.

Linton activated his wristband voice recorder and looked around for somewhere to sit, settling into Brady's swivel barbershop seat, giving himself some height advantage. 'So let's start with the CCTV. You said in your statement that when you left here to go to the cabaret, it was still working?'

Brady shrugged. 'I guess I'm pretty sure; I was kind of distracted – I couldn't find my jester's hat.'

Linton smiled. 'And that would be coming up to 7pm?'

Brady nodded. 'I'd normally have been in there earlier, to get set-up. Guess I was running a little late: totally unprofessional of course, but at the same time maybe no harm in keeping an audience waiting, building up expectation.'

Linton took a mental note. 'And it was only shortly after that the system shut down.'

Brady shrugged: 'So it would seem.'

Linton tested the swivel capability of the barber's chair for a moment while he let his thoughts percolate.

Brady sighed and looked at his wrist for the time.

Linton stopped swivelling and said: 'OK, so let's go through it – which members of your staff have access to this room?'

'I told all this to the police already,' said Brady wearily, trying to get comfortable in his upright office chair.

Linton nodded. 'Sure, maybe in this case I'd like to hear it myself, from the horse's mouth so to speak.'

Brady sat up straight and made an effort. 'Rob himself had a code-ring, so he could come in and check over the monitors to see how all the androids were operating throughout the school.'

'Your sports teacher Howard Trent wasn't given one of those rings I suppose?'

'No,' said Brady. 'Rob was the only teacher with access.'

'I heard Trent wasn't exactly fond of the deceased,' said Linton, scratching an ear.

Brady scratched his own ear in return. 'That was just Howard being his usual bad-ass but mostly harmless self.'

Linton nodded thoughtfully. 'In his statement he said he was at your cabaret event, left not long after it got started – couldn't remember exactly what time – sat in the staffroom for a while thumbing through some sports magazines, then went home, where he lives alone. Unfortunately he met no one he knew on the way who could verify this. However, your external cameras confirmed he left the school at 7.55pm which obviously keeps him within our time frame.'

Brady shook his head. 'I know Howard had a chip on his shoulder towards Rob because of his involvement with the androids…but no, it's too crazy, it had to be an accident.'

'Anyway it obviously still leaves him in the frame, but we might let that one go just for the moment: the guy did stand up pretty well after all to being grilled over the content of those magazines.' The detective allowed himself a pause before continuing. 'So who else is able to stroll in and out of here?'

Brady shrugged: 'No one else except for AJ.'

'AJ?' said Linton, raising an eyebrow.

'You haven't met Android JFX72 – our janitor?'

'Not personally. You allow an android privileged access?'

'He keeps this place in order; I'd be lost without him.'

'Is "he" switched off at night?'

Brady shrugged. 'AJ turns himself off once he's done his final rounds.'

'OK – and his schedule for that evening; was he doing his final rounds?'

'What are you getting at?' said Brady.

'You seem to have a lot of trust in this unit,' said Linton.

'Yeah, I know this bot. He's a good guy.'

'A good guy huh?' said Linton giving Brady another piercing stare.

'Come on, you know yourself: AI units are universally hardwired not to cause harm to a human being under any circumstances.' Brady looked again at the monitors. 'Or mess around with systems outside their remit.' He had a further thought: 'Shame you can't check the footage right up to the point it stopped working; then you'd catch the culprit red-handed coming in here.'

Linton folded his arms. 'I guess whoever wiped it thought of that.'

'And then running it back, you'd also spot any suspicious activity during the lead-up, like someone getting ready to commit a crime.'

Linton sighed. 'We were talking about your android janitor and how you place a lot of trust in him – "it".'

'I can tell you for sure, Android JFX72 has never been anything less than diligent, trustworthy and loyal – to me and the school. I even get updates on how the play is going.'

'The play?' said Linton, pinching one ear lobe.

'Our end-of-year open day presentation; we're offering scenes from *Romeo and Juliet* this time around.'

'Remind me: is that a comedy or a tragedy?' The detective moved on to running his index finger up and down the bridge of his nose. 'So, tell me more about this android janitor; how long has he been employed here?'

Brady shrugged. 'That I can't say for sure, offhand; AJ was here before I arrived...' he broke off, watching Linton's moving finger, wondering if he was being subtly hypnotised. 'I'm telling you again, AJFX72 wouldn't do anything to jeopardise what we have going on here; he'd put himself on the line to defend the school.'

'Like maybe bump off someone who did appear to pose a threat?'

Brady realised he'd walked himself into it. 'And how would Rob have posed a threat to the school?'

'That's what I'm trying to find out,' said Linton, stating the obvious. 'Maybe he was up to no good. Could be your android janitor knows more than you about what goes on in the back corridors of this place. Perhaps you need to get out more.'

Brady threw his hands up in the air in mock surrender. 'What kind of *no good*?'

'Who knows, some kind of industrial espionage: those advanced androids you have here, their software must be valuable. Maybe he was working for another company.' Linton looked around the room as if he might spot a secret passageway. 'Has to be some explanation for the erasure of the CCTV.'

Brady glanced at the monitors. 'Most likely the system was hacked. It's happened before a good few times.'

Linton gave the comment due consideration: 'Strange though it happened that evening in particular.'

Brady shrugged. 'Still most likely it was random, just a coincidence.'

Linton sniffed. 'In my experience nothing's ever random; there's always a reason, some tell-tale connection.'

He paused, checking his wristband for the time. 'Anyway, let's move this on. What was Rob Bennett doing in that area of the school at that particular moment? Why did he leave your cabaret event so early?'

Brady couldn't resist a mock pout. 'Yeah that was a crime in itself.'

Linton delivered a cold stare. 'This is a serious investigation by the way.'

Brady reminded himself this was all about Rob and sat up straighter. 'OK, nothing unusual about being in that area, maybe he was going to the storeroom to get something.'

'Or maybe he had a rendezvous to meet someone?'

'Like you already said, most people were still in the cabaret, behaving themselves.'

'So maybe he was meeting up with some*thing*, rather than some*one*?'

Brady shrugged an acceptance. 'Quite likely he would have been checking in on the android learning buddies.'

Linton's eyes lit up. 'And on the way he came up against your janitor? Maybe it was jealous of Bennett's relationship with the other androids?'

Brady shook his head. 'I can tell you for a fact AJ doesn't have negative emotions like jealousy in his software.'

Linton took a moment to absorb this before asking: 'What about your higher grade android teaching staff – what range of feelings do they have?'

'I guess something not too dissimilar from AJ: a basic set that includes curiosity, satisfaction in doing a good job – then a palette tailored for teaching added on top of that.'

'Are *these* guys allowed access to "negative feelings": anger, jealousy, rage?'

'Only a neutral awareness – like AJ they can't *feel* anything directly.'

Linton took a moment to make another mental note. 'Anyway, they were all interviewed by the police. They must have liked your act, none of them left and all eyes were loyally focused on the stage throughout, so no attention paid to the background comings and goings.'

Brady shifted in his chair. 'Aside from Howard, what did the other regular teachers have to say?'

Linton shrugged. 'The three female members of staff were helpful, but nothing either of them said amounted to anything significant.' Linton paused again, lost in thought, crossing and uncrossing his fingers.

'What about the kids?' Brady enquired, not comfortable with these long silences.

'Again, none were able to offer anything concrete. Sure, people came and went, but memories around times were too vague. And we also checked with both sets of house-parents looking after the two dorms: no boys or girls came and went during the period in question. All house-parents vouched for each other, so unless there was some kind of crazy group conspiracy…'

Brady shook his head.

'No, I agree that's a dead end,' said Linton.

'The android learning buddies – the ones helping out in the play, they were left outside in the corridor.'

'Sure, unfortunately they were switched off. Shame because they might have logged something otherwise. Maybe we'll check their memories all the same.'

The office globe pulsed as a face appeared in the main honeycomb. 'Now here's more trouble,' Brady muttered.

The woman on the screen looked deeply concerned.

Linton offered a half-smile: 'Anxious parent?'

'Worse,' said Brady. 'This one's from the PBA: People before Androids.'

'I'll leave you to it,' Linton said as he left the room. 'I think I might follow up next with your guy AJ. Maybe he'll just confess, save us all a lot of hassle.'

2

arper responded to the beep from her iSpecs with a typical teenager's sigh as her mother's image appeared in both lenses. 'Don't frump like that Harper,' said Sophia Richards. 'I just needed to make sure you're OK: can't get over what happened to that unfortunate teacher?'

'Sure, I'm still alive I suppose,' the girl said with a petulant shrug.

Her mother flinched but let it pass. 'Did he take you for any of your regular subjects? I must have talked to him during that last virtual parent-teacher conference?'

'We only had him a couple of times as a sub: he was mostly in charge of the droids.'

'It's all very sad. What is everyone saying? I gather there's an investigation ongoing, but it had to have been an accident surely. Do you think we should come down there and –'

'– No!' said Harper sharply, but then quickly switched to a more amenable tone: 'I'm OK, really. Everyone here is perfectly safe.'

Mrs Richards sighed. 'Can we move our chat to your

globe Harper – I hate doing this through your specs: it's like you're behind a wall or something.'

Harper folded her iSpecs and palmed her globe. 'Is that better?'

'Yes, now your Italian mama can see her baby girl!'

Harper got up and began to walk around the globe. The great thing about this piece of tech was how it revolved, allowing whoever was on the other end of the conversation to follow you: useful if you were making a meal or doing some rare tidying or whatever. Right now she was simply doing it to be annoying.

'Now you're putting me in a spin!' said Mrs Richards.

Harper relented and sat down; maybe that kind of rebellion was too tiring.

'It's a shame we're not doing this virtual, I could be right there in the room with you.'

Harper frowned. 'You're close enough Mother, thank you.'

'Anyway, what's happening at the moment?'

'We all had to go to a meeting, along with our droids. They normally would have already been in the overnight bays getting re-charged, but just for once they came along with us to Mr Brady's stupid cabaret cus there was no time after the last play rehearsal to dump them off.'

'They were in there watching the show with you?'

Harper raised her eyes to heaven. 'No Mother, we parked them out in the corridor.'

Mrs Richards shuddered. 'I don't suppose they could have wandered off and –'

'No, didn't I just say they were in sleep-mode.' Harper couldn't resist a chance to tease: 'Except of course…Miss

Tracker's been talking about messing with their settings and so there's all this stuff now about letting things go too far and android free will, along with lots of other shit that's been flying around since that whole Mr Milton incident.'

Mrs Richards winced. 'Go easy on the language please Harper. "Mr Milton" was your android English teacher right, until that other unfortunate event which we won't dwell on right now.'

'He was given that nickname after some dead poet who wrote a big epic thing called *Paradise Lost.*' Harper had a thought. 'Maybe that's something I can relate to,' she added pointedly.

'OK...' said her mother, noting the thinly-veiled accusation. 'I think I can hear where you're coming from Harper. Yes...you always liked English,' she added encouragingly.

The girl gave a non-committal shrug. 'I guess it helps to give each droid a name if you're gonna be stuck in a classroom with one for maybe a whole year.'

'Makes them more human I suppose,' said her mother with a sad smile.

There was a pause as Mrs Richards turned to welcome her husband – sitting down next to her to share the globe.

'Hello Father,' said Harper, with a steely lack of affection.

'I just overheard you saying the learning buddies are helping with the investigation into what happened,' said Richards.

Harper shrugged. 'Maybe so; they were taken away for examination anyway.'

'I suppose they'd be useful, their data might reveal things about the evening in question, even tell us something about what their assigned student has been getting up to recently?'

Harper instantly bristled at the suggestion she might be up to more mischief or perhaps not pulling her weight in her studies. 'Let them look, I've got nothing to hide.'

Sophia Richards moved to change the subject to something more upbeat. 'Anyway, let's talk about that drama presentation you mentioned a moment ago, how is it coming along?'

'OK I suppose, until this happened. Anyway we're taking a week off until after the funeral and everything settles back down again.'

'Of course, that's understandable,' said her mother. 'I don't suppose you've been assigned characters as yet?'

Harper sniffed the air. 'Miss Tracker's more or less agreed I can do Juliet.'

'Well that's wonderful. The star part! Your father and I will so be looking forward to seeing it.'

'Yeah, you'll even get to watch me die at the end...'

'Don't spoil it!' her mother squealed, before realising the irony in her words.

'Hey!' replied Harper, acting like she felt aggrieved.

'You know that's not what I meant! Please Harper; we were having such a nice conversation.'

'You mean "civilised for a change"?'

Her mother shook her head in mild despair.

Harper glanced at her wristband. 'OK, this is all very pleasant but I actually have things to do.' She started to get up from her chair.

'Wait, before you go,' Sophia Richards said quickly. 'Who do you think will be playing Romeo? Maybe that good-looking African-American boy we met the last time we came down to visit.'

'Little Stevie? He's a show-off pain in the ass!' said Harper.

'You could do worse: son of a candidate for senator, he'd be a catch.'

'So, who *is* going to be the lucky guy?' her father chipped in, trying to play his part in lightening the mood.

Harper shrugged. 'Apart from me nothing's decided yet. Miss Tracker keeps moving everyone around, trying stuff out – she's always banging on about "the process" – drives us all crazy.'

'I'm sure she means well,' said Mrs Richards.

'We're supposed to be finding out more about the play before we settle for sure on who's playing what: or *what's* playing *who*.'

'Sorry?' said her mother, confused.

Her father moved his face over to take up more of the screen. 'I assume you're referring to your learning buddies being given actual parts in the play – and not just walk-ons it seems.'

'Who told you about it?' said Harper with a scowl.

'A little bird,' said her father, tapping his nose.

As the conversation was winding up, Sophia Richards asked: 'Anyway, you seem to be OK for the moment, Harper. The last time we talked you were demanding we get you out of there.'

Harper shrugged. 'What the hell, maybe I'm getting used to it.'

Before dimming her globe, Harper froze the last shot of her parents on the screen, lingering for a moment on the relieved look in her mother's face, before turning attention to her father's more impenetrable expression, as always his eyes conveying a sense of something hidden below the surface.

❖

The school's janitor stared blankly at Special Agent Linton. They were borrowing Brady's office while he took time-out on the viewing gallery.

'So, AJFX72 – here's a straight question, did you kill Mr Bennett?'

AJ looked suitably taken aback by the accusation. 'In what way might I have done that Mr Linton?'

Linton frowned. 'Did you strike, push or in any way manhandle Rob Bennett, causing him to fall down the stairs?'

The android answered more quickly this time: 'No, I certainly did not do any of that, Mr Linton.'

'You're hardwired in such a way as to make it impossible under any circumstances to harm a human being, is that correct?'

AJ nodded hesitantly, looking a little unsure.

'Unless...?' Linton leaned forward, thinking maybe he was already onto something.

'Unless it was an accident,' said AJ.

'OK...' said Linton disappointed. 'Did you ever hear that old expression, "accidentally on purpose," Android JFX 72?'

AJ seemed bamboozled by the phrase, offering only a stock puzzled expression.

Linton turned his head and glanced at the banks of monitors. 'And I don't suppose by chance you came in here anytime during the evening in question and interfered with the surveillance system?'

AJ dwelt on the question, nodding repeatedly as if going over it meticulously word for word.

'Is that a yes or a no, AJFX 72,' said Linton, pressing.

'*No*, is the answer to your precise question,' AJ said, finally.

Linton looked around the room, conscious of Brady not being present, thinking how to best put the next question. 'OK, so let's come at this from another angle: what if you had to act in some way to protect your boss?'

'My boss?' said AJ

'Mr Brady,' said Linton.

'Yes, I can certainly act to protect Mr Brady,' said the android, managing to look more at ease.

'You mean like push him out of the way of a runaway train, even if it meant causing him a minor injury?'

'If there was a train coming, I would have to take effective action to save him from serious harm – but I cannot leave the school and be near a train track, I am the janitor.'

Linton tipped back his chair, trying to appear casual. 'Suppose instead of a "runaway train" it was a runaway human being, posing a direct threat to Mr Brady and the school?'

AJ frowned. 'The hypothetical level is too high for me I'm afraid.'

Linton sighed and tapped his wristband. 'Mr Brady, can you get back in here and help us please?' He then added in a lower voice, 'Listen Brady, I don't want you to be alarmed: when you walk in I'm going to pull a gun on you. Don't worry it's an experiment involving AJ here.'

'Sure, but I'd prefer to die on stage,' Brady said back faintly.

They waited. Brady walked in. Linton pulled out his gun and pointed it.

AJ remained motionless.

Brady immediately cottoned on: 'You wanted to see if AJ would protect me?'

Linton turned to the android. 'Why didn't you take action when I pulled the gun?'

'There was no action required,' AJ answered.

'Even when I point it again now, menacingly?' asked Linton. Accepting his acting skills might be letting him down he resumed a more regular line of attack. 'A gun is a gun is a gun. Why didn't you intervene to protect Mr Brady?'

'I heard you tell him that this would be a pretend situation and not to be alarmed.'

Linton sighed, admitting defeat. 'OK, AJ, you got me stumped for now. I guess you can go resume your normal duties.'

With AJFX72 heading for the door the detective called out, 'AJ, catch!'

The android turned in time to extend an arm and receive the gun with ease, like a baseball pro taking a low catch. He held onto the weapon awkwardly, clearly not sure what to do next.

Brady turned to Linton looking more than a little concerned. 'What was all that about. And tell me that's not loaded.'

'Just indulging some idle curiosity,' said the detective, calmly taking the gun back from AJ.

'You said a moment ago that I could be excused?' said AJ, equally unruffled. 'I do have a number of things to attend to.'

'Sure,' said Linton. 'We may continue this again.'

'I shall look forward to it,' said the android with a stiff smile.

3

After the autopsy and following all the emotional intensity of the funeral, Kerry spent the next weekend holed up in her condo, content to be alone for a while with a chance to process her personal feelings over what had happened. It was good anyway to get a respite from the subdued atmosphere around the school including a low-level tension that had crept into the staffroom. She was also keen to re-earth herself by doing something practical and wholesome and was in the process of making a banana cake to go with her afternoon tea. She felt extra worthy at finishing off the by now very over-ripe second bunch she'd bought from Greta Pearson at the Fair Trade event.

Even for someone used to the intensity of theatre, Kerry was finding it a challenge dealing with all the emotions feeding into this real-life drama. She was conscious of a lingering aftershock from what had happened, alongside a belated sympathy for Rob, a fellow member of staff who she hadn't really got to know that well, something she now deeply regretted. And even though it seemed highly unlikely, it was still an unsettling thought that someone would have wanted to harm him.

She looked at the coloured mapping of her feelings projecting from one of the globe's honeycombs, predictable as such: mainly sadness, guilt, plus some surrounding confusion and fear. With no concrete evidence to the contrary, the coroner's verdict had been accidental death, but because of the continuing investigation and the uncertainty around the CCTV failure, there was still this uneasy feeling hanging around the whole thing.

As her fingers sifted the cake mixture, Kerry's thoughts went back to the funeral ceremony which had taken place in a hired community hall to accommodate the sizeable numbers attending, including all members of the school population, as well as various outsiders who'd held or felt a connection with Rob. Nearly all of these people appeared to be representing various campaign groups rather than claiming to have known him personally. The proceedings were conducted by a female Humanist celebrant who was both efficient and empathetic, handling everyone's feelings with tact and well chosen words of comfort.

All of Rob's fellow staff had been there of course, along with Liza Woodley, who'd been working flat out over recent days as grief counsellor. Howard Trent thankfully buttoned his lip for once and Jim Brady toned down the humour and allowed his more serious side to take over when giving a moving tribute to Rob both as a lover of history and someone with a passion for AI.

Charles Richards was there as well, commiserating and hand shaking. Kerry got to speak to him briefly and he mentioned how he'd been hearing positive things about the play particularly how they were using the learning buddies. There was no mention of the upgrade, but that wasn't surprising given the sensitive circumstances. She managed to exchange a few words with the kids in the drama group, including Harper. Kerry observed there was little or no communication between father and daughter, at least as far as she could tell.

The only figure representing Rob's family was an older half-sister, Elizabeth, not blood-related: both had apparently been adopted. Elizabeth lived and worked just outside the city on some sort of eco-farm. Kerry found a quiet moment to offer her condolences; the woman had been clearly saddened but also came over as remarkably focused and calm.

Prior to the ceremony there'd been a heated discussion at school management level over whether it was appropriate for android staff to attend. Despite the absence of a formal religious element it was still felt by some that this was a spiritual ritual and relevant only to human beings. But Rob's close association with the androids in the school couldn't be ignored and it was in fact Elizabeth who'd intervened, calling Brady with a request that they be allowed to come along.

As a fitting tribute, an inspired Inez Martinez reassembled the barbershop quartet, who led them all into the final song – an old Irish tune called "The Parting Glass", chosen by Jim Brady himself. A small number of personal items were placed on the coffin, most notably a weathered copy of Darwin's *On the Origins of Species* that Elizabeth had brought along with her: a present from her brother from several years before. She read out a message written on the inside cover, which said: "Together in solidarity – love Rob."

Kerry had cried buckets along with Inez and Meera and she'd noted most people there had tears in their eyes. The android teaching staff looked on with respectful silence. The other member of their fraternity, Janitor AJFX72, seemed to watch the whole thing as if both bewildered and perplexed, caught between sad frowns and then happy smiles when good things were said about Rob. Kerry considered how this perhaps wasn't so different for the human mourners; after all it was both a saying goodbye and a celebration of his life. She added all these musings to her earlier thoughts concerning the seductive power of projection: how meaning, much like beauty, can lie in the eye of the beholder.

Kerry looked at the cake-mix and decided it was ready. She slid it into the oven then palmed her globe and began flitting through various sites and TV channels, wanting to know how Rob's death was being received in the outside world. One report included an interview with a spokeswoman for the school management, keen to point out that despite its reputation for things unusual, no human being had ever died there before, never mind been murdered.

The coverage moved on to Charles Richards standing outside the school gates combating any suggestion this tragedy was related to tensions within the school, especially low morale amongst the small number of human staff. He dismissed the doomsayers and conspiracy theorists who chose to present it as confirmation that with its heavy reliance on artificial intelligence the school was flirting with something dangerous and unpredictable.

Kerry dimmed that honeycomb and glanced again at the one projecting her emotional profile, taking in particularly where fear overlapped with guilt. She had to admit to having her own concerns regarding the spotlight being directed at the school's android population: the implications for the play were all too obvious. She knew that AJ had been interviewed on more than one occasion and while her learning buddies had escaped the same level of scrutiny, realistically there was little chance now of them getting any kind of upgrade that might invite more controversy.

And could there be a connection? Maybe she was deluding herself, promoting her own self-interest and the needs of the play over common sense and restraint. She had to ask herself: what were her own views exactly on AI? Regarding the broad question of androids taking over many jobs and roles previously done by people, she had to admit she was ambivalent. She did of course feel immediate solidarity with those unemployed teachers protesting outside the school gates, aware she'd been fortunate in terms of her current situation. On the other hand she genuinely believed there was a role for AI in education, as well as the performing arts. But it was more than that: she was coming to feel that at some level these beings were exactly that, 'beings' – OK, maybe not sentient like a human, but still present none the less. Notwithstanding the current empathy restrictions inhibiting their range of emotional interaction, her learning buddies had still shown the capacity to somehow be "in the moment," sometimes appearing more tuned-in to what was required than their human companions.

Kerry didn't consider herself to be a political person as such, but in a broad sense she viewed Humanity with a sense of realism. Thinking back to the book by Darwin that had been present at the funeral: how long had *Homo-sapiens* been going as the dominant species on the planet, a few hundred thousand years at the most? Certainly it was a blink of an eye in evolution terms. What was that compared to two hundred million years encompassing the age of dinosaurs, or the billions of years when the Earth had been home to nothing but bacteria.

Despite arriving very late in the day, through their impact on global warming in particular, people now threatened the very existence of the planet. If the evolution of the Earth as a living entity was akin to baking a cake, with bacteria supplying the basic ingredients and the rest of nature acting like a team of Michelin chefs adding to the mix over billions of years, it was as if at the very last moment this amazing creation had been handed over to a wet behind the ears cocky apprentice-cook to pop into the oven, turn up the heat way too high and then fall asleep, allowing the thing to burn to cinders.

Maybe if androids ran things it would prove to be the Earth's salvation. They'd insist on a more rational and enlightened approach; they might even put a stop to global warming, poverty, inequality, war…create a different type of cake altogether.

Later, removing her own modest creation from the oven, Kerry heard a beep outside her door. It was AJ touring the campus with his electric cart. 'Excuse me Miss Tracker: materials for recycling, or anything else I can possibly do for you?'

Kerry found herself briefly musing on the idea of inviting the janitor in for tea and cake; just to be pleasant, a modest enough reward for the android's sociability. In an innocent kind of way the timing of AJ's arrival made it the most spontaneous and natural thing to do. She allowed herself an inward smile then let the thought go: unlike the school's android teachers, AJ didn't have a mouth as such to eat with. Anyway, boundaries were boundaries – some even more complex than others.

4

After waiting more than a week while all the various rituals took place and for everyone's emotions to calm, Kerry finally called the drama group together again to touch base and see how they were coping. Entering the fringe hub she was relieved to see none of the kids were missing, but couldn't help noting how the group was still clearly divided in half; if anything the gap had increased, with the learning buddies far over to one side.

'Hi, it's good to see you all again. I hope everyone's feeling OK after what happened.'

The kids returned her a collective shrug that gave little away of what they might be feeling.

Kerry glanced over at the learning buddies. 'There's something I've been meaning to ask: when you're just hanging out, do you order these guys to take a time out, stand at ease, or what?'

The group looked to one another like it hadn't occurred to them before. 'We don't say anything,' Wanda offered. 'They do what they do automatically. Why do you want to know?'

'Because it's curious, the way they're assembled; it almost mimics the way you're gathered.'

The kids turned to look in unison.

'You mean like they're actively copying us?' said Chuck, his eyes narrowing.

'I just wondered if it was something still hanging over from their old empathy settings.'

'Don't give them too much credit,' said Tania. 'They're not consciously pretending to be us or anything; that *would* be creepy.'

Kerry nodded to herself, making a mental note.

Omar threw in his pennyworth. 'We shouldn't even be saying "they" it's not like they're acting together as a collective; you've seen how they don't have conversations or anything.'

'So why *is* that?' said Kerry. It was true, even in the staffroom with the elite model teaching androids there was no what might be called free engagement between them: all of their commentary related one way or another back to their human companions. OK, Mr Wilde might occasionally address Mr Hubble, but this would concern a point of information. Otherwise they just joined in with the general conversation, adding useful comments, being helpful; experts at blending in.

Harper responded to Kerry's internal musing. 'They're just supposed to be available – to *us*. Like if they're not needed that moment to help you through an assignment or kick your ass for your own good, you don't want them getting in your space. You want them invisible, out of the way.'

'I get it,' said Kerry, 'not drawing attention to themselves: unobtrusive.'

Chuck smirked. "*Un-ob-tru-sive!*" he repeated, underlining each syllable. He grinned and slapped palms with Little Stevie as they slipped into a hip-hop routine from the 1990's, hands cupped over their ears to suggest external headphones.

'Early Eminem!' said Chuck, trying to act super-cool; jabbing at himself with two index fingers.

'Gangsta-man Ice Cube!' Little Stevie responded, making the same gesture.

"*So where's that man – the Invisible Man?*" asked Chuck, rapper style.

"*In the back of the van, being un-ob-tru-sive!*" answered Little Stevie, adding fancy hand and foot movements of his own.

"*On the way to the Can?*" asked Chuck.

Little Stevie shook his head: "*No Man – that's in-con-clu-sive!*"

Wanda and Tania laughed, letting their hips melt as they joined in with the boys, offering some neat moves themselves. The four of them then formed a conga and set off round the room with all the other kids joining in too, swaying their backsides outrageously and punching the air.

"*We're kids from the hood, we don't wanna be good!*" rapped Little Stevie at the front.

Kerry was aware of the learning buddies watching with a detached bemusement, she waited until the conga finally came to a halt and said, 'I was just thinking how it would be great if you could reverse the usual learning roles and teach the LBs something, like how to dance and punch the air like that?'

Little Stevie called over his own learning buddy. 'OK, do this for the teacher: copy me saying, "*Un-ob-tru-sive!*"' He punched the air again to illustrate.

DAK 11 hesitated, then soft-punched the air while pronouncing "unobtrusive" with a distinct lack of conviction.

All the kids laughed, mocking the android's underwhelming efforts.

'Why can't you put some heart and guts into it?' said Chuck.

'There is a conflict of meaning,' replied DAK 11.

'What kind of conflict?' Little Stevie demanded.

'The word, "unobtrusive" sits in direct opposition to demonstrative behaviour that would likely draw unwanted attention,' said the android.

It took a moment for the logic to sink in. 'Hey, wow: that's one clever-assed droid!' said Carlos.

Chuck wasn't to be outdone. 'Hey, you never heard of *acting* Mr Clever? You're actually allowed to say one thing and mean something else. It's part of all the pretending we'll be doing in this play, right Miss Tracker?'

Kerry nodded agreement. 'I guess that's a fair point.'

The boy was on a role. 'Yeah, not just the play, the whole world is at it: look at most of those politicians, great pretenders all!'

'It's the way of the big bad world!' agreed Little Stevie.

Wanda returned to Chuck's earlier remark: 'So if we're teaching them to act, aren't we inviting them to deceive us?'

'Maybe we're already one step behind?' said Harper. 'Like they're looking at us now with those blank faces and thinking all kinds of evil ways to do us harm? Murder us in our beds.'

Kerry decided to take the bull by the horns. 'Are you thinking evil thoughts right now, DAK 17?'

The android answered: 'Evil relates to emotions such as hatred and lust for power. You are aware that we cannot experience these feelings ourselves: only comprehend them as abstract terms and note their effect on human beings.'

'OK, but you know what we're talking about here?' said Tania. 'You're not that innocent.'

As the android paused for consideration, Kerry's wristband buzzed. 'OK, sadly we're out of time; I hate to put a stop to such a fruitful discussion, but thank you all for a really interesting and enlightening session.'

As the group started to break up, she became aware of Agent Linton standing by the door. 'I didn't hear you come in,' she said, taken aback.

'I was trying to remain unobtrusive,' Linton replied, with a dry smile.

❖

Jim Brady slowly poured himself a cup of tea from an old china teapot, using an antique silver strainer. He was getting to love real tealeaves like he loved his replica Chevy, vinyl records and old DVDs. 'Will I pour you one?' he asked Linton.

Special Agent Linton politely refused: 'Just had my third coffee of the day.'

'You should try it,' said Brady. 'I'm a convert myself. It

lowers stress: all about creating a ritual, taking time; being in the moment.'

Linton winced. 'Maybe that's not always where I want to be.'

Brady latched onto this as an opening for fair comment on how Linton was now going to be based in his office, seemingly for the indefinite future. 'Maybe this isn't where you really want to be either?'

Linton shrugged. 'Convenience wins out as always.'

'I don't get it,' said Brady, 'the verdict was accidental death: so why are you still here?'

'Darn good question,' said Linton, throwing up his hands. 'I guess the CCTV failure still leaves us with a few loose ends. Other than that I guess I'm none the wiser. My orders are to continue to probe but keep it nice and low key.'

'Probe for what?' asked Brady, reasonably.

Linton said nothing for a moment, continuing to look puzzled as he nodded to himself about something.

Brady settled back in his barbershop chair to sip his tea. 'So, how *are* things coming along with the investigation?'

Linton sniffed a few times. He appeared to have a cold or some kind of allergy. There was a high pollution warning that day. 'Slow slow slowly…like your tea ritual. Or maybe we're getting somewhere and I can't see it.'

Brady shrugged. 'No one has confessed as yet, even under torture?'

Linton shook his head. 'You've been watching too many movies. We really don't do that sort of thing anymore. You heard about ethics committees?'

'Don't talk to me about committees,' said Brady.

'Anyway, with no CCTV coverage how can we know who or *what* is telling the truth.' Linton sucked his lip. 'I did run a check on those LBs that were left outside the cabaret which confirmed they'd missed everything.' He gave a half-frown at an accompanying thought, 'Unless their testimony can't be trusted; maybe they're prone to walking around in their sleep and getting up to no good without knowing it?'

Brady grinned. 'I thought they were too busy dreaming about android sheep.'

Linton allowed himself a brief smile then switched back to a frown. 'It would help even more of course if I'd had access to your janitor's memory files. I put in a request to the manufacturer, but was denied that crucial piece of evidence by your own Charles Richards.'

Not sure what to say, Brady offered a non-committal shrug of the shoulders.

'Data protection, sensitive commercial interests: the usual baloney.' Linton rubbed his chin, considering options. 'I could apply for the authority to override all that, but between you me and the walls I've been told from on high to back off. It appears your benefactor has a wide sphere of influence.'

Again Brady chose not to comment.

Linton shrugged and let it go for the moment. 'I guess nothing we might have discovered could be used anyway in a court of law, where android evidence isn't accepted. But still, it would be nice all the same to have the inside track.'

Brady put down his cup and leaned further back. 'So at the end of all this there's nothing conclusive. No evidence, no witnesses: no-one saw anything.'

Linton sighed. 'Like we said before, all were conveniently distracted by your compelling show.'

Brady smiled. 'Good to hear you say that again: helps my ego.'

'Maybe Rob Bennett walked out cus *he* didn't like your gags?'

Brady recoiled at what clearly sounded like a loaded remark. He returned to a more sober tone: 'That's quite possible, Rob was a serious kind of guy; according to everyone in the staffroom he didn't exhibit much of a sense of humour.'

'So maybe you had him bumped off because you don't like silent hecklers?'

This time Brady was about to protest when there was a polite announcement from the door as AJ entered carrying some fresh water containers.

'I hope I'm not interrupting?' said the android.

'No AJ, good timing. We were just discussing the case,' said Linton.

AJ didn't reply, starting to replace the old container with the new one.

'Do you want to know if we're getting anywhere with the investigation, AJFX72?' Linton probed.

'Yes, it would be interesting to know if we are making progress, Mr Linton.'

The detective got up and helped himself to a cup of water. 'Just for the record AJFX72: can you tell a bare-faced lie?'

There was another pause.

'Straight question, come on AJ?' coaxed Brady, curious himself.

'I can say false or meaningless words if you instruct me to. Then it would not clash with my loyalty configurations.'

Linton swilled his cup. 'Like if I asked you to say, "The US President is a robot?"'

'Yes, I could say that,' answered AJ.

'But you wouldn't mean it?' said Brady.

AJ smiled. 'I could not really believe that to be true, Mr Brady.'

Linton said, 'OK, fair enough, I guess I did pick what was an obvious untruth. But, can't you tell even small lies, maybe to serve some higher cause?'

AJ looked bemused. 'Mr Linton, I am only the lowly school janitor.'

As Linton looked away in exasperation his eye fell on one of the monitors showing Kerry walking along a corridor. He turned back to the android with a smile. 'Hey AJ, maybe you should ask Miss Tracker for a part in her play: enjoy some of that license to pretend. Even get to play something or someone else for a change?'

'I would be most happy to help out with the play if Miss Tracker or Mr Brady asked me,' said the android.

'But would you like to be actually involved AJ?' said Brady, intrigued. 'Get caught up in all that drama?'

AJ frowned, seemingly unsure.

Linton smiled. 'I get it, you're probably thinking about what happened to your old pal Mr Milton.'

'Will that be all,' said AJ, with almost no expression, not waiting for an answer as he picked up the empty water container and left the room.

'There goes a good honest guy,' said Brady.

Linton looked at the two fresh water containers, one

of which was sending up gassy bubbles. 'Your android actually did say something interesting just a moment ago.'

'What?' said Brady, following the detective's gaze towards…the bubbles?

'He said: "Are *we* making progress with the case?"'

Brady shrugged. 'Like I've said all along, AJ's on our side.'

Linton paused. 'Maybe so: still, I'm curious, from an android's point of view, who or what are '*we*' exactly?'

⁂

Kerry's globe was showing a live TV interview with Charles Richards. 'There was never a question of closing the school down, even temporarily,' he asserted. 'An incident is being investigated; the institution itself was never on trial.'

'We understand that enquiries are still ongoing?'

Richards nodded reassuringly. 'Listen, we're not unfeeling, we know the students as well as the staff received a shock over what happened, but as far as those continuing enquiries are concerned, I understand it's very much a case of filling out the record.'

The interviewer switched the focus: 'You're also facing ongoing criticism over what many consider to be an over-reliance on artificial intelligence?'

Richards puffed up his chest. 'What I can report to your viewers is that our students have benefited enormously from this ambitious program: great progress is being made.'

'And you're fully confident the children are safe? It seems you had an issue with one of your advanced android teachers, some kind of malfunction: the unit actually exploded in the classroom while rehearsing Shakespeare's *Romeo and Juliet*?'

'That was a relatively minor event,' said Richards, brushing it off, 'certainly no-one was in any danger of being hurt.' He decided to risk a light-hearted quip: 'And it did succeed in getting the students' attention.'

The interviewer forced a smile.

Richards held his hands open in appeal. 'You have to expect teething problems with any innovative enterprise. But yes, we've also taken that incident seriously and looking into the root causes.' He moved to strike a more upbeat note: 'By the way, the drama presentation you referred to is progressing extremely well: in particular I'm hearing great reports about how the young cast are being ably assisted by their android learning buddies.'

'I understand your own daughter is involved?'

'That's right,' said Richards, sounding like a regular proud father.

'Can we assume it's a star part?'

Richards allowed himself a full smile. 'I gather they haven't got onto individual casting as yet. But she'll be making a contribution whatever happens.'

'Will this be a musical version?'

Richards visibly relaxed: over the worst. 'As I said, it's at an early stage. No doubt they'll have a few surprises up their sleeves.'

'You'll be there on the big night of course?'

Richards beamed. 'My wife and I wouldn't miss it for the world.'

Kerry shrunk the TV and decided it was time for some more serious thinking about the play. As far as the plot and storyline were concerned she knew it pretty well inside out by now. But the interview with Richards had underlined the pressure they were all under and she needed to take stock regarding the general approach she was taking.

She let her mind drift back to that first meeting with the drama group and her suggestion the learning buddies might represent all the Montague characters. At the time it had just been a way to grab their attention, wrong-foot any negative resistance and she still had her own reservations about the humans versus androids scenario, but what if the play was set in the future as Inez Martinez had suggested, in a society where full android citizenship had become the norm: present a fraternity of androids engaged in an ongoing feud with their flesh and blood neighbours?

Kerry allowed her imagination to take this further. She'd probably need to establish this from the beginning, maybe have one of the learning buddies narrate the Prologue? A few program notes might help in setting the context.

Whatever they did, it had to be relevant to what was happening in the world right now. This interpretation would of course touch on the very real fear that androids might take over more jobs and positions currently occupied by humans and eventually dominate whole sectors of society; maybe even start to form their own communities. Kerry had experienced the protests going on outside the school and there'd also been a number of incidents reported in the US recently involving attacks by individuals or angry mobs, although thankfully so far at least no android had resorted to violence in order to defend itself. This inevitably tapped further into the perennial nightmare sci-fi scenario of full scale conflict between androids and humans, always with the possibility of the latter losing out to a vastly superior foe. Was this the direction they wanted to go in, stoking the fires of unrest? Jim Brady had already expressed his own reservations in this regard as well as passing on Charles Richards's obvious concern.

But putting it in a broader context, did they really need to be so coy, especially given AI was already very much an accepted part of war and conflict in the real world, with intelligent machines commonly used as mine-detectors, or to safely dispose of chemical and biological weapons; drones used for spying and as carriers of warheads. AI was also integral to cyber-warfare. All of this had brought long running tensions to a final crisis for what had once been called 'The United Nations' – re-branded in 2031 with the less delusional title of 'Nations Forum' – its Security Council previously made up of just six permanent member countries side-lined in favour of a more representative body freely elected by all. This wasn't to say that those top wheelers and dealers had been removed from the equation as they still continued to exert undue influence, either overtly or covertly, mostly through tacit support of mega-powerful private corporate interests.

Beyond all of this lay yet another existential concern centring on how differences between people and robots were becoming increasingly blurred, as androids with near-perfect human features and attributes matched the still relatively small yet growing numbers heading in the opposite direction via the acquisition of tech implants, artificial organs and limbs. Kerry was reminded of an old movie, *Edward Scissorhands* – it was still a key question: where did a human being end and an artificial creature begin? And now with the rapid advancement of android emotional intelligence, were there any limits to these quasi-feelings – what happened when you allowed full access to concepts like ambition and self-worth; not to mention injustice, suffering and resentment. Would they soon be demanding equal citizenship: could all this even be a natural evolution into an entirely new species: *Robo-sapiens?*

5

For their next rehearsal Kerry was keen for herself and the gang to move on and try to put recent events behind them. A big ensemble moment like *Act One, Scene Five*: the party at the home of Lord and Lady Capulet offered a good way forward.

Standing just inside the fringe hub entrance, she delayed long enough to observe the whole group. It was always slightly ironic to see the learning buddies waiting on stand-by while the kids looked almost as vacant, expressions blank; inner selves hidden behind the tinted lenses of their iSpecs.

Kerry made an immediate connection with the party scene where everyone would be wearing masks. These would normally be costume if was to be a period piece, but if they were going for a futuristic setting, the plain ones with neutral expressions she'd brought in with her for this session would offer something more open-ended and timeless.

By now she was used to actors taking up frozen poses and the remarkable way in which these neutral masks allowed body-language to by-pass the face as a conveyer of feelings. To start off the session, Kerry got the learning buddies to line up wearing them. For the moment her human crew were observers. 'OK, I want you all to watch while I take up a series of body stances.'

She did a series of five poses, suggesting different emotions; freezing each one for a few seconds, before changing to another. 'Can you now repeat the sequence,' Kerry asked the learning buddies. As they dutifully complied, she turned to her human cast. 'Can you read each of these and say what feeling is being expressed?'

It was clear to everyone the learning buddies were displaying in sequence: suspicion, hope, puzzlement, fear and curiosity. It was startling to watch.

'That's so far out man!' exclaimed Jing.

Kerry noted the energising effect it was having on her disenchanted teenagers as they let their own masks drop a little.

'Are we going to be using these in the actual play?' said Omar, already hooked.

'That's what I want to explore in this session,' said Kerry. 'But let's do some warm up exercises first.'

❖

Jim Brady turned away from the drama activity going on in the fringe hub, switching his attention back to the movie he'd been watching on the office globe. He picked up on *The King of Comedy* at the point where the hapless anti-hero, Rupert Pupkin is trying to ingratiate himself into the company of a famous mega-successful comedian. Rupert is an obsessive joker but unfortunately for him just isn't naturally funny. Nonetheless he carries a deep inner belief that all he needs to break into the big-time is a decent opportunity: something the great Lenny Bruce had parodied in a skit about the legendary London Palladium and the elusive, "Good Room".

Brady knew the true answer of course to the Holy Grail of making people laugh. Yes it might involve a bucket-load of persistence, an indefinable amount of luck, having all the cutting-edge material in the world, even access to the fabled "good room" – throw in the key element of presence and yet…in the wrong hands it could still fall flat and die a death.

There was also the crucial question of timing.

Special Agent Linton had no doubt majored in *bad* timing. Entering, he noted Brady's preoccupation with what was on the screen and how his host was ignoring him and saying nothing for a moment.

'Good movie?' said Linton, after what he felt was a respectful interval.

'Only one of the best,' answered Brady, allowing some irritation to leak through. He finally swivelled his barber's chair around. 'I can't help wanting to pinch myself – that you're still here Detective, taking over half my office. Don't take this personally but there must be more urgent cases out there calling on your fine skills of deduction?'

Linton looked up as if to some higher power. '"*Who am I to reason why?*" – didn't somebody say that?'

Brady allowed Linton an empathetic smile: hadn't they both been sent here in response to some higher calling. 'Anyway, don't mind me; maybe I'm even looking forward to our little sessions.'

Linton glanced at the frozen movie on Brady's screen. 'Funny, I don't believe I've heard you tell an actual gag as such, unless I missed something?'

Brady grinned at the challenge. 'How many Zen Masters does it take to change a light bulb?'

Linton raised his hands: 'I give up.'

'Just one: so long as the bulb is also enlightened.'

Linton scratched his chin. 'OK, maybe if I chew on that long enough I'll learn something.'

'It's the way I tell them,' said Brady, enjoying himself now.

Linton adjusted his sitting position in the lower chair, trying to get comfortable. 'OK, while recognising this may all now be just going through the motions, "friendly fire" so to speak, what happened with the CCTV still has to be suspicious, at least lending support to the notion there was an attempt to cover-up something.'

Brady eased back, waited.

'By the way,' Linton continued, 'why stick with such an antiquated closed circuit and not upgrade to a smarter system?'

'Maybe I prefer its retro feel,' said Brady. 'Besides, I gather they had to contend with some major protests back when that option was first considered: a number of health risks were flagged; a lot of so called "smart" technology was being used by the military to knock people out, as well as killing off wildlife.' He paused. 'Anyway, those fancy systems still get hacked just the same.'

Linton stroked his chin. 'OK, back to the main topic: let's indulge our imaginations and pursue the fanciful possibility this *was* a planned homicide.' Linton paused to allow the other man room to object.

Brady shrugged and indicated the detective could continue for the moment.

'In which case, supposing our assailant was lurking there near the top of the stairs, waiting to strike. So how did he, she or *it* know that the victim would leave the cabaret and come down that way?'

Brady shrugged again.

'Unfortunately we didn't find a signed note in Rob Bennett's pocket saying, "Meet me urgently at the top of the stairs."'

'Seemingly there was nothing of significance recorded in his wristband either,' said Brady, doing his best to contribute.

Linton scratched his chin. 'Now that was an odd thing, how he hadn't exchanged any messages for quite a while. Kind of strange: no communications at all? In fact, aside from the other teaching staff he didn't keep many personal numbers. A suspicious mind might see that as a pre-emptive move to cover up tracks. The kind of thing you'd do if you were engaged in some kind of subversive operation as part of an underground group or cell.'

'Family?' said Brady, trying to keep it on a level he could relate to.

'Both parents deceased,' said Linton.

'There's that older half-sister, Elizabeth – I spoke to her at the funeral.'

Linton nodded. 'Sure, she gave a full statement to the police. I read it through a couple of times. She works outside the city on some kind of hippie eco-farm. Interesting how both her and Rob were adopted, she said they'd been close and yet distant at the same time.'

Brady gave his barber chair a half-spin and waited for Linton to continue.

'So nobody really knew this guy, "Rob Bennett". I said it before, maybe he wasn't what he seemed – which links to our search for a motive: *why* might he have been killed? We already conjectured how he could have been working undercover for someone, maybe spying for a rival android manufacturer, or maybe he was the good guy who knew about someone else who was the bad guy, the real spy…' Linton reached into his pocket. 'By the way, I had another talk with Howard Trent on the way here. He gave me this, said he'd forgotten about it when first interviewed – but one of the other teachers remembered how he'd produced this in the staffroom, shortly before Rob was killed in fact.'

Brady looked sadly at the printed out image of Rob looking like a 1960's hippie and posing with a robot.

Linton continued: 'Seemingly, Rob reacted all mysterious and defensive when it was sprung on him?'

Brady said nothing and handed back the photo.

Linton examined it again. 'From the robot's design it shouldn't be too hard to fix on what year that was. I already have a few notions as to where it was taken.'

❖

'So in this scene, Romeo and his friends Benvolio and Mercutio are gate-crashing Lord Capulet's party. Luckily, everyone is wearing masks. It's like a carnival. This is of course where Romeo and Juliet first meet and instantly fall for one another, although because of the masks it could be said to be love *before* first sight as they sense something even while their faces are still covered. Anyway, Romeo tries to use the dancing to get closer, but Juliet's interrupted by Lady Capulet, who wants her to spend more time getting to know the rich suitor they've invited, Count Paris. But before we start into the lines, we need to get a sense of the whole occasion; this is a party remember, there's loads of other guests. There's also music and musicians, waiters carrying food: it's a big fabulous scene with huge scope for ensemble acting.'

Kerry paused to take in what seemed to be expectant faces. 'I want us to get a grasp of the broad-stroke choreography first: fixed patterns like the flow of the music and the dance steps; the formal behaviour of the characters such as the proper and correct way these people had of behaving, nodding their heads and bowing, moving across the room with style and elegance, their social standing displayed for all the world to see. All of this can have a ritualistic feel, controlled and superficial to a degree, yet there's rich sub-text to those rehearsed smiles, coded signals: that subtle deviance. The masks of course add yet another layer to this social pretence and play-acting.'

'Yeah, cool, we're following,' said Omar, looking a touch left behind, but nonetheless intrigued.

'Weaving through these formal patterns are the more free individual movements of several key figures: Lord and Lady Capulet, Juliet and her Nurse, Count Paris, the Montague gatecrashers. These characters will have a more heightened sense of purpose about them. Our prospective lovers will of course stand out even more: if this was a film, the camera would be drawn to these two.'

'Sure, they're the hero and heroine, right?' said Little Stevie, directing a cheesy grin at Harper.

The girl rolled her eyes and released a despairing sigh in response.

Kerry took note and pressed on: 'Juliet's hot-headed cousin Tybalt is also there, as always on the lookout for trouble.'

'So, let's get started,' said Chuck, ever ready for some action.

'But let's leave lines and individual characters to one side for the moment. First we need to establish our basic *mise en scene* –'

Tania groaned: 'Would you mind trying that again in English, Miss Tracker!'

'Sorry, it just means setting up the general atmosphere. I want you to act as either hosts or guests: mingling in other words.'

'Mingling?' asked Carlos with a frown of his own.

'OK…maybe imagine for the moment you're just at a posh party; forget about the 16th Century, it could be any time period. You might have a drink in one hand; if you want something a little old-fashioned, ladies could have a fan perhaps.'

'What about us gents?' asked Little Stevie. 'What are we carrying?'

'Well, how about a fancy walking cane, not because you have a bad leg, more for show; twiddling with it when you're standing around watching the dancing.'

Chuck brandished his imaginary cane. 'Or fencing; dealing with the enemy imposter!'

'Maybe the cane wasn't such a good idea,' said Kerry.

'Sure, twiddle our thumbs instead,' groaned Chuck.

Kerry breathed in. 'Anyway, let's try it first with just you kids. You simply move around the room, stop briefly to smile at someone; bow politely, then move on to engage with someone else.'

As the human members of her cast went through the motions, most of them looked a little awkward and self-conscious. Maybe mingling wasn't so straightforward for these teenagers, Kerry reminded herself.

'So it might help to establish a rhythmic pattern: let's give each of these meetings and greetings a count of three; then with a smile or nod you move on. We're basically going for rhythm and flow – for the moment you don't have to worry about what you might be saying in these brief exchanges.'

As a pattern became established Kerry found she could up the tempo if required, as well as freeze the ensemble movement and allow the spotlight to fall on a selected couple, as if listening in on their conversation. She turned to the other half of her cast, standing by. 'OK learning buddies, now it's your turn. Same as the others, you move around the space and when you pass by anyone you stop for three seconds, then nod politely and move on. OK, got it?'

The learning buddies did get it. It went like clockwork, so perfect it was laughable: there were a few titters from the onlookers. Clearly some basic elements were missing, a sense of a deeper purpose the most obvious factor. Yet, even without the upgrade, if the worst came to the worst they could do it this way, Kerry told herself. At least they were an ensemble: there was shape, pattern; the scene was almost what you might call alive.

'You know something,' said Wanda. 'Wouldn't it be great if we were doing the whole play; you know, like a full production?'

A look of immediate interest travelled around the room.

6

Charles Richards entered the small conference room arranged for him by the joint US departments of Defence and Homeland Security. The four members of the task-force assigned to this top-secret project exchanged smiles and introductory handshakes with their guest.

As chairperson for the group, deputy head of Defence Tim Wilson invited them all to take their seats looking out onto a viewing platform. In his mid-40's, Wilson was dressed casually in a black polo-neck sweater, redolent of Manfred Mann's Earth Band, circa UK 1964. This laid-back look accompanied a boyish expression but his overall body language suggested someone who could make hard decisions if called upon, who wouldn't be shy of pressing a button and counting down, "5-4-3-2-1".

Also in tune with the current fashion, head of Homeland Security Monica Chan presented her ultra-slim body in a simple-cut mini-dress, along with a man's waistcoat and tie, recalling the iconic fashion model "Twiggy". She had a neat side-parting in the fringe of her hair and despite the lightweight frame came across as a tough woman who wouldn't flinch from dealing with weighty matters.

Still, Richards couldn't help thinking of all that responsibility resting on such thin shoulders and skinny bird-like legs. He was aware of the reassuring feeling he got from the substantial material contained in his well-tailored suit with its broad lapels and sharp lines announcing someone who meant business, recalling roles assumed by his favourite actor, Spencer Tracy, as seen in a number of iconic movies, several of the best made late-career going into the 1960's.

In contrast to the others, General Calvin Macy and Admiral Roy Horne were both dressed formally in their military attire, although to fans of The Beatle's *Sergeant Pepper* album with "Lucy in the Sky with Diamonds" playing in their minds the two men might fancifully have blended in with the overall ambient effect.

Wilson got the ball rolling: 'Before we even get started Richards, I must say it doesn't help how this discussion is taking place against the background of a recent fatality in a certain high school where these androids of yours are so much an integral part.'

'Yes, I'm obviously aware of that,' said Richards. 'That incident was unfortunate. Hopefully we can continue to minimise its impact as far as this is concerned. I'm grateful in that regard to Ms Chan here for her early intervention and ongoing support in helping to keep the formal investigation low key.'

Ms Chan offered a reserved smile. 'The least I could do in the circumstances.'

Wilson added: 'I guess it's in all our interests to allow

you an unhindered run at this, *if* what you've got here actually fulfils its weighty promise.'

Richards brought up a hologram projection of an android soldier, revealing just the basic body-shape and weapon-less for the moment. 'Ladies and gentlemen, I present to you our brand new state of the art *Peacemaker*.'

All four faces looked bemused.

Macy frowned. 'He doesn't look much different from what we have in the field already: the ones driving trucks, clearing mines, forming cordons to hold back rioters and other low-grade duties.'

Admiral Horne proffered a thin smile. 'Sure, I get it: we're going to play "Action Man" and really go to town dressing this guy up?'

Richards shook his head. 'Actually Admiral, with one or two fairly modest accessories, this is pretty close to the finished article.'

The expressions of surprise morphed into mild confusion.

Macy looked again at the android figure. 'If this guy's supposed to keep the peace, how does he have any authority: unless he has secret weapons hidden up his backside?'

Horne frowned. 'I was under the impression we were considering something with the potential to operate at full combat level.'

'That you will have Admiral,' said Richards, 'if you'll just bear with me for a moment.'

Both military men shrugged and decided to hold their fire.

'The crucial point,' Richards continued, 'is what's happening on the inside.'

'Don't judge a book by the cover is I think the appropriate cliché,' said Ms Chan.

Wilson leaned forwards. 'OK, Richards, I'm assuming these units can be "dressed up" as the Admiral says to carry whatever weapons are necessary for any military operation. I guess we *were* forewarned this is all to do with what you're claiming to be a major enhancement in their emotional intelligence. So let's move this on. Maybe you can tell us: does this guy have the same EI level as a human being?'

'Yes and more,' Richards replied confidently. 'Crucially, it understands human beings better than they understand themselves. It knows what provokes a particular feeling to appear in any given context: enabling a fully informed decision on the best way to respond.'

'Emotional-rational,' said Ms Chan. 'Or maybe it's the other way around?'

'It works both ways,' said Richards, pleased with her observation.

'You surely can't be saying he has access to the full range of feelings we have?' said Horne mildly offended.

'OK...' said Ms Chan, intervening. 'Before we get too ahead of ourselves with our gender assumptions, calling this thing a "he" – is this soldier in fact a male?'

Richards smiled. 'Physically *all* these androids would be gender neutral; however, Ms Chan's observation alerts us to an important consideration. If they're to formulate an appropriate response to any emotionally-driven human action, we would want to include those habitually associated with both genders.'

Wilson sat back in his chair. 'I hardly need to tell you Richards that we have other projects competing for the same funding. And on top of the matter mentioned earlier, there's another incident of some concern relating to that school you're involved with. Apparently one of your more advanced teaching androids exploded? Again, it hardly inspires confidence in what you're offering us here.'

Richards nodded to acknowledge fair comment. 'It's important to say the android concerned was an experimental semi-biological model, totally unrelated to what you see here. But the incident you're referring to was actually invaluable; isn't it a truism that you often learn far more from your mistakes? In fact we're continuing to explore initiatives in that area: in many ways the educational front line is a particularly useful proving ground for what we're trying to develop with regard to conflict resolution.'

It sounded reasonable. There were a few nods, even smiles of recognition from those around the table: anyone who had kids in school knew how challenging things were right now.

Wilson continued: 'Anyway, what you seem to be claiming for this creation of yours standing before us is the ability to make the best possible decisions in any given situation, informed by an emotional intelligence that is far superior to the average human?'

'Yes, I think that's a fair summary,' said Richards.

'Even when it comes to life or death situations?' asked Ms Chan – eyebrow raised.

There was a moment of silence in the room.

Richards paused before answering: 'Yes, in those situations especially.'

General Macy, a known hawk, looked around encouragingly at the others. 'So let's not beat around the proverbial bush, this is what we're here to consider right? I for one can see a clear advantage, especially in a situation where a human combatant might allow the heart to overrule the head; let sentiment get in the way of hard pragmatism.'

Wilson allowed himself a small frown of reservation. 'As a first base, are we talking about this "peacekeeper" operating purely in a protective role?'

Ms Chan gave a small cough. 'We're all aware that as far as national security goes that's always an ambiguous term.'

'Whichever way it is,' said Horne, 'why not simply upgrade the EI training for our regular human combatants and continue to allow them to make those kinds of tough decisions?'

Richards shook his head. 'Apart from the fact human recruits to the military will always show mixed ability in assimilating that kind of learning, compared to the uniform capacity for all androids to process it equally, we might also be in danger of inadvertently building in a bias towards what the General has just called "pragmatism"– which could then prove too rigid in variable and unpredictable contexts. What this enhanced EI soldier brings to the table is greater flexibility, openness to the unique challenge of any given situation; no a priori agenda, ideological bias or fixed imperatives.'

'And no emotional baggage,' Ms Chan added positively.

'I suppose it's a fair point,' Wilson acknowledged. 'Aren't we well used to dealing with the fallout caused by some human son-of-a-bitch with a one track mind. We seem to end up with repeated versions of *The Charge of the Light Brigade* – any number of ways to send lambs to the slaughter.'

Macy said, 'There's also the advantage that if a few of these androids do get destroyed at least we have no wives and kids mourning their loss.'

'But what if they're captured and their insides are analysed: don't the enemy get one just like ours?' asked Horne.

Richards stepped in closer to the image. 'There's the usual self-destruct mechanism if anyone tries to access manually, or hack in without inserting the correct code.' He used the control patch on his wrist to make the image explode into nothingness. 'With regard to the second part of your question, I don't need to tell you there are plenty of others out there working towards something similar. It's an arms race after all.'

Wilson stroked his chin. 'OK, if what you're claiming for these units is true, it's obvious the first side to deploy them would have a clear advantage in any conflict; a certain number could even be sacrificed to gain a strategic advantage, perhaps win a first decisive round knowing replacements are coming fast off the production line. We could in theory sacrifice thousands, even millions if it meant we got the ultimate upper hand.'

'And we don't have to hang around waiting for mothers to have more babies,' Ms Chan chimed in witheringly.

'And you get to sell us a whole lot more android soldiers!' Wilson continued. 'You'd be set to make a lot of money out of this Richards; I hope I'm not sounding cynical.'

Richards raised his palms in self-defence. 'You've heard this before, but it really is not about financial recompense.'

'So we'll take a few hundred thousand for free. Try them out!' snorted General Macy.

Admiral Horne offered a thin smile. 'No doubt Mr Richards does have to put food on the table.'

There was a pause, while they all looked to one another.

Wilson nodded his head. 'What have we got in terms of clinical trials?'

'Results are extremely favourable,' said Richards almost too casually.

Ms Chan coughed. 'OK, we've already said how android soldiers have been employed in the field for some time, so that much isn't new: the main point of our discussion here is that up till now we've resisted allowing them the independent *choice* of taking a life, in any circumstances.'

'They have made those kinds of choices in simulation,' said Richards.

'Simulation, be darned!' said Macy. 'You say these guys are super-intelligent, so they're not stupid. They must know when it's real or not. We'll never know how they shape up to making those hard decisions until they're thrown right in there where it counts.'

Wilson leaned back. 'We're not suggesting setting up a real-life trial and asking one of these units to decide whether to kill or not, right before our eyes?'

'Tests and trials always tend to be under the counter or off the beaten track,' observed Horne. 'They didn't test the A-bomb in Times Square.'

Ms Chan exchanged a quick look with Richards before turning to the others: 'OK, so no one is saying we should openly carry out such a test. But hypothetically, just supposing an android combatant had *already* made this kind of decision, taken a life to protect someone or something of far greater importance, of geo-political significance perhaps: can we say one hundred per cent we would reprimand that heroic figure out of hand?'

A s Special Agent Floyd Linton drove his carrier
through a grove of trees, he picked out a line
of replica First Nation totem poles covered in
carvings depicting snakes and other creatures creeping
up their length. On top of the poles were heads of eagles,
bears, coyotes.

When the dirt track came out to run alongside a lake
he wondered if there were any real fish in there. Maybe
these people knew how to keep them alive? Or was it just
as polluted and full of plastic as much of the open water on
the planet. Linton dwelt on the irony of how some of that
plastic was now actually made into the shape of aquatic life
– designed to fill lakes and pools with artificial movement
and colour, so things might not look quite so bad.

'Thanks for making the time to talk. I'm sorry for the
loss of your brother.' Linton looked across the small rustic
wooden table at Rob Bennett's sister, dressed in a tie-dye
vest and baggy Aladdin style pants. Her long hair was
twisted into two beaded plaits and she had a flower tattooed
on each bare shoulder. She looked a year or two older than
Rob and facially a little like him despite the fact they weren't

blood related, or even had the same colour skin. Still, it was almost as if there was a subtle family resemblance.

Elizabeth returned him a bemused smile. 'Thank you Detective, I appreciate your kind words; not to mention coming all the way out here to say them?'

Linton shifted his body weight on the hard wooden seat. 'I know you already talked to the police, but that was a formal interview and I was hoping you might help in giving me a fuller picture of Rob.' He paused, slightly disarmed by her open stare. 'We didn't get a lot from his fellow teachers in terms of his personal life; he appeared to have kept much to himself. You said in your statement you hadn't seen much of him yourself in recent times?'

Elizabeth shrugged: 'Rob and I also led largely separate lives – I guess he was always busy with his own thing.'

'But you'd say that he was a likeable character, not someone who would encourage enemies.' Linton framed it in the affirmative, like there was no real reason for doubt, yet knowing there was sub-text for anyone who wanted to hear it.

Elizabeth examined Linton before answering: 'Does that mean you're thinking maybe it *wasn't* an accident, despite the coroner's verdict?'

Linton tried to fudge his answer. 'I guess we'd still like to build a fuller picture, just for the record; or maybe it's the way I personally like to work.'

If Elizabeth perceived any disingenuousness, she decided to let it go. 'To answer the first part of your question I'd say my brother was a genuinely likeable guy.'

Linton pondered for a moment. 'And you never thought to seek a fuller, more public inquest yourself?'

This time Elizabeth offered a puzzled frown. 'Why invite a cloud of suspicion: wouldn't that imply he was involved in something that might have put him at risk?'

'Sure,' said Linton, backing off, not wanting to put her on the defensive, especially now she appeared to be opening up a little. He reached in his pocket and took out the photo obtained from Howard Trent. 'We were given this picture. Maybe you can identify where and when it was taken?'

Elizabeth looked sadly at the image for a few seconds; turned it over for a moment then handed it back. 'He sure loved robots: I'd say that was at least five years ago; at one of those DARPA conventions.'

'DARPA?' said Linton, nodding. 'That's the department of the military looking at new technology.'

Elizabeth shrugged. 'Those public conventions are open to anyone; they do like to show off their toys. Rob would have gone there a number of times.'

As if on cue, a squadron of military planes appeared overhead, flying low and making their presence felt with the loud roar of their engines. With Elizabeth withdrawing into herself for a moment, lost in thought, Linton took advantage of the break in the conversation to look around and absorb their surroundings: the rustic lodge next to where they were sitting, the nearby gardens and poly-tunnels – orchards extending into the distance. He took in the stillness of the place. The kind of peace you'd want to protect. Regarding his interviewee, he was conscious of how in revealing anything about herself she was potentially offering valuable insight into her brother's character. If Elizabeth was a peace-lover and she expressed a kinship with Rob, it might back up the image of him being a kind, peaceful kind of guy. At the same time it couldn't be ignored how she was an eco-warrior; an activist with a conscious motivation for her actions and maybe a broader agenda. Maybe there'd been more to Rob Bennett than the quiet unobtrusive person everyone seemed to remember.

'Fill me in on what you're doing here Elizabeth,' asked Linton, still looking around at the grounds. He also wanted to get more of a sense whether this woman was a reliable witness, had her feet on the ground. Maybe she had a false impression of her brother.

'We collect and save seeds. We look after the planet's future.'

'Tell me more.' Linton projected what he hoped was a convincing empathetic hippy-dippy smile.

Elizabeth allowed herself a grin at his unconvincing effort; but then her expression hardened. 'It's a beautiful project. But we also know that we're at war.'

'War?' said Linton, his ears pricking up.

Elizabeth sat up straighter. 'Did you know that back at the beginning of the Gulf War, when it became clear the United States and the UK were going to invade Iraq, there were those in that country who had the foresight to move all its precious seeds out of harm's way?'

Linton looked genuinely surprised. 'No, I guess I didn't know that.'

'Aside from the appalling loss of life, damage to infrastructure, not to mention the pollution of the land, looting of artworks and stuff – no one gets to hear about the destruction of the seed banks.'

'Seed banks?' Linton scratched an ear.

'It's a first instinct of warfare. Like a group of male lions when they kill another male head of a pride, move in on his family – they also kill his babies, so the mother will be forced to mate and provide them with their own offspring.'

Linton scratched the other ear.

'And sure enough in the example I was giving, the prediction was correct, the seed banks were "accidentally" destroyed amidst the general chaos of the bombing and fighting. They would have contained strains that Iraqi farmers had relied on for thousands of years, going all the way back to the Garden of Eden; that had grown over time to respond to the local soils and weather conditions. Then once conquest was achieved, the first order from the new ruling American led administration was that from now on Iraqi farmers were not going to be allowed to re-plant their own seeds, but instead had to buy a whole new type of seed from a US based multinational company. These seeds would certainly not be suited to local conditions, would also be GM and the resulting plants would be sterile so the farmers would have to keep going back to the same company for more.'

'Okay, so now I get the lion connection,' said Linton.

'This scenario has been replicated everywhere and not just in war contexts. In India, tens of thousands of farmers committed suicide after their cotton crops failed massively, due to being forced to buy useless inappropriate seeds from the same company.'

'Forced?'

'Maybe the US couldn't march troops into a country like India but it could bully the government into accepting damaging trade agreements…'

Linton had to cut her off – his head was starting to spin. 'I guess we should be grateful then for what you're doing here under the radar in saving our planet. This kind of thing could go by unappreciated, invisible to the rest of us ignorant folk.'

Elizabeth smiled. 'A lot of important work is under the radar I guess.'

Linton let this last comment hang in the air for a moment.

Elizabeth looked up at the Sun overhead like someone else would look at their wristband for the time. 'I'm afraid I'll have to stop now, several things to be done before it gets too hot.'

Linton thanked her as he got up and stretched his legs, saying she'd been very helpful; then turned to walk back to his car.

It wasn't until he got into the driver's seat, slotted the gear into reverse and checked his hat in the rear-view mirror, that it really hit home how during the whole conversation Elizabeth had not asked him the most obvious question: 'Why would anyone want to kill her brother?'

8

Kerry put aside her breakfast bowl and lay back with her eyes closed, her mind running over the implications of that seismic moment at the end of their last session when the kids themselves had come up with the idea for a full production; they'd even volunteered more of their free time if necessary. She'd told them yes, she'd be into it herself, but would have to clear it with the Principal as this was a clear departure from her original brief. But even before that she needed to think it through. Was it a good idea, would they be taking on too much? Up until now she'd envisaged sharing the play's major and minor characters around a good bit, given the limited number of scenes they would be able to present. But doing the entire play right through meant a major re-think regarding how her small troop of actors would cover so many roles.

One big advantage to keeping with the humans versus androids theme was how it would allow the learning buddies to play everyone on the Montague side: Romeo, both his parents, cousin Benvolio, as well as their servants and a number of minor parts. Turning then to the Capulet household, Harper Wanda and Tania could neatly fill the roles of Juliet, Lady Capulet and the Nurse. But that still left the five boys to cover Lord Capulet, Tybalt and other members of that extended family, plus their servants, and then on top of that Count Paris, Prince Escalus, Friar Laurence, Friar John, the Apothecary, not to mention Romeo's close friend, Mercutio.

It was unlikely Jim Brady would be keen on her bringing in more actors, given his original reasons for selecting this group; she felt uneasy herself anyway about going in that direction, it might upset their growing yet still possibly fragile sense of themselves as a collective. So it was clear one way or another most of them would need to play more than one character: the girls would certainly have to take on a few of the male roles. She'd have to consider how best to cast Mercutio who is allied to the Montagues but not actually part of that family; and there was a knock-on issue with the Prince and Count Paris being related to him. Overall it could easily become over-complicated and messy: she'd have to think it through for what were the best options.

❖

'I hope you're not too busy?' said Kerry, poking her head around the door.

Jim Brady held up the cover of the book he was reading.

'You're actually reading the play!'

'Don't act so surprised. I'm doing my homework, just so I can keep up with whatever request you're liable to land on me next.'

'How did you guess?' said Kerry with a smile.

'What's in there?' asked Brady, noticing she had a large carrier bag with her.

'Masks – Miss Angelou asked me to spend today talking to her classes about Ancient Greek Theatre. I've a fair collection back home that I acquired during my travels – luckily I packed a few coming here from California: big sacrifice, I had to throw a load of good clothes out of my suitcase to make room.'

'I admire your dedication,' said Brady with a smile, 'and your foresight.'

'Greek Theatre was full of prophesy, it was a big influence on Shakespeare in fact, including the play we're doing.'

Brady's face revealed a touch of real concern. 'Talking of looking ahead: how is it coming along – we're on track for open day, which is…' He glanced at the calendar on the wall and opened his eyes wide. 'Is that just six and a half weeks away?'

Kerry looked at the figure for "June" – the bubbly but painfully vulnerable face of Janis Joplin.

'There's actually been a new development, the kids are asking for something closer to a full production. I didn't say anything they just came out with it themselves. They're all up for it; even willing to sacrifice time at weekends to rehearse.'

Brady took a moment to respond, looking more than a little wary. 'OK…maybe that sounds like it *might* be good news. But what are the implications here: you don't think there's a danger of overreach?'

'No, I really think we can do it. We've been making some great progress.'

Brady leaned back to give it full consideration. 'Obviously it would be all the more impressive regarding our overall objective to show ourselves off in a good light.' He nodded to himself, warming to the idea. 'Who knows maybe we might even think about taking it out of the day schedule and put it on in the evening?'

'Hey, that would be so great,' said Kerry, before adding quickly, 'But here's the thing: with such a small group of actors and lots of characters to fill, it would help even more now if I could get that upgrade for the learning buddies and allow them more versatility. I know you had some misgivings after that early incident with Chuck, but we really have moved on since then in building discipline and awareness…'

Brady held up his hand to stop her. 'Truly, I was all set to follow up on that until this whole thing with Rob happened. And now our benefactor's right in the middle of negotiating some kind of hush-hush government contract; we just can't risk inviting any more unnecessary attention and controversy: in fact, you might want to re-think that whole humans versus androids angle.'

Kerry looked at the calendar image again, wishing it could speak or sing on her behalf.

Brady began shuffling through a pile of envelopes on his desk, slitting one of them open with a silver-dagger paperknife. 'I thought letter writing had died a death, it seems to be making a comeback. Go on, keep talking, I listen better when I'm distracted.'

Kerry took an in-breath. 'OK, so I'm taking on board what you just said about the humans versus androids theme. As you know I always had my own reservations about that angle anyway. But if I give up on having the learning buddies playing all the Montague tribe, here's what I'm left trying to juggle with. Taking the four female characters first: my three girls can fill Juliet, Lady Capulet and then say Lady Montague; but that would leave the all-important Nurse, just for once Shakespeare went a little overboard on the female roles.'

Brady smiled. 'You could play her yourself? My favourite part in this play, she's real funny.'

'Sure, could be my big moment,' said Kerry deadpan.

'OK…and the male characters?'

'I have five boys to fill eight principal male roles as well as several minor ones.'

Brady locked his hands behind his neck. 'So how do we solve all this?'

'I have a few options, first base is to set the play back in the 16th century when they obviously didn't have androids, so there will be no attempt at realism, the audience will simply see the learning buddies as actors playing parts to serve the drama. That way I can distribute them across the whole list of characters: it would fulfil your original request, reflecting well on how successfully we're using AI here; celebrate what the school is all about.'

'I like it!' said Brady. 'So problem solved; maybe I don't want to hear the other possibilities.'

'Or – maybe I should be standing my ground here and challenge your reservations. Maybe we *could* be taking a leaf out of *West Side Story*, but be really bold and bring it up to date: let the learning buddies play their own kind, make it more immediate and real.'

Brady's frown returned. 'Except we don't have gangs of teenage androids wandering around looking for trouble: not yet anyway.'

'What if it's set in the future?'

'All dark and depressing retro *Blade Runner*? You'll have everyone coming down on our heads, including Charles Richards. The "robots taking over the world brigade" will have a field day. It invites in all that negativity. You acknowledged yourself how important it is to promote something positive.'

Kerry bit her lip: 'The play is a tragedy, after all.'

'Sure, but the ending is still upbeat,' said Brady, waving the book. 'The warring factions learn their hard lesson. The lovers have ultimately sacrificed themselves for peace. This was your original idea for pulling together the whole shebang.'

Kerry checked her time. 'Sorry, I'll have to head for my first class with Miss Angelou in a moment.' She picked up her carrier bag: 'Want a quick preview?'

'Sure why not,' said Brady, curious.

Kerry pulled out a large mask made of light wood covered with some kind of stretched material and held it up to show off a face with a sorrowful expression. 'This is one used by an actor as part of the chorus in a tragedy,' she said, slipping it on.

'You don't look too happy,' said Brady.

She removed the mask. 'The chorus never left the stage during an entire play: it was there as a constant presence to represent the ordinary citizen witnessing the struggle between their more noble betters and the gods.' She dipped again into the bag and pulled out another one, this time with a dignified expression: 'This one might be more *you*. It was worn by a royal character.'

Brady took the mask and put it on. 'How do I look?'

'Like a king,' said Kerry.

'Maybe the King of Comedy?' said Brady, droll.

Kerry smiled: 'Yes, they did of course have comedies too.' She looked at her wristband again. 'Better go.'

Brady picked up his jacket. 'Come on, I'll walk with you, we can talk a little more on the way.'

'Thanks,' said Kerry, gathering up her bag. 'By the way, classical Greek Theatre was full of symbolism: you wore purple if you were a royal character and put on a hat if you were going on a journey.'

'Hmm, not sure about the colour, but I like the idea of a hat; maybe I'll invest in a fedora like my good friend Mr Linton for the next time I take a wander.'

As they opened the door AJ was hovering outside, about to knock.

Brady smiled. 'Hey AJ – is it time to water the plants again? Afraid I'll have to leave you to it old buddy.'

They left the room and walked around the viewing gallery before stepping into the glass dropdown pod. On the way down Brady said by way of appeasement: 'Something I *can* promise is once you're into the final stretch I can arrange for the kids to get a release from most of their regular classes to concentrate on rehearsals.'

'Thanks, that'll be a big help,' said Kerry, still obviously subdued at not getting her request.

As they exited from the pod, Brady took a moment to look out onto the busy plaza, experiencing something like a déjà vu moment. 'Listen, I know where you're coming from with this upgrade Kerry, I imagine even with their current empathy restrictions, any of your learning buddies could play someone like Prince Escalus: OK here's a high status royal with a couple of big long-winded speeches but essentially he just talks down at everyone. Count Paris, Juliet's other suitor? Nice guy but superficial, no one really engages with him. The Friar is admittedly more complex but still more or less static regarding character development.' He paused. 'But I can see how it's a whole different ball game with the likes of Juliet's Nurse and Romeo's pal Mercutio: for an actor to really get inside those characters, especially deliver all that off-beat humour – he, she, or "it" has to connect with a whole range of complex signals and hidden meaning…'

Kerry held her breath.

'OK, so here's the new deal,' said Brady finally. 'If you agree not to present this thing simply as humans versus androids, I'll get onto Charles Richards right away and make a good pitch for this upgrade.'

'Deal,' said Kerry smiling.

Brady looked relieved too. Before heading off he threw her a conspiratorial grin. 'Let's shake this whole thing up, crazy Mama!'

❖

Kerry spent the whole morning with Miss Angelou's classes. The masks were an instant hit, although it served to provoke a wider interest in what her group were doing with the play. Conscious of avoiding too much attention, especially at this delicate stage where a few things were on the line, she chose to play it down, saying it would have to be a surprise on the day.

At lunchtime Kerry entered the fringe hub to find her group sadly reduced. 'What happened to the girls?'

Carlos shrugged. 'Medical officer for jabs, not their fault: compulsory.'

'OK, I must have forgotten, with so much going on...'

'Hey, she's human after all,' said Omar with a grin.

Kerry grimaced good-humouredly. 'Thanks, I'll take that as a compliment.'

'So are we going to get a full production?' asked Jing eagerly.

'Yes...I talked to the Principal earlier – and he's sympathetic to the idea. He just has to mull it over a little. But he'll be back with an answer a.s.a.p.'

There was a chorus of accepting shrugs and nods.

'Shame about the girls,' said Kerry, 'I'd planned –'

'But *we're* here!' declared Chuck, 'along with our trusty droids.' He offered the learning buddies a mock-friendly peace sign.

She realised this was a good opportunity to work with the boys on their own: 'OK...so why don't we look at the all-male scene where Tybalt picks a fight with Romeo and Mercutio subsequently gets killed.'

'At last we get to spill some blood!' said Chuck eagerly, happy to swop his peace sign for the now legendary imaginary sword.

'We'll be taking it slow and with a lot of self-control, after the last time,' Kerry said firmly. 'Oh – I almost forgot,' she added, pulling a camera from her bag.

'Are you filming us today?' asked Jing.

'I thought it might be helpful for me to watch it back later.'

'Sure, so now we're in the movies!' said Little Stevie, acting super-cool.

'But only with your permission of course? It'll be just for my own use, I won't be showing it to anyone else.'

'You have our permission madam,' Chuck said, bowing courteously.

'Aren't you going to ask for *their* permission?' asked Carlos, indicating the learning buddies.

The question took Kerry by surprise. It was a fair point: maybe her android actors *should* have some say in the matter, after all wasn't this part of the all-important process; wouldn't she be guilty of taking them for granted otherwise. She'd have to think that one through later. Anyway, given she'd been put on the spot. 'Do you mind if we film this scene?' she asked the nearest one.

'I cannot hold a personal view in this,' DAK 11 answered, before adding in an even more mechanical voice: '*Basic data protection and manufacturer copyright dictates images are allowed but only for non-commercial purposes. You must also not post them online.*'

It was almost comical. She turned to the kids. 'By the way, I'm assuming no-one here is secretly filming?'

The boys displayed empty hands as a gesture of innocence.

'Great, so let's get started,' said Kerry.

Chuck put up his hand. 'You haven't told us who's playing who in this scene.'

Kerry smiled sympathetically. 'OK, Chuck I guess you've been Tybalt before so why don't you give that part another go. But take it easy, that sword looks just as sharp as last time.'

'She's giving you a chance to redeem yourself, dude,' jeered Little Stevie.

'Little Stevie, would you like to pick up again with Romeo?' said Kerry.

Chuck grinned. 'Congratulations dude: be ready to duel!'

Kerry looked at the remaining three boys: 'Mercutio for you, Jing?'

'Sure,' he said, pleasantly surprised.

'And let's have a second group working on the same scene: with Omar playing Tybalt, Carlos playing Romeo and maybe DAK 14 as Mercutio? In fact I'd like to run it several times with different combinations and the learning buddies trying out all three characters.'

'Fine, give me two droids,' said Chuck, 'I'll take them both on.'

The door beeped to announce AJ entering. 'Excuse me but Mr Brady has asked me to find a space to house a number of chairs. I will bring them in here if that is OK with you, Miss Tracker? I'll try not to be in the way.'

'No, not at all,' replied Kerry, a little surprised but not minding too much especially after all the support and encouragement Jim Brady had given her. 'We'll try and ignore you AJ if that's OK.'

'I'll be as quick as I can,' said the android, stepping outside to his waiting trolley containing the first batch of chairs.

9

Tim Wilson was welcoming everyone back for a second meeting of the military task force. 'So Richards, I gather you're keen to provide some kind of simulation for us: at least we'll get to see our guy in action this time.'

'I thought following the last session it would help to show exactly what we're talking about here with regard to enhanced emotional intelligence,' said Richards, pointing to holograms of *three* figures: two human, one android. 'Bear in mind this could involve scores of individuals, hundreds, even whole armies; but for purposes of illustration we're breaking it down to just three protagonists.'

'Sure, easier to follow,' said Wilson, as all heads nodded acceptance.

'I'm sure you're all familiar with the old western, *The Good the Bad & the Ugly* – the famous final shootout?'

'Good movie! Sure looking forward to what you have to show us,' said Admiral Horne.

Richards waved a remote and all three figures donned cowboy outfits, including hats.

'Nice touch,' said Ms Chan.

'In that famous scenario there are three gunmen standing in a rough triangle. You'll remember the contest is over a stash of gold, whoever remains standing will claim it. In this version our android plays the "good guy" who has the fastest draw but that advantage appears to be offset by the chosen rules of engagement, as none of them have time to shoot both adversaries before being shot by the one he didn't shoot first. It's a game of poker with guns. From the android's point of view, the "bad" guy is probably more of a threat than the "ugly" one; however he can't really know that for sure.'

'We all remember how this ends,' said Admiral Horne, 'the good guy comes out on top. But maybe your android is going to show us something we didn't already know?'

Richards pulled out a thin cigar and chewed off one end, trying to look tough and ice-cool like a hardened gunslinger.

There were a few smiles. Macy grimaced and said, 'OK Richards, very good piece of acting, but let's not go overboard.'

'I'm just trying to give you all a sense of the heightened atmosphere generated for this climatic scene in the movie: the rapid increase in camera shots as the tension mounts, the pulsating swell of the music – all of it obscuring how the good guy doesn't in fact have to be quite that smart. We're conveniently asked to forget or put aside how just a moment earlier he's secretly taken all the bullets from the ugly guy's gun, putting him right out of the equation.'

A couple of the faces at the table looked affronted at the suggestion they'd somehow been duped all those years.

Wilson nodded. 'So the good guy only has to shoot the bad guy. And he knows he's faster.'

Horne said, 'Thanks for that Richards, taking all the mystery out of what was once a great ending!'

Richards continued: 'The truth is without that unfair advantage the good guy can never be certain of the right decision. He's back trying to think it through rationally as well as read their faces and body-language for giveaway emotional signals that might either confirm or contradict this "intelligence". As all these inputs enter his brain they might trip over one another. And remember, it's extremely hot: hard to read through the tension in the faces of the other two, with beads of sweat pouring in rivulets down their –'

'Thanks Richards, we do get the picture!' said Macy.

'OK, so what is the good guy thinking? Maybe the ugly guy will shoot him in the belief that he will instinctively go for the bad guy. But can the good guy take the risk of shooting the ugly guy first and then very likely be killed by the bad guy? And don't forget the ugly guy and the bad guy are also preoccupied with thinking this through. It's a game of treble-bluff, almost impossible for anyone to be certain of what is the best call.'

Wilson narrowed his eyes like he was staring down the barrel of a gun, trying to work it out. 'So what are you saying? If this was your android taking the place of the good cowboy, it's advanced EI and complex algorithms could somehow correctly read the other two faces, all those subtle signals you've alluded to; also make a strategic decision about what false emotional signals to give off itself to scupper their own guesses, lead them to act against their own interests –'

Horne groaned as he reached for the water jug. 'I have to confess this is all a little tricky for an old greybeard like me to follow.'

Macy shook his head. 'OK Richards, at the end of the day surely we're talking about good old-fashioned gut instinct? Our guy simply reads the other two faces, picks up on all the fear, suspicion – and just intuits what they're going to do.'

'In which case we may as well stick with our regular human soldiers, sailors and airmen, the ones who actually possess a set of real live guts,' said Horne. 'Mr Richards may have just pulled the rug out from under his own proposal.'

'OK,' said Richards, 'let's see just what happens when we bring these three up to date.' He flicked the remote, replacing the android figure's cowboy outfit with a modern army uniform, complete with the familiar white helmet worn by international peacekeeping troops. 'It might help to begin with our soldier in this role?'

'Why not, a good place to start,' said Wilson, sitting back.

Richards gave the two human figures indistinct paramilitary uniforms, both of them now holding stun-knives. 'Let's keep the other two guys vague in terms of nationality, for the sake of neutralising unwanted prejudice.'

'Why switch to blades?' queried Horne. 'Why not stick with firearms, or rocket launchers for that matter?'

Richards nodded: 'Yes, we could keep this at a distance, even let them fire drones at one another using computers. But that way it would be harder to get a handle on how exactly emotional intelligence works. Everything would be too removed regarding who makes the decisions; who carries out the orders.'

'We're keeping it up close and personal,' said Macy approvingly.

'It's important to keep in mind the first point of call in this context is diplomacy. It's not a simple question of overpowering these guys with superior weaponry or fighting skills. Observe how our *peacemaker's* own stun-blade is still in its sheath.'

Richards waved the remote and the two human figures began to circle, firing insults at one another. The android soldier gestured for them to stop, but they ignored it, moving in closer for the kill.

'So, let's say our peacemaker steps in unarmed to separate them, finds itself caught in the middle and as a poor reward for this initiative, gets killed instead.' Richards allowed this to play itself out.

'Not good,' said Admiral Horne with understatement.

Richards brought the android back to life: 'So with no other option it draws its own weapon as a show of authority. The other two hesitate for a moment, but then go on fighting. Our peacemaker finally intervenes forcibly but perhaps only succeeds in parrying one of the combatant's lunges, wrong-footing that guy's defences so *he* ends up getting stabbed instead.'

There was a moment of silence as they looked at the frozen tableau.

'So what do we learn from that?' asked Macy, baffled.

'That our peacemaker has blown it!' said Ms Chan. 'It may even have upset what might have remained a stalemate in which each of them had no advantage. Neither would have actually risked the first thrust of the blade.'

'Removing the deterrent of Mutually Assured Destruction,' said Wilson.

Richards summarised: 'Stepping in with a flawed approach has resulted in defeat of one side and victory for the other with all its ramifications. As Ms Chan has said, it's very likely undermined the credibility of the *peacemaking* role. We might even imagine the fatally wounded combatant waving his fists at both his assailant and the peacemaker, cursing them equally with his last breath.'

Tim Wilson looked at the three hologram figures: 'So Richards, any more options?'

Richards scanned the faces of the group. 'Actually, at this point maybe I can throw this back to all of you for suggestions?'

Wilson took up the challenge. 'How about our android steps in as before, but this time his superior fighting skills allow him to parry both stun-knives at the same time: maybe he disarms these guys so no one gets hurt.'

Richards nodded assent. 'So let's go with that.' The scene was acted out. And yes, the plan had worked. Wilson looked pleased with himself.

'But this is a temporary solution at best,' said Richards, 'they may try it again, only the next time they'll be better prepared, more devious. How long can our guy stop them hurting each other? And, with a little image enhancement...' This time the lone peacemaker was dealing with at least a dozen on each side and eventually overwhelmed.

'OK, point hammered home!' said Macy.

'So what is the elusive answer, according to your emotionally intelligent peacemaker?' asked Ms Chan. 'Maybe we should finally let this thing make up its own mind.'

'OK...' said Richards. 'I'm putting this on auto. Let's see what happens.'

This time the peacemaker turned, selected a few combatants on both sides and in a matter of seconds permanently disabled them with clinical efficiency. The others looked stunned and the fighting came to a standstill.

'Hmm...' said Wilson, a little taken aback, 'that was far from peaceful.'

'But it worked!' said Macy approvingly. 'Isn't that exactly the sort of thing we're looking for?'

Wilson nodded. 'So let's consider how we justify that kind of violent action coming from our android friend, convince everyone that it's appropriate and absolutely necessary?'

Richards continued: 'What you've witnessed is a decision made in the round based on all the intelligence available, including EI. OK, in the limited scenario in front of us it might appear random and vague in its likely effects, but think of the broader picture: maybe the rise of a despot who will become a threat to peace and world order. Or imagine he's taking out the guy who was about to assassinate the Austrian Archduke and set off World War 1. One life set against millions?'

'Maybe they'd have had that war anyway,' said Horne.

'That's the road not taken, something we can never know,' Richards countered.

There was a lull in the conversation while everyone took stock.

Wilson stroked his chin. 'The way you've just described it makes *our* guy sound more like an assassin. I'm wondering: could it operate covertly – maybe we should have the CIA on board in these discussions?'

Ms Chan shifted in her seat. 'This isn't a territorial thing but I don't think we should muddy the waters at this stage.'

Richards swopped looks with Ms Chan before continuing: 'What we're considering at this juncture is a combatant that operates fully out in the open, a piece of military hardware that everyone will eventually get to know about.'

Wilson nodded. 'I guess if we're talking about giving this guy the freedom to make life and death decisions on the battlefield there has to be a close monitoring. We couldn't risk losing track of an android operating undercover.'

General Macy pushed out his chest as if to remind himself why *he* was standing there in this room. 'OK, let's say for now we've been given a convincing argument for this android soldier. So here's the sixty-four trillion dollar question: if this guy can show such efficiency within these small operational limits, if its decision making is so superior compared with a normal human being – why stop there? Why not hand the bigger decisions over as well. Let's have android generals and admirals! And then what about our supreme commander in chief: replace the President with an android, isn't that the logical progression!'

Richards could only offer a diplomatic smile. 'I understand where you're coming from General. Like we were just saying, maybe this is all about taking small steps.'

Kerry sat cross-legged on a cushion in front of her globe, eagerly looking forward to reviewing the recording of the three-way fight scene they'd been working on in their last session. She was playing catch-up a little with the play; her talks on Greek Theatre with Miss Angelou's classes had gone down so well Jim Brady had asked if she'd mind fitting in a lunchtime talk for the general school population. As a result she'd had to cancel the following meeting with her group, but it was worth it to spread the theatre vibe around: again the masks had been a great attraction, although she'd assembled lots of hologram images there was nothing like the real thing you could hold in your hands and then slip over your face. Thinking now back to Miss Angelou's classes, Kerry had also been impressed by the way kids listened attentively to the android teacher as she provided further background to the great plays by Aeschylus, Sophocles and Euripides, helping bring to life the heroes behind the masks such as Jason, Achilles, Hercules as well as plucky heroines standing up to various forms of injustice like Cassandra, Antigone and Iphigenia. Kerry still had a particular memory of going into 10th grade English, where Harper had shown remarkably keen interest, soaking it all up, even asking a number of insightful questions during discussion.

She was near the end of the recording and had got to the final version they'd done with Chuck playing Tybalt alongside two learning buddies: DAK 27 as Romeo and DAK 33 as Mercutio.

"*A plague on both your houses!*" cursed Mercutio as he lay dying from a fatal wound delivered by Tybalt: a cowardly thrust below the other's guard aided by Romeo's misjudged intervention. Despite the monotone delivery, helped by the dramatic context the android did somehow manage to convey some of the dark pathos in the lines.

For its part, DAK 27 as Romeo stood rooted to the spot, face impassive; but from Kerry's point of view looking at the whole picture it wasn't too hard to imagine the character's internal self-accusation: 'This was mostly my fault.'

Tybalt lowered his sword, already conscious of the heavy price he'd have to pay for his victory: the original intention had been to fight Romeo, but this could no longer be interpreted as an honour killing on Juliet's behalf, it would only be seen as yet another example of the senseless violence Prince Escalus had condemned…

Now as the angle she'd been filming from changed, another figure caught Kerry's attention: AJ! She'd forgotten all about him arriving in on their session, realising now she hadn't taken in at the time when he'd finished his task and left. But there he was on the screen…and the slightly unsettling thing about it was how after starting off discreetly with his back to their work, he'd come around to the other side of the row of chairs to face them. It was patently obvious he was watching, taking it all in. Surely to God he hadn't been sent there to spy? Kerry couldn't bring herself to believe that Jim Brady could be so two-faced. She couldn't help thinking of a Janus mask. On the other hand it was amazing to think the android janitor could be so interested in what they were doing with the play?

ACT THREE

"These violent delights have violent ends..."

1

Floyd Linton's car weaved its own way through the freeway lanes, while he closed his eyes and tried to think things through. It wasn't easy as he had a raging headache. He'd been getting them for a while, maybe over a year, in fact ever since going on a series of departmental up-skilling courses. They'd worked on a few novel interrogation techniques, lateral ways of getting information out of a suspect: mind games that even for a seasoned cop were pretty close to the bone. None of which had grabbed him, if anything he'd felt propelled in the opposite direction, even found himself imagining being on the receiving end, like he was the one that wanted to spill the beans, to just talk. OK, he wasn't ready for the big old rocking chair on the porch just yet but maybe it wasn't so far off. He sensed there was more going on inside him than he'd previously been aware of – and perhaps it wanted out.

He winced, another streak of mini-lightning forking his brain as he reached into the glove tray for his tablets and popped one. He was lucky, his supervisors had provided them under the counter: medication not yet on the official market, one of the perks of being an employee of the Nation. Or was he being naive? Maybe he'd been set-up as a guinea pig for some drugs company. Perhaps during one of those trance states he'd gone into on the course, he'd been brainwashed like in that old 1960's spy movie doing the rounds again; what was it... *The Manchurian Candidate*.

He shrugged it off. Maybe he really was being looked after.

Linton felt the vehicle veer off sharply to the right and knew he'd left the freeway. He rubbed his eyes and returned to self-control. The asphalt gave way to the familiar dirt track and the long line of trees winding towards the farm. He let down the window and breathed in the almost fresh air. He hadn't realised until now how much he was looking forward to this second meeting with Rob Bennett's sister.

'It's good to see you again,' Elizabeth said a short while later. 'I've freed myself up this time; I was thinking it would be nice to show you around a little?'

Linton felt himself relaxing as he was led along between the rows of plants, the orchards full of fruit, through the poly-tunnels.

Elizabeth picked up a handful of soil from a tray. 'You already know how we protect the integrity of seeds here. Some of them go back to the beginning of agriculture, having adapted naturally over thousands of years to the specific and changing conditions of where they grow.' Seeing Linton's almost innocent expression, she asked. 'So what really brings you out here again?'

'I guess something last time must have planted a seed.'

Elizabeth threw him a broad grin. 'OK…maybe we're going to see a beanstalk come out of your head!'

Linton grinned back then adopted a more serious expression: 'Did Rob confide in you much about his own work?'

Elizabeth continued walking. 'I told you before; I really hadn't seen him for quite a while. As far as I know he enjoyed what he was doing.'

As they walked on between two lines of seed-beds, Linton felt a sudden head spasm and reached into his pocket for another tablet. 'Migraine,' he said in explanation.

'What are those?'

'Medication, they sort of work. Take the edge off anyway.'

'You probably drink too much coffee. When we get back to the lodge, I want you to try something.'

Sitting at a rustic table made from a wooden cable reel, Elizabeth poured them both a drink. With him looking across at her warily, she laughed. 'You'll take that chemical-laced stuff, with who knows what they've put into it. This is a totally natural herb substitute. Here, look, I'm pouring myself a cup too. Keep your eyes peeled in case I do a switch and give you the poisoned one!'

Linton smiled unambiguously for the first time in a long while. He couldn't help liking this young woman; even allowed himself a fleeting fantasy he could fall in love with her. Maybe he'd give up everything and come to live out here: get by on herbal drinks, plant seeds and pick apples all day. He imagined himself being happy, unburdened. But then he would have to be a different person. Or would he?

'You were far away?' said Elizabeth.

'Must be your herb coffee: instant effect?'

Elizabeth chuckled: 'OK – "instant" – I get it!'

It was getting a lot warmer, Linton took off his jacket, loosened his collar. 'Can you tell me some more about your family background? I'm still trying to get a fuller picture of you and your brother as adopted kids.'

'Like even a lot of true siblings we actually didn't have a lot to do with each other as children. Until we lost our foster parents: that did bring us closer.'

'They were killed in a flash flood I understand?'

'I guess it was out of that we both got interested in climate change, global warming: the survival of our planet. My area became food security, the land, seeds – his was education, history; developmental learning.'

'And artificial intelligence?'

'Yeah, later on he got into that in a big way; would have been aware of all the latest stuff going on in that field.'

'He was passionate about it?'

'Sure, in a good way, he wanted it to be beneficial rather than socially divisive.'

'So do you think he would ever have placed himself out on a limb over that?'

Elizabeth looked away, like she was weighing up whether to say something or not.

Linton decided to go for broke and add one more thing to tip the balance: he eased it onto the scales with a light a touch as he could manage: 'I found something intriguing, going back through some old news reports. His name came up in connection with a case concerning animal rights?'

Elizabeth raised an eyebrow then laughed. 'Well, good sleuth you. That was a long way back. OK, to hell with it, confession time. Both of us did almost get into trouble once, as animal rights activists; a *long time ago* I stress again, back in what you might call our more innocent "anarchist" days. We were accused of releasing some poor sad creatures from a fur farm back into the wild.'

'*Almost* got into trouble?'

'The company didn't want too much publicity; the case never got to court.'

Linton waited a moment, before easing back in his seat. 'Anyway, water under the bridge; like you say, it was a long time ago.'

Elizabeth smiled: 'OK I know where you're going with this Mr Detective and notwithstanding your professional brief, I do read you as a guy with a good heart.' She paused. 'All I can say about Rob is he would always have believed in doing the right thing.'

'Rob had privileged access to the android workforce in the school…' Linton looked at Elizabeth invitingly and allowed the comment to hang.

Elizabeth scrutinised him: 'You know for a special agent who keeps his cards close to his chest you're actually pretty transparent.'

'You don't say?' said Linton, raising an eyebrow.

Elizabeth pondered on something else then said: 'You know I talked with that Charles Richards at the funeral, the one who supplies all the AI resources in the school. Now I'd say there's a hard guy to read.'

Later that day, Linton found himself looking over Jim Brady's shoulder at the banks of monitors covering the school. Scanning the top row he got tracking shots of the outdoor recreation area, taking in the periphery wall with its four watchtowers and the main entrance gate. Second row down surveyed all the main buildings, including the central plaza, canteen, fringe hub and all walkways and corridors. Third row went inside individual learning hubs and presented the live action going on between teachers and students.

The detective shook his head. 'It's a mystery how we still can't be sure if the system was accessed internally from here or hacked from the outside.'

Brady shrugged. 'What does it matter, it's immaterial; nothing so far points to even the flimsiest link with what happened to Rob.'

Linton paused for a moment, conscious of how by default Brady had become the only person on the ground he could confide in, as well as bounce ideas off. But wasn't the offbeat principal still potentially a suspect? He had prime access to the CCTV after all. And what level of control did Brady have over AJ the janitor? Then again, why get all fussed about it, following the accidental death verdict the investigation was effectively on ice: all he was required to do was hang around and ask questions, but making sure to keep it all low key. He scratched his head: at the end of the day he was a cop and it was hard to let go now his curiosity had taken over.

Brady broke the silence: 'A devalued dollar for your thoughts?'

Linton surfaced from his musing. 'I talked to his sister,

out at that seed-saving place. Without saying much I think she told me quite a lot.'

Brady turned away from the monitors. 'She gave you a lead?'

Linton folded his arms. 'OK, here's the big question: who would want to hurt a guy like Rob Bennett? Where's the motive? Thinking about it as a personal thing: anger, revenge, jealousy, seems to get us nowhere.' The detective tapped his knee with the palm of one hand as if trying to nail down a thought. 'I'm more inclined to think that like his sister, Rob had some sort of political or ideological agenda, except while hers is out in the open, his was hidden.'

Brady raised an eyebrow. 'So you're still persisting with that crazy idea he may have been a saboteur of some kind?'

Linton got more comfortable in his chair. 'Let's take another look at Rob Bennett's responsibilities as android supervisor: remind me what that involved?'

'Why go over it all again?' said Brady wearily.

'Repetition: one of the best tools available to an investigator. Always a chance someone's story might reveal something new and expose some flaws, cracks, contradictions.'

Brady sighed and gave way. 'Rob followed up on the daily timetables; monitored the drones and made sure students had their learning buddies with them for their classes. He also checked all AI units were docked each night for re-charging.'

'Did that include the higher grade android teaching staff?'

'Sure – I'm afraid there's not much of a night life for any droid.'

'Remind me: what is lights out time for students during the week days?'

'12 midnight – we might be more liberal than some institutions.'

'Are they ever allowed to keep their learning buddies with them overnight?'

'No, that's totally out of the question,' said Brady.

Linton allowed all of this to sink in. 'OK, back to Rob Bennett. Did his job as overseer include Android JFX72?'

Brady sat back. 'AJ answers to me regarding his day to day duties, although he has a fair amount of flexibility in how he gets around to everything.'

'So AJ's practically a free agent, you told me before he even shuts himself down for the night.'

'True: but Rob would have been the one ultimately responsible for making sure that happened; that AJ didn't wander around at all hours, if that's what you're implying.'

Linton sat forward, becoming more alert. 'OK, obviously not the evening in question, but sometime in the lead up to all this, just supposing Rob Bennett had tried to take advantage of the android's sleepy-time vulnerability, made an attempt to get at its files – access the software?'

'That would have counted as a serious data infringement; not to mention overstepping his authority.'

'But what if he *had* tried to do that?'

'AJ would have instantly reactivated and offered minimal but effective resistance and then reported it to me.'

'The android wouldn't have decided to deal with it more decisively all by itself: used its own initiative to come up with a devious plan for a more permanent solution?'

Brady threw up both hands in protest.

'Or alternatively, maybe AJFX72 reported it directly up-line to Charles Richards for further instructions?'

'OK, where's this leading to now?' Brady said, his frown deepening.

Linton shook his head. 'Tell me something: you've never thought it strange how this android has such a sophisticated level of intelligence? I mean for a lowly janitor, as "he" keeps reminding us!'

Brady put up his hands, this time in surrender. 'Guilty: that much you can put down to me. AJ's been the beneficiary of multiple upgrades in his EI that I've requested along the way: I wanted him to be able to tune-in to everything that's going on through the whole school, understand where both students and teachers are coming from.'

Linton rubbed his jaw. 'Sure and maybe this guy understands all too well where *we're* coming from the way he's been running rings around this investigation. Maybe he's even more sophisticated than you realise.'

'So what are you driving at now?' said Brady.

'I'm considering the possibility there's even more inside that android's software than you know about and Rob was set on freeing it up: maybe hoping to "out" your janitor for what it really is?'

'Which is what exactly?' said Brady, bemused.

Linton threw his hands in the air. 'Hell, you tell me! Maybe an experimental prototype getting a secret test-drive under the radar. Something your Mr Charles Richards wouldn't want anyone else to know about.'

Brady couldn't help smiling at an internal thought.

'What's so funny?' asked Linton, slightly unnerved.

'I was just remembering a madcap British TV comedy show: *Monty Python's Flying Circus* – saw some of it recently on a retro channel, there was one hell of a crazy sketch about a dead parrot...'

Linton stroked his chin. 'Is this to do with parrots repeating stuff they shouldn't?'

Brady smiled. 'Maybe you're onto something there; I think there might even be a joke around an old lady having tea with a priest. Actually it was the catchphrase running through the show that came to mind: "And now for something completely different."'

Linton released an exasperated sigh, allowing his attention to wander around the room and onto the monitors. He was instantly drawn to one covering the corridor outside the fringe hub, showing Kerry Tracker with Charles Richards.

'Well now, talking of the devil...'

❖

The school's principle benefactor had just a short while earlier arrived in the staffroom unannounced and told Kerry he'd heard from Jim Brady about the kids wanting to do a full production. He also understood how it tied in with her request for an EI upgrade to the learning buddies. So when he'd then asked could he tag along to their next rehearsal to say a friendly hello and maybe even have a look at what they were doing, she'd felt she could hardly say no. But now as they walked into the fringe hub together, Kerry was acutely aware that amongst her cast was his daughter, Harper and how the girl might react badly, blame her for allowing this to happen, even suspect she'd deliberately invited him in to monitor her behaviour.

Harper looked from her father to Kerry. 'What's going on?' she said, immediately on the defensive.

Richards projected an easy-going smile. 'I happen to have a meeting with your Principal – just thought it might be nice to pop in on the way and see how you're all doing.'

"All?" questioned Harper, eyes narrowing.

Her father turned to Kerry: 'And I've been hearing such positive things around how you've been utilising the learning buddies?'

Kerry tried to relax, her stomach in a knot. 'Yes, it's really helped us with our explorations; we probably couldn't have got this far without them.'

Richards looked pleased. 'That's great to hear. And I understand you intend to really show off that contribution by giving them actual parts in the play?'

'That's our plan,' said Kerry, 'although we haven't made any firm decisions yet around casting.' She glanced at Harper, who returned her a dismissive shrug.

Richards held up his palms apologetically. 'Anyway, please don't let me get in the way of you rehearsing.' He turned to the group. 'Your director said I could watch for a moment, would that be OK?'

He received a group shrug in response, but Kerry couldn't ignore Harper staring at the floor in obvious discomfort, probably both angry and embarrassed at having her father there making a show of her in front of everyone. Kerry was reminded of the teenage girl she'd encountered at their first meeting: sulky, rebellious, yet at the same time vulnerable.

'Anyway,' said Kerry, 'maybe it will do us good to have an audience – so far we've only had AJ in here watching.'

Richards returned her a curious half-smile at the remark.

Kerry decided her best bet was to pick an ensemble moment where everyone could be involved including the learning buddies: that was clearly what the man had mainly come to see. 'OK,' she said, turning to the group, 'we'll set up the party scene improvisation again, using the masks.'

Richards stood at the back and observed the action taking place at the party with obvious fascination, alert to everything that was happening. He nodded to himself frequently, noting how the masks helped minimise the demarcation between human and android actors, and how despite being neutral they combined with body language to convey emotions. In terms of the story itself, he saw how Romeo and his friends used the masks to gain entry to Lord Capulet's home and operate undercover.

He was also pleasantly surprised at the way his daughter took part as just one member of the collective. When they were finished, he thanked the cast for their time and said how impressed he was with their work. Turning to go, he indicated for Kerry to come with him to the door. 'I can see the kids are really responding to how you're approaching the play, and I have to say seeing the learning buddies operating in that way was particularly illuminating.'

Kerry was relieved herself with how it had gone, but still aware of the obvious limitations. 'Thank you, yes, I'm pleased overall. I guess with the LBs it's still a bit wooden and...'

'Robotic?' Richards offered with a smile.

'Well, restrained anyway,' said Kerry.

Richards glanced over again at his androids, once more left to one side while the kids fell into conversations amongst themselves. 'What you're asking for is a restoration of their previous empathy settings along with an enhancement of their overall EI so as to broaden their capabilities as actors?'

Kerry said a silent prayer: 'Yes, I was hoping something along those lines might be possible?'

Richards nodded his assent. 'OK, I think we might be able to do something for you.'

'You're serious?' said Kerry, her heart skipping a beat.

'But I want you to keep it to yourself for the moment; I'd rather the whole world didn't know about it just yet.'

'Thank you for having faith in what we're doing,' said Kerry, a little at a loss.

Richards threw the briefest of glances at his daughter. 'I guess we all have reasons for wanting this project to be a success.'

❖

Brady and Linton turned away from the monitor.

'That seems to have gone well,' said the detective, checking his wristband for the time and picking up his coat and hat. 'Your benefactor looked happy with what he saw.'

Brady looked pretty relieved himself. 'Have to say I was equally concerned with how his daughter would react.'

Linton shrugged. 'She seemed OK about it by the end?'

"Fair face must hide what the false heart doth show," said Brady, cryptically.

'Is that a quote from the play?'

'Shakespeare yes, but no – a different piece of work,' said Brady.

2

Tim Wilson gave his coffee a stir. It was the third meeting of the task force and Richards thought he could read some impatience in their faces. 'OK,' said Wilson, 'let's call a spade a spade, what we're talking about means abandoning what were once quaintly known as the "three basic laws of robotics" – primarily the most important first law?'

Admiral Horne coughed into his fist: 'Can we run over those again for the benefit of those of us who grew up on gritty war comics while some of you guys were enjoying trippy-dippy space-ballet sci-fi.'

Wilson was happy to show off his literary credentials. 'According to the science-fiction writer Isaac Asimov, the inventor of the three laws, they are number one: a robot, or in this case an android, must never harm –'

Macy cut in: 'Come on, I think it's obvious that by now all of that fanciful bullshit has gone out the window. We've long had AI machines in the form of drones with clear orders to kill certain categories of human beings; namely enemy combatants.'

Wilson frowned. 'That may be true General; but let's

not forget they've also been responsible for the deaths of untold numbers of innocent people. I'd still argue these "laws" are useful as a first-base ethical template: maybe somewhere to return to when we might be in danger of losing our way.'

Ms Chan leaned forward. 'It's also important to remember that drones are limited to a narrow field of operations based on orders fed to them originally by a human controller and to this extent are seen as neutral detached machines by Joe Public. Mr Richards is proposing something far more existentially threatening: robots in human-form with their "own minds" – free to make their own choices as to whether someone dies or not.'

Wilson nodded. 'I've been assuming all along these guys will possess an overseeing ethical governor, a safety component ensuring appropriate and proportional response in any given military context?'

'Yes and no, ladies and gentlemen,' said Richards. 'Yes, there will always have to be some form of ethical governor, but this time it won't be located in a single command centre with the authority to override other considerations; instead it will be present throughout the entire fabric of this android's advanced emotional intelligence. As Ms Chan has already alluded to, until now all AI units have had to operate within the constraints of what may be biased ideological parameters set by their human controllers. For example what might be considered proportional in a given military context may be overly influenced by a country's concern with avoiding reputational harm, as opposed to a real possibility of physical damage to vital infrastructure or even loss of life. In other words the human moral high ground on which the ethical governor stands may itself be shaky. With our Peacemaker we are in effect talking about handing decisions over to what we might say is a more neutral and balanced intelligence?'

Macy allowed himself a smirk as he leaned forward. 'By the way, something I've been meaning to ask. What prevents these sophisticated guys from realising how superior they are and simply heading off to form their own alternative community?'

Richards smiled at the comment. 'A self-serving community is out of the question; their programming has a built-in restraint on forming what might be loosely termed "relationships". Yes, they'll communicate with one another, that part of it is essential to maximise efficiency: they obviously must be able to share information, process options, but any "conversations" as such have to relate directly to their operational mission.'

'So they can't just stand around next to the old barbed wire talking about last night's baseball game or the meaning of life?' said Wilson.

Admiral Horne looked a little lost. 'So which android gets the final call in one of these operational discussions – what sort of hierarchy of command do we have here?'

'There is no hierarchy, although that may come at some point perhaps. But like we said the last time, let's walk before we try to run. For the moment android soldiers operating as a group must think collectively and by pooling what they know will arrive at common consent before embarking on a course of action. It guarantees back-up for every decision and no possibility of rogue actions by any one individual.'

Wilson looked puzzled. 'But surely they're bound to have variant views if each of them is bringing different experiences to the table? OK, they might be operating as a unit, but spread out, out of sight from one another?'

Richards nodded: 'Not only will they be identical in terms of hardwiring, their software will also be interconnected so they can continually receive updates on each other's experiences; consequently they'll come to common consent around devising the most effective collective strategy.'

'Like an ant army?' said Macy.

'Something like that,' said Richards cautiously, noting that most faces were by now looking a little doubtful.

Wilson crossed his arms. 'OK, I think we have the general picture. But coming at it from another angle altogether, just for the sake of argument, what happens if sometime in the future an "ant" army made up of these guys came under the command of a ruthless dictator?'

Richards nodded again. 'You may remember: there's one last, key element to all this. We can embed into their hardwiring something our friend Asimov came up with later on as a way of dealing with that kind of question, a fourth law that takes precedence over the other three. To paraphrase: an android's ultimate loyalty extends beyond even the highest appointed individuals to *Humanity* as a whole.'

Wilson rubbed his chin and sat back. 'Yes, that does offer a broader frame; not to mention raising the bar for what we're expecting from these guys.'

There was a long pause while people helped themselves to sips and slugs of water.

Ms Chan eventually broke the silence: 'Perhaps we should look a little more at some of those compelling instances Mr Richards was referring to a short while back.'

Richards took a moment before responding to the invitation. 'OK, imagine a live situation in any conflict zone where it's complicated strategically, politically, ethically…'

'Let's not beat around the bush and throw in *financially*,' said Wilson.

'As it stands, we have a number of choices. We can send in traditional troops with all the risk that entails: loss of lives, body bags; opposition here at home. Plus, human beings are fallible, may even contribute to making a situation worse…'

'OK, we've been through this much already,' said Macy impatiently.

'Or, we extend the deployment of our current range of military robots: less cost, none of the aforementioned disadvantages, but effectively they're just walking humanoid drones, a human being still makes the decisions, more often than not far away from the immediate action. It's too rigid and prescribed: OK for specific tasks like clearing mines, but for strategic interventions that require flexibility – '

'What you're saying in essence is your guys will obey orders, but they'll also know when to deviate,' said Ms Chan.

Richards took time to choose his next words carefully. 'We sometimes call it a *Theatre of War*. So let's use another analogous term borrowed from that same arena. Think of them as like actors on a stage – yes they can follow an agreed script but they also know when and how to *improvise.*'

Jim Brady slipped into his chosen costume for that evening's cabaret, conscious of how it was this ability to adopt an alternative persona that had originally prompted Charles Richards to bring him to the school. These other selves had the licence to do what Jim Brady Principal simply couldn't: as Mr Punch he could act mean, as a medieval court jester with turned up toes and jingly bells on a stick he could be plain embarrassing. He might never fully comprehend how it all worked beyond being fully present and good timing – having read Freud's classic analysis of comedy, *Jokes and the Unconscious* he was probably none the wiser. Anyway, what mattered was that it allowed him to lord it over his largely teenage city. He was the Prince of Verona here; he had the power.

But tonight was the first show since Rob Bennett's death and would be very much a tribute to him, so Brady wanted to offer something softer and poignant; more in keeping with the occasion. Earlier, he'd run his mind through a "lovable rogue's" gallery of his favourite clown characters from medieval fools through to silent-movie icons like Lloyd, Keaton and Chaplin; then into the early talkies with the likes of Laurel and Hardy, before reversing back a few hundred years and settling for the white-faced French clown, Pierrot, a character originating in 16th Century Italian Commedia Dell Arte.

Adding finishing touches to his makeup and taking a last look in the mirror at the sad white face with its downturned mouth, a single tear painted on one cheek, Brady pulled back to get a look at the full picture: the black skull cap, flowing white tunic complete with its oversized pompoms. He was ready.

❖

Agent Linton had taken a seat towards the back of the cabaret, conscious of how there would probably be some audience participation. Let others be hauled onto the stage he was thinking. A detective's place was in the shadows, operating undercover, out of the limelight; all the while waiting for the right moment to act but on his own terms. He'd actually anticipated attending the show from the outset of the investigation, given it was where everyone had been on the all-important evening: he'd now be able to see for himself how conspicuous people were as they came and went; ascertain how easy or difficult it was for anyone to slip in and out with no one else noticing. Once all eyes were on the stage maybe it was the simplest thing?

As if to prove the point, his attention was drawn to someone he could easily have missed coming in, Elizabeth of all people. She was already making her way towards a spare seat on the other side of the auditorium. He thought about waving over to her, but changed his mind, maybe she wanted to be left alone.

An hour into the show, things were moving along smoothly. Several students and staff had offered tributes to Rob. One wacky girl read out a poem written on a paper plate – something about "food for the soul" and "forbidden love". Despite his professional detachment, Linton had to admit to being touched by the whole experience.

Brady the white-faced clown had switched to a lighter tone now, asking if anyone else in the audience wanted to get up and surprise everyone with a routine. Linton knew it was ridiculous but he still avoided looking directly at the stage.

But it was Harper Richards of all people getting out of her seat. As Linton watched the rebellious teenager move down the central aisle he imagined the last time she'd been invited up, full of anger and resentment at facing a public chastisement. But now she looked to be full of cheer, wearing a broad smile, all sweetness and light.

Moreover, this time she'd brought back-up: joining her on stage was her android learning buddy.

'Thanks for coming up,' said Pierrot, looking more than a touch taken aback. 'I had been feeling lonely here all on my own.' The sad frown morphed into a big smile: 'A round of applause for our two guests!'

Harper smiled back and bowed to everyone.

'Well Harper, I see you have company tonight. Is this going to be a double-act?'

Harper gave a cute smile. 'We're here to promote our play. The most amazing thing ever; directed by our wonderful teacher and director, Miss Kerry Tracker!'

All eyes picked out Kerry, sitting anonymously near the middle of the auditorium; who found herself smiling back at a sea of inquisitive faces. The drama teacher was also thinking how this was the first time she'd seen Harper and her learning buddy together in an informal setting: maybe a glimpse into what things had been like before the infamous downgrade?

Pierrot asked: 'So tell us young lady, what is the name of this play?'

'Haven't you heard, Mr Pierrot? We're doing William Shakespeare's *Juliet & Romeo!*' Harper gave a little cough that sounded distinctly like a cue.

DAK 49 replied tonelessly: 'Actually, my dear one, as your learning assistant I must correct you, I believe it is called *Romeo and Juliet*?'

There were immediate laughs from the audience.

'Oh no no no!' insisted Harper, wagging her finger and putting on a frumpy frown. 'I think you have it wrong there learning buddy; it's definitely "Juliet & Romeo" – ladies first after all.'

DAK 49 offered a fairly convincing shrug, then looking upwards said: *"Hush, what light through yonder window breaks!"*

Another laugh rippled through the audience.

To Brady it was reminiscent of the great Stan Laurel. With the room cheering madly, Pierrot put his hands together too, not least to applaud the android's spot on timing.

'Oh Romeo, you're so forward and bold!' Harper exclaimed, eliciting more hoots of laughter. 'Well...' she continued, 'I guess now you'll have to come and meet my parents. I hope they won't be too shocked.'

There was more hysterical laughter.

Pierrot smiled again, but looked more wary this time. 'Is this going to be a comedy version of the play?'

The girl looked out at her captive audience. 'Oh no, Mr Pierrot,' said Harper. 'Our play is going to be unbelievably tragic.'

3

West Side Story was still such a great movie, Kerry reminded herself as she gulped down some muesli and watched Rita Moreno leading her Puerto Rican Sharks across the dance floor to challenge the Jets gang. Thinking about the play and the party scene at the Capulet's home, they simply had to include some dancing. So what kind of moves would it entail? If the play was going to be set in the future and given the participation of her androids, wouldn't it be amiss if they didn't incorporate some elements of robotics?

She'd keep that up her sleeve. First they'd have some fun playing around with some smooth moves from the 16th Century. After clearing away her breakfast things she found a suitable dance-step program on her globe then with ancient lutes and wind instruments filling her ears, stood to face an imaginary partner.

The globe pulsed, moving the dance demonstration to a smaller honeycomb to accommodate the face of Charles Richards in the main hexagon. 'Hi Kerry, sorry to call so early, I just wanted to get you at home and offer some good news on the upgrade. I've checked with your Principal and we can organise it for you later today during your lunchtime session if that suits.'

'Oh, wow,' said Kerry, 'that's amazing; I really didn't expect it to happen so quickly.'

'I'm aware the deadline for opening night isn't so far away.'

'Please, don't remind me!'

'This software package is going to be quite special.'

'So how are you going to do this?' she asked, sitting back down.

'OK, just to fill you in: we've put the play through a program to map its emotional landscape, making sure we've captured all the humps and dips, hills and spills – all the mountains and valleys of feeling,' he added poetically.

'And you can actually do that, even with a Shakespeare play?'

Richards smiled. 'I know what you're thinking: maybe the search will miss out on the emotional subtlety required. OK, so what you'll end up with are all the primaries: happiness, remorse, anger, loss, joy – as well as all more nuanced shades in the emotional palette: different levels of curiosity for instance. You'll also be able to have combinations of these as you would in real life.'

'Wow, it's hard to process,' said Kerry.

'Take an emotion such as *disappointment*: like your football team just lost the final.'

Kerry closed her eyes and pictured her group of actors in a freeze frame. Then she imagined her own expression in response to the curtain coming down on an artistic failure. 'OK…I have a couple of images.'

'You've got a group of guys all feeling disappointment, sharing the same basic emotion. But individually, one of them feels annoyed with himself because he didn't put all his effort in, feels he let himself and everyone else down, didn't play as well as he could. So what would that be: disappointment plus *regret*?'

Kerry tried to picture it on someone's face, as Richards continued: 'Meanwhile someone else is blaming the guy who missed the last minute penalty, thinking he should have been the one asked to take it. So you got disappointment clouded by anger, resentment; an offloading of blame. This is going to look different right, reflect that subtle difference in emotional colouring?'

'Yes, of course.' Beyond being excited Kerry was somewhat taken aback by the depth of Richards's observations. Maybe he had secret ambitions to be a theatre director?'

'There's yet another guy there who always knew they never stood a chance against a far superior team: he's disappointed but resigned. So now you have disappointment plus a degree of acceptance. How does that combination look to you?'

Kerry instinctively allowed her shoulders to droop and released a philosophical sigh.

Richards's face grinned on the screen. 'You got it Kerry. You're an actress!'

She lifted her shoulders again; right now disappointment was the opposite of what she was feeling.

'So, you like the sound of all this?'

'You bet, it sounds amazing.'

'You've got your broad strokes but also some subtlety

in there. Close enough anyway to what you'll get from your human actors.'

Kerry smiled at the irony: maybe this level of sophistication would be a lot more than her human actors could manage.

Richards leaned forward into his control pad. 'Let's put these images up.'

The screen now showed four learning buddies as the football players, all clearly disappointed. Kerry could see which one was angry, which one was accepting…'Yes, it's very clear.'

'And I haven't forgotten how in the rehearsal I witnessed you set up those group tableaus.' The screen image changed as the four figures adjusted their body positions so they were now interacting with each other.

'So what happens once this new software is installed: do I take them through the play line by line, action by action, finding some agreement on an appropriate emotional response?'

'That's basically what you're going to be doing with your regular actors, right?'

'Yes, I suppose it is.'

'With the kids you'll be drawing out all these subtle nuances from whatever basic emotional intelligence the average fifteen year old carries around inside them?'

Kerry felt a small shiver, remembering the challenges that still lay ahead. 'That's what I'm hoping to do alright.'

'What your LBs will have is a tool for understanding and contextualising emotions. You'll already have given them the lines of the play along with any explicit actions. Once all of this is combined in a given moment you should get an appropriate emotional reaction; or rather it's truer to say an expression of an emotional reaction.'

'They're not really *feeling* as such.'

'No. We sure can't have them actually getting angry for instance. You'd have some real-life disaster on your hands.'

'Glad to hear it!' said Kerry, with understatement.

'You'll still have plenty of work to do – teasing out exactly what you want regarding artistic interpretation. The good thing is, once all of this stuff is set, your androids will deliver their parts faithfully on the night, even on a wet Wednesday evening when the only person in the audience is the cleaner.'

'I'm hoping we're going to sell-out!'

'I'm sure you will Kerry. No doubt people will be begging for tickets.'

Kerry had a thought: 'Seeing as you mention "cleaner", will this bring them up to the same level as AJ for instance? I have to say for a janitor he's very, what can I say, tuned-in to what we're doing?'

Richards didn't answer straight away. In fact he looked away from the screen for a few moments, as if collecting his thoughts. 'They'll be around the same level.' He smiled. 'Plus they'll be able to act!'

Kerry allowed herself a smile back. But then a flash of concern crossed her face.

Richards noticed it: 'Something just crossed your mind?'

'What if one of my regular actors slips up, forgets their lines, or jumps ahead and misses half a scene?'

'Were you not thinking of using a prompter?'

'In the past I've tried to avoid it: place my faith in the actors, trust the rehearsal process.'

'So what would you hope for if someone did jump a line or two?'

'By having a sense of the whole scene, between them they'll find a way of rescuing it, get back on track.'

Richards nodded. 'So you want to know if your androids can do the same as the kids: grasp what's happening, see the whole picture; not to plough on but wait until someone rectifies the situation.'

'Yes,' said Kerry.

Richards stroked his chin thoughtfully. 'OK, this is interesting; it's good we're having this conversation. Maybe we can build in something that anticipates the possibility of this occurring.'

'So how is this upgrade going to happen exactly?'

'You'll appreciate this software is hugely valuable, I can't just arrive down there with a pin in my pocket and insert it into their ports. I could be mugged on the way!'

'I see what you mean.' Kerry hadn't quite thought about it that way but it was true: someone could kill for this. She would kill for it!

'I'll do it directly from here, using a safe transporter, cutting-edge encryption. Only your own LBs will be getting it of course.'

'Thanks again for doing all this.'

'I'm only too happy to help. We'll talk again.'

❖

Kerry made her way across the plaza, buoyed up with her good news, enjoying the formal patterns of the 16th century courtly dance music she was listening to through her earpiece. She took in the contrasting random movement of bodies all around her, with their differences in pace, jazz-like counterpoint of changes in direction; chance interactions taking place.

As the 16th century merged into the 1960's, she imagined sections of the crowd breaking into different kinds of dance from that decade: some doing the Chubby Checker Twist, one single file weaving its way through recalled Little Eva's *Locomotion;* other freewheeling individuals flowed along to hippie grooves. Breaking out of the 1960's bubble, she pictured retro hip-hop for some students; eco-warrior dancing for others.

She mused on what her fellow teaching staff would go for: Tex-Mex for Inez Martinez; traditional Indian ragas or even a touch of Bollywood for Meera Patel? Eddie Cochran inspired Rockabilly of course for Jim Brady; heavy-metal country music for Howard Trent…

Kerry paused for a moment and replaced this with another fantasy: a dance floor divided in half aka *West Side Story*: Sharks and Jets either side – everyone finger snapping and foot tapping, primed and sprung, ready for competition; for war.

Setting off again, she was so engrossed she almost bumped into Greta Pearson coming the other way: thankfully the girl's learning buddy pulled her up to stop them colliding. For a moment all three engaged in a shuffle routine: going one way then the other, with Kerry and Greta exchanging awkward smiles and then a synchronised "sorry" before continuing in their separate directions. Strangely, this brief moment of disorientation had the knock-on effect of putting some doubt into her upbeat mood: maybe her gang would throw cold water on the ancient music she was bringing along for them to hear? They might turn their noses up at the stately *Pavane*, perhaps dismiss the lively *Galliard*. She could always resort to the spinning *Moresa* dance used in Zeffirelli's movie, even unleash the sword dance version; although thinking about Chuck, maybe that wasn't such a good idea.

Passing by the fringe hub she converged with AJ, about to enter through the door with replacement water containers.

'Not bringing us any more chairs today, AJ,' Kerry asked, studying the android for a reaction.

'I was making sure you and your cast are well supplied with refreshment for your exertions, Miss Tracker,' AJ replied, betraying no obvious giveaway.

'Thanks, that was very thoughtful of you,' said Kerry, following the janitor in.

Watching AJ fit the containers into position, Kerry asked, 'By the way, what did you think of our rehearsal the other day?'

The android managed to look nonplussed. 'What did I think?'

She wanted to say: 'While you were spying on our rehearsal?' but thought better of it.

AJ took a further moment to respond. 'While I was stacking the chairs, I did observe a small part of what you were doing. Everything appeared to be going very well as far as I could see, Miss Tracker.'

'In what respect?' said Kerry. 'Come on, I need some feedback here,' she insisted with a coaxing smile.

'I would say the young people appeared to be enjoying the task you set them.'

Kerry appeared to let it go. 'OK…thanks for that AJ.' She paused for a second before adding, 'What about the other members of my crew?'

There was another short delay as AJ appeared to be processing the word "crew" – searching through his internal thesaurus. 'They *all* seem to be doing very well, Miss Tracker.'

Kerry pondered on AJ's answer. So the android had added a new term to his informal social vocabulary: did this bring any satisfaction, a sense of growing a little more within himself? Did it make him feel more connected, owning a greater sense of himself.

She looked at the time, coming up to coffee break.

AJ noted the gap in the conversation: 'Unless I can be of any more assistance, I will leave you to it.'

Kerry smiled. 'No, that's fine for now AJ, and thank you for sharing your thoughts with me.'

'Anytime, Miss Tracker,' AJ replied, backing towards the door with his trolley.

'Oh, by the way…' she called after him. 'I'm assuming you'll want to come and see the full show on the big day?' She nearly added: 'You'll be getting a formal invite for the opening,' then realised she'd probably have to clear it with Jim Brady first.

'I would not miss it for the world,' said AJ with a wave and a fully unambiguous smiley.

❖

Jim Brady turned away from the monitor, went to the coffee machine and noticed they were out of cups.

'Hey, wait till I get a hold of AJ!'

'You mean our guy who was just chewing the fat with Miss Tracker,' said Linton.

Brady put on a pouty face: 'Taking his time down there when he could be replenishing my supply of environmentally friendly containers.'

'Maybe Android JFX72's not *your guy* after all?'

'I should get on to maintenance; give his loyalty configurations a makeover.'

'Do you need to get permission for that?' said Linton, curious.

Brady let out an easy sigh. 'Hell, I was only kidding, I'd have to fill out a whole bunch of technical forms, a pain in the ass. Maybe I like AJ the way he is. Let him talk all day long with Miss Tracker for all I care; it's good he's taking such an interest.'

'You said "loyalty" – that's an emotion right?' Linton let the word hang for a moment.

Brady nodded: 'I guess all that matters is that Android JFX72 is a loyal employee of this school.'

'So talking to Miss Tracker when he should have been bringing you a supply of environmentally friendly coffee cups wasn't a question of "loyalty", more a momentary lapse in getting his priorities lined up in the right order?'

'Something like that,' said Brady, losing interest.

Linton spun around slowly in Brady's barber chair, allowing a thought to come through. 'We were talking before about AJ's software. Remind me how it operates on a simple day to day basis.'

Brady tilted back as best he could in the lower chair. 'His "Janitor" programme covers all the tasks and duties for this place. Some of them are tied into time schedules, others are more loosely defined – generally he knows what he has to do, when it has to be done by, with some flexibility in terms of how it's all accomplished.'

Linton shrugged. 'OK, makes sense...'

'Crucial. If he has to stop and deal with an unpredicted event, like a student throws up over the plaza floor from a reaction to the crappy food; that might put him out of sync time-wise, so he has to be able to adjust. Maybe he'll speed up the next few tasks to get back on track, so he's ready and available for anything important up ahead.'

'Like your coffee cups.'

Brady offered a mock-scowl. 'Yeah, like my coffee cups.'

'Are we going so far as to talk about free-will here?'

'I wouldn't put it past that old tin can to keep me waiting on purpose,' said Brady with a smile this time.

Linton smiled back. 'It's a relationship then of sorts.'

'Sure, he's my buddy and right-hand man rolled into one. I've had some illuminating conversations with AJ: we sort of "click" if you know what I mean. You have to remember I'm not your regular principal material: still a rock and roll loving stand-up comedian at heart – wouldn't be here at all if I hadn't had my arm twisted.'

'I can understand why they insisted: I watched you at the cabaret, you've got a handy range of skills, crowd control for one.'

Brady folded his arms. 'Not bragging but the school has gone from being almost out for the count to just about hanging onto the ropes. That has to be an improvement.'

'Anyway,' Linton continued, 'going back to your pal AJ: a moment ago you were saying how you've got...what's that expression: *a partner in crime*?' He delivered it half as a joke, not bothering to hide the double-meaning.

Brady winced. 'I forget I'm still, "helping you with your enquiries". You can get carried away and forget such things while making innocent conversation about coffee cups.' He threw his hands up in mock surrender. 'What the heck, I may as well confess: AJ and me – we're a mean killer double act, just like those 1960's film icons Bonnie and Clyde.'

Linton rubbed his jaw: 'Might be something alright to be up there in that outlaw hall of fame.'

Brady sat up straight: 'Hey! Either this is actually getting serious or you're doing a neat line in comic irony.'

'Maybe I picked up a few tips from you the other night,' said Linton, droll.

Brady's eyes lit up. 'But now you've got me thinking. Why not, there's real potential there for a double act! After all, he's the perfect straight guy. Hell, if Harper Richards and her learning buddy can do it.'

'You'd better get working on it for the next show,' said Linton, this time allowing himself close to a full smile.

Brady picked up his jacket, energised. 'Come on, this is too good to let slip; you can help me brainstorm this with a proper cup of stewed coffee down in the canteen, and maybe throw in a doughnut or three.'

❖

Kerry sat in a quiet corner of the canteen taking tentative bites from something resembling a croissant. Up at the serving hatch everything was delivered by mechanical arms, not even complete robots; then at the pay-bay, meals were scanned and the cost swiped from your account. With no engagement, she found the whole experience alienating. She swallowed a piece of tasteless pastry and flipped through her rehearsal notes. After her talk with Brady she'd thought it through and made a provisional decision on how to approach the play and deploy the learning buddies, but there were still challenges regarding casting, especially with her shortage of female actors.

'Hi there!' said a cheery voice.

Kerry looked up to see Greta Pearson, accompanied by her learning buddy.

'Hi,' said Kerry back to both of them.

'We're wondering if we can be in your play,' said Greta.

'Really?' said Kerry, taken a little by surprise and thinking the girl must be a mind-reader.

'Are we still in time?'

Kerry became wary: she'd kept faith with Richards and hadn't discussed the upgrade outside the staffroom, but maybe news had still got out somehow and Greta was thinking about her LB, simply being opportunist. 'I guess we're still just about in the preparation stage…but conscious of our deadline all the same,' she added quickly.

'Hey, so that's great!' said Greta.

'What made you decide to come to me now?'

The girl gave an easy shrug. 'It's hard to say, could've been watching Harper and her learning buddy the other night at the cabaret…or maybe when you and us met up in the plaza earlier on today: you know, going this way then that way, something just slipped into place…' Greta dropped down into a seat opposite, followed a split-second later by Gaia. 'Will we have to audition?'

'Well, that's probably not actually necessary...maybe you could come along and –'

Greta frowned. 'But we don't want to be wasting everyone's time, how do you know we'll be any good?' She checked her wristband. 'We still have a couple of minutes till our next class?'

Kerry decided to go for it: 'OK, why not, let's give it a try,' she said pulling a hard copy of the play from her bag and handing over a pin for Greta to insert into her learning buddy's port.

'This is so cool!' said Greta.

'Maybe we'll look at *Act Two Scene Five*: where Juliet has been waiting anxiously for her Nurse to return from meeting Romeo; she's hoping for news of his intentions regarding proposals of marriage.' Kerry pushed the play-script across the table to Greta: 'If you'd like to do the part of the Nurse?'

'Sure, hand me the first aid kit!' said Greta.

Kerry turned to Gaia. 'And if you could help us by saying Juliet's lines?'

Gaia said, 'Of course; I will help in any way I can, Miss Tracker.'

'OK, so we'll go from the beginning of the scene where Juliet has that speech talking to herself: *"The clock struck nine when I did send the Nurse – in half an hour she promised to return..."*'

Gaia delivered her lines with a marked clarity. While it was all predictably monotone, Kerry was conscious how reading them cold here in the canteen, even for a human actress it might have been challenging.

For her part Greta immediately picked up on how the Nurse on arrival realises she can keep Juliet waiting, knowing she has this rare opportunity to take advantage of her mistress: complaining about her aching bones, cajoling Juliet into giving her a back-massage before she'll reveal her good news.

The two of them followed one another right on cue, their timing near perfect; even managing a genuine rapport between the characters, with Greta cheekily turning her back to Gaia for the welcome back rub.

'So, are we in the play?' said Greta, waiting for Kerry to say something.

'I guess you are,' said Kerry, still a little taken aback. 'At least as far as I'm concerned, but I'll have to check it first with the Principal and then with the rest of the group to make sure they don't mind, everyone's kind of used to one another at this stage.'

'Better late than never; just doing our duty right!' said Greta, checking her wristband for the time and turning to Gaia. 'Hey learning buddy, would you mind getting us both a healthy fill of water from over there so we can celebrate?'

'Yes, of course,' the android replied and headed over to the drinks dispenser.

'Not the sugary one!' Greta called after her; then leaned down close to Kerry, lowering her voice: 'She did a good Juliet, right? I suppose you already have an idea who's playing her?'

Kerry hesitated before answering. 'Actually…I do probably have someone in mind for that role.' Saying this she wondered if she might actually be closing off an interesting possibility.

Greta shrugged: 'Sure, no problem in asking. Anyway she'll be great in whatever you give her. Me, I'm open too. You're the boss Miss Tracker.'

'Thank you, that's good to hear,' said Kerry, glancing over to see Gaia waiting behind a couple of students dithering at the dispenser. 'You have a very sympathetic understanding with… her… your learning buddy, especially given the current empathy restrictions. There's a lot of mutual respect: how did that come about if you don't mind me asking?'

Greta smiled. 'What did I hear Miss Angelou say in English class the other day with that Emily Dickenson poem about "coming at things slant"? I guess it's like lateral thinking: takes maybe a bit of patience, honesty, sure respect comes into it; a little affection doesn't do any harm.'

Gaia arrived back holding two cups of water.

'Let's have a toast,' said Greta, raising her drink, followed by Gaia.

'So lunchtime today?' said Kerry, raising her coffee cup.

'We'll be there!' said Greta as they headed off.

Watching from across the room, Linton turned to Brady: 'I'm wondering if we're not all just a little out of our depth here.'

'Maybe we are,' said Brady. 'Hopefully Miss Kerry Tracker is the one that still knows her way back to the shore.'

4

Harper sallied along a corridor with DAK 49 on her shoulder. The girl did a neat line in space-taking, at each near-collision uttering, "Excuse ME!" while her learning buddy offered the same words as a genuine apology.

They got to the "lockers": keyless boxes with a palm print control patch. Harper swiped her door panel which opened revealing the contents: a pile of chocolate bars, some small items of clothing, make-up; a paperback copy of *Romeo & Juliet*.

"I just don't know what to do..." she sang in broken-hearted fashion, applying some fresh eye-liner and tossing up her hair, aided by the mirror on the back of the open panel. She took in DAK 49 watching her in a detached kind of way. 'You're lucky you don't have to go through all this,' she said, making a face on receiving a couple of wolf-whistles from students passing by.

Hearing a beep from her iSpecs she tossed away the lipstick as her father appeared in both lenses.

'So what do you want this time,' she said coldly.

'Just thought I'd check in to see how things are coming

along with the play: have to say I was most impressed with what I saw the other day. By the way, I may have a little surprise for you and your group later on today in that regard.'

'Really?' said Harper distracted as she reached into the locker for the play-text and caught her knuckle on the door. 'Ouch!' she cursed, dropping the book on the floor. 'Pick that up!' she ordered DAK 49. When the android hesitated, she was forced into being more amenable. 'PLEASE dear learning buddy, retrieve that object we are *both* working with. Can't you see my own hands are full at this precise moment?'

As the android obliged, Harper returned to a more frivolous tone: 'Yeah, you can hang onto it there for the moment, handsome.' She slammed the locker panel shut and offered her arm. 'Now it'll help big-time if you guide me to where we're supposed to be next.'

DAK 49 led her along – allowing Harper to continue the conversation with her father via one lens of her specs, making her half-blind to where she was going.

Richards's voice cut in: 'OK, I don't want you to have an accident, we can switch to audio?'

Harper sniffed. 'Forget it Daddy, we're sorted. Anyway it's better this way: maybe I need to keep one eye on *you*. Who knows, I might work out what's really behind this sudden fast-growing interest in our play.'

Richards recoiled slightly. 'You know you could be a little more appreciative of how I'm going out of my way to support what is fast becoming an ambitious project happening right there in your very own school.'

'Sure, so glad I'm here and not wasting my time at some fancy upmarket college where I might get to hang out with people of my own rank – the kind with parents who don't mind indulging in a bit of mindless pampering for their only sons and daughters.'

Richards sighed and moved the conversation on. 'Anyway, whatever transpires I'm sure you're going to make your mother and me proud.'

Harper flinched at the thinly veiled implication "making them proud" was something that hadn't happened so far.

'Hey!' she grunted as a similarly distracted student almost barged straight into her. 'Some people are so clumsy and rude.'

'I can see I'm holding you up,' said Richards. 'I'd better leave you to it; bye for now.'

Harper flicked her specs back to normal as they reached their destination. Turning to DAK 49 she snapped her fingers. 'OK, give me a catch-up on what we did here last time.'

❖

Looking down on the plaza, Jim Brady caught sight of Harper Richards being led along by her learning buddy; a cause for optimism, he wondered? He noticed that despite the continuing cold war, a number of students were choosing the lazy option, letting their assistants navigate for them. Brady thought about each android's internalised GPS and how this had once been a novelty, just like every other new-fangled invention: the internet, mobile phones, iSpecs – breakthrough discoveries now taken for granted. These days practically everything that moved, from vacuum cleaners to lawnmowers had a self-drive built in. Your personal carrier announced, "Sit back and enjoy," leaving you free to watch the newsfeed or a movie. Progress: wasn't that the name of the game.

And why waste energy finding your way through a crowd when you could allocate the task? Brady felt saddened at the thought a student's sole concern was getting to a destination while their learning assistant experienced the actual journey; taking everything in, negotiating space, interacting: continuously updating all this data for future reference, adding to the overall storage – the accumulation of a life?

❖

'So, today I'm hoping to introduce two new recruits,' said Kerry, telling them about Greta and Gaia and their audition earlier in the canteen.

There were surprised looks and a number of groans at the mention of the two names.

'I thought we were doing just fine as we were,' said Harper.

'We have kind of got used to it being just our little band,' added Wanda giving her friend some backup.

Kerry held up both hands. 'OK, I know it's a deviation from the original set-up, but then so is going for a full production: it'll really help us to have another girl, Greta's super-enthusiastic; I think she'd bring a lot of positive energy.'

'But how are they gonna catch up with what we've done already?' said Omar reasonably.

'Yes, that's a fair point,' said Kerry, 'we've covered a lot of important ground; then again we're still in the exploration stage regarding our approach to the play, so I think there's room for them to come on board.'

There were a few more token sighs but then surprisingly perhaps the group chose to back off.

'So, I'll bring them in,' said Kerry, hugely relieved having anticipated the possibility of more resistance. She went to the door and beckoned to Greta and Gaia who'd been waiting patiently outside. As the pair entered to join the others she wondered if this meant the group would have accepted just anyone. Probably not, it was more likely their acquiescence had something to do with how these two "oddballs" were a bit like them, fellow outcasts in their own right.

Kerry continued: 'Greta is aware of how much we've already done but no doubt she'll soon find her feet – and her learning buddy will of course be just like the others...'

'Actually, sorry if I beg to differ Miss Tracker,' Greta interjected with a breezy smile.

'Oh crazy,' said Carlos, raising his eyes to the ceiling. 'We've gained two more drama queens in one go!'

'Actually,' said Kerry, 'Greta makes a good point: when all the learning buddies get into character none of them will be like one another.'

'You really should be in politics Miss Tracker,' said Wanda.

Harper frowned. 'Just so long as it doesn't mess around too much with who's playing what.'

'Well...we haven't actually made any hard and fast final decisions as yet,' said Kerry.

The girl looked around the group for support. 'But I'm Juliet, right? I thought we at least had that much decided?'

While Kerry had sensed for a while that Harper's status as leader was no longer clear-cut, this was bound to be a sensitive issue for the whole group and if the girl threw a tantrum and walked out now, there was a chance they all would. Also this was the daughter of the person who'd just thrown them a lifeline. Plus she so desperately wanted the part.

'Yes Harper, I did in fact have you pencilled in as Juliet.'

Chuck latched on straightaway: 'When do the rest of us find out who we're playing?'

Kerry held up both hands. 'I promise the next time we meet I'll have a decision for everyone.'

'Why can't you tell us right now?' asked Tania, reasonably.

'Maybe you still don't know yourself?' Little Stevie challenged.

'Actually I do have it more or less decided. But right this moment I need to give you all a break so we can give the learning buddies an upgrade.' Kerry turned her head with relief to see Jim Brady arriving in through the door, timing his entry to perfection.

The kids looked uniformly surprised.

'This was agreed with Charles Richards after he came in to see us and was so impressed. I've been keeping it as a surprise since. After this they'll be back to their previous empathy levels; maybe something even better.'

'Can't we stay and watch?' asked Tania, eyes lighting up.

'No, I'm sorry, it's a security thing,' said Kerry.

Greta looked concerned. 'But afterwards will it still be "them"? Like will they still have the same identity?'

Kerry looked to Brady for clarification.

'This won't replace their current software,' said Brady, 'it's more an added-on tool. There won't be any memory loss anyway.'

Greta stopped biting her lip, relieved.

'So when do we get them back?' asked Omar.

'You'll have them for the next session,' said Kerry. 'Trust me; this'll be worth the wait. And for the moment I think it's best if we keep this to ourselves OK?'

The kids nodded an "OK" and filed out.

Kerry looked at her android actors standing like a chorus line. 'For some reason I'm feeling nervous,' she said to Brady.

'No need to be: it's just one more giant step for robot-kind.'

'Hi there,' said Richards, appearing as a hologram projecting from Brady's wristband. 'Do these make up your full complement Kerry?'

'Yes I'm pretty sure this will be it.'

'Jim, you've got that acceptance code I sent you?'

Brady tapped his head. 'Here, safe and sound.'

'OK,' said Richards, 'I'm keying my own code now. You can patch them at your end one by one; this part should only take a few seconds.'

Brady walked along the line, inserting his code into each android's receptor, located at the back of the neck.

'I really appreciate what you're doing,' said Kerry, conscious of how this was after all a humble school play.

'It's all for the cause,' said Richards.

Brady finished his tour along the line. 'OK, they're all open.'

'So, we'll start the download,' said Richards, 'this should take less than a minute.'

'Will I be able to come back to you if we have any unforeseen glitches?' said Kerry.

'I don't anticipate anything at a technical level, but for your own reassurance maybe start off with something where you can monitor them as a group. How about that party scene: try it without the masks and see how their expressions are matching up to the feelings implied by the lines and actions. It'll be good to get a sense of how it's all shaping up before you get into any intense one on ones and trickier moments like the fight scenes.'

'It's almost too much to take in,' said Kerry, overwhelmed.

'OK,' said Richards, 'we're done: if you want to go along the line again Jim and close those receptors.'

Brady took his time, making sure they were all sealed.

'Yes, no rush,' said Richards. 'Last thing we want to do is leave them open for anyone to hack in some crazy instructions.'

'Could that happen?' asked Kerry, concerned.

'Sorry, I didn't mean that to alarm you. Anyway, once this is done that code will become obsolete.' Richards had another thought: 'My only concern now is what happens when everyone else gets to hear about this and asks for the same upgrade for their learning buddies. Hopefully the kids in your group will be able to keep it to themselves for the moment, later on we can present this play as a trial run. If it's a success, we can say we've proved a point and then maybe offer it to everyone.'

'That would be great,' said Kerry, even though the words, "If it's a success?" gave her a cold shiver.

Brady indicated he was finished.

Richards concluded: 'So, good luck with your new actors Kerry. We'll talk again soon.'

5

Kerry was lying in bed, letting her mind drift for a while having just surfaced from a strange and intoxicating dream. In it Greta had been Juliet as she shared her feelings about Romeo with her nurse, played by Gaia. Kerry couldn't quite retrieve the fading mental pictures but she still felt the physical sensation of it being so real and alive.

Her mind went back to the audition in the canteen, except on that occasion she'd asked Greta to play the Nurse and Gaia to read Juliet. Like a lot of things in dreamland, it had come out all topsy-turvy. As she slipped in and out of consciousness and tried to re-capture the dream's narrative, it became even more confusing: one moment it seemed like *she* Kerry was Juliet, the next thing she was Gaia playing the part…

Kerry opened her eyes and glanced at her wristband. Time to make a move: she had to go into town to pick up some items for the play and after that drop by Jim Brady. Today was a huge day on two fronts: her group would be finding out what characters they were playing as well as getting their learning buddies back.

Getting dressed, she felt a heightened awareness of her movements, conscious of how like everyone else on the planet she was *"preparing a face to meet the faces that we meet,"* as the poet T.S. Eliot had once put it. She was assuming the mask of Miss Kerry Tracker, teacher and play director: a competent young woman in complete control of her wits, overseeing a project that in all honesty still relied on a lot of hope and trust – a wing and a prayer.

Checking herself in a mirror, her mind went back to the learning buddies. Did they never experience something akin to these thoughts? When placed at ease or on stand-by did they ever daydream; while observing human activity wasn't something inside busy joining up the dots, adding two and two together. Were they not at some deeper level in the process of becoming themselves?

❖

Inez stood at the drinks dispenser entertaining requests from those sitting at the table: 'Hands up for coffee? Mr Wilde, your usual refreshing herbal tea?'

'Yes please, that would be most appreciated Mrs Martinez,' Mr Wilde replied, his polite smile working against what appeared to be intense inner concentration.

Inez and Meera shared a smile between themselves, suspecting the android teacher's expression had something to do with how at that moment he was multi-tasking: downloading and processing information for his classes.

The truth was Mr Wilde was well able to do a gazillion things at once *without* giving them his full attention. Had Rob Bennett been there he might have revealed how the android's prime focus was on finding a satisfactory response to Mrs Martinez. Even the straightforward answer: "Yes please" demanded much consideration; after all, she'd asked him a question, in which case the answer was not a foregone conclusion. Simply by asking, Mrs Martinez had left a door open to the possibility he might just for once say, "No thank you," and astound everyone by requesting a cup of hot chocolate. Other matters of social etiquette needed to be considered such as the probability she'd only asked to be polite. On the other hand, he was cognisant the woman had what was known as a genuine "soft spot" for him bordering on affection. Of course Mr Wilde knew how that emotion related to the broad concept of "love" and as an android had no illusions in that regard, but he also knew about his namesake Oscar Wilde and that some human females had a platonic fondness for gay men. But at 10.43am on a so far uneventful day, for the android teacher the concrete circumstances were much the same as usual: familiar staffroom, the same chair he always sat in, surrounded by the same company. There was no rational compelling reason for him to make a change in what had become a predictable and comforting pattern…

As if reading his thoughts, Inez continued: 'I wonder if one day Mr Wilde, you'll arrive in here having had a terrible time with your students and demand a double-shot of black coffee!'

Mr Wilde allowed this to penetrate then said: 'Hopefully I will never have to suffer such a dreadful experience.' He added a gracious smile for her benefit.

Meera sighed. 'I'm thinking back now to poor Mr Milton. Perhaps *he* should have come in here and taken a stiff drink of something strong before having to face tenth grade English.'

'Anyway, I'm sure our Mr Wilde is made of more resilient stuff,' said Inez comfortingly.

"*The stuff that dreams are made of*?" replied Mr Wilde, with a grand wave of his hand; 'as taken from the novel, *The Maltese Falcon* – borrowing heavily of course from Shakespeare himself.'

'As in *The Tempest* – my favourite play by the Bard!' said Mrs Martinez, delighted with all the link-ups and wordplay. 'Along with *Romeo and Juliet* of course,' she added out of loyalty to the current cause.

❖

Kerry looked out through the window of the shuttle-bus, aware of yet another protest taking place outside the school. She half-regretted taking a trip into town, although it had been good to get off campus for a while.

As the bus drew nearer she saw that on this occasion there appeared to be two distinct groups of protesters, separated from one another by a security barrier. "People before Androids" formed the larger presence, while opposing them were banners representing a more fringe grouping: the "A.R.S.N – Android Rights & Support Network".

Kerry glimpsed someone arriving, holding a placard reading: "Rob – R.I.P – we won't forget you!" She was unable to see which group this person belonged to before the bus veered away, picking up speed.

She entered the Principal's office to find Jim Brady staring into his globe, getting an earful from somebody. He grimaced and motioned for her to take a seat. Turning, she realised that AJ was also there with his toolkit, about to do some handyman work.

'Good day, Miss Tracker,' said the android. 'Please don't mind me; I'm just putting up some more shelves for Mr Brady's expanding DVD and vinyl record collections.'

'No, please, carry on,' said Kerry.

'Mr Brady has amassed some rare items of interest so he tells me,' AJ added as he continued to survey the task, his eyes automatically measuring width and height. He bent into his toolbox to select the right sized screws, picked up his drill and then put it down again. 'I shall desist from making noise until he has finished this conversation.'

Kerry forced a smile. Maybe it was a spill-over from the protests outside, but today there was something about the android janitor that made her feel uncomfortable. He was perhaps too nice – too good to be true?

'Yes, I'll keep all that in mind,' said Brady. 'Yes, I do appreciate your call. Sorry, would you hold there for a moment.' He muted the speaker and whispered to Kerry. 'Everyone out there's got something to say.'

'The PBA – and some other groups, I passed them outside.'

'This one's from the ARSN. They want to make sure we're treating our androids fairly, not exploiting them.'

'OK...' said Kerry.

'Yes, I'm still here,' said Brady, un-muting the speaker. 'Would you like to hear some words from one of our android staff?' He motioned for the janitor to come over to the globe: 'Talk to them AJ.'

'What would you like me to say?' asked AJ.

Brady lowered his voice again: 'Just tell them the truth goddamnit!'

'The truth: Mr Brady? Could you be more selective for me?'

'Say you're happy in your employment and that we're not exploiting your boundless good nature.'

AJ looked at the globe hesitantly. 'Hello, this is Android JFX72, the school janitor speaking. I am perfectly content in my work, thank you.' AJ listened to the next question. 'Yes, I can testify that I am not being exploited.'

Brady made a gesture and whispered, 'OK, that's enough AJ; wind it up.'

AJ said, 'Well thank you for your considerate enquiry regarding my well-being which is much appreciated. Goodbye.'

Brady allowed himself a guffaw: 'Good job AJ. "Testify!" I should get you to field complaints and enquiries more often.'

'Will you be adding that to my duties, Mr Brady?' said AJ innocently.

Brady's grin turned to a frown. 'Sure and have you getting into serious conversations with these people? Next thing is you'd be asking for a raise!'

'A *raise:* Mr Brady?' said the android, puzzled.

'Forget I said it,' said Brady with a smile. 'A slip of the tongue old buddy.'

'Will I *raise* these shelves now you are off the phone?' AJ continued, having found and successfully repositioned the metaphor.

Brady chuckled: 'Well said again AJFX72, you old devil!' He turned to Kerry. 'Just let me check something first with Miss Tracker. Are we ready for the big moment?'

'I have to say I'm a little nervous. They'll be getting back their learning buddies *and* finding out which parts they're playing.'

'So we won't make them wait any longer. And I don't want to hold our good friend AJ up either in fulfilling himself and his duties. You go on ahead Kerry; I'll bring the LBs along shortly.'

As Kerry closed the door behind her, she could still overhear Brady talking to the android. 'OK AJ, enough of the fancy talk; let's get those shelves up.'

❖

Just for once Kerry allowed herself to be late. She didn't want to be there first as they entered in ones and twos asking what character they'd be playing. It was good the kids had a moment together as a group, waiting collectively. She wondered how much they'd missed their learning buddies. "Absence makes the heart grow fonder" – wasn't that a saying?

Entering the fringe hub she immediately sensed the anticipation, palpable in their body language as they turned towards her. It was a reminder of the freeze-frames they'd done in one of those earlier sessions when they were exploring the effect of the masks, such as waiting to hear news, good and bad.

But today there were no masks, whatever was going on inside reflected itself in their faces: one or two showed barely concealed excitement, expectation; others wore half-smiles, preparing for disappointment, wounded ego.

Kerry picked out Greta, confident but relaxed. In contrast, Harper looked edgy, standing hands on hips, expecting to be given what she was due and yet despite her self-assurance there was still a hint of doubt, vulnerability.

Jim Brady entered, followed by the learning buddies walking in a line. Was there anything obviously different about them? A more pronounced step perhaps, increased awareness as they looked around?

Gaia walked straight over to stand next to Greta. The other learning buddies followed this lead, smiling empathetically. The kids looked befuddled, most of them taking a moment before smiling back.

Brady grinned and said, 'I'll leave you to it, Miss Tracker.'

Greta dropped down onto the floor followed immediately by Gaia. The other learning buddies did the same, followed hesitantly by the rest of the kids. They all sat there waiting for Kerry to say something and bail them out of this awkwardness.

'Well,' she said cheerfully, 'here we all are, re-united. And you'll soon have a chance to get fully reacquainted, but before that I'm sure you're also eager to hear my casting decisions? I very much want to share my reasoning for this. I've done a lot of –'

'Awe, come on Miss Tracker,' Wanda protested. 'Leave out the tearful stuff and just give it to us straight.'

'Yeah, call a shovel a shovel,' added Little Stevie.

Kerry breathed in. 'Please, I think it's crucial to see the whole picture. This isn't just about individuals and who gets what. It's about the play after all. "*The play is the thing*," Shakespeare said himself. And it's a team effort.'

'Yeah, that's what gets said when they're picking you for sports,' said Carlos. 'All the fat and nerdy ones and the rest of the freaks kept waiting till last. Half the time you're told to stand on the side-lines and cheer on the chosen ones getting all the attention and praise.'

'I certainly don't intend it being like that. But I understand by saying "team" perhaps I set up the wrong comparison. Making theatre isn't a sport; it's not even supposed to be competitive. We're all creating this together cooperatively, me included. And this isn't just about the "star" roles. Because we're a small cast and there are lots of parts to go round, you're all going to be busy. Several of you will be playing more than one character. No one is going to be watching from the side-lines. It's safe to say the only spectators will be our lucky audience.'

Wanda sighed. 'Well done, Miss Tracker, you've succeeded in bamboozling us as usual. Will you just get on with your explanation so we can know what's happening?'

'I bet you're getting Romeo,' said Chuck, giving Little Stevie a nudge.

'And going back to what Carlos said, I don't want this to be like announcing the team sheet for a match. As I reveal who you'll be playing, I want you to stand and take up a position as if you're onstage. That way you'll get a clearer sense of how you relate to everyone else in the context of the play.'

❖

Jim Brady was back in his office and pouring out two cups of coffee, one of which he handed to Charles Richards, who'd just arrived and was now looking intently at the monitor covering the action going on in the fringe hub.

❖

'So, we're in an unspecified future, in terms of exactly how far off,' said Kerry. 'In the opening scene there's a meeting of the Montague and Capulet servants, with lots of bragging, and mutual hostility. I want these characters to be played by learning buddies.'

Chuck thumped Little Stevie on the shoulder: 'Robot wars! We'll get to see the servants knocking lumps out of one another.'

'So, DAKs 14, 33, 17, 27 – I want you to take up positions in an imagined public space. DAK 14 and DAK 33 will play Sampson and Gregory, servants from the Capulet clan, while DAK 17 and DAK 27 will take on Abraham and Balthazar who are their equivalent on the Montague side.' She glanced pointedly at Chuck before clarifying: 'Just to make it crystal clear, we don't need any action for the moment, we're merely walking this through.'

❖

Richards shook his head and frowned at the monitor, already concerned at what he was seeing. 'I'm not too impressed with the casting for the opening scene.'

Brady looked up from watering his plants. 'I guess you've become pretty familiar with the play by now.'

'I had to check it right through for the new software. I have to say I didn't expect to see such a negative presentation of AI right from the start.'

❖

Kerry continued: 'Just as the servants begin fighting, Benvolio of the Montague clan arrives, played by Jing.'

'Yeah, I got Benvolio!' The boy held his arms aloft in celebration. 'Cool dude.'

'The young nobleman steps in to stop them…'

'But Benvolio has his weapon drawn right Miss Tracker?'

'Yes, good intentions undone by, what shall we say, youthful exuberance?'

Jing restricted himself to a modest flourish of an imaginary sword.

'Because, who comes along next but Juliet's cousin, Tybalt –'

Chuck stood up. 'That's got to be me!'

Kerry nodded her assent and continued. 'Next, enter the older generation: Lords Montague and Capulet, also armed – played respectively by Carlos and Omar.'

'Far out!' the two boys exclaimed in unison, giving each other fist-bumps and high fives before taking their places in the scene as sworn enemies.

❖

Brady looked over Richards's shoulder at the screen. 'OK…so while she has androids playing the servants, their masters are flesh and blood, who far from acting superior, wade straight in with their weapons adding fuel to the fire?'

'Yes…interesting,' said Richards, visibly relaxing.

❖

'So,' said Kerry, 'let's consider what the audience has witnessed so far. The play is set in the future, but the status quo is much the same as today: robot servants with their human masters.'

'It'll be reassuring to some,' said Omar.

'This should lure the audience into false comfort. Because arriving to impose his authority we have Chief of Police Escalus – played by DAK 16?'

'You're giving that important part to a droid?' said Chuck, taken aback.

'Yes, and if it's a surprise to you it will be even more of a jolt for the audience. It will alert them early on to expect the unexpected and we'll have established a society made up of humans and androids where some of the latter have managed to elevate themselves up the social ladder, even to the highest position in the land. It's a land of opportunity right?'

'I get it,' said Wanda, 'like back when Obama became the first black man President. High hopes, right Miss Tracker?'

❖

'Well now, I'd say our formidable drama teacher has even managed to surprise *us*?' said Brady looking pleased with himself, his decision to back her vindicated, so far at least.

Richards stroked his chin. 'In as much as we have an android given the highest status role, taking on responsibility; in full command of the situation…yes, this has to be positive.'

❖

'Now we meet Benvolio's two friends, Romeo and Mercutio. OK, so who's going to be our romantic hero – Little Stevie, are you up for this?'

The boy tried to give the impression it was no big deal, but it was clear he was relieved: 'The main dude? Sure, why not.'

Chuck aimed a smirk at Harper. 'Stevie's the boy now, no more dreaming of kissing your droid.'

Harper rolled her eyes, giving Chuck a look of total disdain.

Kerry pressed on, wanting to keep the energy positive: 'Mercutio will be played by your learning buddy, DAK 43 – if that's OK Tania?'

Chuck did another double-take. 'What? That's two of the biggest parts gone to them already!'

Kerry glanced at the characters already in position. 'Yes Chuck – and see how we're starting to fill our stage. Don't forget the play tells us that Mercutio and the police chief are related.'

Chuck shook his head, flummoxed. 'I guess it makes sense then.'

Wanda frowned. 'But if Tania's droid is playing

Mercutio, how's it going to handle saying all that crazy sex stuff?'

'Yeah, like all that "Queen Mab" whatever,' said Tania. 'How can it get even close to knowing what that's all about?'

'I still don't know what it's about,' said Jing, 'and I'm human.'

'These are all good observations,' said Kerry. 'We might have similar questions in a moment when it comes to deciding who or what will play another key character.'

❖

Richards took a sip of coffee, his eyes still on the monitor: 'Anyway, so far so good with the upgrade; the learning buddies look focused and for want of a better term, *relaxed*'.

'And the kids are into it – asking some pertinent questions.'

'You're right, it's a real consideration: how *does* an android actor deliver a line that relates to a biological drive it can't even remotely own? We allow them simulated activities such as eating and drinking, but our learning buddies can never have a sexual identity, and for good reasons: we're working with young and vulnerable people.' Richards shook his head. 'We can't forget there's some weird and frankly scary stuff out there in the wider world that doesn't have such inhibitions.'

Brady nodded his agreement and chose not to add anything.

❖

'So we're really moving along,' said Kerry. 'Let's jump to Romeo, Mercutio and Benvolio gate-crashing the party at the Capulet's house. This is where Romeo gets to meet Juliet for the first time, played by...' Kerry delayed her announcement just long enough to give the impression it had been her free decision, '...Harper.'

The teenager duly stepped forward to take up her position, looking around like she'd been awarded a well-flagged Oscar.

❖

Richards knocked back the rest of his by now cold coffee. 'You have no idea how much depended on that.'

Brady gave the other man a heartfelt pat on the shoulder. 'I guess I'm relieved not to be a father.'

❖

'So Wanda, are you happy to play Lady Capulet?' said Kerry.

'Hey, don't say I'm going to play your mother, white girl!' Wanda said as she took up a position next to her friend.

'Yes,' said Kerry, 'we're obviously ignoring any attempt at realism on that front; although I was thinking we could have it in the back of our minds that due to falling fertility rates and stringent adoption policies denying choice based on racial profiling, families of the future might be more of a mix.'

'Groovy,' said Wanda, her eyes wide.

Kerry looked again at the group. 'And while we're talking about mothers: Tania, will you be OK with Lady Montague?'

'Yeah, fine with me,' said Tania, pleased at not being asked to play too big a speaking part.

Kerry looked back at Juliet standing with her mother and father. 'And there's one very important person still missing from the Capulet household. So, Gaia, would you care to take up your position as Juliet's Nurse?'

A ripple of bemusement swept around the room; except for Greta who unashamedly jumped for joy. 'Hey that's so brilliant Miss Tracker!'

Kerry looked at Gaia. 'Do you think you can take on this part for us?'

'Yes Miss Tracker,' said the android with a bright smile, taking up her position. 'I will do my very best.'

Chuck was determined to make his objection felt this time: 'She's got to say a whole load of that crude-sex stuff; same as Mercutio.'

Tania frowned too: 'Yeah, remember how in that punk movie we saw the Nurse kept wiggling her butt. She's got to have been around the block a bit right?'

'A woman of the world,' added Wanda.

Kerry nodded. 'These are all valid points. Yes the humour in the play is often risqué and crude; in fact we can see the Nurse as a female counterpart to Mercutio in several respects. Anyway, I thought we'd achieve an artistic balance if *both* characters were played by learning buddies? In terms of characterisation I think the new EI software will make all the difference, as far as our Nurse is concerned, Gaia should now be able to process the admittedly complex human feelings you've alluded to relating to her sexual and maternal memories, even if she can only comprehend it all in theory.' Kerry looked at her female doubters. 'I guess that would have been true had I picked any one of you?'

'You've got an answer for everything Miss,' said Wanda, squirming along with the others.

❖

Richards checked the time and put on his coat to go, happy with what he'd seen. 'OK Jim, it's all very interesting. Your director appears to be well on top of things and no doubt the play will prove to be a success. So keep me posted; I'm especially looking forward to hearing how the new software shapes up.'

❖

Kerry noticed Harper staring off into space. 'You look like you're thinking about something?'

'I'm just trying to get my head around this whole reality-pretend thing,' said Harper, glancing at Gaia. 'She's going to be an actual *android nurse* right? She's not an android playing a real person?'

'Yes, it's the same with Mercutio, Police Chief Escalus and the Montague servants, all of whom are android characters.'

'So how can she have memories of being a mother and all that other stuff, like she even remembers being Juliet's wet-nurse?'

Again Kerry nodded appreciatively at the observation. 'Yes, this is also something we'll need to clarify, both for ourselves and our audience.'

Omar put up his hand. 'No problem, it'll be just like those old *Bladerunner* movies where the androids got given false memories; even fake photos and ID to back it all up.'

'I always thought it was cruel the way that happened,' said Tania, 'giving them false hopes and everything.'

'But as you say, those films were forerunners in speculating a future where such things might happen. No harm in borrowing from that,' said Kerry.

'Anyway, it's already here,' said Carlos, 'Doesn't every child's doll have its own bio.'

'What about Mercutio and the Prince?' asked Jing. 'Will they have started off with some kind of memory implants too?'

'I think we can say it will be different for them,' said Kerry. 'The Nurse has been programmed to serve a specific purpose regarding her employment, she's low status compared to Mercutio who is a much freer agent. The same thing would apply to the Police Chief, probably even more so.' She paused for a moment. 'Anyway, it will be interesting when we juxtapose these ideas against the text.'

Wanda said, 'I guess in the Nurse's case anyway, it makes a crazy kind of sense of some of what gets said.'

'Do you have an instance in mind?' asked Kerry keen to hear support for what was after all, a radical interpretation of the play and characters.

'When we read through it the first time I thought it was plain weird the way the Nurse is so outright cheeky and goes on about her own daughter: no way would a posh woman like Lady Capulet have taken that kind of backchat.' Wanda nodded to herself. 'But now I'm seeing it different: maybe she has to put up with it for Juliet's benefit because it's all part of the pretence.'

'Yes,' replied Kerry, impressed. 'That would certainly fit into what we're saying.'

Greta snapped her fingers. 'And it's also why she talks so crude: because another part of her role is giving Juliet some necessary lessons in life, including her sex education, so the girl doesn't end up being *too* innocent. Maybe that's something Lady Capulet would have been uncomfortable with doing herself?'

'So what's new,' said Wanda, rolling her eyes.

Harper took it in, looking thoughtful. 'So this means that when Juliet was small, she would have believed all that stuff about the Nurse, until she got older and found out the painful truth?'

Wanda nodded: 'Loss of innocence; like the Tooth Fairy or Santa Claus.'

Kerry looked around the group. 'So are we generally OK with this interpretation for the android characters?'

'Yeah, it's cool,' said Omar. 'It's gonna be different anyway.'

Kerry turned to the learning buddies. 'Have you been able to follow the logic of this conversation?'

They all nodded in unison.

Kerry was conscious there was still one person left sitting down. 'OK, I also want to try something a little left-field with Friar Laurence.'

'You want me to play a man?' said Greta.

'Actually I'm thinking a woman priest – *Friaress* Lauren? We know the character is experienced in using herbs and potions which is traditional female territory; so in a way we're just reclaiming that.'

Chuck grinned. 'Will she have to shave her hair?'

Greta looked horrified.

'It's OK, we'll give her a bald pate wig,' said Kerry with a jokey smile.

Kerry continued: 'We also need a Friar John. Tania, you have a relatively small part as Lady Montague, so you could double up: Friaress Johanna for you?'

Tania smiled. 'Sure, as long as I can keep my hair too.'

Kerry noted there were two learning buddies still seated. 'DAK 11, will you please play the Apothecary?' She glanced back at the figures collected around the Capulet household. 'There's one more important character we'll have met even before the party scene. Carlos, you also have a small enough part as Lord Montague, we only see him near the beginning and at the very end. In between maybe you can double-up as Count Paris?'

Carlos looked pleased. 'Yeah, that's cool – it means I get to go to the party *and* have a duel to the death.'

'Finally we might ask DAK 49 to play the Count's pageboy servant,' added Kerry. 'DAK 27 is already playing Romeo's attendant, Balthazar.' She surveyed the whole assembly of characters. 'And that's more or less it – we have one or two small speaking parts yet to fill as well as several non-speaking roles: musicians, waiters, but those can be sorted out when we go through the relevant scenes.'

'Is that it, are we done?' said Tania, looking amazed.

'Yes, it's great we've all that established and now you

can go away and learn your parts. Also you can try out your learning buddies with their new software: and don't forget even though they now have their own characters they can still play any of the others to help you with your lines. Oh, and you'll be glad to hear that you're all excused from non-core classes from now through to our opening night.'

'Because we're the cream!' declared Chuck, speaking for everyone.

'*The Cream*,' said Jing, snapping his fingers and turning to Carlos and Omar. 'UK band...first hit single, "I Feel Free" – second one..."Strange Brew" released 1967?'

'B side, "Tales of Brave Ulysses," said Omar not missing a beat.

'Jeez, "Strange Brew", that's certainly what we are!' said Wanda with a grin, looking around to take in the new-look ensemble.

'Maybe it's not a bad description,' said Kerry smiling along too as they all began to shuffle out in high spirits singing the song's chorus.

ACT FOUR

"A faint cold fear thrills through my veins..."

L inton's daydreaming was interrupted as his carrier pulled off the freeway, slowing as it left the slipway and hit the now familiar dirt track. He opened his eyes and switched to self-drive, allowing the drifting thoughts to continue. Given the formal investigation concerning Rob Bennett's death was now effectively dead in the water, the only reason he could think for him being kept on the case was that his superiors were interested in something still ongoing, maybe something dramatic yet to happen?

Being kept in the dark continued to niggle, but he was starting to accept his life in limbo, perhaps even enjoying it. After all he was a "free agent" in how he filled the void – like getting out of the city and visiting Rob Bennett's sister for a third time. Right this moment, as the car passed by the tree-lined lake, he was feeling something strange... hard to put a finger on it: happy?

'So you're back for more dandelion coffee and herbal remedy for migraine?' said Elizabeth, examining him with a smile.

'They've been happening a lot less frequent, thanks,' said Linton, feeling strangely exposed, even a touch embarrassed.

'So, maybe it's working,' Elizabeth said as she got up from her chair. 'Would you care to help me inspect the goats and pick out some of the best cider apples?'

'Can't think of anything I'd like more,' said Linton, actually meaning it.

'So, let's go do it, soldier,' she said, making a mock military salute.

As they started to move off, a few of the other farmers and seed-savers arrived, taking in Linton with curious looks.

'Some of you may not have met Mr Floyd Linton,' Elizabeth announced. 'Watch yourselves, he's a cop.'

There were a few delayed smiles; one of them said: 'You're welcome, we're police too of sorts; you protect people, we look after seeds.'

Elizabeth pulled Linton along by the arm. 'So detective, maybe we'll discover along the way a little more about this notorious suspect named "Floyd" – who he really is?'

❖

"*What's in a name? That which we call a rose, by any other name would smell as sweet...*" Harper's globe pulsed and she signalled for DAK 49 to hold off from prompting her next line. Her father's face was in the main hexagon, his lips moving, but with no sound as she still had him on mute.

She indulged herself for a moment before flipping up the volume. 'Oh yes, there you are Father; I can hear you now. I was actually busy going through my lines. Well, I have to say this really is strange, the way I'm suddenly getting all this attention. What is it this time?'

Richards released a trademark sigh: 'I only wished to congratulate you on getting the part you wanted.'

'Well news certainly travels fast around here. Sure, isn't it great, looks like I'm playing one of the servants.'

Richards's expression changed. 'But I thought you'd been given –'

Harper grinned. 'OK, you can calm down, I was only fooling. Anyway, what if I *was* being asked to play a servant, should that make me any less in your eyes?'

'You know that isn't what I meant; it's more I always believe in going for what offers the highest challenge.'

Harper put on a "dumb" expression. 'Maybe you're forgetting I only got roped into this cus of what happened to poor Mr Milton.'

'Well, that's all in the past,' said her father, magnanimously. 'Mistakes were made, let's just be positive about this now. And don't insult your own intelligence, Harper; this is a chance to move on and make an important contribution.'

'Yeah sure…' Harper took out her gum and casually stuck it onto the nose of her learning buddy.

Richards winced. 'I'm telling myself I didn't see that.'

Harper shrugged. 'We're not allowed to stick it under the desks anymore.'

Her father chose to bite his tongue. 'Anyway, I'd better let you get back to your script.'

'Sure, I don't want to be letting you, the school and the entire universe down.'

'By the way,' said Richards trying to sound more casual. 'Have you noticed much of a difference with your learning buddy since the upgrade?'

Harper sniffed the air. 'Not so obvious that I can tell… maybe a negligible something here and there…'

Richards recognised the game she was playing and called a timeout: 'Anyway, early days yet, hopefully once you get going on the play in earnest it'll show through.'

❖

Hot-seating was one of Kerry's favourite ways to help actors explore their characters. Right now it was Gaia's turn as she waited to field questions from the rest of the group, sitting on the floor facing her in a semi-circle.

Kerry kicked it off. 'So Gaia, which character are you playing?'

'I am playing the Nurse, Miss Tracker, as you know,' said Gaia.

Kerry smiled. 'I suppose it really wasn't a question if I already knew the answer. Maybe it's more that I wanted to hear you say it.'

Gaia smiled back. 'Yes, I understand your need. Would you like to hear it again?'

'Yes please: and this time with more feeling perhaps?'

Gaia nodded her head and said brightly, 'I will be playing the Nurse.'

'How old are you?' asked Carlos.

'My age is not actually specified in the text.'

'So guess,' said Omar.

Gaia thought for a moment. 'From what is said about

me and suggested by my own words and actions…I would probably be at least forty years of age.'

'Do you like pizza?' asked Chuck.

Gaia sighed like an elementary schoolteacher responding to an infant. 'There were no pizzas in Shakespeare's time Chuck, even in Italy. The pizza wasn't invented until 1889. However, with our version of the play being set in the future, we can take a calculated risk that the people in the play would still be eating pizza.' Gaia paused as another thought arrived from somewhere. 'And while I cannot be sure what my character's food preferences are, I can speculate she is possibly quite plump in build, suggesting plenty of carbohydrates –'

'Hey, when does one of us get a turn?' interjected Little Stevie.

'Yes, we'll be coming to you in a moment,' said Kerry. 'I hope you've done as much research on your own character?'

'I'm lover boy, that's all anyone needs to know,' the boy replied with a cheesy grin.

'Give me strength,' mumbled Harper, putting a finger in her mouth in the obligatory gagging gesture.

'What's your favourite colour?' asked Tania.

This time Gaia seemed a little unsure. 'I think I like… blue?'

'Is that you or the Nurse talking?' said Greta with a smile.

Gaia smiled back. 'Perhaps we share the same preference.'

When they'd gone around the whole group, Kerry had one more question. 'Who are you most loyal to in the Capulet household?'

'My loyalties are divided. Most immediately to Juliet of course: firstly as her nurse, but also as her friend and confidant, someone who understands and sympathises with what she is feeling.'

'Wow!' said Wanda, genuinely impressed.

'Even if it means deceiving your employers Lord and Lady Capulet by helping her meet with Romeo so they can get married in secret?' said Kerry.

'Yes, at that point I believe it is the right thing to do.'

'So, you make a conscious decision over whom to be loyal to?'

'Yes,' said Gaia. 'As the Nurse, I have my own mind and must decide for myself.'

'How do you decide? What informs your decision?' Kerry probed.

Gaia frowned. 'The answer to that question is more complex. It may take a moment to consider all the possible contributing factors.'

Greta stepped in protectively. 'Hey yeah, some of these are hard questions, hope I don't get the same grilling!'

'Actually,' said Kerry, 'Gaia is helping us all here by showing us how it's done. We can apply this level of interrogation to our own characters. Think of it like an onion: peeling away the layers.' She turned to the android actor. 'That's right isn't it Nurse: your behaviour towards Juliet and your employers results from a complex mixture of thought and feeling. You are a human being are you not, complete with underlying contradictions?'

Gaia smiled. 'I did say I was probably over forty, but I was a young girl of fourteen too once upon a time.'

Kerry was dying to ask more questions, but sensed it was

time to move on to questioning another character. Anyway, what the android had said already was revealing enough.

❖

After his morning trip to the eco-farm, Linton was back in Brady's office, taking off his coat and hat and looking at the monitor covering the fringe hub. 'Hmm, it's definitely sounding more and more interesting.'

Brady stroked his chin. 'Yeah, now there's some food for thought. Not sure how long we'd last ourselves in Miss Tracker's hot seat.' He grinned at the detective. 'She sure knows how to get someone to spill the beans: you'd better watch your back; she'll be coming after your job.'

Linton gave a half-smile: 'Sure, maybe it'll be vacant soon.'

'I notice you've already been a little absent without leave just lately,' said Brady with a grin.

'Sure,' said Linton, 'getting in a little practise at leading the easy life.'

'Anyway,' said Brady, 'going back to Miss Tracker, it's good to see she's getting a good handle on the upgrades.'

There was a knock at the door, followed by AJ entering carrying a potted plant.

Brady beamed. 'Oh yeah, good man AJFX72, I'd forgotten all about it; how about over there on the desk.' As the android did this, Brady turned back to Linton. 'I'm going all out for a healthier atmosphere. That's my cue for a cup of green tea.'

Linton was momentarily distracted, thinking back on something as he watched AJ carefully put down the plant.

After a moment he snapped out of this reverie: 'Sure, maybe I'll join you in one this time.'

Brady did a double-take. 'Hey now, what's the big bad world of crime coming to? Where have all the hardnosed, divorced, alcoholic, coffee-swilling, disgraced cops gone? You can't buy one these days for love or Bit-coin!'

On a screen an animation figure representing a lone US soldier was dodging a fusillade of spears and arrows, then fireballs and rockets, laser beams – defending itself against wave upon wave of attackers from hordes of medieval warriors to flying drone insects and gigantic mechanical monsters.

The interactive war game came to an end and General Macy's face took over the screen. He removed the helmet he'd been wearing, his eyes bulging, looking exhilarated, even high. 'Maximum points, ladies and gentlemen,' he announced with immense satisfaction.

Richards looked at the other three screens filled by the remaining members of the task force: due to various work pressures the group were conducting this session via a virtual teleconference. Richards hoped this wasn't a tacit downgrading of his proposal. While they still maintained a positive front towards him, he sensed in their eyes and body language there was still a good deal of reservation.

'OK Richards,' said Wilson, 'it seems we've got a straight contest for funding approval between your android Peacemaker and this latest version of the Warrior Helmet, ably demonstrated by General Macy. No doubt you're already aware of the Helmet's proven worth: thanks to its newly enhanced neural connectors, faced with multiple hostile threats even rookie recruits have been able to make better split-second choices, kill more combatants up to a success rate of ninety-four percent.'

Wilson paused before continuing: 'You'll also appreciate that in contrast to your android soldier, this means jobs for human beings; it'll help ease unemployment figures, offer less hostility here at home. Your guy's gonna have to trump all of this in some way.'

Richards allowed the challenge to hang in the air for a moment. '*War and Peace*, ladies and gentlemen: isn't that what all this boils down to? OK, so this super-trooper helmet can be part of an improved war machine: it offers an enhanced ability to kill, but nothing else. Perhaps we're in danger of getting away from the main point. What I'm offering would place us back at the centre of things, not just regarding military operations but in our key humanitarian role as peacemaker. These two roles shouldn't be incompatible; in fact they should go together like hand and glove. Isn't that what we've always claimed to be doing, acting as the world's policeman, righting wrong? Yes, we might intervene with force, but always towards ending conflict: isn't this the only thing that allows us to assign the moral high ground to ourselves?'

Wilson leaned forwards into his screen. 'Can we clarify something here: you're not suggesting this would be limited to a Nations Forum peacekeeping role?'

'That should offer a first base of course,' said Richards. 'But I also mean this to be our regular foot soldier in all conflict scenarios. Yes, this is a peacemaker but it will use force if necessary.'

There was a general nodding of approval. Richards hoped this indicated he wasn't so far away from winning them over as he'd earlier thought.

Macy picked up the helmet again, cradling it in two hands like he was weighing up its value in gold.

Richards thought back to the war game he'd just witnessed and how the faces of those watching the action had been so alive and viscerally involved, seeing it all through Macy's eyes. They'd been drawn right into the drama, while Richards's own offering, his earlier simulation of the three person gunfight, just hadn't fully captured them in the same way. OK, they'd been intrigued, intellectually connected perhaps but not emotionally engaged. He was aware that he needed to fight fire with fire.

'Anyway, I think we've covered some important ground,' said Wilson, stretching out his arms and then stifling a yawn, 'maybe we can all get some lunch and come back again afterwards.' To Richards there appeared to be a clear sub-text hinting that maybe they weren't really getting anywhere. As if he might be reading the man's mind Wilson added: 'I think we're still going to need one more final piece of evidence to fully convince us of everything you've been saying.'

Richards nodded to accept the challenge. He appeared to mull something over, then smiled and said: 'OK, so here's something to go with your burgers and salads: how long is it since any of you saw a production of *Romeo and Juliet*?'

❖

At the start of their next session Kerry wanted to give a moment to running over the play's main themes, but there were immediate protests.

'This is still a hell of a lot of talking,' said Chuck. 'We waited all that time to find out our parts: I seem to remember this had something to do with *acting*? You know, like moving around with swords?'

Little Stevie said, 'Forget it dude, if this is set in the future it'll be more like laser beams, drones and even more weird far out stuff.'

Chuck wasn't giving up his sword so easily. 'So who's to say in the future they won't be even more retro than we are – like totally stuck looking backwards.'

'Actually,' said Kerry, 'maybe we can find a way to incorporate both perspectives?'

Omar groaned. 'OK, but we need to decide or no-one's gonna get killed.'

Kerry nodded. 'Well seeing as we're focusing on this aspect of the play, let's take the duel scene we already worked on. Going by the text, the fighting has to be at close quarters if we're to believe Tybalt can slip his weapon beneath Mercutio's guard.'

'So stuff like drones and laser beams will make them too far apart,' said Little Stevie.

Wanda sighed and shook her head. 'Can we please get away from all the competitive talk about weapons for a moment? Here's a different question: if Romeo knows he's to blame for getting his friend killed, why doesn't he feel sad and guilty instead of just getting mad and taking it out on Tybalt?'

'OK…we'll try to answer that,' said Kerry. 'Let's

remember, while Romeo is the hero he's far from flawless: we've already seen how his emotions run ahead of him. So in this instance wanting to get even and avenge his friend overrides any self-awareness regarding his own mistake. The truth is for the play to work, Romeo has to be seen as impetuous: if he'd dwelt even for a moment longer on his own culpability, it might have disarmed him. Then we wouldn't have this crucial turning point where the play begins to fulfil its destiny as a tragedy: it wouldn't be the play that Shakespeare wrote. No, our hero has to be a hot-bloodied male who wants immediate retribution. The heart overrules the head and he does something without thinking of the consequences.'

Chuck grinned. 'Yeah, he acts stupid. Isn't that's why you gave the part to Stevie.'

'Hey!' said the other boy, giving Chuck a hard jab to the chest. 'Tybalt's the one who starts the fighting you moron!'

'Boys, that's enough,' said Kerry, firmly.

Chuck and Little Stevie separated themselves, with a parting shove for good measure.

Tania raised her eyes to the heavens: 'So immature, right Miss?'

'Anyway,' said Kerry, 'getting back to the original question, whatever weapons we end up using, they'll have to be toy ones or replicas, just in case any of our actors get too carried away.' She looked pointedly at the two boys.

There were a few good humoured jeers.

'And yes, Wanda's right to draw our attention to the all important feelings behind each action and maybe this is a good time for us to focus on the flipside to all that anger and rage, remind ourselves that this play is also about *love*?'

❖

'Do we have to do this in front of everyone?' said Harper, a short while later. They were looking again at the now familiar party scene and had arrived at the moment when Romeo and Juliet first kiss. 'You could always give the others a timeout.'

Kerry did feel some sympathy for the teenager with her whole image at stake. This would be the first time since casting the play that the spotlight was focused so closely on the two lovers.

'OK, I get what you're saying,' said Kerry. 'It would be tempting to give everyone a break and work with just yourself and Little Stevie, but remember that although this scene has these moments of intimacy where the world stands still as it were, we still have to bear in mind how the general party action is continuing on around you: you're not entirely alone and that is crucial to how you must behave.'

Chuck smirked. 'She just doesn't want to puck Stevie in front of everyone.'

Harper threw Chuck an evil look; then almost as if to spite him, turned to Little Stevie and planted a kiss full on his lips. 'There you go Romeo.'

The boy was so surprised he nearly toppled off his Cuban heels.

'Woaah!' a round of applause went around the group.

Greta turned to Gaia and gave the android a quick peck on the cheek. 'We're all in this together right Miss Tracker?'

'Actually yes,' said Kerry, making an immediate connection, 'it *is* a party: so in amongst the dancing there will likely be more exchanges of affection. We could even allow for more flirting to be going on, courtship in the air. Romeo and Juliet wouldn't be the only potential lovers in a situation like this.'

'Yeah but there's only two in the actual spotlight right?' said Harper, reversing her earlier coyness. 'We don't want everyone kissing and hugging all over the place.'

Kerry got the point; the star actress was protecting her special status. 'Don't worry we'll be sticking close to the script in that regard. But it's still good to keep in mind as background: in any social gathering the speeches and action we witness are just the tip of the iceberg beneath which there's a whole world of sub-text and implicit meanings. That's why our attention to *process* has been so valuable so far –'

'Miss, will you never give that thing a break!' wailed Tania, backed by a chorus of supporting good-natured groans.

❖

'OK, Richards, I'm intrigued,' said Tim Wilson, back on screen picking up on the earlier session. '*Romeo & Juliet:* true it's been a while since I saw it, but as far as emotional intelligence goes I seem to remember that play contains more than a few cock-ups. It's a tragedy right?'

'*Human* cock-ups,' Richards replied, 'combined of course with the cruel hand of fate. I have to confess this came to mind because my daughter is currently involved in a school production.'

Ms Chan raised an eyebrow: 'Do I hear a proud father talking?'

Horne aimed a wink at the other three: 'Is this by way of offering us all an invitation?'

Richards proffered a thin smile. 'Maybe it'll suffice to take you through the play here and examine those "cock-ups" just mentioned from an EI perspective, focusing on how they link-up together as a chain reaction. Remember how it starts with two warring families and two young people who make the cardinal mistake of falling in love with someone from the wrong side. First you have to acknowledge they're following an admirable impulse, innocent love reaching across a great divide: a potential for healing, conflict resolution in other words?'

Richards waited for a tentative nod of heads before continuing.

'Then in order to protect that love and enable it to blossom, Juliet's nurse colludes in keeping it a secret. That's also human judgement informed by good intentions. Was it the right call? Her loyalty is obviously divided between the girl's parents who are her employers and this young woman she's raised from a baby. And who's to say she's not right to side with Juliet and help this well-meaning project along. And then into this comes the Friar, who takes a big gamble because he's loyal to them too. He gives Juliet a potion to knock her out so it seems like she's dead, but he's going to tell Romeo the truth so that he can sneak into her tomb in time for when she wakes up and they can both elope.

'OK, by now admittedly the outcome is starting to look very shaky and unpredictable: too many accumulating factors that might lead to it all going wrong. But again, let's be reminded, the Friar is only acting to help a good cause. You might argue the mistake is keeping it a secret and yes, that of course adds to the risk. But think about it: Normandy Landings?'

'OK, we can hear where you're going with this,' said Wilson, prodding his ears to indicate they were buzzing.

'And despite the risks, there *is* a plan: it could work. Who can foresee the crucial letter to Romeo telling him that Juliet's not really dead will go astray due to some almost ridiculous providential bad luck.'

Horne gave it some consideration: 'OK, so let's move this to the battlefield. We know about letters going astray or being misinterpreted, *The Charge of the Light Brigade* has been mentioned before. As for bad luck, the Normandy landings could have been scuppered by the unsettled weather at the time.'

'So staying with the play, what would your android have done that was any different?' asked Wilson.

'To answer that I would of course have to be one of these androids myself,' said Richards modestly, 'I'd need access to that superior level of intelligence: maybe that's the whole point, I can't answer it adequately because I too am human and fallible.'

'Try – give it a shot,' Macy insisted.

'OK,' said Richards, 'let's suppose in our play scenario we make the Nurse an android. And she or "it" if you prefer, makes the same calculated but emotionally informed decision this relationship is all for the good, has the potential for conflict resolution. Sure, there's a risk it will worsen things, but the situation is inflamed already:

the volatility has been there for a long time. "Ancient grudge" I think it says at the beginning.'

Horne frowned. 'So Richards, you've just undermined your own argument, the android makes the same mistake as the human.'

Richards shook his head. 'No Admiral, this in itself was not necessarily a mistake. All might have gone well had it not been for the next intervention by the well-meaning Friar.'

'And this guy's a regular bumbling human being I suppose?' growled Macy.

Wilson cut in: 'Just before you answer that Richards – if I remember right, isn't there also the small matter of a fight in which a couple of important guys get killed?'

Richards nodded: 'Yes, that too has to be taken on board. Juliet's nephew Tybalt is in attendance when the two lovers first meet and witnesses them falling for each other. Afterwards he comes looking for a showdown with Romeo, family fidelity on his side. But our hero's so full of true love he doesn't want to fight, especially with one of Juliet's own clan.'

'A good decision that offers to diffuse the situation,' said Ms Chan.

'Crucially we also have to factor in Romeo's friend Mercutio being there as well with his own emotional axe to grind. He and Tybalt square up to one another, which draws well-meaning Romeo into making a clumsy intervention, upsetting Mercutio's guard, who takes a cowardly hit from Tybalt and dies hurling *a curse on both their houses.*'

'Romeo gets it all arse-ways in other words,' said Macy.

'Funny, this reminds me of that three-way simulation you showed us.'

Horne looked puzzled. 'Didn't your guy on that occasion end up making the "emotionally intelligent" decision to kill a few rival combatants?'

Richards paused to allow the moment to breathe.

'OK Richards, put us out of our misery,' said Wilson. 'Bearing in mind we're talking about a work of fiction and trying to see its relevance for a concrete situation, what might your android peacemaker have done in Romeo's position?'

Richards shrugged: 'Maybe it would require something right outside the box. Could be Romeo offers a temporary diversion, just to take the heat out of the moment, allowing everyone to calm down?'

'Sure, maybe he swoons into his hanky and faints!' snorted Macy.

'Why not?' said Richards, surprising everyone. 'If it succeeded in saving two, three lives, stopped the feud from escalating? A regular human soldier hardened for combat and full of machismo could never envisage doing such a thing: recognise it as an emotionally intelligent action.'

'Maybe we should send in more female troops, who are more used to fainting?' said Macy.

'That's sexist General,' said Wilson. 'Once your regular female trooper has been through her training she'll be as tough as the guys. Anyway Richards makes a valid overall point: chased by a bear, aren't you supposed to lie down and be still?'

'I'm getting lost,' said Horne, scratching his head. '*Bear*: are we talking about the Russians now?'

'Yes I think we're in danger of losing track of where

this conversation started,' said Ms Chan. 'We were talking about a school production of Shakespeare's play, *Romeo and Juliet*. Mr Richards added in the hypothetical scenario of an android playing one of the characters instead of a human being, potentially making different decisions –'

'Except...maybe it wasn't hypothetical,' said Richards.

'Jeez, I think you've left us all way behind,' said Macy with a weary sigh.

Richards put a finger to his lip. 'Only if you promise to keep it to yourselves, I can let you in on a little secret: "top secret" in fact. Android actors will be taking a full part in this production. I was fortunate enough to witness a rehearsal myself.'

There was a bemused silence; a mixture of smirks and smiles as everyone took in the new information.

Wilson said, 'These are your own make I take it?'

'Yes, the regular learning buddy models we have in the school, but with their EI now greatly enhanced: modest perhaps compared with our Peacemaker, but maybe not so far off at the same time.'

'OK, so here's a question,' said Horne. 'Given their now superior EI, what stops these android actors from seeing all the disasters coming and changing what appears to be a flawed script to make it turn out better? I mean, isn't that exactly the kind of initiative we're looking for here?'

Wilson jumped in: 'Wait, let me guess what the answer will be this time. The laws of theatre dictate you don't mess with the Bard's text, right? If the Nurse reveals what Juliet is up to for example, the parents intervene and that's the end of the story. You've got one hell of a disappointed audience, not a tear in sight, all those dry unused tissues?'

Richards held up both hands to suggest they were finally getting close to understanding him. 'The key to all this is these androids are *aware* that they're acting. It's a core input within their enhanced software. They accept having to act the play as written, even if the behaviour of the fictional characters they're playing goes against their own intelligent reasoning: because their highest loyalty in this instance is to the production.'

Wilson looked perplexed. 'But then that means we bypass any opportunity for them to display that wonderful flexibility you were previously talking about? That was your main ace in all this as far as I understood it.'

Richards paused, knowing his next reply was crucial. 'So this is the thing – they do have room for manoeuvre to depart from the script if necessary, to *improvise* in other words. If a human actor forgets a line for example, an android can delay its own response so as not to compound the problem; allow space for the scene to be rescued.'

Looks passed from face to face, everyone caught between fascination and bewilderment.

'These guys must be a theatre director's dream!' declared Ms Chan.

'Exactly,' Richards replied. 'So I guess all you have to do is substitute theatre director for general or admiral? What did I say to you earlier: *Theatre of War*?'

Macy held up his hands in mock surrender. 'Listen Richards, this may sound hunky dory to you but I'm not exactly a theatre-goer: if we're gonna draw analogies, can't you make it something an action guy can relate to – like sport, incorporating some good old-fashioned red-bloodied competition?'

Richards sensed he'd made crucial ground in establishing the logic of his proposal, in setting the stage as it were and yes, perhaps it would do no harm now to offer something closer to a military mind's comfort zone. 'I appreciate what you're saying, General. Let me get onto that for you right away.'

Harper was checking herself in her locker door mirror as DAK 49 watched her movements with curiosity: sympathy or empathy, it was hard to tell.

Harper allowed herself a joke: 'You want some mascara?'

DAK 49's smile in response seemed to say, "Come on, I know you're kidding me."

Harper stuck out her tongue, amused despite herself. Glancing along the corridor she caught sight of Greta and Gaia collecting things from their own locker.

Her eyes narrowed slightly. 'Let's go,' she said, heading in the direction of the other couple.

Just as they were approaching, another girl came hurrying by checking her wristband – tripped and was heading for a nasty fall until Gaia reached out and caught her. The girl lay supine in the android's arms for a moment before being lifted up to vertical and allowed to gently find her feet again. 'Thanks,' she said, embarrassed, not sure whether to direct this at Gaia or Greta.

'Don't mention it,' said the learning buddy with an easy smile.

The girl went on her way again, a little more gingerly. Greta gave her comrade a high-5 before they moved off themselves.

Harper stayed rooted to where she was standing, taking time to run a slow motion replay of what had just happened: the android's lightning speed in reacting to a totally random event – its first instinct to protect *any* human being from harm. Her countenance betrayed some envy at the close bond between Greta and her learning buddy. She turned and caught DAK 49 observing her. 'OK, what's so fascinating? Hey, maybe I should give *you* a nickname too: how about "Nosey Parker?" Whatever I'm thinking right now is none of your damn business.'

❖

The school's basketball hall was packed to the rafters. Jim Brady had responded to Charles Richards's request for an exhibition of androids playing sport – preferably a game that would be competitive but also involve teamwork and highlight cooperation. The school's benefactor had specified that it should be the learning buddies from the drama group with the new upgrade taking part. He'd been a bit cloak and dagger about it all, just saying it would be good promotion for the school's AI policy. He couldn't attend personally, but would be watching along with unspecified others via a live-streaming.

Brady had gone for a limited-contact sport, better safe than sorry. A selection of Kerry's android actors were formally designated the "away" team and pitted against a "home" side made up from kids on the fringes of the school's junior basketball squads that included Little Stevie, Jing and Wanda from the drama group.

Floyd Linton took a seat next to Brady and looked around the hall. 'I don't see any learning buddies in the audience to cheer their side on?'

Brady flinched, taking this as a mild criticism. 'They're normally left outside. We've limited room in here.'

Linton was clearly in the mood for banter. 'I read once that in Ancient Greece, when they had those big open air dramas, showing plays by Sophocles and those other guys – everyone got to attend: the women, even the slaves.'

'Sure, so maybe we're not so perfect,' Brady replied gruffly.

Linton grinned. 'You know you come over as a serious kind of guy sometimes for a stand-up comedian.'

Brady couldn't resist a corny joke: 'Sure, but right now I'm sitting down.'

Linton's grin morphed into a grimace. 'Ouch...'

The two men sat back, more relaxed after their verbal jousting. Linton looked out at the court as the two teams warmed up. 'So how will this work – how do you avoid anyone getting hurt?'

'The learning buddies have downloaded all the rules and general etiquette of the game, as well as gazillions more stuff on strategies. We've added in a zero-contact rule for both sides, just as a precaution. Even a knuckle-rap from an android could have us in court with parents taking us to the cleaners for damages.'

'Are your home team kids any good: who's going to win this?'

Brady shrugged. 'Hard to know; Howard Trent tells

me the whole basketball squad are no great shakes, but I guess there must be worse schools out there.' Brady pointed: 'Look, our star guy is a five foot tall giant.'

Linton looked down at Little Stevie, bouncing the ball, showing off with some flamboyant moves. 'He looks confident anyway.'

Brady winced at the boy's antics. 'The boy fancies himself, especially now he's got the star part in Miss Tracker's play.'

The teams were lined up ready to start; the referee getting ready to blow his whistle.

Linton raised an eyebrow. 'Doesn't having a human ref give unfair advantage to one side? Or maybe you're planning on switching to an android umpire for the last two quarters?'

Brady made a face. 'Maybe we'll do that for the return fixture.'

'Give your guy AJ the job maybe?' said Linton, pointedly.

'Sure, good idea,' replied Brady. 'Now let's watch the match.'

The ball went up...Little Stevie rose and caught it, giving a quick pass to Wanda, who moved it down the court. A couple more passes and the ball was in the opposite basket. It looked all too easy, compared with games of chess the learning buddies were clearly at a disadvantage: for one thing they couldn't jump off the ground.

Now it was the android team's turn. The ball was successfully passed out from the baseline and moved methodically from one player to another. Half way down the court the home team made an easy interception; a couple of passes and it was back in the same net.

'That's four-zero to the kids already,' said Linton. 'Slow learners: I thought your androids would be quicker on the uptake.'

Brady folded his arms. 'Let's not be too hasty. Wait and see.'

One of the DAKs threw in again. The ball was worked up the court until Jing, with a superior grin on his face went for what he thought was another signalled pass, only to witness the android changing its mind at the last split-second, giving it to another player instead. They repeated this improvisation until one of them threw an immaculate basket, the ball sailing perfectly into the net, not even hitting the ring.

'4-2' said Brady, smiling approval.

The home team worked it down the court and scored again, only it was noticeable this time that the defending androids got nearer to the ball and almost made some interceptions of their own.

'6-2,' said Linton.

As the game re-started, the kids responded to a signal from their coach and moved up to form a high defence pressurising the opposition at their own end. The android holding the ball, seeing what appeared to be an impenetrable wall, simply threw a basket from where it stood, straight into the net: a fantastic three-pointer.

That made it 6-5.

The home team waved their arms in protest. 'Hey, that wasn't fair!' screamed Little Stevie.

The referee shrugged. 'It's allowed; read the rules buddy.'

And so it continued like this, tit for tat, each side scoring on their own restart, until finally the sequence was broken when, on their next foray down the court, the home team, a little over-confident, managed to lose the ball. It was Little Stevie going for a layup, attempting one bounce too many when an android arm reached out – the next thing the ball was in the opposite net for another three-point score.

There was a huge cheer from the crowd. Little Stevie looked livid.

'Now the home team are two points behind,' said Linton. 'If I ever saw murderous intent on someone's face it's that guy.'

On the next play Little Stevie sauntered with the bouncing ball as far as the opposition's zone-defence, feinted to go for a short pass and as an android defender put out a hand to intercept, barged heavily into the outstretched arm. The android registered a mild rocking movement, indicating minimal contact, but Little Stevie collapsed as if felled by a karate chop. He lay stretched out on the ground, writhing in apparent pain; then switched to waving his arms in the air, appealing to the referee, who took a moment to decide then whistled for an offence.

As the crowd booed the decision, Little Stevie jumped up unscathed to take his two free shots.

'Miss Tracker has herself an actor alright,' said Linton.

'This can tie up the match,' said Brady.

Little Stevie steadied himself, took aim and scored a neat basket. The clock signalled the next shot would be the last action of the game. As he prepared to throw a second time, there was a loud shriek from someone in the audience.

All eyes turned to pick out Harper, apparently oblivious to what was happening on court, lost in her own world behind darkened iSpecs.

Little Stevie lobbed the ball and missed; the ball clattering off the ring.

With the match over and the androids winning by a point, the crowd shuffled out. Once they were in the corridor, students woke up their learning buddies. As Howard Trent arrived with the ones that had just been playing, Harper turned to welcome back DAK 49: 'Hey good looking, congratulations, your side won!' She said this while exchanging looks with Little Stevie: barely suppressed rage from him, hard to believe innocence from her.

❖

Richards looked mortified. 'I have to say that was more than excruciating: sincere apologies for my daughter's appalling and unforeseen behaviour.'

'I guess we all have sons and daughters,' said Ms Chan, her comment endorsed by several nods from the others.

'*Rebel without a Cause*?' remarked Wilson. 'Won't teenagers always be the same?'

Richards relaxed a little, comforted by their show of empathy. 'On a more positive note, while my daughter has embarrassed me on a personal level, I'm actually grateful to her for helping to prove my point regarding the unreliability of human emotional intelligence.'

Macy sighed. 'OK, so what did we learn from the actual game?'

Horne stepped in positively: 'Well, we have to acknowledge these standard model androids were at a clear disadvantage from the start in their motor skills, plus they'd never played basketball before; yet incredibly they still won. I guess this was partly down to a quick mastering of the basics, but no doubt Mr Richards will be telling us it was their enhanced EI that allowed them to adapt to a changing and fluid situation?'

Richards looked pleased with the observation. 'And contrast the opposition's failings: the prime example being the player taking the final shot finding himself overwhelmed by feelings of anger, resentment, embarrassment – causing him to become flustered, lose his focus and miss. Had that been an android it would have retained a cool head.'

'So if this was a battlefield...?' said Macy, a little more impressed.

Wilson nodded. 'And there was something else we should take on board; something that might easily have gone unnoticed. When the home team lost, did we see any over the top victory celebrations from the android side?'

The group became more attentive to what Wilson was saying. 'There were no fist-bumps or punching the air, nothing to accentuate the other's side's defeat, rub their faces in it; no attempt at humiliation that might give cause for come-back, revenge, retribution. These guys won, but with one eye on the future. Might we call that emotionally intelligent thinking aimed at conflict resolution? Would it have been the same the other way around?'

❖

Entering the fringe hub, Kerry knew straightaway something was wrong: it was like one of their freeze frames – portraying division, conflict.'

'Is everything OK?' she asked.

Tania shrugged. 'We can't do the play anymore.'

'Why not?' said Kerry, her heart missing a beat.

'Because our star-crossed lovers have fallen out and aren't talking,' said Wanda.

Kerry looked at Harper, then at Little Stevie – receiving a mix of pouts and sulks from the two of them.

'Ask *her* –' said Little Stevie. 'Little Miss "I'm the centre of the universe."'

'Some people are easily offended,' replied Harper, 'especially sore losers.'

'Anyone could see how she put me off!' continued Little Stevie, incensed.

'OK, so this is about what happened at the basketball match?' said Kerry.

'You bet it is,' said Little Stevie.

'OK, I can understand that feelings got hurt. Is there any way we can remedy this?'

'You want *me* to say I was sorry?' said Harper.

'Well yes, that might help a little,' said Kerry.

Harper turned to face Little Stevie, placed her hands on her hips and offered a mealy-mouthed "sorry". It was as close to an apology as another slap in the face.

'There, see!' said Little Stevie. 'It's a joke: I'm not putting up with this kind of shit.'

'OK…' said Kerry, more determinedly, 'whatever's going on, maybe it will take a while to smooth things over, but in the meantime can we leave this disagreement at the door and get on with the play?'

'So how am I supposed to work with her after that?' the boy demanded.

Harper smirked. 'I wouldn't be fussing too much over it Romeo, maybe your kissing's as bad as your shooting.' She added, 'I'd be better off with my droid, at least they WON!'

'Hey!' said Little Stevie, verging on apoplectic. 'That's it she can find another sucker to put up with her craziness.'

'See,' said Tania. 'We've got ourselves a problem.'

Kerry couldn't help feeling deeply disappointed in Harper; it was almost as if the girl had deliberately set this row up. Part of her would dearly liked to have given the brat her marching orders, but it was very late in the day now to be re-arranging the whole play, having to ask Wanda or maybe Greta to play Juliet. It would make a complete mess of everything.

There was also Harper's father to consider – and the school. Kerry knew she had little room for manoeuvre in trying to salvage something from the situation.

'OK, it's too late to start switching everyone around. Maybe this is going to have to be part of our overall learning curve: in fact we might even see it as an opportunity?' She looked at Harper. 'You just said you'd be "better off" with one of the learning buddies?'

Harper attempted to feign a casual shrug, but it was clear from the look in her eyes she knew she'd boxed herself in.

Kerry continued, 'So I think the simplest solution would be a straight swop between Romeo and Mercutio. That's if Stevie's happy to play Romeo's friend?'

'Fine, he's got better speeches anyway,' said Little Stevie.

'And DAK 43 will play Romeo. It means of course we'll have to tweak perceptions of our hero a little: establish that as an android, Romeo has been brought up as an adopted son by Lord and Lady Capulet, the implication being perhaps that they couldn't have children themselves. It'll be something like that old movie *AI*.'

Looks spiralled around the room with everyone more immediately focused on what Harper's response would be. The girl looked uncertain about her next move, probably aware that if she backtracked now she'd lose face and it was quite possible no-one would support her this time.

For her part, Kerry was now concerned that in calling the girl's bluff as well as taking a gamble with this sudden re-interpretation of Romeo, both decisions might appear too rushed, that she'd be seen to have lost control. They might lose confidence in her and maybe back off from the whole project.

Harper's blank expression gave little away. Finally she said, 'Sure, no problem, at least the droid will have all the lines learnt.'

This time the remark was too predictable and fell flat. Little Stevie just shook his head. Besides diffusing the situation, it also let Kerry off the hook, at least for the moment.

But Omar was already thinking back as well as ahead. 'OK, so now *Romeo's* an android: will he have false memories or be free like Mercutio and the Prince?'

Kerry nodded thoughtfully. 'We can imagine Lord and Lady Montague wanted him brought up just like a regular human child, so in his case there wouldn't be a central core of pre-set memories, only his lived experience.'

'And he does know he's an android, right?' asked Wanda.

'Yes, I think we can assume that,' said Kerry.

'Hey, it all fits together with what we said before,' added Greta, already won over. 'If he was adopted as a small child maybe around age five, OK so he'll be missing all that deep down stuff from when he was a baby and a toddler, but it means he'll be just like Juliet cus she'll have memory blanks too around everything the Nurse says around that early time in *her* life.'

'So like attracts like!' said Kerry. 'Wow, that's such an astute observation; it's definitely something we should explore more.'

There was a pause as they all took a moment to catch up with where they'd got to.

'OK, that's Romeo's inner-core sorted,' said Carlos, more down to earth. 'But what about his outer body – how do we – and our audience, believe he can actually *grow*; get older?'

'Guess that'll be the same for all the other android characters,' said Tania, frowning.

Kerry picked out several bemused faces. She was feeling a little dizzy with it herself.

'No problem,' said Jing, 'it won't be long before androids have bodies that can be regularly updated: just like a kid getting new shoes as their feet grow bigger.'

'Genius!' said Chuck, caught halfway between praise and mockery.

'Why not?' said Omar. 'And they'll have faces that can be micro adjusted to show age.'

'Maybe even something close to a living skin that can stretch by itself,' added Carlos.

Tania smiled again. 'Hey, we're really piecing this thing together.'

'Yes…I think all of this can make sense within the play,'

said Kerry, hugely relieved. She checked her wristband for the time.

Chuck coughed into his fist. 'OK so now that's all sorted, what are we gonna do in the next session: hopefully not another round of nothing but talking?'

'Actually,' said Kerry, 'while I was watching the basketball game –'

Wanda groaned. 'Let's not go there again!'

'No, it's just that I was taken by the general movement and flow: the choreography. It made me think of the dancing in *West Side Story*. If our play is set in a future where there's free interaction between humans and androids, it begs the question: what kind of moves will it involve?'

'Guess we'll have to work in some robotics,' said Tania, offering an impressive demonstration.

'I love it!' said Kerry. 'But like we said about the weapons, let's use our imaginations to invent a whole new way of moving for this hypothetical future. Sure, we can include retro influences like robotics; maybe even add in some elements of 16th century dance? But hopefully it will all come out like nothing ever seen before.'

Wanda shared a look with Tania. 'Why not, it'll be fun making it up.'

Greta added: 'And like you say Miss Tracker, the learning buddies can feed in their ideas as well.'

'OK,' said Kerry, 'let's see what moves we can come up with for the next session. Hopefully we'll have lots to try out.'

As they filed out, Harper made a point of catching Kerry's eye. 'Sorry about what happened earlier, Miss Tracker. It's funny how things turn out though. Maybe it's all for the best huh?'

4

'To whom or what am I ultimately loyal?'

'Yes, AJ, that's the question Agent Linton, asked you. Let's not have any brass neck this time you old tin can.'

'Those are very mixed metaphors Mr Brady.'

'Now come on AJ,' said Brady, feigning disapproval. He turned to Linton. 'Some out there might think AJFX72 has ideas above his station. But I say, "why not" – it shows a bit of gumption.'

'And a neat line in how to avoid answering a direct question,' said Linton, less impressed. He offered the android a way back: 'OK, let's keep it to the main point. Who or what…'

AJ said, 'My primary function is to look after the school.'

'And protect it from harm?'

'Yes, that is correct,' said AJ.

'Give me some examples…'

'Dust, damp, dangerous obstacles, litter, soft-drink spills, chewing gum –'

'OK, that's enough, we get it,' said Linton. 'Let me ask you something else, coming at it another way.' The detective paused, knowing his earlier questions had merely been a way of building up to what was coming next. 'Don't you also have a duty to protect *yourself* from harm?'

'Yes,' said AJ, 'otherwise I would be of no use to either Mr Brady or the school.'

'And would that compulsion to self-protect include resisting someone trying to gain illegitimate access to your internal mechanisms – your memory?'

'Yes, I would do whatever I could to prevent that from happening.'

'Would that include physical resistance?'

'Yes Mr Linton, but only up to the point where I might be in danger of doing direct harm to a human being.'

Linton sat forward. 'So was there ever an occasion when you had to apply physical force or *action of any kind* in order to prevent someone from trying to access the secrets of your programming?' Linton paused. 'Rob Bennett for instance?'

AJ almost started to nod, but then switched to a shake of the head.

'What is that?' said Linton, 'a yes or a no?'

'I was merely considering your question, Mr Linton,' said AJ.

'Well I need a clear answer, pronto,' Linton pressed.

There was an extended silence, before the android finally answered, 'I have no actual recollection of such a thing happening.'

Linton threw his hands in the air. 'Now where did that come from? Hey that's just dandy! Most convenient: you'd certainly make a fine politician Android JFX72!' He leaned forward again. 'OK, I'd really like to know AJ: in your own words, take your time; what lengths would you go to on behalf of Mr Brady and the school?'

AJ shrugged. 'I would do whatever was required. Water the plants, put up shelves…'

'OK…what if there was a choice say between looking after the school and protecting Mr Brady?'

'My main tasks involve the school. But if there was danger to Mr Brady, I would have to see to him first.'

'Again, can you give me an example?' asked Linton, patiently.

AJ thought about it. 'I would certainly stop putting up a shelf if I saw he was having a heart attack.'

Brady chuckled. 'Thanks AJ, good to know that.'

Linton wasn't so amused. 'OK, supposing I go to take a swing at Mr Brady, right now, hit him hard on the chin: what's going to be your response AJFX 72?' He pulled an arm back, fist clenched; then in slow motion aimed a haymaker at Brady's jaw, dragging it enough to allow for an intervention.

AJ watched as Brady played his part by following the arc of the fist and leaned back as if to cushion the blow.

The two men looked at the android. This time Linton said nothing: just let the moment hang.

AJ smiled. 'You were pretending again Mr Linton. You did that once before, except on that occasion you used your gun. It's called "acting". I believe Mr Brady was too.'

Brady couldn't resist another chuckle.

Linton said, 'You've got us going in circles again AJ; all credit to you, you're one clever-assed guy. I think you *should* ask Miss Tracker for a part in the play. She could do with a fellow that can handle things like comic irony.'

'I think Miss Tracker has decided on her cast,' AJ said, innocently.

'Sure,' said Linton. 'But there's always a chance someone might, what do they say in the theatre business: "break a leg", like fall down some stairs?'

AJ expressed a frown. 'I am the school janitor Mr Linton. I'm not sure I could really spare the time…'

Linton seemed to have finished his interrogation, but suddenly he turned on a sixpence, swinging a left hook at AJ's chin – and found his wrist restrained in a vice-like grip.

Brady said, 'OK AJ…I think it's safe to let go now.'

AJ let go. 'Were you acting that time as well, Mr Linton?'

Linton gave a half-smile. 'Yes Android JFX 72, I guess I was.'

AJ took a moment then smiled too. 'You certainly had me fooled. You're the one who should be in the play Mr Linton!'

After AJ had been dismissed to continue his duties, Linton checked his wrist, realising it wasn't even sore. 'Amazing, not even a hint of a bruise.' He turned to Brady. 'So, after that dramatic interlude let's get back to earth and do a quick re-cap on something. Charles Richards has kindly given an EI upgrade to Miss Tracker's android actors, right?'

Brady nodded agreement.

'And this new software was downloaded directly by him from his company HQ? He wasn't actually there in the room with you?'

'No, for security reasons,' said Brady.

Linton rubbed his chin. 'So anytime in the past your kind benefactor could have added more up-grades if he'd wanted to, re-configured their EI settings without you or anyone else knowing anything about it?'

'No,' said Brady, emphatically. 'I had to key in a code first at my end.'

Linton's eyes narrowed. 'Unless that was just a lot of smoke and mirrors – to fool you into thinking it was necessary. You only have his word for it, right?'

Brady shrugged. 'I'm not an expert: how am I supposed to know if he was telling me the truth or not?'

Linton sat up. 'Come on, this is important Brady. If such a thing *is* possible there could be a whole bunch of potential implications relating to this hard-wired command androids have to both look out for themselves and at the same time serve the wishes of human beings who might need protecting.'

'Maybe I'm missing the point,' said Brady.

'Just supposing AJ's emotional palette was secretly enhanced to somehow include "jealousy" after all, and this was then targeted towards Rob Bennett because of his closeness to the other androids,' Linton waved his finger, 'towards wanting to remove his rival?'

Brady sighed wearily. 'Even if such a thing was possible, we've said it over a number of times: an android is hard-wired never to intentionally inflict harm on a human being –'

Linton cut in: 'Unless it's to protect other *more important* human beings?'

Brady went to say something in reply, but then decided to bite his tongue and let Linton continue.

'What if an android is somehow "persuaded" by a higher authority that it's legitimate to inflict harm on one particular human being to avoid untold damage to others who are serving some kind of noble cause and then finds itself facing a direct accusation it just can't wriggle out of, meaning someone is about to find out *their* important secret. It will have failed to protect those it serves – caused *them* harm.'

Linton snapped his fingers. 'But, there is of course a simple way through this. It temporarily overrules the normal injunction against doing physical harm, maybe goes into some kind of AI trance state to do the deed – and then, returning to "normality", it conveniently *forgets* what it's done thanks to some new failsafe feature wired into the programming. Maybe we just saw that happening – right in front of our eyes?'

Brady shook his head. 'You're obviously dumping all this fanciful stuff at Charles Richards's door.'

'I'm just letting it all stack up, that's all. You know I decided to make a formal application after all to by-pass his refusal to allow me access to AJ's hard drive?'

'And what happened?' asked Brady.

'My superiors told me in no uncertain terms to back off. So what does that say?'

Brady sighed. 'OK, if you're insinuating some sort of cover-up, that for some reason your people in Homeland are in cahoots with whatever you think Mr Richards is trying to hide, preventing you from gaining direct access to AJ – why have they kept you here, knowing full well you'll be gnawing away at their guy like a pit-bull with all these goddamn questions?'

Linton held his hands open, lost for a definite answer. 'That is indeed a mystery. Who knows, maybe my role in all this is simply to stress-test this guy, keep him under observation and report any weaknesses in the armour. Could be I share something with AJ – just being played along here like a puppet on a string.'

❖

"Critical distance?" said Charles Richards. He was checking in with Kerry to hear how the upgrades were impacting on the play.

'It's a term sometimes used to describe the theatre practise of Berthold Brecht, the German playwright and director active from the 1930's to 50's. I studied him in college; it came back to me while I was thinking through how my actors should develop their characters from an emotional point of view. I want an approach that will be equally applicable for both kids and androids.'

'I think I'm with you so far,' said Richards genially.

'The standard way into acting a part is what was once popularly known as a Method approach, linking back to the great Russian director, Stanislavsky. In a nutshell the actor tries to get inside the mind of the character he, she, or in our case "it" is playing, to see things from the character's point of view; to look at the dramatic context and ask themselves, how would I feel and act in that situation?'

'OK, so this clearly involves empathy?'

'Yes, plus imagination: often the character's situation is way beyond the actor's own life experience. They then have to find something from their own memory that comes closest to what the character might be going through.'

'Does that mean the actor tries to directly feel what the character is feeling?'

'Yes and no. Even for Stanislavsky, it's more the case an actor must understand the emotion, rather than be overtaken by it. While being fully alert to the character's motivations and desires, he she or it must also take a step back in order to retain a level of detachment.'

'OK, now I'm getting the *critical distance*,' said Richards, intrigued.

'Brecht extended this concept by placing it at the centre of his theatre practise. It was also a key part of his politics, being a committed Communist.'

Richards flinched slightly. 'You'll have to fill me in on the connection.'

'He saw parallels in theatre with what was happening in the real world with the rise of Nazism; especially the danger posed by a charismatic leader appealing to the people through their emotions while at the same time feeding them propaganda, or false facts and fake news as it's come to be called in more recent times. Brecht argued the same thing can happen on the stage when the acting is too naturalistic: the actor becomes invisible, inviting the audience to share the character's emotions directly, leaving them open to adopting a single narrative, only one interpretation of the situation which then leads on to only one ending and "solution" to the problems outlined in the story.'

'I see what you're saying. I'm impressed.'

'Brecht tried to get his actors to distance themselves from the characters they were playing by "presenting" rather than inhabiting these roles. Likewise, contrary to the usual attempt within the production to set up a seductive atmosphere – lights, music etc – lulling the audience into forgetting they were in a theatre, Brecht wanted his audience to be continually reminded this was an artificial situation –'

'I like it,' said Richards, '*artificial intelligence!*'

Kerry smiled, pleased at her unintentional pun.

'OK, I think we're on the same page with this Kerry. The term you're using is extremely useful for conceptualising how the learning buddies will operate within their new enhanced EI. Rather than saying they can now "feel" things better, it's more useful to stress how they're able to stand back and observe themselves as they act out a feeling with a certain detachment: your "critical distance" in other words. In fact it's a safety mechanism. If we applied this to an everyday context such as road rage: once you recognise what's happening and realise you don't have to be taken over by your emotions, you can resist getting mad and hitting somebody.'

'Anyway, it's good to talk this through,' said Kerry.

Richards smiled. 'I guess it's useful for both of us to be able to articulate how the androids are operating.' He adjusted his tone slightly: 'And how's my daughter getting along? Maybe I shouldn't ask, it's *her* space after all, but I have to say I was concerned you might have had some fallout after that unfortunate incident during the basketball game.'

'Yes…we did,' said Kerry, 'there was some initial falling out; but I'm glad to say we managed to weather that particular storm.'

Richards returned to being upbeat: 'Anyway, who knows, could be the whole thing was simply about them getting into character; maybe putting in a little of that critical distance? Hell, maybe they're more dedicated and professional than we give them credit for!'

Kerry smiled back awkwardly, conscious she was keeping something back.

Richards misread the signal. 'OK, I know I'm indulging myself here. I won't hold you up any longer. I'm aware that the clock is ticking on this. Well good luck, Kerry. Keep me informed and let me know if I can do anything more to help.'

Kerry dimmed the globe. Overall she felt good about the conversation, but guilty nonetheless at being economical with the truth. She wasn't exactly sure why she'd not told him about the character switch, what was on the face of it a positive development – one of his protégées being handed one of the star parts. On the other hand, it was *his* daughter that would be playing opposite an android Romeo...

5

Greta frowned into the girls' bathroom mirror as she inspected her face.

Gaia stood beside her, looking at her own reflection; more bemused than critical.

'You've got a hell of a lot to learn Honey-babe,' said Greta. She took out a lipstick and applied a fresh gloss before passing it to her companion who looked at the object hesitantly.

'OK, maybe nurses didn't wear lipstick in the 16th Century, but our play is set in the future right?'

Gaia offered a tentative nod.

Greta continued: 'And if we're seriously thinking about getting into character, it's good you get a general sense of how women look at themselves and think about their image and all that other ridiculous female stuff.'

Gaia raised what would have been an eyebrow had she possessed one.

Greta laughed: 'Hey...maybe you don't approve of make-up; our Nurse is a feminist!'

Gaia looked doubtful.

'I guess she *is* pretty outspoken and liberated in her

own way. Anyway, might be fun to try this, even once? Call it general research.'

Gaia gave way and applied the lipstick, trying to copy the way Greta had rolled her lips.

The door opened and another girl walked in, taking up her place at the mirror. 'Hi there!' she said, starting to top up her eye-shadow.

Greta winked at Gaia's reflection in the mirror.

Gaia's reflection winked back.

The new girl said: 'She's got the new upgrade, right? After the basketball match it's all around the grapevine how the ones in the drama group are back to how they were before?'

'Except it's even better than last time,' said Greta, aiming another wink at Gaia.

'Could be all our droids will be getting the same,' the other girl said, hopefully.

'Maybe this play we're doing is like a trial run,' said Greta. 'You'd better be giving us all your support on the night.'

'Sure, I'll be there cheering along with everyone else.' The girl offered a two-handed peace sign before she left.

Greta grinned into the mirror: 'So, it's still *you*?'

'It's still *me*,' said the android.

'Still *us*,' they said together.

With the whole space to themselves Greta and Gaia started to practise their dance moves.

❖

'Before we get into the dancing,' said Kerry, 'because this is all about people coming together on a social occasion, I quickly want to identify the different relationships within the play. We have boy-girl, mother-daughter, father-daughter, father-son, mother-son, husband-wife, girl-nurse…what else?'

'Girl-girl: boy-boy?' Wanda volunteered.

'Sadly there isn't much girl-girl,' said Kerry, 'Juliet lives in something of a bubble; her closest "girlfriend" is probably the Nurse. The only other young female who gets a mention is Rosaline, but we never get to meet her. On the other hand, boy-boy relationships *are* central to the play: in the all-male gang thing and the individual friendships Romeo has with his friends, most notably with Mercutio.'

'And do you think the two of them are maybe more than just *friends,* Miss Tracker?' asked Tania, with a quizzical look.

'Well, certainly with Mercutio there's enough in what he says to suggest his feelings quite probably go beyond platonic affection.'

'You mean he's gay!' said Omar. 'Call it like it is Miss, we're not in kindergarten.'

'Yeah, in one of those movies we watched he was black and gay,' said Chuck. *"Queen Mab is here!"* he pronounced, trying to camp it up. He got no response from the others; even Little Stevie just rolled his eyes.

Tania screwed up her face, continuing her train of thought: 'Guess it might be a challenge for an android to understand that kind of thing?' She let her eyes flit for a moment in the direction of Gaia. 'Maybe it helps if it's kind of well, leaning in that direction already?'

Chuck released a guffaw.

'I don't see why there should be any problem,' said Kerry, 'especially with the new software.' She paused to let them know she was taking the question seriously. 'Besides being gender-neutral, I'm pretty sure the LBs don't have any built-in sexual orientation. They do of course understand the term "gay", but obviously they can't actually *feel* what it means.'

'So even after the upgrade they still don't really have any feelings of their own,' said Wanda, sounding half-disappointed.

Greta couldn't hold herself back any longer: 'It's more like they're just not allowed to *own* their emotions. But they can still *show* feelings – because they know how *we* feel, through what we show *them*.' She shared a look of solidarity with Gaia.

Chuck groaned. 'Hey, when are we starting this session? Little Stevie and me have been working our asses off on some cute moves.'

'My fault as always,' said Kerry, cheerfully. 'OK, enough of the talking, let's dance!'

❖

'What is *that* they're doing?' said Linton, looking over Brady's shoulder.

'Good question,' said Brady. 'A mix of robot-punk, hip-hop, eco-warrior, the Chubby Checker Twist and maybe throw in some old-time Texas line-dancing.'

Linton winced. 'Wouldn't like to try it myself; looks dangerous.'

Brady eased back into his chair. 'These are the two

feuding tribes right. Maybe they get to fight each other with their dance moves.'

Linton stroked his chin. 'Could be that's what happened with poor Rob Bennett. His two left feet got in a tangle when an android assassin stood on his toe.'

Brady sighed despairingly. 'You're just not giving up on that.'

'All options have to remain open,' affirmed Linton, but with little enthusiasm this time. Brady watched a bit more of the action. 'You have to admit it's impressive the way they're all working together, even bold Harper Richards: I have to keep pinching myself.'

Linton nodded. 'And everything seems to be working out fine with the androids and their upgrade.'

'That's exactly what I want to hear. I'm starting to get calls from the media: along with Charles Richards and his wife it looks we'll have the whole world in attendance on the night.'

❖

'Wow, that's so amazing!' Kerry declared as she clapped along to the rhythm of one of the dances they'd just put together. 'We'll definitely have this in the party scene; it'll be even more startling with the masks.' She paused, thinking. 'I know this is stealing from *West Side Story*, but maybe there could even be a hint of it in the opening scene when the two sides meet and fight?'

'So it's a kind of dance, as they circle round each other?' said Carlos.

'Exactly; but maybe we'll keep it a little more subtle,

closer to a subliminal thing for the audience.'

Chuck was immediately into the idea: 'We could use it again for the duel!'

'Why not!' said Kerry. 'A kind of motif offering something ritualistic and a way to slow those action sequences down. Thank you so much everyone, perfect!'

'We're doing great aren't we?' said Tania. 'I hope you're passing all of this on to Mr Brady, putting in a word for us right?'

'I can tell you now Mr Brady is already very impressed,' said Kerry. 'OK, to end this session I want to do a short mirroring exercise to explore the learning buddies' new software a little more.'

'We did something like this before,' said Jing.

'We did. But this time I don't want you partnering your own learning buddy.'

'Why is that Miss Tracker?' asked Greta.

'It's an exercise in "critical distancing" – which will work best if you're paired with a stranger as it were: don't worry, it'll become clear once we get started.'

6

From that point on, with just around four weeks left to go, the formal rehearsal period began in earnest as they worked methodically through the scenes, sorting out the lines and actions while continuing to explore character and the underlying themes within the play. Things moved along smoothly and Kerry thanked her goddess, namely "the process" for helping prepare the way, bringing her teenage gang along with her thus far.

Several moments stood out. In one rehearsal they reflected on attitudes to girls and boys in Shakespeare's time, making comparisons with their own world. Greta remembered Harper and DAK 49's double act at the cabaret and suggested the title of the play *should* be changed to "*Juliet and Romeo*". The other girls backed her up, which set Chuck and Little Stevie off trying to defend the status quo. Kerry tried to be diplomatic in suggesting it might fit in with their adventurous interpretation of the play?

There was a call for a vote and surprisingly perhaps Omar, Carlos and Jing sided with the girls.

So the play became *Juliet & Romeo*.

Then Carlos proposed updating the title to give it a more technological feel, especially given their version was now going to be set in the future. Omar agreed, but remembered how someone else had suggested that people in the future might still be heavily into retro. So it morphed again to become *Jules & Rom* – with DAK 43 acquiring the affectionate moniker "CD-Rom".

Kerry did meet resistance when saying they'd be using a minimal set and to forget about stagehands coming onto the stage to move stuff around, they'd be doing everything themselves in character, the whole thing stylised. Some of the kids were a bit miffed, having anticipated other students or learning buddies being brought in to do those menial tasks. But when she got them to try it out, moving props themselves between scenes along with the music, they fell into it, accepting how it made the whole thing move along snappier.

The music was another journey of discovery. They recalled the songs in *West Side Story* and the way popular numbers were inserted into the Baz Luhrmann movie, but Kerry argued they should approach it the same way as the dancing: how it would be far more interesting if they devised their own music, tried to imagine what this future time might *sound* like. And they were blessed with having a number of musicians in the group: Omar played guitar, (a bit rusty but willing to give it a go) Carlos (messed around with) various kinds of percussion, Wanda played piano (grade nine) and Greta was teaching herself tenor-saxophone.

Everyone contributed towards coming up with original melodies, chord progressions and beats: even non-musicians could call out random notes and their learning buddies were able to play it back with the sound of any instrument.

They also had to consider costume. 'What are we all going to wear?' asked Tania. 'What'll people look like in this future?'

Everyone brought in magazines and all kinds of esoteric stuff from the Web showing fashion forecasts. Some wanted to give the play a shiny metallic, outer-spacey feel, with clothes made out of silver foil; others argued for a more earthbound dystopian design based on retro-styles and recycled materials. All agreed however that with both options it could look clichéd.

Jing came up with the idea that in this future time there might be a reaction against how retro offered up such a mix-up of styles, a hankering instead for some kind of uniform simplicity like the simple tunic and trousers many south-east Asian peasant farmers still wore; maybe it could include a belt? The other boys liked the image of something that leaned towards a martial arts look. The girls went along with the idea so long as they could add their own amendments: servants and other low status characters might wear a simple outfit, but the upper echelons could allow themselves more personal touches – raised shoulder wings, pleats in their tunics. Kerry was happy to have found something that would be economical, as well as relatively easy to design. Meera and Inez offered to help make the costumes.

The play's director was most impressed with how they were all working as a team. At the same time she felt she was getting to know them a little better as individuals, even if she could never really be sure what was ticking away inside their young minds and hearts. For that matter, did they have any idea what was going on inside her?

Kerry reflected on how it wasn't all that different in the staffroom. What did she really know about Inez Martinez, Meera Patel, or Howard Trent? How much of their inner-selves did anyone reveal: probably very little except during bouts of stress or excitement, when the mask momentarily fell. With Jim Brady she'd had some meaningful conversations around the play, but on a personal level he too remained little more than a stranger.

Within her troop, some appeared more transparent than others. Of the boys, Chuck's nature was the most "what you see is what you get" – wearing what was often a juvenile self on his sleeve. But in some ways this was deceptive, Kerry was coming to appreciate he used this to mask his intelligence and that there was a lot more to him.

Little Stevie was temperamental and behind the surface swagger, a little shy; a sort of extrovert-introvert, trying to live up to some kind of projected image of himself. Despite having a touchy side he was generally good-humoured and a positive influence in the group.

Jing, Omar and Carlos were all easy-going: while saying little in the early stages, they'd always been cooperative and willing to go with the flow. Each came more into his own as the project progressed and it occurred to Kerry they might even have been mistakenly tagged as accomplices in the assault on Mr Milton: victims of a group sanction. But if that had resulted in them being sent to her to take part in the play, she was happy to view it as a kind act of fate.

Amongst the girls, Tania had been the most reticent in pushing for a leading role in the play. Kerry sensed a lack of confidence around acting, but when the girl danced almost another self appeared: she could really move her body, a couple of times the whole cast stopped to watch and applaud. Tania helped work out some great choreography for the movement sequences.

Wanda was super-smart and very astute. She had a strong sense of herself as a person of colour. She offered a continuing thoughtful presence and more than anyone else had held them all together in difficult moments. On the other hand, she was well able to let her hair down when she wanted to.

While Greta was still considered a "weirdo" within the wider student population, inside this little band she'd now been more or less accepted. She was always happy to speak out and own her space. Her close relationship with Gaia embraced something way beyond what Kerry could assimilate. Clearly the girl had managed to create a close bond of some sort even before the EI upgrade. Greta spoke to Gaia like the android was her equal; she was unashamedly fond of her.

Harper was by far the hardest to read: yes, there were fleeting glimpses into what was going on beneath the surface, but Kerry could never be sure she wasn't projecting her own interpretations. Since the row with Little Stevie and the resulting character changes, the girl had noticeably parked her brat self, had in fact become remarkably positive within the group. OK, she was still protective of her status, but that was hardly unusual for a teenager, never mind an actress. More to the point she'd become highly protective of the play and keen on promoting it. As the performance date got closer she threw her energy into putting up posts and spreading the word.

The newly enhanced learning buddies were continually fascinating. Mingling with their flesh and blood compatriots during the scenes, they became less and less differentiated. If Greta said something affectionate, Gaia responded with a look that was uncannily close to human; even when Greta said something complimentary about someone else, the android still smiled, although with a subtly different expression. And while they appeared not to own negative feelings such as jealousy, these darker emotions were clearly available to them within the context of the play. Kerry was witness to how adept they were now at switching between actor and character, truth and fiction.

There were moments when she witnessed her human cast watching appreciatively as one of the learning buddies delivered a line or added a movement. In terms of stagecraft they had an instinct for doing the right thing, especially the way they often paused and allowed time for a moment to breathe. She thought again about her conversation with Richards concerning critical distance; what Brecht had called his "alienation technique" – an elusive concept that even in his own day, actors had struggled to fully grasp.

Kerry had never worked with androids quite like this before, but nonetheless it held an odd familiarity. Trying to put a finger on it she recalled some teaching practise she'd done while at college, working in a centre for children who were visually impaired. It had presented a real challenge for her at the time and opened her mind to some of the assumptions she'd brought in with her. Her abiding memory was the way they'd explored everything through sound and particularly touch; there'd been a constant movement of hands feeling the air, boundaries and surfaces. One child was fascinated with the contours of Kerry's face; at first she'd felt uncomfortable, but then found herself giving in and enjoying being explored and discovered.

In contrast with those children, her android actors had everything you could want in the sensory department, with absolute confidence in how they occupied space. Yet it was a paradox of sorts, like they'd been around for a very long time – old hands full of life's experiences – but at the same time possessing an almost child-like quality to their actions, as if they were just starting out. It was strange to think they'd internalised knowledge a human being might take several lifetimes to acquire – and still managed to act like innocents with no baggage or agendas; entering each day blind as it were to their futures.

One immediate bonus was how they instantly knew their lines, never to be forgotten. Their total commitment was infectious and the kids now saw them as a support rather than being annoying: even Chuck was prompted to offer a few jokey backhanded compliments. Overall it meant Kerry was able to speed up the line-learning, giving her more time to work on character development and tease out deeper meaning and subtext.

As a demonstration of the positive use of AI in the school it was already a success. She was confident Jim Brady and Charles Richards would be pleased with how things had gone so far; their faith in her and the group amply rewarded.

C harles Richards felt upbeat if a little apprehensive. This time the four members of the military task force were coming to him.

Allied Robotics was housed in a building the size of an airport terminal. In one hangar various types of android bodies were assembled, mostly by other robots, parts being added piecemeal until, finally brought to life, they walked the last few steps unaided to where hundreds were already waiting in line.

In a second area, human technicians and programmers walked and talked individual models through a variety of tests: checking motor skills, balance, responses to a wide range of stimuli. Some units did heavy lifting while others carried out delicate procedures like threading needles with cotton which required sensitivity and skilled eye-hand combinations.

A few technicians sat down with their subjects, asking questions and recording the answers; some of these interchanges came across as relaxed conversations, with the observers leaning back casually in chairs, smiling, drinking coffee.

It was much like a cafe area in the arrivals or departure lounge of an airport: people and androids catching up and sharing their news.

In some instances a conversation involved two androids and one technician, no doubt testing the potential for cross-lines and misunderstanding: the subtle nuances of three-way communication.

Some androids sat in pairs talking eyeball to eyeball, apparently removed from any human presence, until on closer inspection a technician could be seen eavesdropping. Despite the veneer of informality, it was clear this was a highly controlled environment.

Richards led his entourage around the rim of the gangway. 'As you can see, these units are being prepared to fulfil multiple functions, depending on their future roles; each software programme will relate specifically to duties such as traffic cop, surgeon, gardener, childminder, teacher, hospital porter or whatever the calling might be. As you can see, our trademark body shape is much in evidence but there are also numerous variations to dovetail with specialist tasks.'

'Can you pick out some examples?' said Monica Chan.

Richards pointed to one extremely sleek version being put through its paces. 'That one over there has been designed to go into very narrow spaces: caves, pot holes, drains, even collapsed buildings. It has an exceptionally flexible torso, designed to manoeuvre around tight bends.' He picked out a few more examples: 'Others are extra heavy, or ultra-light. Some are absolutely water-proof.'

'Could that be our new line of Navy Seals?' Admiral Horne mused, showing immediate interest.

Tim Wilson pointed: 'What are those guys doing over there – just sitting talking to their technicians?'

Richards smiled. 'Some androids require a high level of social skills: those that might end up being a nurse, teacher, play worker, even a secretary. Think of the nuanced behaviour expected from any android where diplomacy and tact is involved.'

Macy scanned the room. 'So where do you keep those guys we've done so much talking about – our Peacemakers? I hope they're stashed away somewhere safe?'

Richards nodded. 'You can see we have a certain level of visible security, but there's a lot more going on behind that. Clearly any competitor would be more than happy to be a fly on our wall, eavesdrop. As well as asking visitors to leave all potential recording devices at the door, we have a state of the art disablement field as back-up. Our security is air-tight, as far as we know we haven't been compromised as yet.'

He gestured for the group to follow along the gangway. 'OK – so our guys who are going to save the world are kept in a separate hanger. Only I have the entry code: no-one goes in there without me keying it in. I want you to be assured these units cannot be accessed without my knowledge.'

'So our future combat troops are safe in your hands, until we get *our* hands on them,' said Wilson.

'That's correct,' Richards replied.

'Unless this is all just an elaborate charade and you're secretly working for the other side?' Horne said it as a joke but with a straight face.

Richards smiled. 'Do we know who or what "the other side" is anymore? Not so long ago it was the Russians,

North Koreans – China, Iran; even the European Union: it used to be so simple. Now you wouldn't know who it is: we're not really even talking about countries.'

'A fair point,' said Wilson. 'Once upon a time war was about rivalries between kings and queens and emperors; heads of state – now it's more a case of the stock market deciding who's going to be enemies.'

'So, let's go in,' Richards declared, swiping the security patch with a medallion hanging around his neck, adding his name as voice recognition.

As far as the eye could see, standing in squadron formation, were row upon row of androids with the same body shape.

General Macy looked initially impressed, but then doubtful. 'Individually they don't look that scary.'

Admiral Horne agreed. 'I guess we were still expecting something along the lines of Iron Man or Mr Indestructible – even the Terminator?'

'And that, ladies and gentlemen underlines a key point,' replied Richards. 'The aim is for them *not* to be scary. Yes, we want them to have real authority, but of the kind which can only be built on trust. People have to believe that these guys are firm but fair.' He paused to let this sink in. 'But don't think for a minute that undermines their capability to hold their ground. They have a near indestructible body casing that is heat resistant and waterproof; they can hop six feet in the air or be dropped from a helicopter without damage.

'And yes, they can of course fight if necessary, with access to every martial art going. These guys can crawl through mud and wade through water and fire; then disable an attacker – all without blinking an eye.'

Admiral Horne threw Macy a wink. 'Yes, Richards, but can they whistle? You know, for signalling: Morse-code perhaps.'

'Better than any canary, Admiral,' said Richards confidently.

'And on top of all that, they have your coup de grace: your enhanced emotional intelligence,' said Wilson.

'It's the key factor: otherwise these guys are essentially just efficient fighters,' said Ms Chan.

Horne frowned. 'But how can we be absolutely sure our competitors haven't somehow piggy-backed on all this; stolen our secrets? What if they do have something similar in the pipeline?'

Ms Chan said: 'From our intelligence we believe no one else is quite there as yet; but it's a limited window.'

'Anyway, who knows, maybe handing over our secrets wouldn't be such a bad thing in itself?' said Wilson, taking everyone by surprise.

All eyes turned to him as if he'd committed a treasonable act.

The Defence Secretary held his hands up in self-defence: 'Let's remember the immediate result of us achieving such a critical advantage will be to seriously raise the fear threshold for those we oppose. If we appear to have gained the upper hand, the last thing we'd want is to provoke a hasty response, make them trigger happy with whatever weaponry they do possess – nuclear, chemical, biological?'

Horne frowned. 'Doesn't that just take us back to everyone being equally matched: Mutually Assured Destruction?'

Before Wilson could respond, General Macy let loose with some pent up outrage: 'Well if that's where we're going, why bother with all this hush-hush bullshit; let's take down that firewall and hand over all our secrets right now!'

'Maybe *they* won't be quite so generous when they've got their noses in front,' said Horne acidly.

'Anyway,' said Wilson, 'I was only offering it as a thought. Even if anything was ever officially to happen along those lines it would clearly have to be reciprocal and encompass a focused and choreographed release of information.'

Richards nodded agreement. 'Yes, no one wants freewheeling misguided zealots giving up our secrets to just everyone and anyone.'

❖

Jim Brady spent a good deal of his time in those final weeks fielding calls from various anti-AI campaign groups like the PBA, although there were a few voices coming from other perspectives praising what they were trying to do in the school. On a personal level he could easily sympathise with the many unemployed teachers out there protesting, imagining how he'd feel if his own hot seat was taken over by an android version of himself.

At the other end of the spectrum were the android-rights groups like the ARSN; still confined mostly to the fringes, but gaining traction all the time. It hadn't been that long since an orang-utan had won a court case awarding it legal status as an honorary "non-human person" so maybe it was just a matter of time before androids also achieved some level of acceptance as "new citizens". The irony wasn't lost on Brady that by promoting a benevolent view of AI, the play might become a victim of its own success and invite a sting in the tail: android sympathisers might soon insist that "acting" like any other employment should involve wages and regulation of work conditions. Brady could even imagine a scenario where janitor AJ downed tools and led the rest of the android staff in a demand to join a trade union.

Still by far the biggest existential fear for most people was a future society run totally by and for androids. Probably the clinching moment would be their full takeover of the global stock market. This institution was of course already nominally controlled by AI machines in the form of computer algorithms: it didn't take a huge leap of the imagination to envisage just one more giant step for robot-kind.

It was enough to force a decent hard working ex-comedian to drink, Brady mused. But somehow he was managing to get by on herb teas, some of them now being supplied by his new pal Floyd Linton, plus the occasional double espresso when things got too stressful.

Thinking now about Linton, Brady mused on how little he'd seen of him in the last while.

❖

Special Agent Floyd Linton was in love. At least, that's what it felt like to him. By now he was aware that it wasn't so much with Rob Bennett's sister Elizabeth – he was sober and realistic enough to realise this was happening at the level of an intoxicating daydream – more to do with a whole new vista she appeared to have opened up.

In his last communication with his superiors he'd asked how long this current deployment was going to last and been told to sit tight just a little while longer until the end of term. Connecting this with Charles Richards's growing interest in the drama production, Linton could only assume the sub-text meant until after open day had passed off safely? He'd suspected for a while that the ex-governor might have influence with Homeland: it could even be the detective had been kept there all along simply as additional security for the man's valuable android acting troop. But that had to be some stretch of logic; surely if there was any potential danger they could come up with more efficient ways to ensure their protection?

Anyway, this was still all idle conjecture as long as communication with his bosses remained one-way traffic. Clearly they were content to have him supplying them with reports and updates and just hanging in, close to whatever may or may not be about to transpire.

So he'd finally given in. Yes he'd still be here, or hereabouts, not too far from the action, if there was going to be any. He wouldn't be too far away…

❖

In those last few weeks Android JFX72 was busier than ever. If such a thing was possible the janitor was even more industrious when it came to ensuring everything in the school would be shipshape and ready for the big occasion. Floors and walls were cleaned with what seemed like almost religious devotion.

'Atoning for one's sins?' Jim Brady quipped on one occasion, watching AJ apply floor polish to a surface you could already see your reflection in. The android merely smiled back and continued to shine away.

One small task involved periodic replenishing of the drink containers in the fringe hub. Entering the group's latest rehearsal, the android took a moment to observe how they were progressing with the play and couldn't help noting two key casting changes, one of which involved the part of Romeo, now apparently being played by one of the learning buddies. AJ detached and re-attached the water containers while he checked again to make sure he wasn't mistaken.

❖

With only two weeks to go before opening night, Jim Brady called Kerry to come and see him urgently. Arriving in his office she was surprised to find Charles Richards there, along with Harper.

Brady arched his eyebrows, indicating this wasn't his doing.

Richards was cordial, but with a concerned look on his face.

'Has something happened?' asked Kerry.

'Mr Richards has been made aware of some recent casting changes in the play?' said Brady, still looking somewhat removed from what was happening.

Kerry looked at Harper who sent back a "don't look at me" shrug of the shoulders.

'Please,' said Richards inviting Kerry to sit, while he remained standing himself, along with Brady. Harper plonked herself down in the vacant barber's chair, turning her back to them.

Richards said: 'It transpires that following what I now understand to be a complete falling out between the two leads, the part of Romeo was transferred to one of the learning buddies?' He said it as if this signalled the end of the world.

'Yes,' said Kerry. 'At the time it was the best way to minimise disruption to the group.'

Richards folded his arms. 'OK, you know I'm fully behind you using the learning buddies in the play, by now that goes without saying. And I'm also supportive regarding the futuristic setting, even though we might be walking a bit of a tightrope presenting androids that have risen right to the top of the social ladder.' Before continuing he stole a glance at Harper's scowling reflection staring back out of the mirror facing the barber's chair. 'However, there may be those who'll draw the line when it comes to a human girl falling in love with an android: they might not accept she would first of all – and even if they do, still react strongly against it. I don't want to throw away hard-won good will, invite unnecessary controversy and jeopardise the whole project over one element. Let me make it clear this has nothing to do with my own daughter being involved.'

Harper rolled her eyes in the mirror.

'What will the audience think when they kiss?' said Richards, glancing again awkwardly at his daughter's reflection.

Harper finally spun the chair around to deliver a scathing response. 'It's a play, Father. You know – like, pretend duh?'

Richards flinched slightly and knowing she'd scored a hit, Harper added: 'I don't recall you kicking up such a fuss that time I played Sandy in *Grease* and had to get very personal with a boy you'd always said was a complete louse.'

'That was different and you know it,' said her father.

'Is it?' said Harper. 'As far as I can see it involves the same kind of make-believe.'

Richards released a world-weary sigh. 'Is there some way around this Miss Tracker?'

Kerry shrugged. 'Not without undoing all our good work, as well as undermining the integrity of the whole process by reversing a decision that won everyone's agreement and which got us through a very precarious moment. By now they're all well attached to their roles, it would certainly have a very negative impact to switch someone else to play Romeo again at this stage. To be honest, apart from Little Stevie none of the other boys would be able for it. We might also take note of how DAK 43 is actually handling the part exceptionally well.'

As Richards was digesting this last point, Kerry continued, 'Responding directly to your concern, I'm confident the audience will get the bigger picture and see this for what it is: a humble school play that happens to have young people and androids working together, playing their respective parts in an ensemble production.'

Richards glanced at Brady, then turned back to face Kerry. 'What if your Principal was to have a talk with the boy concerned, I know his parents are ambitious, he might be persuaded to change his mind.'

Kerry's eyes flitted around the room, taking in the calendar on the wall now showing July with Jim Morrison of the Doors staring back at her. Their song "*The End*" came to mind. She felt an impulse in her gut to just walk away in protest; clearly this was emotional blackmail if not outright bullying. On the other hand this wouldn't be the first time she'd been forced into making last minute changes to a play; usually it happened when an actor got sick or had an accident and there was no choice but to bite the bullet and somehow pull something out of the hat. On those occasions she was conscious how this ended up reflecting unfairly on her personally as the director, with everyone forced to adapt at such a late stage everything inevitably looked under-rehearsed, the flaws showing through. Kerry gave an inward sigh: at the end of the day it was probably only ego that took a lasting hit, with even an outright embarrassment a home audience still clapped politely and supported the overall endeavour. Yes, it was only another school play after all.

Harper gave a little cough. 'Ah hum, I see no one is going to ask me how I feel about all this.' She turned to aim full venom at her father: 'Am I simply to be sacrificed along with the play; just to suit your own ambitions, *as always*?' Before he could answer she turned to Kerry, 'I was just thinking there of another old play you and Miss Angelou talked about recently in English, the one about some king of the ancient Greeks who wanted to go off and fight a war? There's a wooden horse involved at some point if I remember the story right.'

Seeing her father's face freeze for a moment, she continued on. 'Anyway, this king has a big problem: there's no wind for the ship's sails, so the army has to sit around for weeks, all his soldiers getting restless and agitated. He assumes the gods are behind it, this stalling of his ambitions plans, so he consults the fortune teller or whatever they called them back then...'

'The oracle,' said Kerry.

'Yep, that's it, thank you. So this oracle says to the King: "There will be no wind for your ships unless you sacrifice your own daughter." What was her name again, Miss Tracker?'

'Iphigenia,' said Kerry.

'That's her. She just has to be killed, to appease these, so called "gods". And even when her own mother pleads with him to save their daughter's life, he goes ahead. She's sacrificed, just so they can go off to fight another stupid war!'

'You know that I'm against war,' said Richards.

Harper shrugged. 'Sure. Anyway, maybe I'll get to play the lead if you ever decide to do that Greek play, huh Miss Tracker. I'll be well able for that part if it ever comes around.' She finally came to a halt, caught between anger and suppressed tears.

Richards flinched. 'Harper, I'm sorry you feel like this –'

Harper raised her hand: 'Please Father, enough, just do the right thing and let the play go ahead as is. And when you attend on opening night, I want you there close to the front so the world will see how you fully support your daughter: so when she kisses her robot Romeo they'll give her the benefit of the doubt. They'll say she's only doing that because it's part of the play and because she's a good actress. Along with you they'll be impressed and say "this girl really has something to offer". Alternatively you can announce to the school and the rest of the world that the whole thing is off, your own daughter has thrown a tantrum because she resents being stuck here, hates having to be around your scary droids. Oh, I can see the reports: android manufacturer's daughter this and ex-Governor's daughter that –'

'OK, that's enough,' said Richards, putting a final stop to it. He looked first to Brady, and then to Kerry. 'For the sake of the production and the school we'll stick with what we have.' Before turning to leave he added: 'Good luck Miss Tracker. You have my full support. We'll all be there on the night cheering you on.'

ACT FIVE

"Now the two hours' traffic of our stage..."

A nd so finally it comes to fruition: after all the hard work learning lines, nailing down of movement sequences, tying up of loose ends – the opening night of *Jules & Rom*. Everyone's there: friends, fellow pupils, parents, brothers and sisters, grandparents; plus Jim Brady along with all the other teaching staff. Inez and Meera have ensured their android colleagues are dressed up for the occasion – Miss Hideko stands out in a traditional kimono, the gold medal exchanged for a cherry blossom in her hair. An extra special effort has been made with Mr Wilde who is sporting his namesake's iconic flowing cape and broad-brimmed hat. 'Be sure to take that off your head once you're seated,' says Inez. 'Don't worry, you'll still stand out,' Meera adds genially.

And yes, Kerry Tracker has kept her promise: Android JFX72 is there too, seated in row five next to the Principal.

Kerry herself is up in the lighting box, there in case she has to abandon preset cues, improvise the changes manually. Looking down into the auditorium she feels so far away from the stage. There's nothing she can do now to help her cast, if anything goes wrong it's up to them to fix it. She can see TV cameras, adding to her nerves. No doubt there will be any number of mobile devices hidden away in pockets and handbags – the production will be up on social media in no time.

Special Agent Floyd Linton is sitting half-way back, both on and off-duty. He assumes one way or another it will be the final night of his watch. Next to him is Elizabeth; looking a little lost amidst the venue's painful associations. She must be conscious of how much Rob would have wanted to be here to see this. Linton offers a comforting smile, but his mind is half-distracted by something that happened only a moment earlier just as they were queuing up outside waiting to come into the auditorium.

Despite being dressed up in his evening tux, AJ had been called back into janitor mode to deal with a liquid spill. Linton had watched with interest as the android carefully cordoned off that section of the floor, placing a sign saying, "SLIPPERY SURFACE" before cleaning up the mess and applying a quick drying agent. A minute later the floor was deemed safe. After this innocuous interlude the protective barrier was removed and AJ returned to being a guest at the show.

The detective is now racking his brains trying to remember if he'd ever used the description, "slippery customer" in reference to AJ. He pictures the scene at the top of the stairs from which Rob Bennett hurtled to his death. Linton's also trying to recall the precise words he'd used when interrogating the android: something along the lines of, "had AJ *pushed* or *manhandled* the teacher?" The words, "*by chance*" are echoing too somewhere.

❖

Charles and Sophia Richards enter accompanied by a surprise guest. At the last minute General Macy had been in touch asking for a ticket saying maybe he could do with a trip to the theatre after all, broaden his horizons? Richards's immediate guess was the task force had delegated Macy to do this. There hadn't been any news since their visit to see his production line so it could even be they were viewing this as a final test for his proposal. He'd calmed down since the showdown with Harper and told himself to sit back and enjoy the evening, but now with Macy there apparently ready to give the thumbs up or thumbs down, he's back on full alert. It's likely the show is being relayed back to the rest of the group watching in another venue.

Macy is dressed in civvies for anonymity, but despite the informal attire, Linton recognises the four-star army general when the man takes his seat next to Mr and Mrs Richards. Most of the detective's hunches appear to be confirmed as he joins up the final dots connecting AJ and Charles Richards with the military, along with Rob Bennett's presence at the DARPA weapons conference. It's now Linton's sure guess that the teacher must have been a threat to some kind of high-level military project and strategically "removed".

Linton looks over to where AJ is sitting next to Brady, as another implication hits home. If the android had indeed played the part of an assassin in this real-life drama and then for no good reason been relieved of its duties and sent back to company headquarters, this would have inevitably drawn suspicion, so it had to remain in situ. But that begged further questions regarding its "mental state" afterwards? Was it even cognisant of what it had done; couldn't the same quasi-emotional buttons be pressed again, *randomly* this time? These uncertainties would surely have presented an unacceptable risk to both students and staff; so maybe *that's* why the detective had been asked to hang around keeping a watchful eye, reporting dutifully back to his superiors, enabling them to make a continuous assessment of the android's state of mind.

❖

Lights up on an almost bare stage: perhaps an immediate disappointment for anyone hoping for a lavish set depicting 16th century Verona.

But then, seeping in like an aural fog, music from another time, from the future. A strange new world, although certain key elements are immediately recognisable: the beating throb of the streets; the driving pulse of male energy, volatile and dangerous.

Boastful banter from offstage – before two rival groups of young men enter from either side. Or, are they "men"? There's a noticeable intake of breath from the audience with the realisation these are androids *acting* like men. It's not a total surprise: rumours have been doing the rounds, participation by the learning buddies had been flagged; and yet…

The dialogue reveals them to be servants of two grand and influential families, the Montagues and Capulets. They begin provoking one another: pointing, mocking –

"Do you bite your thumb at me Sir?"
"I do bite my thumb at you Sir!"

Now they draw out long daggers, weapons of choice seemingly for these mean streets of the future; echoing the current retro obsessed times. The two groups circle in slow motion, cat and mouse; each feint with the blades getting closer as they tease and goad, inviting the other side to go that little bit too far...

Despite the tensions on stage, the audience settles, reassured by the familiar. Heady youth yes, violence yes, boys will be boys, yes: this is simply what males do, have always done since time immemorial. Next to him, Richards's military guest visibly relaxes.

Now two human actors appear on stage: Jing playing Benvolio of the Montague clan and Chuck as Tybalt from the Capulet side; these youthful figures turn out to be masters to their squabbling subordinates.

But this aura of superiority is immediately undermined when Benvolio, in an attempt to play the peacemaker, unwisely draws his sword – and Tybalt in turn brandishes his own weapon, making the volatile atmosphere rise up a notch.

"Turn thee Benvolio, look upon thy death," declares Tybalt.

"I do but keep the peace, put up thy sword," Benvolio protests.

"What, drawn and talk of peace?" sneers Tybalt in return.

Richards sneaks another glance at Macy: so far so good, at least the General looks engaged.

Next, the head patriarchs of the two warring families appear on the scene: elderly Lords Capulet and Montague played by Carlos and Omar. They flourish their own weapons: ornate looking long-bladed cutlasses. It's all set to descend into a full scale riot until Chief of Police Escalus arrives. There's palpable surprise, even shock in the audience at seeing the city's highest authority is an android.

"You men, you beasts!" the Police Chief declares, addressing the warring factions with a mix of pity and disdain.

Richards exchanges looks with Macy, as the army man nods back sagely. What kind of society is this, the audience must be thinking. But regardless of any misgivings, they're certainly hooked; the sheer power of the story, wanting to know what happens next.

❖

The end of the first scene anticipates the arrival of Romeo. Prior to his entry, Lady Montague expresses concern over her adopted son's recent behaviour –

> *"Away from light steals home my heavy son*
> *And private in his chamber pens himself,*
> *Shuts up his windows, locks fair daylight out*
> *And makes himself an artificial night..."*

The word "artificial" resonates with new meaning when Romeo appears. Silence emanates from the auditorium. But when the hero speaks he is both eloquent and convincing. Those watching have to acknowledge this android can act.

Through the power of words he appears tender as well as foolishly romantic, pining for an unobtainable love called Rosaline. Some of the audience will probably be wondering if she too is an android.

In the following scenes, it's clear from Romeo's words and actions he feels different from his human friends in a way that goes deeper than surface appearance. While they accept him for what he is, he chooses to separate himself off and his profound existential suffering comes over as self-inflicted. There appears to be an identity issue. Romeo lacks inner-belief; he constantly dwells on the negative –

> "O anything of nothing first create!
> O heavy lightness, serious vanity...
> ...this is not Romeo, he's some other where."

Kerry looks down from the lighting box, trying to read the audience's body language. They seem to be relaxed, so far sympathetic to what the play is offering. While some may have skimmed through the program notes, only now will they fully understand their meaning.

❖

The play moves on to Romeo and his two friends hearing about the party at Lord and Lady Capulet's house. Here Little Stevie as Mercutio gets an actual clap from the audience when he delivers the "Queen Mab" speech as a futuristic form of hip-hop rap. The play progresses to the party scene itself, which goes without a hitch, the ensemble movement so full of life, everything heightened by the masks so that subtle nuances of social interaction are achieved through the mere tilt of a chin, the nod of a head. The futuristic music adds to the overall magic and wonder.

The dancing is literally out of this world, with the actors moving in sync to rhythmic patterns that seem to have come from the minds of both humans and robots.

Kerry breathes out, unclasps her hands. She has to marvel at it all. All her cast are doing well and the sheer presence of the androids on stage is compelling, the way they follow the action, how they listen with what appears to be heightened attention when others are speaking to them. They're just that bit slower to react, always allowing a slight delay before responding.

Charles Richards has more mixed feelings: relieved the play is going well, but also ultra-conscious of his special guest. So far so modest, the world is full of robots that can walk, talk, dance and play musical instruments – fulfil creative but benign tasks, but when it comes to participating in a stage-fight where weapons are used in earnest, how will his prototype peacemakers shape up?

For him personally, another moment of truth arrives first. He feels his wife grip his hand as Juliet and Romeo finally get a glimpse of each other across the dance floor and experience an immediate mutual attraction. And when Romeo lifts his mask and Juliet's interest grows there can be no doubt that she is *knowingly* falling for a non-human. It comes over as a natural impulse, almost as if she was already primed for this moment. Romeo's low key presence clearly appeals to her, how since arriving at the party he's chosen to "carry the torch" for the others, apparently too self-conscious to join in the dancing. Has she simply been won over by this shy awkwardness and vulnerability? Juliet is only 14 and still clearly innocent in many ways, but this also gives her a more knowing side; ambivalence towards the social world she inhabits – a mirror-image of how Romeo feels estranged within his own community?

Unfortunately for the would-be lovers, Romeo has also been spotted by Juliet's cousin, Tybalt – who, incensed by the presence of this Montague imposter seeks to challenge him. Chuck has augmented his character's typically scary presence with what looks like a silver artificial ear: perhaps the intention is to invite the question as to which one he turns when playing "deaf" to sensible advice. Thankfully on this occasion the young hothead is restrained by Lord Capulet who doesn't want a scene in his own home, especially after Police Chief Escalus's warning against further outbreaks of violence. The situation is diffused, but it feels like only a temporary respite.

Despite the close attention, Juliet and Romeo manage to engineer a quiet moment together and there's an open steal from the Luhrmann movie: the "fish tank" scene – with the two of them isolated under a single floodlight. Kerry has set plastic fish dangling on invisible threads in the hope this will add a further layer of meaning: of species threatened. She's thrilled, the acting here is especially intimate as Harper and DAK 43 manage through mime to create the presence of the indoor tank, moving themselves around it and viewing one another through its transparency, holding this magical scene together through a shared belief.

And then it's time for the first kiss…

Afterwards, Juliet playfully chides Romeo: "*You kiss by the book…*"

Yet it's clearly an empathetic observation. How else would an android have learnt? Leading such a protected life until now, Juliet has also probably had to rely on such second-hand sources for guidance.

❖

The well-known balcony scene follows: as always outrageously charming and poignant, but with many of the lines acquiring new meaning in this radically altered context. Despite his initial bravado in climbing the wall back into Juliet's home, Romeo's self-doubt is still there: he remains hidden while she declaims her love to the universe. He can't believe she's talking about *him*:

"*I am too bold, tis not to me she speaks…*"

But when she fondly repeats his name, "*Oh Romeo, Romeo*" – he gains confidence and reveals himself, returning her affections. After much poetic talk and romantic wooing, they arrange to meet the next day to be married. Against all this joyful optimism, the audience hasn't forgotten the risks they are taking, including the danger for Romeo if he is discovered. The words of the play's opening prophesy echo in his earlier premonition that there may be a price to pay for all this new found joy:

"*…My mind misgives*
some consequence, yet hanging in the stars…
…some vile forfeit of untimely death."

The play moves on and there are more surprises for the audience to contend with, including Juliet's nurse also being an android. While this can't be a shock in itself as artificially intelligent nurses are already an accepted and staple part of society in 2040, as acted out by Harper and Gaia new layers are added to the close bond between the two characters.

Looking down from the lighting box, even Kerry is taken aback by the depth of their relationship, appreciating how well this works in helping to make sense of Juliet's love for Romeo: in a way the girl can be seen to have transferred her natural affection from one android to another.

※

When Greta appears as a female version of Friar Laurence, Kerry catches sight of someone in the audience leaving. Perhaps this person is just going to the bathroom, but it could be an objection to the characterisation, there are still all kinds of traditionalists and fundamentalist out there. Could it be others did the same in response to that first kiss between the lovers? Kerry can't be sure, having been so preoccupied with the stage lights. If so she prays there won't be too many more. On stage, Juliet and Romeo are wed in secret by Friaress Lauren and for them there's optimism and hope.

※

But soon the action moves back onto the streets and the inevitable confrontation between Tybalt and Romeo, who is out walking again with Mercutio and Benvolio. While his friends are armed with their long daggers, the android only has a small ornamental version tucked into his belt that looks more like something kept there for decoration. He refuses to fight anyway with Juliet's cousin, wanting to reach across the divide to heal the ancient quarrel. Mercutio however is not so restrained: he steps in, insulting Tybalt – throwing fuel on an already raging fire.

Richards receives a look from Macy that tells him the army man remembers this scene from its exploration by the task force: hopefully it will now send out all the right messages. But here comes android Romeo clumsily trying to get between the two adversaries and play the peacemaker, inadvertently allowing Tybalt to slip his sword under Mercutio's guard with a cowardly thrust.

As Mercutio in his death throes curses friend and foe alike, Macy leans over and whispers: 'I seem to remember that was one of your examples of how *not* to do it?'

Richards tries to project an unfazed smile: it's clear that while the learning buddies may be proving their worth as actors, as far as his proposal is concerned this modest gain is in danger of being undermined by their behaviour as characters, especially now with an android Romeo in the mix. It's certainly not following the seamless logic of the way he'd portrayed it previously to the task force.

Macy adds a throwaway line under his breath, 'Maybe he *should* have fainted after all.'

And now before there's time to draw a breath, distraught over his friend's death and further provoked by Tybalt, Romeo abandons all restraint and takes on Juliet's cousin. He picks up Mercutio's weapon: the fighting is brief and the young Capulet is killed.

There's an audible gasp from the audience when it happens; a noticeable shuffling of bodies in seats.

Macy's instinctive reaction is to shake his head, appearing to share the audience's discomfort. But then, if this isn't wishful thinking and Richards is reading it right, the expression changes as the military mind transposes this to the Theatre of War, considers the possibility it might actually have been the most expedient decision. Firstly an android peacekeeper has acted prudently to protect itself from harm, recognising the need to remain standing for the good of the broader campaign. Secondly, the main threat to any hope of a permanent peace has been removed – Tybalt had not only initiated this round of violence, he'd always been the leading antagonist in maintaining the conflict and might never have gone away, constantly threatening to stir up trouble with his propaganda and warmongering.

Richards is even daring to hope that if an audience is willing to override its initial disquiet and accept an android taking a human life as part of a work of fiction, they might apply the same reasoning to the real world, making this a genuine litmus test for what he and the task force are considering?

Unfortunately all of this is undercut when Police Chief Escalus arrives on the scene: for here is another android but with far higher moral authority. Verona's law enforcer promptly reminds everyone that Tybalt would have received a death sentence for the cold-blooded murder of Mercutio and while Romeo's individual action was partly mitigated by wanting justice for his friend, it was nonetheless a rash decision that will deny the State an opportunity to make an independent ruling which might even have put a permanent end to the long lasting feud. The scene concludes with the formal decree that Romeo must be banished from the city henceforth on pain of death if he breaks the terms of this sentence.

Richards silently curses at how two android figures acting at cross-purposes have added to the ambiguity regarding his proposal. He glances at Macy and receives a puzzled frown that suggests the General is now finding it a challenge making any useful sense of it all and may be as far from convinced as ever.

The action moves on to a distraught Juliet in her room as she hears all the terrible news via the Nurse. Meanwhile, Romeo pays a last visit to Friaress Lauren and believing he will never see Juliet again, throws himself to the ground in despair.

The Friaress challenges the android hero to put aside such thoughts and regain some moral courage:

> *"Art thou a man? Thy form cries out thou art.*
> *…Fie, fie, thou shamest thy shape…"*

❖

Romeo regains hope and despite the looming shadow of his banishment, manages to steal one night with his new bride. The audience discovers them in Juliet's bedroom just before dawn the following morning wrapped in one another's arms, wanting to extend these last precious moments together, musing on whether the birdsong they can hear is a lark or a nightingale.

It is all so innocent and those watching in hushed silence are acutely aware this couldn't ever have been about sex – only platonic love. Or perhaps this is a completely different kind of "love" requiring a new definition? What does come across in this extraordinary moment, as Juliet sorrowfully embraces her android Romeo, is that she weeps for all species, not just Humanity.

Watching the scene from above, even Kerry is struck by Harper's interpretation of the character – suggesting Juliet is a kindred spirit, how they are both only answerable to their own laws.

❖

Jim Brady is also impressed by Harper's performance, but he's aware too of another drama taking place right there beside him: how Android JFX72 has taken to mouthing the lines of the play. This even becomes faintly audible when Friaress Lauren seeks to advise a distraught Juliet, who has arrived with the news her arranged marriage with Count Paris is being brought forward. The girl says she'd rather commit suicide than let this happen.

Brady tilts his head to see more of AJ's face, just enough to take in the intensity of the android's expressions as Juliet's on-stage protector hatches the plan for her to take a sleeping potion that will simulate death. Meanwhile a close associate of Friaress Lauren's – Friaress Johanna is asked to deliver a letter to Romeo in exile, telling him the truth so he can return in secret to the city and come to

Juliet's tomb in time for when she awakes and the two can elope together.

But neither AJFX72 the school janitor or AJ inhabiting the character of Friaress Lauren, can prevent this plan from unravelling when the letter to Romeo fails to arrive: instead the news brought to him by his own servant Balthazar is that Juliet is truly dead. As Friaress Johanna outlines the unfortunate circumstances, there's a further background irony to what is usually taken as an incidental story about being caught in a lockdown, due in this instance to a sudden outbreak of the Black Death "pestilence".

❖

So finally, the play approaches its climax with Romeo arriving in the churchyard ready to break into the crypt containing Juliet's tomb. He has with him a vial of "poison" purchased earlier from a back-street dealer: this future time's version of an apothecary. The audience must assume this is a substance that can disable and destroy an android. He is ready to kill himself to prove his love.

But the hero's momentum is stalled when confronted by Paris – who had been his rival for Juliet's hand. He has come now to place flowers outside the crypt's entrance. Shakespeare portrays this young man as a noble upstanding citizen of Verona – and he too loves Juliet. He's also been led to believe that she died of heartbreak as a result of her cousin Tybalt's death at Romeo's hands. He draws his sword and tries to do the right thing by making a citizen's arrest and bringing Romeo to the authorities.

Romeo of course cannot allow himself to be led away. While wishing no harm, he's forced into protecting himself.

As she watches, Kerry remembers telling her cast how despite his innocence Paris has to be sacrificed for the sake of the story, even if it means Romeo is once again shown to be a hostage to his feelings, not to mention possessing a ruthless determination. In objective terms it's a selfish decision given he believes Juliet to be dead; nothing can be done about that, yet he'll dispense with Paris just so he can enter the chamber and then kill himself, a double waste! Kerry recalls how this scene was cut completely from both the Luhrmann and Zeffirelli movies, each director no doubt conscious of its potential to distract from the main romantic agenda.

Richards glances again at Macy, trying to read him. The General's body language says it all, leaning back into his seat apparently having given up trying to make any clear sense of what this all merits in terms of the proposal. Instead of the alert "critical distance" Richards might have hoped for, the army man appears now to be a mere spectator, simply caught up in the story like everyone else.

'*Have at thee!*' says Romeo, as is the custom of the day, but with little enthusiasm, drawing his short ornamental dagger to ward off Paris's more lethal looking weapon. Kerry has choreographed the fight so Romeo is at least backpedalling, doing his best not to be the aggressor. But faced with the irresistible force of Paris's intention to apprehend him, by causing injury if need be, Romeo knows there is only one way out of this.

❖

Romeo enters the crypt and finds Juliet lying on top of a raised tomb, supposedly dead. The timing of what follows is agonisingly cruel, for just as he swallows the poison she awakes. For a heartbreaking moment Juliet sees him and is full of hope, this is what was planned, it has all worked out: she is with her love at last, her husband, her Romeo.

They kiss…

But then his body slumps across her lap and she sees the vial of poison.

There can be no choice now for Juliet but to join Romeo in death. She curses the vial for being empty, but then her attention is drawn towards the dagger tucked into his belt.

She lifts a hand to caress his face one last time, before dragging her arm with its long sleeve slowly down his upper body, twisting him in the process so the side with the dagger is briefly hidden; the moment is painfully extended before her hand reappears holding the handle, pointing the blade towards her breast.

"This happy dagger…"

Harper's acting has been compelling throughout the play but here she is mesmeric. Richards finds himself held spellbound by this unexpected vision of his daughter; he has to admit to feeling intensely proud of her, what she has achieved. Now, as Juliet prepares to strike and the dagger glints for a moment under the stage lights, he recalls the argument in Brady's office over the casting changes, her referencing the story of Iphigenia and he feels his heart involuntarily chill…

Sophia Richards is conscious of her husband's hand gripping hers; she too has a cramp in her gut.

Juliet closes her eyes, bracing herself...

For some reason AJ chooses this moment to stand up, almost as if alarmed – and is immediately told by those behind to sit back down. Someone rasps, 'It's only a play, you dumb fool!' Brady turns his head to give the android a mild visual ticking-off, but is halted by an expression that suggests deep concern.

In an instant everything changes as Romeo's eyes flick open. He raises himself just enough to take hold of Juliet's wrist.

She allows him to gently part her fingers from the dagger and then drop it down out of harm's way behind the tomb.

The action hangs suspended until Romeo slumps again and is still.

There's a hush – the audience instinctively senses this time he is truly dead. If they didn't already know beforehand, they will remember the opening prologue and know this is a radical change from the anticipated ending: here Romeo hadn't totally succumbed to the poison; he still had one noble action left in him.

A bold move to risk an almost "happy" conclusion, but looks on most faces say they have been won over.

Looking down, Kerry is still pinching herself: where the hell did that come from...it was *not* what they'd rehearsed! It's hard to believe even Harper would have the nerve and audacity to go on a solo-run like that. And there's something strange too about the dagger...

The tragic couple stay briefly frozen in a tableau

before the curtain falls. The spontaneous clapping is unambiguously rapturous – the play is a resounding success.

Along with everyone else, Charles Richards rises from his seat when the curtain opens again to reveal the whole cast standing in a line, re-directing the applause upwards towards Kerry in the lighting box. But there's clearly something else going on: even while enjoying their moment of triumph, Harper's friend Wanda sends her a distinct, "What's up?" Richards's attention is drawn to the ornamental dagger still tucked into Romeo's belt. He glances at Macy and senses the army man has noticed it too.

The actors take several more encores before finally disappearing into the wings. When the house lights come back on, Richards turns to his guest and sees Macy's normally stony face holds a new expression: what looks like comprehension, appreciation – could that even be a nod of approval?

Sophia and Charles Richards make their way slowly towards the aisle, both receiving all kinds of compliments and pats on the back.

'That daughter of yours is one hell of an actress!'

'Great production, whoever saw that coming. That was some neat twist!'

Richards tries to return the smiles but he's still inwardly distracted. His wristband has been on silent and now he feels it pulse. He glances down and from the colour code and cheery icon knows it's a "Congrats" message from Wilson.

Kerry is also trying to pull everything together: her initial assumption had been that Harper and DAK 43 had somehow collaborated on the new ending, but surely the learning buddy would have resisted such a fundamental departure from something Kerry and the whole group had agreed on? She thinks again about that very real looking blade and the penny finally drops. Her mind spins back to the earlier confrontation between daughter and father: no wonder the girl had fought like a tiger to keep DAK 43 in place as Romeo, it looks now like her forward planning even went back to the decision to upset Little Stevie at the basketball match, perhaps even earlier. But what then was her motivation in setting up this surprise finale: simply to prove something – to Kerry, the world, her father?

Even while shaking hands with everyone, Richards has been asking himself the same questions – and has now moved on to wondering what was the point of switching the daggers unless...along with everyone else, android Romeo had also been kept in the dark regarding Harper's intentions. So on hearing that final line, "This happy dagger", the learning buddy had picked up a change in Harper's voice-tone, detected something in her body-language sending out a subliminal message, all of it raising a suspicion this might somehow be happening 'for real'. DAK 43 had been tempted enough to open its eyes, saw what looked like a very real blade in Harper's hand and been convinced that action was necessary to save the girl from possible harm. Was that what she'd been out to prove: how she could ultimately fool the android, her human intelligence winning out over AI – one in the eye and 'heart' for her father? Was this further punishment for downgrading her in his affections; to underline her own importance?

But now another thought: whatever Harper's motives, if the android really had been taken by surprise, then she couldn't have known for sure what it would do next faced with such a radical change to the script. She'd managed to place it in a perfect Catch 22 position of having to choose between her and the play: protecting her would mean committing the unpardonable sin of coming out of character, ruining the final scene and probably the whole production. But amazingly, in the blink of an eye the learning buddy had neatly resolved both challenges: removed the threat of harm and then providing an alternative ending that was truly inspired. It was more than anything Richards could ever have dreamed up himself, a supreme illustration of the kind of emotional intelligence he'd been claiming for his Peacemaker.

Kerry feels her knees wobble as she leaves the lighting box and descends the small flight of steps leading to the auditorium. There will have to be a serious post-mortem session at some point but right now her focus has to be on enjoying the moment, meeting up with her gang and telling them how wonderful they all were. Memories of their little journey together flash by in a second: all the discussions and improvisations; the crisis session following the basketball game – how they emerged from that even more united and focused. Once again she offers up thanks to "the process" for helping to bring them through. But more than anything she's thinking back to whatever prophetic star inspired her to introduce those early trust games.

ACT SIX

"My dismal scene I needs must act alone..."

"*A glooming peace this morning with it brings; the sun for sorrow will not show its head...*"

AJ knows this line by 'heart'; they are the words of summary normally used in bringing together the final assembly of characters and setting up the play's formal ending. But like many directors before her, Kerry had early on decided to cut this drawn out epilogue-like scene with its lengthy parade of witnesses involving the Friaress, Paris's servant, Romeo's man Balthazar, even the graveyard watchman. And no room either for pious outpourings of remorse from Lords Capulet and Montague bemoaning their joint contribution to this tragedy – no grandiose speeches about building golden monuments to lost youth. Not even a rhyming couplet from the Police Chief to tidy it all up: "*For never was a story of more woe, than this of Juliet and her Romeo.*"

As everyone continues to take their leave of the auditorium, the school's janitor steps out of line and approaches the stage – ascends and turns to face the front.

AJ is conscious of how this will be breaking something known as the "fourth wall". The android searches for the best term to describe the final soliloquy about to be delivered: confession, disclosure, unveiling, an unburdening – or simply the right moment to say no to secrets and "spill the beans", to tell all? AJFX72 chooses a suitable expression and proceeds to fill the audience in on everything they have missed until now; leaving nothing out, sparing nobody…

ALSO BY THE AUTHOR

Poetry
Zen Traffic Lights (Lapwing Press 2005)
A Father's Day (Salmon Poetry 2008)
Session (Salmon Poetry 2011)
How to Bake a Planet (Salmon Poetry 2016)

Stage Plays
Cinders 2000 (musical)
Trust Games (2003)
Red Lorry Yellow Lorry (2004)

Radio Plays
Running on Empty (1999) (science-fiction)
The Bughouse (2005)
Butterfly Wings (2012) (science-fiction)

Non Fiction/teaching resources
Know Yourself Know the World (Learning Horizons 2003)
Just a Second! Exploring Global Issues through Theatre and Drama (Afri 2014)
Interdependence Day: Teaching the Sustainable Development Goals through Drama (Afri 2020)

ABOUT THE AUTHOR

Pete Mullineaux lives in Galway, Ireland, where he teaches global issues in schools in association with AFRI (Action from Ireland) and Poetry Ireland's *Development Education through Literature* project. A science fiction thread runs though several pieces of work, including the radio plays *Running on Empty* (RTE 1999) with its quantum physics theme and *Butterfly Wings* (RTE radio 2012), again featuring a quantum reality where the leading protagonist acquires a parallel life and persona. The stage play *Red Lorry Yellow Lorry* (Galway Youth Theatre 2003) might be seen as a forerunner to *Jules & Rom,* set in the near future and featuring two warring families, (who run rival waste disposal companies). A devised sci-fi piece for schools *Equalonia* was included in the Babaro International Children's Arts Festival and a Star Trek influenced play, *The Scream* presented in Galway Art Centre's Nuns Island Theatre. Sci-fi themes also appear in three published resources for teachers: *Know Yourself Know the World* follows a storyline where a computer virus has made the jump into the human body and an intrepid team of 'Micronauts' have to enter the bloodstream to find and deactivate it before the human race is literally 'shut down'.

In the AFRI publication *Just a Second: Exploring Global Issues through Drama & Theatre,* the play "More!" explores food security at an inter-galactic level. *Interdependence Day*: *Teaching the Sustainable Development Goals through Drama*, (AFRI 2020) includes a scenario where Earth is threatened with destruction by visiting aliens unless the pupils can show their understanding of the UN's Sustainable Development Goals. Pete's poetry also reflects themes that surround global issues such as war, climate change, species destruction, most recently in *How to Bake a Planet* (Salmon Poetry/Ireland 2016) "A gem!" – *Poetry Ireland Review.*

ACKNOWLEDGEMENTS

I wish to thank my partner and fellow writer Moya Roddy for her creative support, astute observations and all round comradeship. I'm also deeply indebted to our daughter Cassie whose insightful comments as well as encouragement proved vital in helping me pull it all together. I offer a big thank you to Sean Crosson for reading an early draft and giving me invaluable feedback. The novel has many connections to my work exploring global issues in schools and in this regard I owe a huge debt to Joe Murray, Larysa Karankovich, Roj Whelan, Rose Kelly, Lisa Patten, Gary Whitedeer, Donal & Katie O'Kelly, Ruairi McKiernan and everyone associated with AFRI; similarly Moira Cardiff, Jane O'Hanlon, Anna Bonner and all involved with Poetry Ireland's Writers in Schools scheme. I want to thank Youth Theatre Ireland for supporting youth drama in general and in particular for re-commissioning my play *Trust Games* and including several other works in their "Play-share" online resource; Galway Youth Theatre too for some great memories over many years; Jessie Lendennie and Siobhan Hutson at Salmon Poetry for their ongoing creative support; finally Clann Resource Centre and all in the Oughterard Writers Group past and present for their camaraderie.

"Entertaining, thought provoking, engaging...with a cast of meticulously drawn characters, Jules & Rom shines a fresh and innovative light on one of Shakespeare's finest plays, re-imagined to have contemporary resonance and impact in an age of AI and challenges to humanity such as war and catastrophic climate change."

Dr Sean Crosson – Huston School of Film, National University of Ireland Galway: author of *Hollywood Hurling, Horror and the Emergence of Irish Cinema* (Cork University Press, 2019).

'An exceedingly interesting piece of science fiction that deftly navigates empathy and artificial intelligence in a novel way...manages to suck you into its thoughtfully crafted world. If you have been thinking about the emotional side of our relationship with artificial intelligence, I recommend checking this book out.'

Rose Smith – *TwentyTwoTwentyEight Magazine*, USA.

'Jules and Rom creates a future that is simultaneously both familiar and scarily strange, an intriguing world where android technology and the human spirit must coexist. This original and highly entertaining story is also perhaps a little cautionary as it nods towards an unnerving place that may be lurking just up around the bend.'

Gerard Hanberry – author of *On Raglan Road: Great Irish Love Songs and the Women who inspired them* (Gill/Collins).

 Matador